"*The Truth Against the World* is bloody amazing—a wild, enchanting ride across an apocalyptic America with characters who will steal your heart and surprises you won't see coming. The best novel yet from one of today's finest writers. I absolutely loved this book."
—Deborah Crombie, best-selling author of *A Killing of Innocents*

"David Corbett's *The Truth Against the World* delivers terror, hope and redemption with incredibly-drawn characters, exquisitely-written cross-country settings, and sorrowful lessons in the history of the world. This book is reminiscent of King's masterpiece, *The Stand,* but with a very human—and very American—bogeyman. A fantastic read!"
—Rachel Howzell Hall, bestselling author of *We Lie Here*

"David Corbett weaves together myth and prophecy in a way that makes *The Truth Against the World* feel both timeless and frighteningly relevant. And it carries his hallmark of elegant writing and deeply considered, compelling character work. A fantastic read you'll struggle to put down."
—Rob Hart, critically acclaimed author of *The Warehouse* and *Paradox Hotel*

"A sharply written thriller that gives readers a peek at a future that doesn't seem all that far from reality, *The Truth Against the World* comes pre-baked with plot twists, suspense, and compelling characters. Corbett has outdone himself."
—Alex Segura, bestselling author of *Secret Identity*

Praise for David Corbett

The Long-Lost Love Letters of Doc Holliday

"[J]ust terrific … Highly recommended."

—*New York Times* bestselling author John Lescroart

"Fresh and inventive … exploring the territory where legend, lore, and fact collide."

—*BookPeople*

The Mercy of the Night

"Tierney and company are so real they seem to step off the pages."
—*Booklist* (Starred Review)

"Corbett doesn't stint on either narrative or psychological complexity."
—*Kirkus*

Do They Know I'm Running

"Corbett delivers a rich, hard-hitting epic … an unforgettable journey."
—*Publishers Weekly* (Starred Review)

"A major work of literary art that breaks all genre borders."
—Bestselling Author Ken Bruen

Blood of Paradise

"Corbett, like Robert Stone and Graham Greene before him, is crafting important, immensely thrilling books."
—George Pelecanos, Producer, *The Wire*

"I would say of *Blood of Paradise* what I said of *Done for a Dime*: it's an example of the best in contemporary crime fiction—or, if I may be so bold, in contemporary fiction, period."
—Patrick Anderson, *Washington Post*

Done for a Dime

"Corbett's fluid pace is enhanced by his elegant writing and his focus on characters."
—*South Florida Sun-Sentinel*

". . . one of the three or four best American crime novels I've ever read."
—Patrick Anderson, *Washington Post*

The Devil's Redhead

[A] compelling, shocking and beautifully written tour de force."
—*The Irish Independent*

"Corbett's prose dazzles, cutting across the page with passionate force."
—*Publishers Weekly*

THE TRUTH
AGAINST
THE WORLD

A NOVEL

DAVID CORBETT

ISBN: 9781960725004
LCCN: 2023903522
ebook ISBN: 9781960725011

Cover designed by Tim Barber, Dissect Designs
Interior designed by Ellie Searl, Publishista®

SQUARE TIRE BOOKS
Austin, TX

For Mette, my Better Half, my Best Friend, my Bride
A stor mo chroí

AUTHOR'S NOTE

A glossary of pronunciation for the Irish names and terms that appear in the text can be found at the back of the book.

Consume my heart away; sick with desire
And fastened to a dying animal
It knows not what it is; and gather me
Into the artifice of eternity.

—William Butler Yeats, "Sailing to Byzantium"

"The truth against the world!—Yes. Certainly.
. . . the truth is a matter of the imagination.

—Ursula K. Le Guin, *The Left Hand of Darkness*

SOLAS AGUS DORCHADAS

WITH tens of thousands engaged online—Hong Kong to Tel Aviv, Manhattan to Berlin—Georgie reads from her scrawled notes, reciting the litany of names, linking them to their atrocities:

The plutocratic sociopaths who bankrolled the Capitol bombing.

The homegrown *sicarios* murdering governors, mayors, members of Congress.

The freelancers targeting journalists, bloggers, filmmakers, poets.

The paid provocateurs turning marches into riots, the arsonists torching courthouses—

Outside, a caravan of vehicles rumbles up the abandoned vineyard's winding gravel drive, headlights piercing the fog of airborne ash in the darkness.

A sheriff's squad car, followed by three pickups.

I switch off the overhead lights. The only illumination in the room now comes from the laptop. Its glow sharpens the angles of Georgie's small, indomitable face. Her penumbral shadow hovers like a ghostly avatar in the giant mirror behind.

A bullhorn voice: "Whoever's inside that building: Come out through the front door. Move slowly. Show your hands. There will not be a second warning."

I signal to her: keep going. She leans in closer to the laptop's camera and microphone.

"I'm going to be ending this broadcast shortly. They've discovered our location … If you're hearing my voice, rise up. Take back your lives."

Pickup doors slam shut. About a dozen men altogether, armed with long guns, inch forward up the shallow grade. I grip the pistol in each of my hands a bit more purposefully, breathing slowly in and out, emptying my mind, silencing what remains of my conscience.

1

THE PRISONER IN THE TOWER

Begin, be bold, and venture to be wise.

—Horace, *The Odes*

—1—

A ND so, there I am, secretly following the bastard home. What alternative did he leave me?

I'm speaking of Wilburn Kurth, senior VP at Merchants & Traders Trust of Philadelphia. Earlier in the day, I'm there at his bank, pleading my case. Georgie's case, rather, for it's her funds, essential to her care, that have inexplicably vanished.

Bulwarked behind his antique desk, hands folded before him on the blotter, our Mr. Kurth—bespectacled, portly, razor-straight part in his ash-brown hair—responds to my entreaties with the conscientious steeliness that commends a man who guards the money of others, especially in times such as these.

Meaning, of course, he gives me nothing, wandering around the barn about the sanctity of client privacy and such, ending with a cold, helpless smile.

I thank him for his time, spank the crease back into my slacks, show myself out.

Then wait, sitting in my car the remainder of the workday, while storm clouds the color of overripe plums gather overhead, a real pelter rolling in from the Atlantic.

Five on the dot, our Mr. Kurth scuttles out to his car, briefcase for an

4

umbrella, rain lashing down in blinding sheets. I slip into gear as he pulls into traffic—headlights carving a path through the blur, wipers slogging back and forth. Maintaining a steady three-car distance all the way across the Schuylkill River, I end up in one of those staid and sleepy purlieus often mocked as hotbeds of social rest.

Puts me in mind of the Belfast suburbs, always so peaceful, even at the height of the bombings.

I make a mad dash from car to doorstep and stand there, damp as a rat, when the door finally opens.

It's not the man of the house who greets me, however, but his wife. Even in flats she stands over six feet tall.

My banker married himself an amazon, a bohemian to boot: hair coiled behind in a thick dark braid, a paint-stained denim shirt knotted at the navel.

Her thin brown eyebrows slice like darts toward the wrinkled bridge of her nose. In return, I venture a smile in the porchlight.

"Might I possibly share a word with Wilburn?"

She glances past me toward the rainswept yard, practically vibrating with fright. Given the danger that stalks the land, who can blame her? I could be walking point for a murderous squad of brigands, a wandering strangler, a humble thug. There's no relief in her eyes when her gaze snaps back.

"Does he know what this is regarding?"

"That he does. We spoke earlier, but I didn't get the chance to—"

"If this concerns work, you need to meet with him there." She shakes her wrist for a glance at her watch. "My God, I mean . . . With everything going on, seriously. And how on earth did you find—"

"Melissa, who is it?"

The banker himself at last appears, strolling up from behind, drying his hands on a dish towel. The necktie has fled, shirt collar open, sleeves rolled up from the wrist. It does little to redeem the steeliness of eye.

"No," he says, seeing it's me.

"Mr. Kurth, I'm sorry to disturb you at home—"

"Then leave." This from Melissa, the wife. Arms crossed now, one of the darting eyebrows cocked.

"I don't believe I had a chance to explain my purpose fully."

The wife's face tightens like a fist, but before she can comment, her husband says, "This is highly improper." Ever so subtly, he eases himself in front of his bride. Protector. Defender. Two inches shorter. It's only then I notice the apron: flower print, ruffled edges.

"I mean utterly, absolutely no harm. But I'm here on behalf of a young lady in dire need."

"You told me at the—"

"Not enough so you'd rightly understand."

I pull from my breast pocket the pictures I've brought, printed out on glossy stock.

"I'm calling the police." The wife turns away brusquely. As she does, I spot the girl.

The first sight of a child, it invariably breaks my heart. Blame the sight of too many wandering war zones, starving, dressed in scraps.

This one seems fourteen or so, wearing a private school uniform, white blouse with Peter Pan collar, vest and pleated skirt of Marian blue. Catholic. I picture the classroom, crucifix high on the wall, the imperious nun. Little Sisters of the Rich.

Our eyes meet. I offer a timid wave, which she returns.

"Don't make this difficult," her father says. "I don't want trouble any more than you do."

The mother moves toward the girl, tries to collect her, turn her away from the door. From me. But the young one remains where she is, transfixed.

I cast no spell, I swear, conjure no magic. As if I could.

The girl eases forward. Lanky of build, legs like posts, she'll grow tall like her mother. She possesses as well her mother's chestnut hair, the same dark eyes, but the brows, not yet plucked and sculpted, possess a gentle shapelessness about them that renders perfectly the lonely bafflement of the precocious child.

She slips her hand casually into her father's. "What's your name?"

I offer a courteous glance to the father, a tacit request for permission to respond. "People tend to call me Shane."

Her head lists to one side. "You're . . . "

"Irish, yeah. As wet grass."

From behind, her mother utters a blistering, "Djuna, get away from the door."

Speaking of names. I can't help but grin. An arty appellation for the doomed-to-be-special daughter—from which I surmise there are no other sprogs about. Djuna is an only child.

The father interjects a bit of throat-clearing. "Mr. Redmond?"

"Riordan."

"I'm sorry. Mr. Riordan, it really is improper, visiting me like this. At home."

Behind them both, silhouetted in a rearward archway, the mother holds her phone aloft, a warning: Don't make me finish the call. Be off.

"How old are you?" It's the girl again.

Odd question. I keep my eyes trained on the mother. "Thirty-three. Thereabouts."

"You seem much older." She crinkles her nose. "It's your eyes. They're sad."

> *From his eyes of flame,*
> *Ruby tears there came*

Good old Billy Blake.

"Djuna," the mother barks, "I won't say it again, get *away* from the *door.*"

The rain's worsened, drops the size of apricots.

"Who's that in the picture?" Djuna points to the topmost snapshot I'm holding.

"Her name's Georgie. She's a dear and precious friend, who's sadly fallen on difficult times. That's why I've come to speak with your father. I need his help."

You can feel it, the melting of the man's resistance, the girl's long fingers twined in his. She glances up with wily fondness. "If that's all he wants, Dad. I mean, it's pouring."

The stern banker answers with a sort of growling sigh, which seems a cue between them. The girl unlatches the screen door and nudges it open for me.

Oh, the mother's truly going to hate me now. Inwardly, I'm laughing like a drain.

$-2-$

USING my handkerchief, I mop my face and hands as I stand in the entry, a quick brush across my hair, a flick here and there against the larger droplets clinging to my sport coat and slacks.

In the corner of my eye, I catch a glimpse of a wall-mounted monitor in a study off the main hall—a white cupola appears on the screen, shrouded in churning black smoke. Some sort of newscast—another government building attacked?

The mother rushes forward, slams shut the door, and points me toward the living room.

I lay out my photos on an antique painted chest, turning the pictures so they can be viewed from the roomy Chesterfield couch. Djuna sits in the middle, the parents looming to either side like watchful bookends. Paintings crowd the wall behind them, frenzied slashings of color that only an utter plank wouldn't recognize as the mother's.

I sense no lingering spirits about, no wandering ghosts. They tend to gather where there's hope of something to learn from the living. I keep their absence in mind as I plead my case.

"I met Georgie at Liguorian College over in Lansdowne."

The snapshots begin from the time when I first met Georgie, fresh as a field of bellflower, then advance over three years to the unfortunate present, where she stares back at the camera from the hollows of her haunted state.

"She's very unusual looking," the girl remarks.

"Djuna," the father says, "don't be rude."

"I'm not. I just mean, well, her hair, it's like ink, but her skin—"

"Black Irish," the mother says.

"Actually," I reply, "that's not a term we use ourselves. It's said about us, not by us."

"And the eyes," Djuna says, "they're, like, Asian."

"Seriously, Djuna!"

"That's not at all uncommon," I reply. "Squint-eyed, it's called back home, not kindly. Truth be told, there's as wide a variety of types in Ireland as anywhere, dark to fair. We're not all ginger-haired, blue-eyed, and freckled. Regardless, her people left the old country long ago, banished to the Caribbean as indentured servants when Cromwell drove them off the land. Since then they've moved and mingled and intermarried like all the rest. She's pure American mutt, though the Irish does shine through, not just in her name. Stubborn people, stubborn genes."

The mother seems unperturbed at my having corrected her—no more agitated than before, at least—a good sign. As for the father, he just keeps his eyes locked upon me, as though any moment I might lunge.

"Georgie and me, we met in a class on Celtic myth given by a gent named Reginald Feely."

The father stiffens at mention of the name. As well he should.

"Georgie—and here her Irish shone through—she was mad for the old stories, about Queen Maeve and Cú Chulainn, the Brown Bull of Cooley, the sad fate of the children of Lir. She practically sparkled when we read them out loud."

My voice softens as I remember. A happier, more radiant time.

"But she's a fragile thing, perhaps too fine a spirit for this world. And, as many young people do, she fell in love unwisely."

"With you," Melissa, the mother, presumes.

"No, no. Georgie and me, we're friends—and not 'merely.' Friendship is my sacrament. 'The immortal good that dances round the world,' if you know your Epicurus. Fierce close we are, tight as twins, even in her current state."

I nod toward the most recent picture, honoring the pause the sad image deserves.

"But the romance in question, that was someone else entirely, no need to mention who. It ended brutally, and it wasn't just poor Georgie's heart that broke. Her mind shattered as well, like a crystal glass filled with false hope."

I gaze up into their silence. The girl lets go with a heartfelt sigh.

"What exactly," the mother says, "was her diagnosis?"

"Schizoaffective disorder, which tosses a lot of syllables at a loss for an explanation. I tend to call it *Cú Sidhe*."

"Coo she," the girl whispers, mimicking the sound.

"The old black dog. Depression, but the wickedest sort."

The father says, "Let's get to the payments, shall we?" Banker to the bone.

"Mr. Feely, the professor, went on to be quite famous. Wrote a quartet of novels, two per year, beginning with *The Truth Against the World*, under a cryptonym, Rory Fitzgerald."

Djuna practically levitates. "I love those books!"

Aha. Another mark in the scam. Hardly coincidence, that. The books have sold in the tens of millions worldwide, especially among girls in this one's cohort. If only they knew what I know, the poison secret at the heart of the matter.

"They can make for a ripping read, I'll admit, though the first is best by far."

"I agree."

"After that, he plays a bit too loose with the facts for my taste."

The mother shutters her eyes with a faint guttural moan. "The *facts?*"

Not a fan, I'm guessing.

"You're just jealous," the girl says, "because he's famous and you're not."

"That's not even remotely true, young lady."

"Oh, please."

"And those books are little more than Crypto-Christian agitprop in Celtic drag."

"What I meant," I sneak in, "regarding the facts—I was referring to how the stories were originally told. And understood."

The father glances up at the wall clock. "But the *payments*."

"Yes, sorry. Mr. Feely, or Fitzgerald, learned of what befell Georgie, his former prize student, and quite generously sent money to her stepmother every month. For her care."

The girl narrows her eyes into mine. "Stepmother?"

She doesn't miss much, this one. "Her birth mother died when Georgie was just a wee skitter. The father, well, let's just say he's no longer in the picture."

And thank mercy for that, for he's not worth a thimble of piss.

"Anyway, for the better part of the past two years, Georgie's been in the hands of the Franciscans at St. Dymphna's out near Valley Forge."

"It's a commendable facility," the banker says. "Very devoted people."

Spoken like a man with a lunatic in the family woodpile.

"Yes, indeed they are. But though the good friars are charitable, they don't come cheap. The money from Mr. Fitzgerald, it wasn't just welcome, it was crucial."

"I understand, but—"

"I merely thought to see what might be done. As I said, the funds came from your bank, the very branch, until two months ago. No forewarning, no explanation—"

"I've read about this." Djuna's eyes shimmer. "Rory Fitzgerald, he's disappeared."

"Retired from the limelight." A delicate bit of shading. "So say his publishers, though even they profess to be in the dark as to where he's gone off to. Or exactly why."

"It was very sudden. And mysterious. His readers are furious. *I'm* furious."

Truth be told, the girl looks more fascinated than incensed. Meanwhile, poor bohemian Mom has that look of pained indulgence one gets when it's all been heard before, and not just once or twice. I steal another glance at the paintings lining the walls, the feverish will to abstraction. No spooks and faeries for her fine mind.

"You're making an assumption," the father says, "that Mr. Fitzgerald's disappearance is linked somehow to the checks stopping. What if, instead—"

"He has full right to do however he pleases. I'm not suggesting otherwise. Nor finding fault. But with his vanishing, yes, the money went south as well. And without it, Georgie's stepmum is in a savage state. The cost of care, it's sky high."

The man leans forward, as though by coming closer his point might be rendered irrefutable. "As I told you at the bank, I can't possibly divulge any information concerning his current whereabouts—Mr. Feely, I mean, or Fitzgerald, whatever—even if I knew."

"If I give you a letter to forward along, no word to me as to where it goes?"

The girl's face tightens. "Dad, you never told me you had anything to do with this."

"You never asked."

"I had to *ask*?"

The father refocuses on me. "How can I be sure of your motives?"

I withdraw the letter I've written. It's somewhat damp, but not beyond use. I had it with me when I visited his office, but he'd just have waited till I was gone to toss it in the bin.

Better to wait. Just the right time.

"I've not sealed it, so you're free to read it yourself. I'd like to toss in a few of these snaps as well, so he knows this is all on the level."

Wilburn Kurth, father and fiduciary, gently slips the letter from its wilted envelope and reads. The cast of his eyes as they scan the page reaffirm my first impression of the man, that he's firm and old-fashioned but not senselessly obstinate.

"My contact information," I tell him, "lies there at the bottom."

He folds the letter closed again.

The daughter reaches out. "Can I—?"

"No." He nods toward the photographs. "Which ones would you like to include?"

I pick the oldest, the most recent, two in between, and hand them to him.

He slips them inside the envelope, then fixes me with a stare. "What if he doesn't respond?"

I'm not one for fiddly plans. Seen far too many crumble into dust— first contact with the enemy, God laughing behind your back and so on. I prefer to improvise, sniff the air, look for signs.

"To be perfectly honest," I tell him, "I've not thought that far ahead."

MAKING my retreat from Casa de Kurth, I switch on my radio—a good old-fashioned shortwave set, tucked under the dash, secretly installed by the same crew of streetwise renegados that stealth-stripped the vehicle at my request, removing all tracking devices, neutralizing the surveillance state's efforts to pin down my location minute-by-minute. Tuning the trusty old device to one of the few pirate stations still providing marginally credible reportage, I let the young, earnest voices of the urban underground catch me up to speed on the latest.

A moment later, I'm pulling over, turning up the sound—are they having me on?

Capitol Hill, a massive blast, reportedly a dirty bomb—they're recovering bodies from the rubble and charred debris: staffers, journalists, members of the security and janitorial details, some no more than a limb, a foot in a shoe, a severed arm belted with a wristwatch.

That glimpse of the wall-mounted screen off the Kurths' hallway— the white cupola, the roiling black smoke. *With everything going on . . .* Small wonder the amazon wanted no part of a stranger at her door, no matter how drenched or charming.

Congress itself is out of session, which only makes the feckless hucksters all the more despised. Should have been them that died—so goes the general view.

Reports addressing the real danger of a dirty bomb—not radiation, but fearful rumors—go largely unheeded. Panic's taking hold. Fleeing vehicles choke the roads leading out of D.C.

As for the Noble Leader, Blatherskite-in-Chief—nominal head of the national faction variously known as Nativists, the First Order, Meatheads—he remains quite safe, thank you very much, tucked away, a secure and undisclosed location.

Wherever he is, the gobshite hasn't stopped yammering, issuing vague and ominous decrees on every platform imaginable. State of exception—boots on the ground, guns in the streets. Time for the old iron hand.

Left unsaid: he's the third president in a row dubiously ensconced in his chair. One ended up assassinated, the second fled abroad amidst scandal like a Peruvian *caudillo*. This one seems inclined not to let the present crisis go to waste. Assuming he didn't gin it up himself.

Next on the air comes six new reports of mutinies, adding to all the others that have taken place over the preceding weeks—military commands, National Guard units, feds, police, sheriffs, down to the constables and crossing guards. Anybody with a gun has chosen a side.

And there are a great many guns.

Finally, a travel advisory: avoid anything longer than a cross-town jaunt. Armed gangs and khaki-clad militia are roaming the highways—pro-regime, anti-regime, and good luck if you can tell the difference.

As if that weren't worrisome enough, in the mere few hours since the bombing:

A Haitian family, dragged from their car, hacked to pieces along an Everglades backroad.

A school bus, hijacked outside Colorado Springs. All thirty children missing. No claim of responsibility. No ransom demand.

At least twenty teachers from small-town schools in Michigan's Upper Peninsula, dragged from their classrooms, tied together in pairs—and pitched off a barge into Lake Huron, drowned in the name of saving children's minds.

The bombing, it's like the God of Revelation himself fired a gunshot in the air, alerting all parties: the race is on. The race into the cataclysm, the long-awaited cleansing fire.

Meanwhile, surprise surprise, the rump government already has its suspects—a Muslim prison gang, the Black Rascal Rangers. Those in the know claim they've never heard of such an outfit—and even if it exists, such a massive act of terrorism from relative unknowns beggars belief—setting off a whole new round of conspiracy theories, accusations, threats.

None of which qualifies as the official word. There is no official word.

Hoax Americana.

Is Georgie, alone in her room at St. Dymphna's, at all aware? Even if she has no access to the particulars, she'll be sensing something. Her internal storm glass, always hypersensitive, never fails to detect such atmospheric shifts.

As I head toward the city center, the easterly horizon glows red against a backdrop of stormy darkness—Camden across the river continues to burn, whole blocks afire from ongoing riots. Hazard a guess what will happen once word goes round that a black prison gang's been scapegoated for the terror attack on the Capitol.

Here and there down darkened side streets, more modest conflagrations appear—a delivery van set ablaze, a giant mound of trash turned into a roadblock bonfire, a corner mailbox spitting flames.

Lending an air of the surreal, a digital megaboard lights up the rainy night like a massive pixilated fever dream. Nonstop ads blend seamlessly into one another—memory supplements, malware protection, eczema cremes, funeral insurance.

Beneath the monstrosity's flickering glare, a band of homeless has fashioned a camp. Men, women, whole families huddle inside giant shipping cartons, seeking shelter from the rain.

Half a mile on, I encounter my one and only checkpoint—somewhat surprised there aren't more, given the news.

Gratefully, it's manned by a lone policeman, not some ad hoc band of camo-clad goons.

The officer—plump older gent, gin-blossom nose, raingear rattling in the wind—takes one look at me, waves me on, not so much as a glance at the ID panel on my handheld phone.

Something to be said for a man who recognizes that, as matters turn from bad to worse, he'll likely prove useless. So what's the point of vigilance?

—4—

As I pull into the parking lot of St. Dymphna's, the barred windows glow dully in the rain, while a vivid lightning strike, off to the north, carves a jagged white scar across the darkness.

Originally an orphanage for girls, St. Dymphna's became a home for troubled women sometime after Vatican II, a refuge where the shunned ladies could wander the grounds beneath the stately elms and pretend they weren't prisoners, at least until they reached the tall, wrought-iron palisade fence encircling the grounds, its rails spaced so tightly only a cat could slip through, each shaft of iron capped with a spear-tip finial.

Franciscans technically run the place, but only three actually live on the premises: Friars Daniel, Anibal, and Bayani. As for the daily ins and outs, that's left to the secular staff, who by and large employ a measured hand.

Favorite joke among the patients: "The employees here are very committed."

Who says the mad lack wit?

Gentle gargantuan Derrius is manning the door, anchoring the security desk with his heft. I shake off the weather, offer a smile.

"Can't let you in," he says. "Visiting hours done came and went."

I glance up at the clock: sure enough, ten past nine. "Has Georgie's mum left as yet?"

He replies with an imperious shrug, staring at his phone. Perhaps he's following the day's events. If so, they don't appear to trouble him terribly. Then again, nothing much ever does.

There's history for you—so much of it happens when the vast majority of humanity is otherwise engaged.

"Mind if I sit here for a spell? It's raining hogs and halfwits out there."

Interpreting his silence as consent, I take a seat on a nearby bench. Leaning forward, hands folded, I glance down from time to time and catch my dull, blurred reflection staring back at me from the freshly polished oak flooring.

I try thinking through what I've accomplished, if anything. Wilburn Kurth seems a man of his word, but what if he's not? Or what if this latest uptick in the national turmoil inspires him to inaction? Even if it doesn't, even if he sends my humble letter on, what if Reginald Feely, now the famous and widely beloved Rory Fitzgerald, lacks any desire to reply?

The echo of oncoming footsteps interrupts my ruminations.

Georgie's stepmother, a thin, dowdy woman with nunnish hair turned gun-metal grey, materializes from the shadows at the end of the central hall.

The short, stout heels of her derby brogues clatter against the hardwood. Her vinyl car coat flutters open as she makes way toward me, revealing her usual visiting garb—workaday frock, floral-pattern scarf, the kind to be found at any discount outlet.

Once, I happened upon her out in the world, trolling the shops at an upscale mall. She was dressed to the nines and stared back at me in fright when I said hello, as though I'd discovered her terrible secret. I did indeed wonder—where did the money come from? Maybe Rory Fitzgerald was bankrolling more than Georgie's care.

I rise in greeting. "Evening, Missus. And how is our lovely girl this fine night?"

She stops in her tracks. The look on her, like the shadows are conjuring horrors.

"She asked where you were." Brushing past me toward the exit, she adds, "Wondered why you hadn't come to visit."

"I was chasing an errand." I follow her past the security desk. "I may have good news on the money front."

Again, she stops. Bickery eyes, narrowing into mine: "What do you mean?"

We stand just inside the heavy wood doors, the cascading thrum of rain outside. "I spoke with the banker in charge of the account where Georgie's funds have been drawn."

"God, please, no." She takes a step closer, shooting a glance back at Derrius, then lowering her voice to a flogging whisper. "You can't do this to people."

"Do what, exactly?"

"You don't know when to stop, you just keep pushing and pushing and pushing—"

"All things considered, I think it went well."

"Ha! Like you're one to judge." She withdraws a small collapsible umbrella from her shoulder bag. "Slap a smile on a rotting corpse if you could."

She nudges the door outward with her hip and the umbrella flares open. I hike up the collar of my sport coat and follow, wondering if news of the Capitol bombing hasn't wound her up tighter than usual.

"Not sure I understand the hostility. All I've done is try to help with—"

"*Help?*" She stops and turns. "Do you have any idea how many times they," she points back at the facility, "have asked me—no, begged—to have you barred from visiting? Every time you show your face, Georgie becomes agitated. They need to subdue her, medicate her."

Not true. In fact, a blatant lie. If anyone prompts agitation, I'm looking at her.

"And if I didn't show up at all? You said it yourself, she's wondering where I've been."

Her arm hasn't dropped, and it trembles now with rage, finger still pointing back at all those glowing barred windows. "You should be stuck in there with the rest of them. If life was fair and God was in heaven. Locked away like the lunatic you are."

You've no idea how many times that's come to pass.

"If I thought staying away would do her good, I'd oblige." The rain's slogging down now, I stand there soaked, hair glued to my head, right hand clenching my lapels together, while miniature streams cascade from the curved black edges of her umbrella. "Whatever you may think of me, you know in your heart she looks forward to my visits. Take that away, do you truly believe she'd get better? Send me away—*poof,* like magic, she's happy?"

Her eyes flash with contempt. She drops her arm and takes a small step forward to hiss, "*I'd* be happy," then spins about and marches toward her car.

Two years back, when Georgie first got admitted here, I surveyed the premises, identifying various weak points. At the same time, I studied the routines of the staff, with similar intent.

A man like me, a history like mine, you learn how to slip about.

There will be but one other guard on night duty besides Derrius, and neither will bother to patrol the grounds given the evil weather. Half the time, fair or foul, they spend the hours within earshot of each other, cracking jokes, sharing tales, or one of them slips off to steal a nap while the other keeps the watchful eye.

Yes, arguably they're irresponsible, derelict of duty, especially given the times, but can anyone honestly blame them? Who but me has ever bothered to break *into* the place?

At the rear of the building, down a shallow concrete stair, lies the door to what once served as the furnace room. I long ago jimmied the lock, the better to enter and leave at will.

The giant cylindrical oil tank from the previous, ancient heating system, long empty but still redolent of petrol, stands beside its old companion, the squat black boiler. This is my private bolt-hole, for nights like this when visiting Georgie after hours.

Knowing the storm might vex her, above and beyond whatever effect the news might have, I'm prepared to sit up with her till daybreak if need be, provide a comforting presence.

First, though, off with the wet clothes, drape them against the warm thrumming flank of the current HVAC turbine. I wrap my skivvied self in a thin scratchy blanket, plop down on the concrete floor, and close my eyes, letting my thoughts come and go, appear and disappear, like fireflies winking in the dark.

Come midnight, my clothes are toasty warm, dry as a bone. I collect an apple from my wee stash, a pocketknife to peel and slice, and gingerly make my way upstairs.

It never fails to fascinate me how casually nurses and other staff punch in their codes on security panels, at least when visitors are near. The patients, well, they're devious and clever, so precautions must be taken. But no one gives a moment's thought to protecting the place from the likes of me.

For the sake of simplicity, they use a single four-digit code throughout the building, prompting the question: Who, indeed, are the crazy ones? Within the first hour of my initial visit, I had the run of the place, no corridor forbidden, not a single door barred.

I tiptoe up to Georgie's floor, where they board the depressives—Despairados, per the staff.

Sneaking up to the edge of the door to Georgie's ward, I peek through the window with its crisscrossing mesh. No one walking the hallway. No one in eyesight at all.

At the panel I tap in the magic four numbers, stealthily turn the handle, ease open the vault-like door.

Cocking an ear—nothing but the hum of the overhead fluorescents, dimmed for night shift—I step softly toward Georgie's room, third door on the right.

Another application of code, another heavy metal door clicking open.

I'm in.

THE room is spare, like those one encounters on spiritual retreat: small wooden desk with a crane-neck lamp—shatter-proof plastic bulb, for suicide prevention—plus a bockety wood chair, narrow bed. A picture of St. Dymphna, her very self, hangs on the wall.

The luxury suite.

When she first arrived, they stuck her in a padded cell. Privileges come with proving you're not a danger to yourself. And Georgie has never threatened others. Not her nature.

The bedsheets are bunched and scrambled in chaos, evidence perhaps of one of her signature nightmares.

Pages from her sketchbook lie scattered about the room, each with the tentative start of a drawing—a moonscape, a self-portrait, formless abstractions floating in space—or just a frustrated whirling scrawl.

We're not alone. I sense a lonesome spirit lingering in the room somewhere—nameless, invisible, but present. I can tell by the hint of wet-dog scent.

Georgie stands barefoot near the window, back turned to me: white T-shirt, blue PJ bottoms. She's staring out at the rain through the window's iron bars.

"Hello."

She does not turn in fright. Instead she moves slowly, meticulously, as though savoring each twinge of muscle. Her almond-shaped eyes loom large in their deep-set sockets.

"You've come."

It should feel better, the welcome. Something seems off.

"I thought you might want some company, in case of thunder."

She musters a grateful smile. "I was about to do a little stretching. Do you mind?"

Pressing her palms together at her breastbone, she bows. What follows is a series of slow, methodical movements she calls her Krazygirl Kata—half tai chi, half improvised dance, gliding arms and one-legged poses, deep crouches and dove-like hands drifting back and forth before her face or fluttering over her head. She's given each pose a symbolic name:

> *Angel cradles hummingbird*
> *Noah denies the mammoth*
> *Stealing gravity from the moon*

Somewhere in the middle of the routine, I happen to glance downward. One of the sheets of paper torn from her sketchpad catches my eye, crumpled up. I reach down, gingerly open it. Instead of a picture, it bears writing:

> *My holy man, wholly man, enters:*
> *Let the ceremony commence.*
> *Sacrament? Sacrifice?*
> *Trick question.*
> *Rather, say instead that*
> *the I in anxiety,*
> *the me in blasphemy,*
> *shall once again consecrate*
> *the harm in charm,*
> *the hint of hate in whatever and*
> *the laughter in slaughter,*
> *confirming once and for all*

the sin in sincere,
the mask in masculinity,
the male in malediction

She returns to her original position, feet together, arms at her sides. Then, seeing what I hold in my hand: "Don't read that!"

"But why?"

"Shane?"

"I thought it rather clever."

"You're obscenely easy to please."

I offer it to her, but she makes no move to take it, so I begin to crumple it up again only to discover three words scrawled at the bottom that I failed to spot before.

Wheezy. Sniffles. Grunt.

With that, I'm smiling. It's a game we play, coming up with names for the unfortunate dwarves who didn't make the cut for Walt Disney's *Snow White.* Salty. Dumpy. Punchy. Stuck. Perhaps her turn of mind isn't so dark after all.

"I rather like these here at the bottom. Grunt especially. I can just see the wee fella."

I get no smile in return, merely a whispered, "Is that so," a statement, not a question.

"I've had a few of my own of late. Been meaning to share."

She just stands in place, flexing her hands. Waiting.

"Poxy and Doxy. They're twins."

"Doxy—that means something, right?"

"A woman of the night, mistress, secret lover."

"Interesting." She drifts away into distraction. "Remind me—there's an Irish word for dwarf that isn't quite so . . . "

"Pejorative?"

"Yes."

"The standard word is *abhac*, which is used for both dwarves and midgets. It does, sadly, have a bit of a taint."

"Not that one."

"I'm assuming then you mean *duine beag*. It's gained some currency of late."

"And it means?"

"Little person. Literally."

"Ah."

"As yet it lacks the usual baggage."

Her eyes drift upward to a corner of the ceiling, where the cracks in the plaster resemble an elaborate river system in some mythic nowhere. "What a lovely idea. A lack of baggage."

She shambles toward her bed, lying on her side, knees tucked up, ankles crossed—as though the poem, my reading of it, my clumsy attempt at the game, have one by one ruined any sense of peace her kata might have provided, creating instead some kind of inner storm, mirroring the one beyond the window.

—6—

I pull the desk chair bedside and sit, taking a moment to look at her—the narrow face, jutting cheekbones, a haircut that practically screams *Loony*. I do wish she'd eat.

"Saw your stepmum earlier as she was heading off for home."

The light in her eyes shutters further. "What do you mean, exactly, by 'home?'"

"Is something wrong?"

A soft, miserable laugh. "Everyone always asks me that. Everyone. Always." She flips over in bed, her back to me now. The whole of her body sighs as she makes a pillow of her folded hands. "I am so very tired of being dreary."

"Stop now. You're never that." Outside, the sky emits an inclement moan. The ongoing rat-a-tat of rain. "Would you like me to sing something?"

She's keen on my voice, with a special fondness for the dusty old tunes: *Bean An Fhir Rua* (The Red-Haired Man's Wife), *An Poc Ar Buile* (The Mad Puck Goat), *Casadh An tSúgáin* (The Twisting of the Rope).

"No," she says softly, rubbing her nose like a hare. "Thank you, though."

Suddenly I remember. "Here, I have something for you." I reach in my pocket, bring out the apple, tossing it up with a twirl. Using the pocketknife, I begin by peeling the skin, then make slices, trimming away the core.

She says, "Why do you come to visit?"

Like a kick in the shin, that. "There's a hell of a thing to ask."

"I'm serious. Dead serious."

"As am I. Christ on a cake, you're my dearest friend."

Is this because I didn't come sooner?

She glances over her shoulder. "You're very sweet. And kind. And handsome, by the way, I've told you that."

"Now who's being kind?"

"Don't be glib, okay? I'm trying to, I don't know, trying . . . " Her words follow her gaze, both drifting off. "There are times—when you come here and sit with me, talk to me—there are times I'm not sure I know what you mean. Like my ears are tuned to a different language."

I glance up at the picture of St. Dymphna hovering over the bed. The saintly virgin martyr—she fled from her pagan father after he demanded, in the madness of his grief, that she take her dead mother's place as his bride. Patron saint of incest victims, the mentally ill, runaways, portrayed with her iconic lily, sword, and fettered imp.

"I shouldn't have waltzed in so light-hearted, all mindless small talk, jabbering away."

A moment's silence. Then, in a whisper, she chatters, "Small-talk jibber-jabber small-talk," snapping her fingers in rhythm. It's one of her tics, the finger-snapping.

"Would you like me to go?"

"Yes. And stay away. Find a beautiful wife, have sweet little babies."

"Haven't we flogged this nag enough? How many times, this awful talk—"

"I know you're not gay, I've watched you flirt. Why haven't you fallen in love?"

But I have. A very long time ago. "Georgie—"

"Do you know what it's like not only to be stuck inside this place but to feel like I might have stuck you in here as well?"

"Why do you badger yourself like this?"

She says nothing, back still turned, her body utterly still. Then: "I miss you."

The heartbreak of that. "I'm right here."

"It doesn't matter. I miss you and I miss my life and I want to leave here. Now."

Another gust of rainswept wind rakes the outer walls of the building.

"I'm going to be dreary again, okay?"

"You are never—*never*—dreary to me."

She shivers, tenses. "There was this dream." Said as though the thing arrived like a visitor, which is how it happens to the especially keen. "It went on forever."

I notice again the state of her sheets.

"There's this family—mom, dad, girl, boy—the kind you see in commercials. Wholesome. Happy. They're singing."

Taking a guess, key of E flat: "Oh, we ain't got a barrel of money . . . '"

"I don't remember which song. But it's raining. Like right now, outside. Really, really hard. The windshield wipers, they're thumping right and left. Right and left. That screechy little groan they make against the glass."

She winces, as though that small detail renders the memory all the more vivid. Too much so.

"The singing—it's meant to make them less afraid."

Which is why you can't remember the tune.

She rises up, braces herself with one arm, and reaches out with the opposite hand. "Can I have that?"

I offer an apple slice.

"No. The knife."

That doesn't strike me as the grandest idea. I imagine passing it over, handle first, her inspecting it like a jeweler appraising a diadem, then before I can stop her she's slashing away at her wrist, blood gushing from the wound, a struggle for the knife, a ghoulish scream, the door swinging open, a nurse storming in, a call to security, then the police, after which . . .

31

Speaking of bad dreams. *Not a danger to herself.*

And yet if I deny her request, which seems quite guileless, what signal gets sent then?

I reach over, hand her the knife. To my great relief, she sets it down on the bed, turning it this way, then that, an object of study. The steel blade glimmers dully in the plastic lamplight.

"They won't let us have these, you know." She slips an idle hand under the sleeve of her T-shirt to scratch. "Knives, scissors, nail files. 'Sharps,' they call them. Take them away when we check in, search our purses, our bags."

I picture the scene, the humiliation, the relief. "Back to your dream, the family."

"They were driving on this windy mountain road." She reaches up and with a fingertip draws an invisible rectangle in the air, as though to frame the recollection. "There's this wicked uphill turn, and these giant headlights appear, coming straight at them. So incredibly bright. Like looking straight into the sun. Or at God."

Just then, the door to her room clicks open.

A figure slips in. A hushed snick as the door locks shut behind.
A stunned exchange of glances—eyes big as eggs, the three of us, me
to him and him to her and her to the two of us back and forth.

Not one of the nurses.

Friar Daniel—stubbled for want of a shave, mournful sullen
greyhound eyes.

He stinks of old sweat and recent gin, sniffling as though from onions.
Judging from the waist-high tenting of his cassock, I doubt he's come with
a rousing decade of the rosary in mind.

I murmur, "Jesus fucking Mary in Hell." How to explain—it just slips
out.

My holy man . . . the male in malediction . . .

Remind me what Doxy means . . .

Wheezy . . . Sniffly . . . . Grunt . . .

I'm piecing this all together, my mind like sludge, Friar Daniel
pouring his stare into mine, as Georgie rises from the bed, collects the
knife, pads barefoot across the floor and, with a face as blank as polished
stone, plunges the blade into the stunned Franciscan's chest.

Not a threat to others.

He does not cry out. I get the impression he knows he has it coming.

Elsewhere in the room, however, I sense a madcap laugh from the lone, invisible, wet-dog ghost.

Georgie shoves the friar aside, turns to me, hisses, "The door. Hurry!"

In a snap I do as commanded, punch in the numbers, wait for the liberating click.

She grabs her sketchbook. We slip out and dash for the exit to the stairs.

From behind, a voice calls out, "Hey, hey! You! What the—"

But we're already through the next coded doorway, rushing down, vaulting landing to landing, gripping the railing for balance as we whip around every switchback turn, gathering speed like dervishes.

On the ground floor, Derrius, apparently already alerted from upstairs, stands waiting, blocking the way. He holds a stun-gun in one massive hand, the other gripping a nightstick that he taps ominously against his leg. Still no clue where the second guard is.

Georgie slides to a barefoot stop on the freshly waxed floor.

I make a fateful, split-second choice.

"Derrius, thank heavens." I reveal my empty hands and stride briskly toward him. "Help me, please. I don't know what's gotten into her, all of sudden she made a break and—"

I grip his shirt, yank him forward, and crack him good with the crown of my head. I follow up with a swift knee to his midriff. The big man's eyes roll back, his knees buckle under—he drops, emitting a thunderous moan.

Georgie's already hit the door.

I lean down to whisper, "Sorry, mate," add a pat on his shoulder, then follow her out into the storm.

A moment later we're speeding down the desolate streets.

She glances about, chafing her arms for warmth, her filmy T-shirt and PJ bottoms utterly soaked, her short dark hair plastered to her skull. "We heading for your place?"

"What? No. Of course not, no, they'll be there any minute, looking for you. And me."

"They won't bother."

"They've already rung up your stepmum. Bank on it."

"She'll be relieved."

"Georgie—"

"She'll finally be rid of me."

"That's not how she feels."

"Yeah. Only on the inside."

"Besides—"

"And no one back there at that miserable place will bother to look for me, either."

"You can't be serious."

"They won't want the scandal."

I turn toward her. The question asks itself.

"That wasn't the first little visit, no."

"Georgie, I'm sorry. I had no idea."

"Why should you?"

"Why on earth didn't you tell me?"

"You would have done something noble. And it wouldn't have helped."

"Why not tell someone else, someone you trust, the therapist—"

"You think I *trust* that clown? Hears what he wants to hear. That's how I talked him out of the old juice-jolt."

Electroshock. "They weren't—really?"

"Changed my meds instead. California rocket fuel, Effexor and Remeron. Which, between you and me, I stopped taking."

"And all this is when?"

"About the same time the Friar Daniel business started, oddly enough. I know, it should have sent me into a tailspin, but, whatever, it didn't. Just made me . . . confused."

"Not confused enough to tell me, though."

"It only started, like, last week, week before." She drops her head, fiddles with the T-shirt's hem. "Maybe the week before that."

"Christ in Cleveland—it's been going on all that time?"

"Please don't yell."

"What, were you punishing yourself, or—"

"Please please please just *stop*!"

"All right, I'm sorry, I'll calm down."

I turn off the main drag, figuring it best to stick to the darker side streets, less likely to encounter functioning surveillance cameras.

"But Georgie, honest, I mean this with all my heart. Never again—don't keep something like that from me. There is nothing, nothing in all the world more important to me than that you're safe."

"It's not like he raped me, okay? Not his mojo. He was more, I dunno, sad than scary. Liked talking art, poetry—"

"In the middle of the night. With a rock-hard pecker."

"It didn't turn creepy till the last two visits."

"Jesus wept—meaning what? Three's a charm, tonight's the night, time to get lucky." She no doubt, on some level, knew that—why else pick up the knife? "A little frottage in the cottage, squeeze the weasel—"

"Shane, please please please can we not talk about this? It's just . . . " She turns away. Shortly her fingers snap furtively as she stares out at the lashing rain. Whipcrack of lightning, followed by growls of thunder.

She takes a trembling breath. "Anyway, it's over now."

Sure. That's the hope. Depending on what you mean by "it." And what is hope but the pretty little sister of fear.

A Gift and a Curse

We are each of us angels with only one wing,
and we can only fly by embracing one another.

—Lucretius, *On the Nature of Things*

—8—

PERHAPS you're wondering how such a curious pair became so close, and why I remain devoted.

As earlier related, we met at college. That's not to suggest that I, like Georgie, enrolled in classes as a student. For reasons that should clarify shortly, it's not my privilege to enjoy even the middling entitlements of normal society.

I typically drift from this place to that with nothing but my name—and even that is my own invention, a convenience of pronunciation. From time to time I change it up, if I fear someone, seeing my face, might think they've set eyes on me before.

No documents, scant money, no past I can admit to: my life.

I take whatever work gets offered. Gang bosses have long been known to look the other way for the sake of cheap labor—such have been the methods of digging your average ditch for thousands of years, long before capitalism made it a science. So too laying rail, hammering lumber, quarrying stone. Soldiering.

Not that I'm complaining. Power, fame, wealth—pursue them if you wish. I find them gaudy recompense for the job of survival. A ploy to stand out at the funeral.

If fortune blows at my back, or I make a well-placed friend, I move up in station once skill or leadership or the simple gift of putting words together acquires relevance.

Never for long, however.

Typically I commit some insubordinate outrage to get knocked down again, all the way to rock bottom if possible. That's where I thrive, the better to help the misfortunates around me.

Regardless, one way or another—and sooner rather than later—I'm obliged to move on.

In the current instance, after returning from the ongoing quagmire in the cradle of civilization—serving as a humble rifleman in a New York unit with bloodlines back to the original Irish Brigade—I do all in my power to avoid returning to that godforsaken mess.

Ireland's had far less need of men with my unique skill set since the Good Friday Accords. Besides, I've lost all sense of kinship with the diehard cranks, crackpots, and crazies presently thinking the odd bomb blast will at last unite Ireland—or keep it partitioned for good.

I'm sensing something very much like the Troubles in the current American uproar. That partly explains my decision to remain in the States, my second home as it were. It's here I'll be needed.

There's not just blood in the air. It's in the streets—half the country pitted against the other, coasts against the midlands, natives targeting immigrants, neighbor turning on neighbor.

It's said that once such divisions dig in—once the tribalists shout down all compromise, once those who disagree become not just the opposition but the enemy—democracy's pooch is screwed. Enter anarchy. Or tyranny. Assuming there's a difference. From the pooch's perspective.

In time I wander my way to Philadelphia, and it's there I make the chance acquaintance of a kindly old professor of history named Nils Hovstad.

Through the scholar's good graces I gain work as a janitor at the college where he teaches: Liguorian, in Lansdowne.

As fall term begins I'm roaming the halls, gathering trash and mopping floors, glazing windows, a great clanging ring of keys on my hip as I croon away quietly to myself, songs to keep me company.

The class on Celtic Myth, Legend, and Folklore taught by Reginald Feely meets daily in the late afternoon, and with the instructor's blessing I gain permission to audit.

An utter lark on my part, like revisiting my youth.

It's there I meet Georgie. And feel an instant connection.

She sits in the far corner of the classroom, adrift in her solitude, staring out the window at the red-leafed maples.

She's just yanked off her woolen hat, so her thin, dark, pixyish hair crackles with static. Her cardigan, several sizes too large, slouches off one shoulder, and the blouse underneath has the buttons awry, as though she dressed in darkness or a state of abstraction. She wears high-water trousers and men's shoes with thick grey socks that squat around her bone-white ankles.

The seats all around her lie empty, so I choose one on her right, a little behind, far enough so as not to crowd, near enough to whisper a joke.

Once our instructor arrives and class begins, I get the opportunity to make myself known by gently correcting his mangling of the old names: Muirthemne ("Moor-hev-neh"), Eamhain Macha ("Ow Ma-ha"), Labhraidh ("Lauw-reh"), and so on.

He's miffed at first, of course, a challenge to his authority, but once it's clear I mean no offense he's gamely playing along.

My efforts serve to amuse Georgie; she chances a smile. There's nothing flirtatious about it, but her cat-like eyes glimmer.

After class, we sit on a bench beneath a sprawling old dogwood and run through the course outline, me pronouncing every name and she transcribing the sounds phonetically, syllable by syllable, including the ones that will become so crucial between us:

Oisín (Uh-SHE-un)
Finn mac Cumhal (Finn McCool)
Niamh Chinn Óir ("Neev Heen Orge")
Manannán Mac Lir ("MONN-aw-non Mok LUR")
Tír na nÓg ("Tier-nuh-nogue")
Gabhra ("GAHV-ra")
Tech Duinn ("Chagh DOO-een")
Donn Fírinne ("Don FEAR-neh")
Almhuin ("AL-win")
Bran ("Brahn")
Sceolan ("SHKO-lahn")
Sadbh ("Sahv")
Fear Doirche ("Fahr DOR-eh-ha")
Beinn Gulbain ("Ben GUL-ven)

She beams with gratitude once we're done, and though her skittish nerves persist, I can tell by the warming in her eyes we've launched a solid alliance.

Not long after that first encounter, we meet for tea at a nearby café.

She seems oddly withdrawn. Not sullen, though. More like she's bursting with a perfectly scrumptious secret.

Finally, I say, "One more pump and the well should draw water."

"Excuse me?"

"You've got something to tell me. Out with it."

The twitchy grin playing at the corners of her mouth gives way to a timid smile.

She opens her purse, digs around for a moment, then takes out an item no larger than her palm, wrapped in light blue tissue paper, garlanded with flows of curling ribbon.

"Something for you." She places it on the table. "To say thank you."

"For what?"

"Being so nice. Helping me." She scrunches up her shoulders, hands folded in her lap. "Everything."

I undo the sprawling ribbon, peel back the paper.

It's a salmon, a mere three inches long, carved from cedar and painted by hand with masterful delicacy, each scale multicolored, the most intricate brushwork, vivid pinks and reds with blue and green accents—so small, so precise, like a gem.

"Where did you find this?"

"I made it."

"Get out." My eyes pop. "Your very own self?"

She nods. "It's the symbol of wisdom."

Oh yes, I know. The ancient impulse calling from within: return. The desperate endless upstream fight. So many hundreds of restless miles, even where streambeds have turned to dust. All for a promise of hope. And rest.

I marvel at such perceptive innocence: How does she know? What have I done or said to let her see so clearly into my nature, my fate?

"It's brilliant," I tell her, and her smile at last breaks open.

The bond between us deepens as the weeks pass.

Given her fondness for my singing voice, I entertain her with everything from old Irish ballads to songs of the uprising to dance hall numbers.

In time, she confides to me her struggles with the Old Black Dog:

The shock of her kind and gentle mother dying so young.

The recreant father's prompt remarriage simply so he can abandon the girl.

Thereafter, living alone, day in, day out, with a scolding, resentful, vindictive stepmother.

All that, combined with her own dark chemistry, have led to weeks of bedridden isolation, paralyzing doubts as to her reason for being—watching the spider of existence tend its web—crowned by one attempt, age fifteen, to take her own life.

"That doesn't bother you?"

We're sitting on a bench shaded by birches with their chattering leaves.

"Hardly," I tell her. "What honest person who's awake to the world hasn't considered it?"

"I went beyond considering."

Me as well. I restrain the admission. "I won't be one of those to fault you for it. Nor will I ever tell you to buck up, feel better, think positive."

"I get that a lot." She affects a mincing, carping tone. "'You can't really be feeling as bad as all that.' 'Maybe if you stopped thinking about yourself so much.'"

"'Why don't you go out and catch some bloody sun!'"

That conjures a laugh, bright as altar bells.

"That's the kind of stuff she tells you, your stepmum?"

"Are you kidding? It never stops. She's not alone."

With that image, of being relentlessly flogged with fault—cursed, as it were—I sense our lives weaving together tighter still.

"Well, here's a promise. You never have to pretend with me. I'll never try to 'fix' you. You are who you are—who can claim different? Besides, I happen to think you're grand."

Turns out, I'm not the only one.

Georgie forges another bond as hers and mine progresses—this one with our teacher, Mr. Feely.

Adrift in his thirties, he's a bit of an awkward bird, dressing for class like an Ivy League refugee, the tweed jacket with leather elbow patches, stiffly starched button-down shirt, pressed jeans with the telltale crease, straight as a razor, down to the tasseled loafers. His chestnut hair erupts in tussocks no comb can cure as he peers uneasily from behind tortoiseshell glasses. Gangly and tall, his large hands flap and dangle from his shirt cuffs, lending added nuance to his nickname, "Touchy."

Touchy Feely.

Maybe the bond between Georgie and me calls to him somehow, and he feels driven to elbow his way in.

Perhaps he doubts my true intentions and has decided to swoop in protectively.

Regardless, in time his attraction to Georgie seems genuine enough, if a tad overbearing. And it quickly ripens with passion, something Georgie desperately craves. And deserves.

Ardor transforms her. She laughs more openly and often. Her hair, meticulously brushed each morning, magically thickens. Her skin begins to glow. I even detect from time to time a subtle whiff of Chanel.

Perhaps I should show more concern, knowing Georgie's past. The attraction to an older man, given her father's abandonment, it's one of those red flags people love to wave in retrospect after the battle's been lost.

Not to mention the power imbalance—teacher and student, at a college named for Alfonsus Liguori, founder of the Congregation of the Most Holy Redeemer. No telling the trouble if they're found out.

Also, admittedly, Touchy's endearments often possess an imperious, loftier-than-thou tone that gives me pause. I can't help but hear an echo of the inner voice of self-doubt that Georgie's stepmum nurtures at every turn.

But who am I to judge? The heart wants what it wants—and our friendship hasn't matured to the point I've any right to question her choice of lovers.

As her relationship with Reggie intensifies, she and I naturally spend less time together. Nothing to lament in that. Besides, there's good use elsewhere for my presence.

I double my visits to the local VA, sitting in on rap sessions among the vets—the broken ones, the haunted, the guilty. My brothers.

I even contemplate re-enlisting, taking the place of some young buck hoping to prove his manhood. Spare him the discovery that it lies on the far side of a nightmare.

Before I'm able to reach a decision, Georgie tracks me down, seeking advice.

With semester's end approaching, a project is due: an ambitious essay, a chapbook of poems, a novelette, anything that shows the course has left an impression.

She refuses to content herself with just any effort—she wants to produce something breathtaking, an illustrated manuscript worthy of the Book of Durrow, to make her secret lover glow with pride, show with every word on the page and every elaborate interlaced drawing that her feelings go far beyond a mere schoolgirl crush.

I'm a sucker for such obsessions. Life is bloodless without them.

And so I suggest a premise, a variation on a standard tale, but not far afield from plausible conjecture.

What if, I tell her, the story of the warrior bard Oisín, son of Finn mac Cumhal, ended far differently than recounted in the usual renderings—specifically, the one presented in class?

For those unacquainted with the tale: Finn and his *fianna* are a roving band of hunters and warriors in ancient Ireland, known for their courage and cunning.

One day, while returning from a hunt, Finn and his troupe encounter a beautiful fawn who runs off before them. They all give chase but the fawn darts too swiftly ahead, and finally it's only Finn and his two favorite hounds, Bran and Sceolan, who continue on.

Once the fawn sees it is just those three behind her, she lies down in the grass and waits. Bran and Sceolan approach gently, sensing something unique about this creature, and they lick her face and neck.

The fawn follows Finn back to his home at Almhuin, and that night before the fire she transforms into a beautiful woman. Her name is Sadbh, and she tells Finn she was turned into a fawn by Fear Doirche, the dark druid of the Men of Dea, when she refused his love.

Finn takes Sadbh for his wife, and he lives so happily that his prior love of the hunt and battle withers away.

When the men of Lochlann invade Ireland, however, Finn and the battalions of the *fianna* march off to confront them.

After seven days, the invaders are at last repelled, and Finn returns home to Almhuin.

When he does, he expects to see Sadbh, who is now with child, rush out to greet him. Instead, all his people emerge from the dun with terrible news.

While Finn was away, Sadbh saw his figure approaching across the field, and she ran out to greet him—but the figure was Fear Doirche magically transformed into Finn's image. He struck Sadbh with a hazel rod, turning her once again into a fawn, which he dragged off.

The people tried to run out and save her but when they reached the place where last they saw her, she and the druid had utterly vanished.

Finn grieves terribly for seven long years, and he never stops searching for Sadbh in his journeys.

Then one day, as he and his men are hunting near Beinn Gulbain, Bran and Sceolan come upon a naked, long-haired youth.

As with Sadbh, the dogs sense something unique in the boy, and set about nuzzling and licking him.

Finn, seeing something of Sadbh's aspect in the boy's face, takes him in, and once the boy learns the *fianna*'s language he tells them of his life up until the day they discovered him.

He used to live, he says, with a deer he loved fiercely, who cared for him, sheltered him. They lived in a cave above a vast green valley with thick woods and clear streams, surrounded by high, impassable cliffs.

A dark-looking man in a hooded cloak often came to the place, and spoke to the deer, quietly at times, more harshly at others.

Regardless of his tone, the deer shrank from him in terror.

The last time he saw the deer, the ominous hooded figure was speaking to her at length, and as he did his anger rose and rose until he struck her more viciously than ever before and dragged her off.

The deer stared back tearfully at the boy she'd nurtured and gave out the most mournful cries. He tried to follow, but was struck by a spell that rendered him motionless.

When he regained his wits, he lay in the grassy place where Finn's hounds found him.

Finn embraces the youth as his son, and names him Oisín: "Little Deer." He grows into a great warrior, hunter, and poet, and is among the most famous and beloved of the *fianna*, proving himself one of the fiercest and most capable fighters in their many battles.

But like Finn, he too would continue searching, wherever he wandered—not just for the deer, but for the beautiful valley walled off by cliffs, the cave where he'd been loved.

Not everyone sings the praises of the *fianna*, however, for they demand payment for their fighting, at a rate some find extortionate.

The King of Ireland assembles a great army, not just from among the island clans but from all over the world. They meet Finn and his *fianna* battalions at the great Battle of Gabhra.

Thousands on both sides die, and neither Finn nor the King regain their former power.

After the fight, Oisín and Finn and the remaining members of the band are hunting in the west country when they spot a strange apparition coming toward them from the horizon through the mist across the sea.

As the figure draws closer, they notice it's a young woman, stunningly beautiful, wearing a long silk robe, a golden crown, and riding a grand white horse.

When she comes ashore she directs her words to Finn, explaining that she is Niamh Chinn Óir, Niamh of the Golden Hair, daughter of Manannán Mac Lir, God of the Sea and the King of Tír na nÓg, also known as the Land of Victory, the Land of the Ever-Living Ones, the Land of Youth.

When asked why she has traveled so far, she explains that it's to ask for the hand of Finn's son, Oisín of the Strong Hands, for though other princes seek her as wife, none have earned her love like him, whom she finds braver, nobler, more handsome than all the rest.

If he agrees, he will live with her and be young forever where all is plenty, and she recounts the numerous bounties he will know: the feasts, the swords, the horses, the loyal hounds. Not to mention her bridal bed.

Hearing all this, Oisín promptly jacks himself up behind her on her horse, whose name is Embarr, and the two depart for Tír na nÓg. As they head off, Finn and the *fianna* give up three sorrowful shouts, for they know in their hearts they will never see Oisín again.

The two riders journey west across the waves, beholding many wonders, great cities and courts and lime-white houses, a girl with a golden apple in her palm.

Then the sky darkens, the sun disappears—the winds grow strong on all sides, the sea catches fire. They ride on beneath the lonesome stars until once again the sun brightens and a stunning country appears in full blossom.

Oisín asks if this is Tír na nÓg, and Niamh confirms it is, and soon he will see that all she promised is true.

Her father, Manannán, comes out from his great castle to welcome them, and assures Oisín he will be forever young and enjoy every blessing the land offers.

Here some of the stories vary as to how Oisín passes his days with Niamh, whether in splendor or trial or sleep, but all converge with him aching to see Finn and the *fianna* again, asking finally if he can return home for just a short while to take pleasure in their company.

Niamh responds to Oisín's request with a sigh of heartbreak.

Though she agrees to his request, even giving him Embarr to ride, she warns him—under no circumstances can he touch the ground when he returns, or he will never see her again.

With this caution in mind, he rides back across the waves, but once home he finds none of his old companions. The land has changed—the raths and duns of antiquity have vanished—he recognizes nothing. The humble men he discovers working the land or mending their nets by the sea bear no resemblance to the great warriors he remembers.

When he asks the strangers if they know where Finn and the *fianna* might be found, they look utterly puzzled. "We have heard of Finn and the others in tales the old folk tell," they say, "but such men as them are long gone from the land."

Only then does Oisín realize that what felt like the mere passage of days or weeks in the Land of Youth in fact has been hundreds of years.

With great sorrow he rides to the Hill of Almhuin where Finn's great fortress once stood, but it too is gone, turned to rubble. All he finds is the great stone trough where the *fianna* used to wash after battle or the hunt.

As he leans down to dip his hands in the cool clear water, the cinch strap on his saddle breaks.

He reaches out to break his fall, and the second his hand touches solid ground he ages three hundred years, turning withered and weak—like "a wolf sucked under a weir," to borrow a great poet's phrasing.

Embarr, startled by this transfiguration, gallops back riderless over the waves to his home in Tír na nÓg.

Some versions of the story stop there. Others continue with Oisín meeting St. Patrick, who confirms that Finn and the others are long dead—worse, they now reside in Hell, scourged by eternal fire, as Oisín himself will be upon his death if he does not accept Christ as his Savior.

Hearing this, Oisín responds he doubts he will find old friends among the blessed.

He tells the old saint that when he dies, he intends to bypass heaven and rejoin the *fianna*—be they at feast or in flames.

"But there is still another version," I inform Georgie. "One rarely told, except now and then among the hermits living on the island crags off the westerly end of Connemara."

In this lesser known rendering, as Niamh sees Embarr returning riderless across the waves, she runs to her father, Manannán, and begs him to intercede.

"My devotion to Oisín was not rash or misplaced. It came from the core of my heart."

The old god, however, has no patience for fools, especially mortal ones. He dismisses his daughter's entreaty.

So she kneels before him, eyes welling with tears, and grips his hand.

"I know how frequently it is said that vengeance is stronger than gratitude. But that is not a sentiment worthy of us. Revenge, though fierce with life at first, becomes its own executioner. And no act of vengeance garners greater esteem than one not taken."

Manannán, despite his pride, feels moved by these words. Even so, he cannot bring himself to forgive the faithless ingrate, who had every delight at hand, not to mention a goddess as bride, the great god's very own daughter, only to throw it all away in a meager fit of homesickness.

"I will promise you this," he tells her, lifting her chin so their eyes meet. "He will retain the gift of eternal youth—but not here. He will live and suffer as any other man, since that apparently is his wish."

Niamh begins to speak but he stops her.

"And since he fashions himself a soldier he will have his fill of battles, the likes of which he cannot foresee, too horrible to imagine, a harvest of blood, for that is the path of his race. And he will bear troubles that will shake his soul, all without aging a day, until he himself is stricken down, and dies like those of his kind."

Again, Niamh tries to speak. Again, he prevents her.

"Upon his passing," he continues, "he will journey to the island rock of Tech Duinn and watch Donn Fírinne cull the noble from the common, then ferry the first group of souls across the waters of oblivion while the others dissolve in the wind, or wander the earth as ghosts. But Oisín of the Strong Hands' fate will be neither of those."

"No, Father, no—"

"Instead, Donn will send him back—still young, but without the balm of forgetfulness. He will remember absolutely everything that has befallen him, down to the wickedest fault, like an old man hounded by regret."

Niamh, still clutching her father's hand, refuses to be silenced any longer.

"You're saying he and I will never meet again. To let him live and live again but always alone, preyed upon by a thousand remembrances—such a curse is far too cruel for any offense, let alone his. And he will not be the only one punished—how does that not qualify as vengeance?"

Manannán replies, "I cannot keep you from the consequence of your own poor choice. Let me, however, grant you this: Upon each visit he makes to Tech Duinn, you and he can visit, languish for a spell, enchant each other, until he returns once again a young man to the land of want and death he misses so much—and I alone will determine when and where that return occurs. That cycle will continue for all of time until he learns what was his for the asking here with you: the wisdom of all the world."

I can tell from Georgie's expression as I finish that I've given her what she's been hoping for. She goes away with fire in her mind, eager to render what I've said into her project.

And that project proves a marvel—a handmade book, leather-bound, with parchment pages, on which she's written the tale I told her and more, much more, bits of this and that lifted from the old stories—the Pigs of Angus, the House of the Quicken Trees, the Lad of the Skins—all woven together in her own unique rendering, mad with invention, plus imagined tales of Oisín wandering the earth, beset by his curse over the centuries.

The end result exceeds 400 pages, the script as florid as that of the Irish monks, the illustrations bold in color, intricate in design, the enlarged first word of every chapter an artwork in itself.

The interlaced borders framing each page form elaborate, chainlike vines giving birth to ravens, wolves, and serpents, a pattern that in the original was meant to ward off the Devil.

Working through trial and error, she's matched her inks to the ancient, startling blues fashioned from azurite, lazurite, and indigo; warm greens derived from verdigris and malachite; golden yellows from buckthorn; brick-hued reds from bedstraw root and cudbear.

For a title, she's chosen *The Truth Against the World*, the motto of Finn's *fianna*, and as she reads bits and pieces of it aloud to me, her voice breathless with the fascination of secrecy, I hear as well her love of the old tales' themes—the wonder of this world, the grace of sudden kindness, the pitiless indifference of fate.

It has taken a feverish month to complete, the work filling both day and night, during which she's barely slept or eaten. Her color has blanched to a spectral pallor, hands cramping up from hours of clutching her pen and brush—and yet an inner flame of triumph enlivens her eyes.

As you can imagine, however, given what I've already said, things do not end well. It isn't just fate that proves pitiless. And kindness, sudden or otherwise, offers no grace.

Reginald Feely is the lover who shatters not only Georgie's heart but her mind. I'm not there when the words get said, but I can only imagine how harsh and cutting and cruel they are, given the aftermath.

Georgie's promised to call and let me know how her gift is received, and when I don't hear back by midnight, I go looking.

Searching high and low, I find her at last curled up beneath a great hickory tree on the south end of campus, nothing on but a skirt and camisole, chilled to the bone.

She's unable to register my voice, clawing at her inner arm. It's bloody and raw, like scored meat, with bone visible through the gore.

I tear the sleeve off my shirt, wrap her arm tight, then lift her in a fireman's carry and bolt off to the nearest ER, remaining there beyond daybreak, till I learn she's stable and resting.

It's said you can never turn away from a life you save. From that day forward, through the crests and hollows of her misery, I am there. I could not live with myself if I did otherwise.

As for the stunning gift, the masterpiece, with its central story of the curse placed upon Oisín and his ill-fated wanderings, life after life?

I imagine you've already guessed—it forms the basis for a quartet of international bestsellers penned by a humble college instructor who has taken the pseudonym Rory Fitzgerald.

And how exactly did I come by that unorthodox rendering of Oisín's fate?

I imagine you've guessed that by now as well, and it has nothing to do with island hermits.

I have lived that curse. I am the faithless ingrate.

I am Oisín.

THE MIRROR THAT BECOMES A DOOR

Come away, O human child!
To the waters and the wild
With a faery, hand in hand,
For the world's more full of weeping
than you can understand.

—William Butler Yeats, "The Stolen Child"

—9—

THE rain slams down in howling sheets, my feeble wipers barely able to clear the windscreen no matter how crazed their pace, while the wail of distant sirens competes with thunder in the stormy darkness.

Hunters learn how to think like prey. That instinct kicks in as I zig-zag along the dark Philadelphia backstreets, hoping to avoid any and all patrols, checkpoints, roadblocks.

Mere hours after purchasing my car, when I visited the clandestine garage specializing in stealth-stripping—removing, neutralizing the various surveillance devices embedded in its machinery—I also had adversarial-imagery decals attached to my plates. That renders them indecipherable to the scanner algorithms used by automated license readers blinking away at every corner. No doubt my registration info is on a hotlist already, but the car remains all but invisible given these countermeasures.

As for facial recognition cameras, a special glaze on the window glass scrambles the signal from image to mainframe database. Yes, the system's notoriously underfunded, unreliable, and compromised by hackers, but why take chances?

I've also turned off my cell phone and zipped it inside an anti-track pouch, to make doubly sure no signal can pinpoint our location.

The Fourth Industrial Revolution, with its robot armies and tracking satellites, handheld retinal scanners giving police access to the most intimate details of our lives—it all sounded so intimidating, full-blown corporatism, the fearsome surveillance state. But it failed to take full account of political passions, the "systematic organization of hatreds." Paranoid hackers launching malware attacks, accelerationists targeting the power grid, sabotage from all sides. All those pesky gremlins.

And yet the hunt's no joke. Georgie's confidence no one will bother trying to find us seems beyond wishful thinking. Fear of scandal? Ha! If ever there was a case of "he said, she said"—him a man of the cloth, she an unstable depressive. Old story, I can hardly be shocked. And yet I am.

Meanwhile, she'll ruin herself if I don't find her something more substantial to wear—shoes and socks, a proper shirt, pants. She looks like a whippet dragged from a stream.

First, though, one more precaution.

Mid-block on a dark residential street, I pull to the curb, kill the ignition, the headlamps. Moldering sofas and tables litter the dark yards, cast-off clothes hanging from tree limbs sway in the gusty wind, all left behind in the pelting rain, remnants of abandoned yard sales—the great sell-off, anything to make ends meet as the economy craters.

"Need to stop for just a tick, check something."

I remove a small black device the size of a light dimmer from the front console. When I point it her direction, her eyes balloon.

"No worries," I tell her. "Just a frequency monitor. Won't hurt, I promise."

It's not just cell phones tracking people these days. Subdural implants, "under the skin surveillance"—anyone admitted to medical care receives one.

Sure enough, right around her fifth cervical vertebrae. "You're hot."

"One of my demons."

"Not quite. Giving off a GPS signal. It's okay, there's an easy fix—short-term, but it works."

I withdraw a small unmarked tube from the console.

"It's a salve, called JAM. Contains an aluminum particulate and other stuff I can't begin to explain so don't ask me, but it blocks the signal. For a while, anyway. It'll feel cool on your skin, but nothing more. May I?"

She nods, and as I apply the ointment, she sniffs, wrinkles her nose. The stuff has the smell of fresh solder. "How do you know about this?"

"One great advantage of hanging out with vets. Everyone who enters the service these days gets an implant. And a lot of those folks aren't the kind to entertain being tracked every minute of every day for the rest of their lives."

"'Those folks'—meaning you?"

Among unsavory others. "Hadn't been decommed more than a week before I knew about this stuff. But we'll need to keep reapplying it until we can find a more permanent fix."

"Like what, cut it out?"

"Nothing so drastic, though that does get done. Just turn it off. Electronically. Like mine. But I'll need help with that."

I employ the frequency monitor once again, to ensure her signal's now dark, then check the rest of her, looking for other implants, find none. Everything returns inside the console and I start up the car again, crank up the heat.

Gradually, she settles into herself. In time the steady in-and-out of her breathing suggests she's nodded off. Her angular face, the feline eyes, they look saintly in repose.

My mind tries to sort our situation.

Given that Friar Daniel likely received prompt medical attention, I doubt we have a murder to answer for.

Regardless, *attempted* murder's bad enough, deadly weapon and all, with extra points on my end for breaking and entering, the assault on Derrius—and will I be deemed an accomplice in an escape or a kidnapper?

"You okay?" Georgie, not asleep at all, reaches over, gives my arm a tender squeeze.

"Lost in thought, is all." I drag up a smile. "Seemed you were slumbering."

"I've made things impossible, haven't I?"

"Oh, stop. Not even."

"You're just being kind."

"Nothing criminal in kindness. But no, not impossible. Bit sticky, yes."

She shrinks back into her silence, resumes the finger-snapping—catches herself, stops.

"They'll lock me up for good next time."

There won't be a next time. You're not going back. Ever.

—10—

I need a helping hand—someone to trust without question, tuck us away for a few hours as I scrabble up a plan. Only one name comes to mind. He lives in the urban No Man's Land between Forgotten Bottom and Devil's Pocket.

Not so long ago, gentrification began its intractable creep into this part of the city. It's long since crept away again. The Junior Black Family Mafia controls it now, in a truce with the Razor Boys, a Vietnamese outfit, and they keep the makeshift militias and rival gangs away.

The local firehouse and police station stand deserted—budget cuts, the city says, not retreat, not surrender. That absence, given Georgie's and my predicament, feels oddly reassuring.

Shabby, chockablock storefronts pass by in a blur, an occasional smear of barroom neon. The going's slow, the street littered with nails, bolts, broken glass—ghetto confetti, meant to slow down squad cars. Lookouts appear in high lamplit windows, staring down as we pass, murmuring into their handheld phones.

Despite the scrutiny, no one emerges to block the way. Call me sentimental, but I offer up a little prayer of thanks to Saint Barbara, patron saint of thunderstorms.

Peering past my wipers into the slogging rain, I turn toward the chancier neighborhoods along the riverfront.

It's there I see it—something hanging from a lamppost.

Correction: not something. Someone.

A woman. Naked, thin, small. Like Georgie. A large white cardboard placard hangs from her ankle: "Snitch." Black ink running in the rain.

Slathers of tar obscure the woman's eyes and mouth. So too the hands, the feet. Prevent identification. Doubtful, though, that the authorities, let alone anyone living nearby, won't know exactly who this is.

A mother perhaps, a sister, a wife, hoping to save a loved one with that stubborn faith in the law. Now a martyr to that faith.

For a moment I sit blinking, trying to believe the storm's playing tricks.

The mob responsible might be watching. I should get away.

Georgie stirs, rubbing her eyes. "Why have we stopped?"

"Just getting my bearings, is all." I slip the car back into drive. But I've waited too long.

She looks out past the smeary windshield and sees the figure swaying in the rain. No expression of shock or horror—she might just as easily be gazing into a mirror. Her hand flashes across the space between us, clutches my sleeve.

"I won't betray you. Okay? Ever."

The thought hadn't crossed my mind—how sad, it crossing hers. "Nor I you. That's a promise." I ease my foot off the brake pedal. "Let's be off now, yeah?"

The end of the maze appears at last, the right street, the proper unit in the string of rowhouses down the block.

We scamper through the rain up the walkway, arriving like two shipwrecked castaways beached on the porch.

Checking my watch—it's just past four. No idea how to explain our presence. Simply ring the bell and hope.

Nothing at first. The man who lives here, he's nearing his ninth decade of life on this earth, and though still sharp he's no longer nimble.

Perhaps I've rousted him from sleep. Perhaps he has the sense not to answer the door at this hour, especially given where he lives, this part of the city.

Another ring.

Silence. Just the rain, the wind, the whining groans of pre-dawn traffic from the nearby throughway. Another distant siren.

Finally, the faint slap of slippered footfalls beyond the door.

The Judas-hole racks open. A single eye, electric blue behind the rimless lens, flares with shock at the sight of us.

The tiny peephole closes again, he throws back the deadbolt, pulls open the door.

A small and wiry man, white-haired but humming with Nordic vigor—and fully dressed, even at this hour: ancient wool trousers baggy at the knee, shaggy knit cardigan, plaid shirt buttoned to the wizened throat.

We've not rousted him from sleep at all. Blame senescent insomnia, I suppose.

Nils Hovstad, renegade sage of Liguorian's history department, the irksome iconoclast of the faculty—socialist, atheist, genius.

On his salary he could live quite comfortably elsewhere: a posh suburb, a townhouse in Center City. Instead he chooses to live down here among the underclass, a gesture of solidarity.

When I first arrived in town, sleeping in a shelter a few blocks away, he ambled in one afternoon bearing an armful of clothes for the homeless. Something about the man appealed to me, so I struck up a friendly convo. It lasted three hours, after which he graciously found me a job at the college.

The long chats have continued. Often at the close of day I'll mitch off work and duck into his office. The contrarian professor and the custodian savant—over strong black tea and ginger biscuits, we'll knock the ball about as twilight looms, arguing anything and everything, history, philosophy, politics, art.

He marvels at the breadth and depth of my knowledge, takes me for a voracious reader, a self-made scholar, not a cursed soul who's actually lived the things of which he speaks.

"It's obscenely early, I realize, to come—"

"Stop." He leans out into the lamplight to peer left and right down the block. Rain streams off the awnings, rumbles in the gutters. He waves us inside. "Come along, quick-quick."

Once the door shuts behind us, I close my eyes and welcome the bracing rush of warmth.

"First," he says, "the clothes. I will give them a quick wash, then pop them in the dryer."

I take heart from the kind familiarity of the voice, chesty despite his homuncular frame, and still graced with its Bergensk lilt.

He turns to Georgie, shivering as she clutches my sodden jacket tight around her shoulders. "And young lady, you would appear to require something beyond your current attire. I will see what I can rustle up, as you Americans so colorfully put it."

He points us down a long hall pooled with lamplight from successive doorways. "Second room on the right. You will find blankets in the dresser. Wrap yourselves in those for now."

I let Georgie go first, waiting in the corridor till she re-emerges cocooned in a duvet, its forest green color a fierce contrast to her pinkish gooseflesh.

I go in after, strip naked, find a scratchy Hudson blanket and drape it around me.

"Unfortunately," the professor says as we rejoin him in the living room, "the fireplace is on the blink. Permanently, it would seem. Terribly expensive to fix." He flutters his hand at the imagined bother. "Regardless, I have cranked up the furnace. That should ward off the chill."

"I'm sure you've gathered, well, we're in a bit of a spot."

He collects our sopping clothes. "Later, my friend."

"In particular, you may hear from the police."

"Really? How exciting. I will greet them in my native tongue, then play dumb."

With that, our elfin protector vanishes, leaving us alone.

The furnishings—mismatched, comfy, worn—testify to an untroubled bachelorhood, though he once confessed to me his solitude is not voluntary. "There once was a girl," he told me. "Her name was Rikke. She had the wisdom to choose a man who could afford her."

Folk art from a life of solitary travel graces the walls and bookshelves—Uighur masks, Russian *khokhloma*, Day of the Dead figurines—most of it coated in a thin pelt of dust.

The air smells of tinned fish, mentholated ointment, pipe tobacco.

A small monitor propped on a tray, tuned to Al Jazeera World News, flickers in the corner, the sound muted.

We each try to find a place to sit, but first need to clear away a tome or two to make a place. Very old school, the professor, still devoted to physical books.

As I'm putting away the last of those currently occupying my chosen chair, I can't help but notice it's one of his own works. Letting it fall open naturally in my hands, I let my eyes descend upon a random passage.

> *Orwell, so right in so many ways, in one regard at least understated the threat we face. He maintained that, as long as one held to the truth, being a minority of one, even against all the world, did not make one mad. And yet history, with its supple ironies and seductive contradictions, has shown us time and again that the most expedient way to drive a man insane is to isolate him—and what better way to accomplish that than to drum into his brain that insidious term "self-reliance"?*

> *Pound the drum relentlessly, hour after hour, day after day, and you can cut him off not just from society but from*

his brothers and sisters, his friends and comrades, convince him his few real achievements and innumerable failures are due to no one but himself.

It is this peculiar delirium, commonly mistaken for individual liberty, that makes it so easy to destroy a movement, a resistance, a rebellion. One by one, the leaders succumb to the corrupting delusion of their own magnificence. And one by one, the followers drift away, descending into cynicism, ennui, despair.

Georgie, wriggling herself into the spot she's cleared on the sofa, notices me reading. "Book of the Month?"

"Not quite." I close the thing, set it aside. "An international history of labor movements." An ancient history, given the last half century, as the invisible hand snatched away the overwhelming share of the planet's wealth from the workers who produced it.

As though on cue, the author himself appears, bearing mugs of steaming tea that he sets down before us, along with a plate of the seemingly inevitable ginger biscuits.

"Now," he says, easing down into an armchair of his own, "in response to your earlier remarks—yes, I am aware of your difficulties. You have, in fact, made something of a stir, my learned friend."

—11—

THE professor picks up a handheld remote and points it toward the small monitor on its corner tray. "Not in the international news, obviously." The screen jumps and zags as the channels change. "But the local outlets, yes. You're quite the sensation."

"I can only imagine what's being said."

"You don't honestly think I believe them."

"Professor—"

"Attacking a man of the cloth? Bah. I am sure he deserved it."

"It wasn't Shane." Georgie shivers beneath the green duvet. "It was me. I stabbed him."

The professor turns to her with a cunning eye. "That would explain why you do not appear all that abducted, my child."

"Is that what they're saying?"

"Better still, the man who snatched you away," he nods my direction, "is deeply and dangerously disturbed."

Georgie raises a finger in protest. "No, no, no. That's just—"

"I believe they were quoting your mother on that point."

"She's *not* my *mother.*"

The professor blanches at the sharpness of tone.

"Bit of friction on that point," I offer quietly. "Stepmother."

"Ah. My apologies." He nods contritely. "By the way, just to be clear, your little adventure is no more than a sideshow at the moment. Almost comic relief."

"I'm sorry?"

"There is something else much more important occupying everyone's minds."

As though drawn by a spell, we follow the professor's gaze as he turns toward the tiny screen. Shortly, the crawl at the bottom reads: *Four Suspects Arrested in Capitol Bombing.*

It takes a moment, but gradually the faces appear—mug shots of four black men, each more thuggish than the last. Fresh from prison—having done time for armed robbery, manslaughter, distribution of heroin, ketamine, fentanyl.

Right out of central casting. Poster perfect, if fright's your purpose.

"Arrests? No one's even heard of them, not before yesterday."

The professor taps his mug. "Assuming you believe this gang, these Black Pascal—"

"Rascal."

"Strangers."

"Rangers."

He offers an impish grin. "I know. I am just making a joke."

Georgie glances back and forth between us, like we're suddenly speaking Mandarin.

"Ten will get you twenty," I say, "they don't even exist, this gang."

"Do not tell me that you are one of those who cannot fathom how a handful of common criminals could pull off the greatest terrorist act in the history of the republic."

"Anyone can get lucky once, I suppose."

Georgie, still confused, turns back to the silent TV, squinting at the words whisking along the bottom of the screen.

"This isn't Argentina," the professor says. "Not yet."

"Meaning?"

"I doubt, if this entire scenario is contrived, that the fine minds behind it would exhibit such shoddy statecraft as to fashion their culprits from thin air."

"You think these Black Rascal Rangers are legit, then."

"Their existence has been 'verified,' shall we say, by official decree. And so now they not only exist, they have always existed, 'enemies of decent people everywhere.'" He tugs a shirttail out from beneath his belt, uses it to wipe a smear from his eyeglass lenses. "As to their actual influence, their verifiable numbers . . . " The words trail off into a shrug.

"What about mutinies? There've been a few more, I hear. Two whole brigades of the 82nd Airborne, half the marines at Camp Pendleton."

"That has not been confirmed." He returns his glasses to his face, hooks the earpieces into position, blinks as though to focus. "Even so, it is not exactly Potemkin. As yet."

"Maybe so. But given we now have our Reichstag fire—"

"The whole country's a Reichstag fire, my boy."

Georgie turns from the TV screen and raises her hand—ever the respectful student. "Please, I don't mean to interrupt." The duvet slips off one shoulder. She tugs it back up. "I'm feeling a bit in the dark. Bombing, the Capitol—this happened when?"

"Yesterday evening," I reply. "I would have mentioned it, but . . . "

Her eyes swell expectantly. "But what?"

"Seemed, well, honestly, enough on your plate. As is."

She stares at me like I've become someone else. "I don't know whether to take that as chivalrous or condescending."

"I meant it as—"

"Don't. I'm sure you had only the best intentions. Who doesn't?"

The professor watches this back and forth like a helpless referee. "The point," he interjects gently, "is that the police are understandably preoccupied with this other situation. They will be rousting every gang they can name."

"Then they'll be coming down here."

"Not this soon. Too dangerous. They lack the manpower, not to mention the will. In time, certainly. But the fighting will be door-to-door once they try."

Like Baghdad. Belfast. The imperial wars slouching back home.

"Even should they come here," the professor continues, "they will not be wasting time on the hunt for the likes of you two."

Georgie's mug of tea slips from her hands. She leaps up from her seat.

"Omigod, I'm so sorry, I—I'll clean that up."

The professor rises from his chair. "Sit down, my child. Please." He holds out a reassuring hand, skin like parchment, riven with veins. "That rug has suffered much worse."

Turning back to his chair, he digs beneath the seat cushion and shortly produces a dish towel, like some treasure he's hidden away, wrinkled with an oft-used look, the legacy of multiple stains. He drops it onto the wet spot, begins pressing with his slipper.

After a moment, Georgie whispers, "Holy Hell . . . "

"Seriously, my dear, don't concern yourself, it's nothing."

"Not that," she says, pointing at the monitor in the corner.

—12—

WE turn in unison. The image of Friar Daniel fills the tiny screen. He looks years younger and infinitely happier than he did in Georgie's room. Beneath his serene and pink-cheeked face, these words appear: *Catholic Clergyman Attacked Earlier Dies at Temple University Hospital.*

Georgie turns ashen. "I killed him . . . "

I take the remote from the professor, turn up the volume. Just as I do, my picture replaces Friar Daniel's on the screen. It bears the caption: *Suspect At Large.*

An offscreen newscaster's voice: "The clergyman was resting and in stable condition according to nurses in the unit, but upon checking in on him sometime in the early morning hours they discovered him non-responsive. Attempts to revive him failed. He was pronounced dead at—"

I click the sound off again.

Georgie sits there trembling. "I need to turn myself in."

"No, no. Not at all. That's rash. Instead, let's—"

"They're blaming you—*you.*"

"Yes, well—"

"I need to tell them what really happened."

"Why? Better all around they think I'm the one to go after, yes?"

70

"If I might." The professor reaches down to collect the tea-stained rag from the floor, groaning slightly as he straightens again. "There is something curious about that story."

Georgie's fingers begin to twitch, but before the customary snapping can begin, she folds her hands tightly in her lap. "Meaning what?"

"That man was doing quite fine earlier. The knife had barely penetrated, struck muscle, not arteries. Lungs, heart, fine. A few stitches, antibiotics. . ."

Georgie cocks her head. "What are you saying?"

"Is there anyone else you can think of who might have wished him harm?"

"In the hospital?" Georgie turns to me as though I might have the answer, but I'm an utter blank. I'm also aware that the professor delights in conspiracies.

I say, "It's possible he simply suffered a heart attack. You know, the strain."

"Which brings us back," Georgie says, "to I murdered him. More or less."

"I know someone who might be able to help you," the professor says.

We both turn. Georgie speaks. "A lawyer?"

"A friend. To get you away."

"That sounds . . . You think we should disappear?"

"Until you're better aware of the circumstances confronting you, yes. Lie low. Wait."

"Until?"

"Indefinitely would be my guess, given the general state of things."

Georgie utters a sound like that of a moan smothering a sigh.

"And this friend, he can help?" I try not to sound too encouraged. "Is he trustworthy?"

"Better still—paranoid."

Georgie's head drops into her hands. "This doesn't seem real. Can't be real."

"There is no way he will meet you, none," the professor continues, "unless I assure him you are, shall we say, 'one of us.' Or arouse some other sympathy."

I can only imagine what that means. I wonder if it wouldn't be wiser to simply gather our clothes and head off into the storm. If I were on my own, perhaps.

The professor adds, "He is part of the new underground."

Georgie's head jerks up. "There was an old underground?"

"A former student of mine. One of my favorites, actually. Very keen, very *engagé*."

"You can arrange it," I say, "a contact, a meeting."

"I can try. And will, of course. But unless I am misreading signals . . ." He steps back to take both of us in at once, a look of pitying tenderness. "I believe the two of you have some matters to discuss. I will leave you to it."

—13—

A few years ago, as I trooped through Europe for several weeks, I encountered a pair of buskers in Manchester—lad on guitar, lass on fiddle, stationed just beyond the moving walkway at the Piccadilly concourse. Lovely harmonies, original songs. One refrain in particular stayed with me:

> *Stop trying to protect me*
> *You might just respect me*

The part of me those lyrics touched wakes again as I suffer Georgie's stare.

"Some matters to discuss. Yeah. I bet." Her almond eyes flare with sad fury as she points at the tiny monitor. "I mean, mother of fuck."

I try to take heart from that particular obscenity, one she hasn't used in some time. Means she's feeling stronger.

"What, there's like full-blown civil war now?"

More like competing rebellions—one to defend an illusory past, the other to create an unknowable future.

"You know how they exaggerate."

"Stop. Please, just . . ." She readjusts the duvet around her shoulders. "There's something else. Something you're not telling me. Or a lie that you're—"

"I have never—*never*—lied to you." Have those words ever convinced anyone of anything? "Might we sit?"

"Why?"

"I'm thinking we should sit."

"You're scaring me."

"Absolutely, positively, not my intent."

"Just tell me."

"Standing up, then. Like this."

"*Mother* of *fuck*!"

"All right. Okay. Fine." I take in a long, guilty breath. "It concerns Reggie."

Ever so slightly, her lower lip begins to tremble. "What about him?"

"After things ended between you."

"After he dumped me."

"And your . . . difficulties . . . returned."

"I went crazy, just say it."

"I would never say that. Never have."

"Whatever. Fine."

"The book you so lovingly designed and crafted, the one you gave him as a gift."

Her jaw goes slack. The trembling descends into her throat, her shoulders.

"It got published." Thinking it might soften the blow, I add, "Just the text. Not your beautiful pictures."

If eyes were wounds, she'd be bleeding all over the floor. "Under his name?"

"A pseudonym. Fitzgerald. Rory Fitzgerald."

"Oh my fucking God."

"He's written three more, in the span of eighteen months, given the first's success."

"It was a success?"

"Christ in a catapult. Sensation, more like."

"And you never told me this."

I want to say: Just as you never told me about Friar Daniel.

"I was waiting for the proper time."

"And when, exactly, did you think that would be?"

"I had no idea. He was sending money to your stepmum."

"He paid her off?"

"For your care."

"Pretty much my point. And?"

"I think your stepmum was skimming."

The wounded eyes harden. "What do you—"

"I caught her out and about once, not in her usual drearies. Primped to the nines. From where, I wondered, did the money come if not Reggie? And so I needed to tread carefully."

It isn't just the eyes hardening now. I detect a general stiffening of spine. The trembling, it's anger now. "She was stealing from me. Just like Reggie. Everyone—"

"Until the money stopped."

"Stopped—when was this?"

"Two months ago, give or take. When Reggie—Rory Fitzgerald, that is— when he disappeared."

"He *what?*"

"Vanished. No one knows why. Or where. I was trying to find all that out from the banker in charge of the money right before I came to see you at St. Dymphna's last night."

"What did he say?"

"I gave him a letter. For Reggie. He promised to send it on."

From the kitchen, the clatter of water from a spigot, a tinny echoing splash. The professor, readying another kettle for tea.

"And what do you think—this banker, will he send the letter?"

"No idea, to be honest. If I were to lay odds, given the night's events . . ."

Her gaze drifts down into the pool of her thoughts. It stays there for quite some time, more than a minute, then two, making me wonder if she'll ever touch bottom. Or come up again.

The emptiness of that gaze concerns me. I've seen it before. An episode often follows—abject despondency, wicked fright.

She eases past me and walks toward the entry. Opening the front door, she stands there as the rain slashes down in the darkness, her shallow breath clouding faintly about her head.

Go to her, I'm thinking. Hold her.

She lets the duvet fall from her shoulders. It drops softly around her feet, like a robe discarded before the shower. Maybe that's what she thinks she's done.

She stands there naked, snapping her fingers.

I start toward her. Before I can cover even half the distance between us, however, she says, "I want to go home."

"To your stepmum's?"

"That's *not* my *home!*"

"I'm sorry. Of course."

"Know what I think? That woman, she made sure I was misdiagnosed, made sure I was overmedicated, lied to the nurses and doctors about what I said in private, all to make sure I remained stashed away. For money. Reggie's fucking money."

The same thought had occurred to me. One more thing, with 'only the best intentions,' I chose not to share.

"That house of hers is no more my home than that hellhole she stuck me in."

"You saw the news, they're saying I'm the one to blame. I can walk in, give myself up, you can—"

"No." She rakes her dark wet hair with trembling fingers. "I've no idea where home is. None. But I can't imagine it not including you. I'd scare myself to death alone."

A helicopter whoops and thunders low overhead, moving slowly through the mist, scouring with its searchlight the puddled street, the parked cars, the broken empty sidewalks.

The slanting radiance of the downward beam in the churning haze— it's strangely beautiful, like the glimmering wand of some great angel.

I'm reminded then of the salve on Georgie's neck, wonder if it's washed off. Maybe the police are tracking her signal this very minute.

The glaring down-strike of the beam crosses the porch steps a mere few yards from where she stands in the doorway. She eases back into the shadows, until the light and the chugging rotors overhead, ever so gradually, move on.

"We can't stay in this city," I tell her. "We need to connect with the professor's friend."

"The paranoid? Fine. Sure."

On tiptoe, blinking against the rain, still jaybird naked, she stares out at the disappearing helicopter. Then, glancing over her shoulder, she pins me in place with her gaze.

"I want to find him. Reggie. I want to hear him say it. Everything he did. He's going to tell me to my face."

R ESIST the obvious.

The expression leaps to mind as we wait on the threshold of a modest walk-up in Fishtown—Lower Kensington to the snobs. The professor's mysterious protégé opens the door—Bartosch, we're told to call him, his *nom de guerre.* I anticipate confronting an unkempt, fire-eyed bandicoot—what other image springs to mind at the juncture of "paranoid" and "underground"?

Silly me.

He could be a tennis pro, or a security analyst—slender, vigorous, tall, dressed in a French placket shirt, worsted slacks, oxblood bluchers. A soft mouth and Slavic eyes, full of irony and grief—they evoke an air of clandestine romance. And gravity.

He gestures us inside, promptly secures the door behind.

Harboring the same misconceptions about his lair as I did the man himself, I'm expecting to find a rat's nest of interlinked computers and cast-off furniture, complete with burn marks and disgusting stains, bristling with cat hair, not to mention enough conspiratorial literature thrown about to placate a Trotskyite hoarder—maybe even a lingering scent of rancid marzipan, indicating the presence of nitrobenzene, essential in the making of improvised explosives.

To the contrary, the flat is immaculate: shiny wood floors and bare white walls, sparsely furnished, with that bright clean scent of emptiness. A safe house, not a home.

In what passes for a living room, Georgie and I situate ourselves on a couch that's little more than an upholstered platform with a back. She's dressed like a scarecrow: bulky plaid shirt, gabardine trousers cinched high and tight with a belt of twine, slippers far too large for her tiny feet even with two pairs of socks—the professor's offerings, along with an old waterproof shell, the best he had under the circumstances.

Our host takes a seat across from us in a chair no less minimalist than the sofa. His manner turns lawyerly.

"I've heard the media's version of the trouble you're in," he says, "as well as the professor's. If you don't mind, I'd like to hear from the two of you what actually happened."

Georgie defers to me, chipping in only here and there, when a certain point needs emphasis—Friar Daniel's lurid fascination with her, for example. We both admit to being stunned at his death.

"Then you haven't heard," he says.

"About me being the suspect? Yes, we—"

"Oh, it's gone well beyond that."

Before he can explain further, a voice calls from a rearward room, "Who wants to be first?"

A woman's voice, deeply pitched. Shortly its owner appears, standing in the doorway to the hall leading back toward the rear of the flat.

"This is Michaela," Bartosch says. "She'll be working on you."

"Excuse me?"

"Changing your appearance." The woman again, that same dark chocolate voice. She steps forward into the room. "From what I gather, you're going to need that now."

Michaela—no doubt another *nom de guerre*. Then again, it's her least mysterious feature.

She stands six-foot-five at least, and that in ballet slippers, wearing a simple black dress, flattering in its cinched modesty, accented by burgundy leggings. I flash on Mrs. Kurth, my other tall Bohemian of recent acquaintance, but for all Big Melissa's imposing artiness, she comes nowhere near this one's commanding presence.

She towers over Georgie like a redwood. Multiple bracelets circle each wrist, an onyx ring on one long and delicate hand, a faux sapphire the other. She's drawn her brown hair back in a high, proud ponytail, which sharpens the lines of her cheekbones. Her eyes are so dark the pupils vanish. A voluptuous mouth, perfectly etched in glistening lipstick, distracts from what otherwise could only be called a curiously strong jaw—calling to mind the Sarmatae, half Scythian, half Amazon.

She extends one of her long slender hands, the nails blood red, bracelets jangling dully on her wrist. "Ladies first? Georgina—love that name. Come with me, my dear."

Once they're gone, Bartosch withdraws a sleek black laptop from a thin valise, boots it up. Rising from his chair, he nods politely to the empty space beside me on the couch. "May I?"

Settling in to my left, he clicks on a bookmarked web page. The screen snaps to life—a video. He clicks again. The grainy image twitches and shudders then proceeds to move.

It's a hospital room, a single bed. In it lies Friar Daniel.

"He's alive?"

"Security footage. From earlier this morning."

"You hacked into—"

"Just watch."

I lean in closer. There's nothing for a moment, just Friar Daniel hooked up to various monitors and fluid drips. He lies there blinking, unshaven, a leather-bound breviary in his hands.

A figure appears—male, medium height and build, back to the camera. Hard to make out much else about him given he's dressed in full scrubs, booties to bouffant cap.

The man removes a syringe from his pocket, slaps a hand across Friar Daniel's mouth, plunges the needle deep into the Franciscan's neck. Shivering, then stillness. Eerie how quick.

The camera remains zoomed in as the murderer turns. His face is clearly visible.

My jaw goes slack. "Fucking Hell . . ."

"Yeah," Bartosch says. "That was pretty much my reaction."

It's me, clear as day. Except it isn't—I wasn't there. Couldn't be. I suffer a momentary, nightmarish unease, as though I've lost possession of my own body.

"Who's seen this?"

Bartosch closes the laptop. "Pretty much everybody paying attention to local news."

"Right. But you don't honestly think—"

"What I think," he says, "is that you're a very curious man. You served with the Wolfhounds, New York 69th, correct?"

And so it comes. "You're knowing that how?"

"You honestly think I'd let you in the door, the professor notwithstanding, without checking you out?"

"Fair enough."

"But here's the thing—I've searched the web everywhere and there's nothing about you whatsoever until that day you enlist. Everything before that seems to have vanished."

Something can't vanish if it wasn't there to begin with. "My being here, in the US, it has some document deficiencies. Can we leave it there?"

"The armed services don't normally accept—"

"I said nothing about my enlistment being normal. The reserves aren't picky, the Wolfhounds no more so than any."

"Why them—why a New York unit?"

"It's where I found myself when I landed stateside. I was broke. Soldiering pays."

"That's it?"

"Admittedly, there's sentimental reasons—they descend from the original Irish Brigade under Tom Meagher, fought at Antietam, Chancellorsville, Gettysburg." I know, I was there. "And the famous Fighting 69th, as they came to be known, sent to France in the Great War, Chateau-Thierry, the Argonne, Wild Bill Donovan and the poet Joyce Kilmer among them." And, again, me. "Bit of a sucker for that sort of thing."

"Where were you deployed?"

"All across a mountainous sliver of territory tucked between Iran and Kurdistan."

"Doing . . . ?"

"I manned the turret in our Humvee. Roamed rat lines, rocket boxes, weed-choked canals. Here's an irony for ya—guess whose counter-insurgency model we borrowed?"

"The Russians."

"I said irony, not farce. No, the Brits—aggressive patrols, random searches, the very same methods used against the IRA in Ulster. Find, fix, and destroy the enemy."

"That didn't offend you?"

"The perversities of history. Truth be told, we tried to inflict only as much harm as needed for the task at hand. While not getting killed ourselves in the bargain."

"Any civilians?"

"Not that I'm aware. One doesn't always know."

"No disciplinary actions?"

"You're the one scrounged about in my background—you tell me."

"Any contact with your old unit?"

"None. Left New York upon discharge, floated down here. I've done some group sessions with vets in the area, just to lend a hand."

"How so?"

"Some lads deal with it badly."

"Killing."

"It's not as natural to the species as some think."

"But it's natural for you."

"I'm better at letting it go, let's put it that way."

"And why is that?"

"Proper breastfeeding, solid toilet training—how the fuck should I know?" In truth, I've been doing it a very, very, very long time. "No one truly comprehends his own nature—only fools think so. What is it you're really after—some secret tidbit that will convince you I'm unreliable? Damaged goods, too comfy with combat, possibly mad. There's no guarantee to the contrary, sorry, except my word."

Ever so slowly, he blinks, like an owl. "Then, one day—voila! You magically appear at Liguorian, a janitor."

"Thanks to the professor. Ask him yourself."

"I have. But it still doesn't add up."

"Tell me who I am, then."

"I really don't know. Maybe just a drifter. Or a killer on the run."

"Oh for the love of cripples and Christ—"

"What I know is that someone is out to get you. Someone with serious resources."

"That makes no sense."

"Whoever's out to frame you knows how to use digitized neural networks to create synthetic images."

Easy for him to say. "You'll need to explain that."

"It's software that can slap a person's face on any image or footage it wants. Insert an entire person into a manufactured scene. The common term is 'deepfakes.'"

That, I've heard of.

The technology got outlawed after a spate of divorces, firings, scandals, suicides. Cranks ginned up footage of their exes, their neighbors, their bosses—and no small number of public figures—performing unspeakable acts. But, of course, no ban is totally effective. There are always ways. And people who know those ways.

"Welcome to the dystopian now," Bartosch says. "Usually it requires a large number of samples to get right, especially for expression-dependent textures and pose detection, and that's why yours looks a little rubbery. The finished product is definitely sub-par."

"Looked plenty par to me." And would to a great many others, no doubt. Like a jury.

"My guess, they accessed the security system at Liguorian, grabbed footage of you sweeping the halls, cleaning the rooms. Or maybe there's video of you from elsewhere. Your tour of duty. Your mysterious life before enlisting."

Momentarily I'm inclined to say something like, *This is terrifying,* but given the long view, from trial by combat to ordeal by fire, tossing me into a frozen lake—or boiling oil—to determine guilt or innocence, it seems pretty much in keeping with the annals of justice as I've known them.

"That isn't me. On that footage. You know that."

"The truth is irrelevant." He slips the laptop back inside his valise. "The truth is for suckers—try that for irony."

"I'm not a mad dog on the run. Nor am I suffering from some strangely murderous form of PTSD, if that's where you're heading."

"The point," he replies, "is that you've made some powerful enemies. Who, why? I don't know. The professor swears by you, fine. As a favor, I've obliged. But on top of everything else, in the wake of the Capitol bombing, the purges have escalated."

"I would never do anything to endanger the professor."

"Bit late for that. And it's not just him I'm concerned about."

"Nor do I wish you harm. Your friend, Michaela. The lot you're in with."

"Good. Because we don't exist." Rising from the couch, he snaps shut the latches on his thin valise, while from the back of the flat, down the hall, that distinctive sultry voice calls, "Next victim!"

—15—

OFF to the chamber of transformation—Michaela leans against the doorframe, running the chain of her necklace back and forth across her chin. "The fabled Shane." She eases into the room, making way for me to enter. "I've been learning just lots about you."

Hoping no doubt to fill in the gaps of my "enigmatic" past. If they only knew.

An old-fashioned steamer trunk brimming with clothes and cosmetics stands open in the corner, its drawers pulled open, all manner of scarves, chemises, jumpers spilling out.

"And where might Georgie be?"

"I'm right here, eagle-eye."

The Sarmatian and her artifacts dominate the space so entirely I missed the diminutive figure standing at the other end of the room, near the lavatory door. Then again, she looks nothing like herself.

"Michaela does costumes and makeup for the opera."

"Repertory." Michaela blushes modestly. "Not the Met. And some local TV—which is more to the point here, given the need to make sure you pass close-up scrutiny. You know, checkpoints, high-definition surveillance cameras, that sort of thing. And we have a former member of what you might call the intelligence services in our ranks. He's been a great help. What they do with disguises puts my work to shame."

"You're still pretty amazing. Shane, don't you think?"

Georgie does a slow pirouette. She could pass for a schoolmarm—all neutral tones and modest simplicity: grey jumper over a plain white blouse, herringbone skirt, sheer tights, black flats. There's some kind of padding underneath, suggesting a heft she's never possessed, and a curly brunette wig combines with a pair of gargantuan square eyeglasses to completely transform the contours of her face.

"You're . . . rounder."

"That's kinda the point."

"Because she's so slight," Michaela remarks, "it seemed the best way to go. Easy to make a slight person look, you know . . ." She gestures to conjure girth.

"She's plump as a shrub. And her face looks different."

Michaela takes a seat at the vanity table, crosses her long, sturdy, burgundy legs. "I needed to work in some shading and highlight to make her features softer, blur the angles."

"It does that, surely. And quite subtly, too. Nicely done."

"Facial recognition software focuses on bone structure and minor details—distance between the corners of the eyes and mouth, size of the earlobes. I used semipermanent eyeliner to extend the shape of her eyes, make them seem farther apart. The glasses should accentuate that. Sad, really. Her eyes, their shape, she reminded me of a fawn."

As sudden as that, my mind flees elsewhere—an ancient cave, the one where my mother, Sadbh, in the form of a doe, tried to hide me, protect me. And she did, until the day Fear Doirche dragged her off. And those eyes, staring back at me in terror. So many, many years ago, so very far away, and yet the recollection carves right through my mind.

"I actually considered making her male, change her completely."

That snaps me back. "Excuse me?"

"They're looking for a man and a woman—why not make you two men? Given how small she is, though, that would mean making her a boy, and when I saw her walk, I realized that just wouldn't work. She's too graceful."

"You're up now," Georgie says. "Unless you're hungry. Michaela brought sandwiches."

They rest on a plate atop a side table, cut into triangles. "All I could slap together, last minute," she says, "sorry." Yes, the bread is stale, the jam all sugar, the cheese a mystery. And yet even the simplest thing, depending on circumstances, can taste like mercy. Especially when you're hungry enough to eat a reverend mother.

Michaela taps a finger against her pursed lips, studying me as I eat. "I want to put some years on you. Older men, they're less threatening. And, you know, given what they're saying on the news . . . "

Downing the last of my sandwich, I spread my arms. "Do with me what you will."

As though to celebrate the process, I indulge Georgie's request to sing a few songs for Michaela: Sean O'Casey's "Oh Me Darlin' Juno, I Will Be True to Thee," Yeats-and-Britten's "Down in the Salley Gardens," Thomas Moore's "Oft in the Stilly Night."

Michaela sighs. "I know people in the theater who'd kill for that voice."

"Interesting," Georgie responds. "It's what I want to hear when I die."

I clear my throat. "Conversation's turning a bit darkish, no?"

"Not at all," Georgie replies. "I've actually dreamed about it."

Meanwhile: a salt-and-pepper wig fitted over a mesh skullcap, a false grey mustache the size and shape of a child's pocket comb. Some highlights get brushed into my eyebrows as well, then rimless spectacles.

Georgie cocks her head this way, that. "You look . . . avuncular."

The effect gets enhanced by my own layer of body padding, secured beneath a button-down shirt, a sweater vest, a frumpy black sport coat. Baggy slacks and loafers complete the ensemble. Both Georgie and I look heavier: Portly and Pudgy. Speaking of passed-over dwarves.

She gestures toward a floor-length mirror. "Have a look, Unc."

I behold a man I barely recognize. I could sell you insurance—or a casket.

"I think that will work," Michaela says. "Just to be sure, I want to add a knee brace, to alter your gait."

I retreat to the bathroom to slip off my trousers, tug on the elasticized device—the thing's snug as a tourniquet. I'll practically be dragging my leg. I won't be less threatening through age alone—I'll come off as lame.

Back before the mirror, I take one last glance at my reflection, marvel again at the transformation, then turn to leave. Michaela makes way for me to pass, but Georgie just remains standing there, fixed to the spot, staring at nothing. A shadow has fallen across her mood, so playful only seconds before.

It's sinking in, the situation, the peril. This isn't a masquerade. It's a manhunt.

W E'RE about to head back toward the living room when a thought
occurs. "Go on without me," I tell them. "Need to gather a few
things from my pockets."

It's the key fob for my car I'm after, but I also encounter the anti-
track bag with my cell phone inside. I wonder who might have been trying
to get in touch—the police, naturally, some hostage negotiator reaching
out to forge a bond. Maybe Georgie's mother, offering to stand up for us
should we turn ourselves in. Everyone lying.

As the gizmo flickers to life, I remind myself: Thirty seconds, tops.
And get ready to move immediately—if anyone's tracking, they won't
arrive until you're long gone.

Sure enough, I have a message—not on voice mail. A text.

And who might you guess it's from?

Djuna Kurth. The stern banker's daughter.

> You've been busy. Thanks for the
> entertaining visit last night. Wow.
> Dad practically had an aneurysm
> when he heard about the priest.
> Mom says we're lucky
> you didn't murder us all.

I don't think you did it.
Know why?
Your eyes.

Meanwhile, guess what I found in Dad's safe.
(The combination's my birthday backwards
—he thinks he's so clever).
P.O. Box 76199,
Napa CA 95558
(Rory Fitzgerald's using the name
Robert Brown now, btw.)

You're welcome. Don't be a stranger.

P.S. If you find him, tell him to write
more books like the first one.

Ignoring several other messages flashing their presence—four on voicemail, a handful of other texts—I quickly commit the info to memory then switch the thing off, stuff it back in its bag of invisibility, hoping I've not given our location away nor endangered the girl by opening her communiqué.

My impression of her from the night before—the lonely precocious bafflement, the curse of being doomed-to-be-special—no longer seems adequate. A shrewd old soul bangs on the door of her youth, demanding her jailer bring the keys.

Robert Brown. What better proof that Reggie hopes to remain unfound. If your plan is to hide, choose the commonest name imaginable, a needle in a veritable Everest of hay.

As for the address, it's the opposite end of the continent. Might as well be the moon.

"Anything wrong?"

It's Michaela, looming in the doorway.

"No, nothing. Just needed a tick to collect myself. World's blown its stitches the past few hours. Wanted to gather my thoughts, such as they are."

An eyebrow arches. Gradually, a wan smile. "I've come back to tidy up. But you're wanted up front with Georgina—such a perfect name. So sad she can't use it anymore."

In the living room, Bartosch holds out his hand. "Your phone."

Was he sneaking a look as I checked for messages? If so, and it bothered him, he'd have interrupted me, yeah? "No need, it's fine. I've got an anti-track bag."

"Not good enough, not now. The GPS has already been spoofed, incidentally. As far as anyone can tell, your phone's on its way to Maryland."

Good news, in the event Djuna's messages are indeed being monitored. "How did that happen?"

"There's a scrambler on the porch. Detects all tracking devices, responds accordingly."

The professor was right. Despite the perfectly pulled-together façade, his Underground Man is indeed paranoid. And proficient.

"By the way, Georgie's got a subdural tracker in her neck. Put JAM on it earlier. I'm assuming your solution is more permanent."

"It is."

"And she's on her way to Maryland as well?"

"Vermont, actually. You've parted ways. At least as far as your signals are concerned."

He gestures for us to line up against the bare white wall, then snaps pictures of us individually, using two separate burner phones. "I'll work up new ID panels for the two of you," he says, "as well as some other documentation you'll likely need. It shouldn't take long." He gestures toward the cocktail table in the middle of the room, where his laptop lies open. "I've left my preferred source for news open on the screen—in case you'd like to get yourself up to speed with what's happening out there. Might be wise, all things considered."

Georgie and I, in our bulky disguises, take up position hip to hip on the Spartan couch. Despite the relatively small size of the PC's screen, its images lack nothing in terms of clarity—network reportage, underground video, guerilla journalist postings, phone footage from citizen witnesses. The clips cascade one after the other in some sort of automatic rotation.

In Miami, a torched car turned on its side blocks a city street. Looters rampage the nearby businesses, shattering windows, dragging shoppers and shopkeepers alike into the street for a thrashing, while kids rush about playing hide and seek in the chaos. An open fire hydrant gushes water so the youngsters can body-surf across the asphalt. Others jump up and down on an abandoned box spring like it's a trampoline.

Just across town here in Philadelphia: the Trenton commuter train barrels down the track, the last two cars on fire. Plumes of thick black smoke boil out of broken windows licked by flame. Passengers leap from the rear platform onto the tracks, several themselves on fire.

Farther away, a small town in North Dakota called Lidgerwood: a federal task force sent to capture the leader of a militia called the American Cossacks, which now controls most of the upper Midwest— the Christian Caliphate, they call it—instead gets ambushed. The agents, bunkered inside the town hall, stare out at barricades of mounded tires soaked in petrol and set on fire. Militia units have formed roadblocks throughout the region to deter reinforcements, while others have stormed a nearby federal barracks, confiscating the weapons, holding hostage the military families on base—those not already in league with their captors.

Finally, from Washington: thirty-seven members of Congress, including fourteen senators, have been arrested, charged with seditious conspiracy, inciting violence against the state. Other arrests are immanent.

In his announcement justifying the sweep, the President, speaking from his spider hole, says with his usual ponderous flair, "My fellow Americans, we are in a fight to the death against treacherous forces and criminal elements that do not believe in freedom, nor do they value our way of life. They're in league with a shadowy faction within our own government seeking to weaken and topple this presidency, which you, the people, chose in a free and fair election. Tonight, however, you can sleep well. Many of the leaders of the plot are now in custody. More will follow, until each and every traitor is rooted out. Your support, which I see so vividly springing to life across the land, warms my heart, and gives me strength. United, we shall prevail. God bless you all, and God bless the United—"

I lower the laptop screen. Mentally, I'm recalibrating my comparison of what's happening here with Northern Ireland's Troubles. A backwater fracas in a dying empire's shadow, even with centuries of precedent, that's what that was, in a region smaller than Connecticut.

This is something else altogether.

—17—

MICHAELA rejoins us shortly, with Bartosch following mere moments later bearing the two burner phones, now complete not just with official ID panels but digitized library cards, insurance cards, organ donor cards—all in the names of Gerald Thomas Meyer and Marjorie Angela Meyer, maiden name Burke.

"Fresh from the wizard's lair," he says cheerlessly, as Michaela produces two costume jewelry wedding bands. "Not sure they'll fit," she says, "but it's all I have." We slip them on—mine's snug, Georgie's will need some attention, a bit of tape for padding.

"They'll do quite nicely," I offer.

"It just seemed wise, make you a married couple. No questions as to why you'd be traveling together. The age difference, well, yes, it's greater now, but older husbands, younger wives, it's hardly uncommon."

Bartosch produces an envelope stuffed with cash. Thanks to a thriving black market, it remains in vibrant circulation—no purely plastic or altcoin economy as yet.

I do a perfunctory count. At least a thousand dollars, maybe twice that, fifties and twenties.

"Let me guess—the professor?"

"He really does think the world of you," Michaela says. She takes a seat in one of the minimalist chairs and curiously seems only taller.

94

Bartosch crouches beside her, and they share one of those awkward glances only those newly in love can manage.

I'm about to tuck the envelope away when I notice a slip of notepaper amid the bills. I pluck it out, unfold it.

My Dear Mysterious Friend:

> *I had always hoped that someday I might finally learn how it came to pass that you became so knowledgeable about so many things in such intimate detail. I imagined a brilliant education in your past, a doctorate in history at least, kept secret from others—from me—for reasons I could only guess at. It appears I will be obliged to keep on guessing.*

> *I cannot say goodbye without expressing my fondest gratitude for the time we shared together. Our afternoon colloquies so very often proved the highlight of my day. I cannot adequately express just how much you brightened this old man's twilight.*

> *I fear for what you now face. Innocence is no defense against the mendacity into which this country has descended. The short-sighted selfishness of U.S. capitalism, combined with the sanctimonious self-congratulation of this latest wave of religiosity—believing as it does, among other heresies, that wealth signifies virtue, as though the invisible hand belongs to God—they cannot abide the self-restraint, communal spirit, and commitment to reason required of democracy. They worship certainty and strength, which inevitably find their purest expression in violence.*

> *You are walking into a whirlwind, with your lovely gifted friend as charge. I cannot begin to imagine the dangers you will face, and what you will need to do to survive them. Know this—you will be in my mind and in my heart every step of your journey.*

> > *Ta godt vare på hverandre,*
> > *Nils*

I fold the note over again, tuck it back in among the bills. *Take care of each other.* So Nordic a sign-off.

"Incidentally," Bartosch says, interrupting my reflection, "your car."

"No worries." I slip the envelope inside my jacket's vest pocket. "I've camouflaged the plates, glazed the windshield, dismantled all the trackers."

"Sorry, not an option." He digs a key fob from his pocket. "Out back, ten years old, American-made. Economy sedan. Virtually invisible, it's so nondescript. And like yours all the tracking software's been stealth-stripped, the license plates decaled, the glass treated. Most importantly, it runs. Well enough to get you far away. Which is where you have to go now."

Not a suggestion. A directive.

"I have an address," I say. "In California. That far enough?"

I might as well have said Tahiti. "You're not serious."

"I rather wish I wasn't."

"I meant New York, Boston, some big city where it's easy to get lost in the numbers. Not all the way across . . . That's madness. You'll hit roadblocks everywhere, especially in the middle of the country. Christ, middle of the state. On top of which . . ." His voice trails off, as though in despair of all the other factors he feels I'm ignoring. "Seriously, I can't think of a worse idea."

Georgie looks at me with a pinched, puzzled expression, rendered vaguely comic by her new appearance, the big square glasses.

"I've not had time to explain," I tell her. "I have an address for Reggie. It's just a P.O. box, but I think—"

"You're not honestly thinking," Bartosch says, cutting me off, "of trying to find Reggie Feely?"

"He owes Georgie an explanation. At the very least."

"About what?" He glances back and forth—me, Georgie, me again. "You do realize what's happened since he left Liguorian, how successful he's become."

"We do," I say. "And are you aware he stole not just the idea but the actual words, the text, the story, the whole shebang, from Georgie here?"

"Just the first book," she says modestly. "And the stories, for the most part, I learned from Shane."

Bartosch reflects on all that in silence. A shock of sunlight, having burst through the storm clouds outside, pierces the window blinds and striates the hardwood floor, creating what resembles a ladder of light.

"You're going to get caught," he says finally. "Get yourselves killed. Get *us* killed. California—that's insane. Find somewhere closer, at least till the worst blows over."

"And that means what—days? Weeks? Never?"

"Look, you owe us at least—"

"You said it yourself, the people trying to frame me have considerable resources—who else could they be but the people cashing in on Reggie's books? Who else would go to such bother?"

"I don't know, but—"

"His disappearance is no doubt costing someone money. Maybe a great many someones. I'd be amazed if there isn't a keen hunt for his whereabouts. Somehow they dredged up Georgie's name—from the checks he was sending, I imagine."

He shakes his head in disbelief. "You've already made up your mind."

"It's not me they're after, it's Georgie. Maybe they think she'll lead them to Reggie. Maybe they intend to use her as bait. Regardless, if they're willing to rig up a video to make me out as a ruthless murderer—"

"Which, for all we know, you are."

"Oh, stop now. You're right, my past before arriving here in the states, enlisting with the Wolfhounds, is sketchy for a reason." *Far beyond your capacity to understand.* "Back home, I was involved with some characters of, shall we say, lackluster morality." *Not just of late, but for centuries, nor just in Ireland.* "But a cold-blooded killer, that I'm not." *Not recently.*

This recitation, cryptic as it is, earns me another pinched stare from Georgie.

"And if they catch you?" Bartosch glances over his shoulder at Michaela, who stares absently at the dust motes swirling midair, nervously finger-combing her ponytail. "They'll have questions. About who helped you. Why they—"

"For what? If they already have *us*, what good are *you* to them?"

"You're not seeing the bigger picture. Whoever is after you isn't acting in a vacuum. I can't imagine they don't have sources, connections—and we have enemies."

"Do for yourselves what you've done for us. We don't know your real names, clearly. Abandon this flat. We have no address for you."

"Oh, so you're in charge now?"

"I won't insult you with promises. But our best hope, maybe our only hope, is to go to the source, Reggie himself. Find out the truth. Otherwise we're just waiting to be found. I don't care for that option." I turn to Georgie. "Do you?"

She gazes up through the phony glasses with an expression even more puzzled than the last, as though I've just suggested an overly elaborate suicide pact. Then her features soften, the alarm dissolves. She reaches for my hand, turns toward our pseudonymous helpmates.

"I understand the risks you've taken," she tells them, "and for two strangers. You did it at the request of a lovely old man, but that's no protection, I know. Nor is our gratitude. I won't bore you describing what the past two years have been like for me—and then to find out I've been robbed, lied to, by everyone, absolutely everyone except this man here." She glances up at me with tight-lipped conviction. "I need to find Reggie, speak to him, hear him out. It's that or go back to living in a cage. I've done that. I'm tired of it. Done with it."

Her voice quavers, but not from fright. Something else, something I've not heard in a very long while.

"I know how much trouble we've been," she continues. "I'm sorry for that. But we have something to do now, and it will require more than simply disappearing." She squeezes my hand, bracing herself. "On our way to the professor's, we encountered a woman hung from a lamppost with a sign around her neck reading 'Snitch.' I'll say now to you what I said to

Shane at the time: I won't betray you. I mean that will all my heart. I'd rather die. Regardless, wish us luck. You'll never see us again."

—18—

I T'S late afternoon as we head off in the nondescript sedan. The interior reeks of chemical cleanser, the odor like a waxen orange magically overripe, presumably from a recent detailing—to remove all trace of previous passengers, I imagine—against which a pine-scented air freshener, dangling from the rearview mirror, feebly competes.

All in all, the perfect vehicular manifestation of its inhabitants, Mr. and Mrs. Meyer.

Strapped into the passenger seat, Georgie sits quietly, hands clasped tight in her lap, staring out at the passing housefronts as I negotiate the side streets, aiming for the interstate. The rain has stopped, the streets and sidewalks fill up with others as anonymous as we hope to be.

"I think it's finally hitting," she says after a moment. "I've not slept in—well, I can't remember exactly. Do you mind if I drift off for a bit?"

I slow to a stop to allow a bedraggled young mother—oversized topcoat, neckerchief, wellies, gripping the handle of her pram like a lifeline—to jaywalk left to right. "You needn't ask permission."

She tucks her wigged, bespectacled, and padded self into the nook between seat and passenger door. Her eyelids flutter shut.

My inner drummer beats to quarters—all hands, man your stations. A steady calm comes over me. From the moment I first felt aware of the world and the eyes of my mind cracked open, I knew what it meant to fix on a target, locate my prey. The fact that, in this instance, the quarry lies three thousand miles off matters not at all.

On a main drag I accelerate, swim into traffic. The world drifts into the slipstream blur.

The going's slow on the expressway—rush hour, undiminished despite the state of emergency. Apparently the titans of industry have been urging folks to shake off their dread and don the mask of normalcy. Step out onto the stage of daily life, America! Play your part, hit your mark, recite your lines! And so we find ourselves joining the general slog, heading toward the burbs, off in the dusty red distance.

Like ours, over half the cars around us remain little different than their gas-guzzling forebears. So much for the fabled green revolution. The previous regime strangled it in its crib. This one's disposed of the body.

As for the drivers, a sizable number still wear the air-filtration masks so prevalent during last year's outbreak, a lung-ravaging bit of retroviral mayhem that bubbled up from the equator. After dozens of friends, co-workers, family members fall sick and die, there's something reassuring, I suppose, about the sour warmth of one's own breath.

Soon enough, traffic stalls, always a danger. Red taillights flash in the sepia haze.

Then, off to the right, war cries.

Several dozen raggedy teens burst from the roadside woods wielding hammers, crowbars, hacksaws, charging through the high grass toward the motionless trucks and cars.

Georgie sits up straight. "What's happening?"

"Looks like we're in for a bit of bother."

Not so long ago, they were just urban folklore, avatars of the *becchini* of plague-era Florence, the Ukraine's *beguny*, ragtag bands of homegrown barbarians taking full advantage of the failing state. Now they're a daily menace.

In a flash they're all around, pounding on bonnets, shrieking through windshields, threatening damage unless paid. Horns start blasting, as though that can ward the hooligans off.

One of the youths, pale and scrawny and rat-haired, takes up position in the space between our car and the station wagon just ahead.

He's shirtless, his skeletal torso blazoned with crude tattoos. Screeching something meant to be fearsome, he reveals a maw of nightmarish teeth while holding a machete over his head, two-handed, ready to bring it crashing down.

I ease off the brake, just enough to budge forward, and tap the station wagon's rear bumper, pinning him in place.

He stares down in panic at his legs.

Georgie says, "You crushed him."

"Not in the least. Stay put."

Getting out of the car in my homely disguise, slowed somewhat by the knee brace, I head for where he stands trapped. My left hand snatches the machete away—he's too stunned to resist—as my right hand hammers his nose.

His head snaps back. Threads of blood fly. The driver of the station wagon, having watched the action in her rearview mirror, edges her vehicle forward.

The boy drops to the pavement, shaking with fright.

A trucker several car lengths ahead reaches out his window and fires a pistol shot. The marauders snap to a halt. In the smoggy distance, the wail of a siren.

The youths begin to peel away, jogging back toward the woods.

I pull the bloodied scrap of flesh to his feet. He staggers but stands, legs no worse for the bumper nudge. Desperation whirls in his eyes—how long since he's eaten?

"Keep on like this, you'll be dead come winter. And you really should see to those teeth."

I nudge him toward the roadside. He stumbles, falls to one knee, then scrambles back to his feet, looking back with naked hate.

I wait for him to scarper far enough away into the tall grass that he's unlikely to turn around to retrieve the machete when I toss it toward the gravel berm.

A few nearby drivers applaud from behind their steering wheels. Others merely stare in dumbstruck confusion, like I represent something they've forgotten. Only then does it dawn on me that I've made myself conspicuous—a gimpy old man acting the hero.

I scramble back inside the car, strap myself in behind the wheel. Using a napkin dampened with hand sanitizer, I wipe my knuckles clean and dab away the few spots of blood on my sport coat.

Georgie's staring. "That was . . . wild."

"Hopefully, once traffic thins, we'll be—"

"You made it look so easy, so la-di-da."

"In fairness, the boy was barely more than a shadow. What worries me—"

"I know so little about you."

The hairs on the back of my neck stand up. "You needn't worry, I'm not—"

"No, I'm sorry, that came out wrong. What I meant—I owe you an apology."

I slip the car into drive. "Whatever for?"

"The thing about depression, it makes you totally self-absorbed. It's like your head's a prison, all you can think about is how to get out—when will this be over, why me? It never crossed my mind that I should ask about your life before we met."

Oh, but I told you. You're just unaware, thought it a mere story. "If I thought any of that mattered—"

"Is it true, what you told them, Bartosch and Michaela?" She turns toward me in an awkward jerk. "Back in Ireland, before you came to the states—you said you were involved with some people of . . . how did you put it?"

Lackluster morality. "I've my dark spots, like most anyone, if that's what you're asking."

"I just always found you so charming it never dawned on me that you might have, you know, your own . . . Stupid of me. Selfish."

"Georgie—"

"But we've got all the time in the world now. I'd like to know."

"About?"

"What happened. In Ireland. Why you left."

I stare out through the windshield, gathering my thoughts. Traffic finally eases a bit. We begin to move at a middling clip. In the distance, a stark red sun hovers in the choking haze, calling to mind the deathly eye of Balor the Fomorian.

"I promised to do something that, in the end, I refused to carry out. The people I promised were none too delighted with my refusal. It seemed best we part ways."

"Who were these people?"

"Volunteers, they call themselves. Rebels to some, terrorists to others. The Brits prefer 'ordinary decent criminals,' sucks the political wind out of their sails."

"What did you promise?"

What else? "To kill a man."

"Who?"

A nagging itch beneath my wig creates an urge to slip a finger underneath and scratch. Somehow I resist.

"A tout," I tell her. "Informer."

"A snitch."

And just like that, the woman hanging from her lamppost once again rises in our shared mind's eye.

"What was his name?"

"It's of no importance."

"What was his *name*?"

"McCann. Quinn McCann."

"How did you get involved with . . . ?"

104

"Same as anything. One step at a time."

"That's not really an answer."

"Mistakes beget mistakes. I chose a friend poorly. By the time I saw him for who he was, there were others as well. A whole gaggle of friends. And a favor to be repaid."

"Like what?"

"I tried to break up a nasty fight—bicycle chains, straight razors, broken bottles. Got arrested as one of the brawlers, charged with assaulting a peace officer—and attempted murder."

Behind the phony glasses, her almond-shaped eyes grow round.

"Anyway, these friends, they bailed me out, arranged to have the matter dismissed."

"They were behind the whole thing, the fight, the arrest."

"Very astute of you."

"And this Mr. McCann?"

"Supposedly he'd been the tipster in an arms raid at a farm in Armagh. I was to take him to a place on the bank of the River Blackwater. His grave lay waiting, freshly dug. I put the gun to his head, pulled back the hammer. He dropped to his knees, sobbing. But that's not why I felt moved to spare him."

She's barely breathing now. "What was the reason?"

I offer a helpless shrug. "Didn't see the point."

"That's it?"

"Forgiveness isn't a crime, though you'd hardly know it given the state of the world. I told him to run. I did the same. Found my way across the water and into a recruiting center in New York. They were desperate for bodies—all that was washing up on their doorstep was the usual flotsam of drunks and druggies. I was able-bodied and willing. No questions asked. And so off I went, like so many Irishmen before me—the Wild Geese, the San Patricios—fighting someone else's war."

She sits there chewing her lip, studying me for a bit. Finally, with a trembling sigh, she settles back into her silence, satisfied for now.

Shame, really. Because, except for here and there, it's mostly lies.

A Brief Aside on the Wording of Curses

War-battered dogs are we.
Fighters in every clime;
Fillers of trench and of grave,
Mockers bemocked by time.
War-dogs hungry and grey,
Gnawing a naked bone,
Fighters in every clime—
Every cause but our own.

—Emily Lawless, "With the Wild Geese"

—19—

Now, given Bartosch's suspicion that I might be a murderer on the run, the short work I made of the scrawny hooligan, my response to Georgie's queries with elaborate deceit, I can imagine what you must be thinking. This Shane character, he's not at all the man he makes himself out to be. He's a slick, smooth-talking monster.

Draping himself in false concern for a fragile young woman. Making up gibberish about being cursed by a god, while heading off on a cross-continent trek into a country descending into chaos. All to indulge—worse, justify—a lust for violence.

Let's be clear. I never claimed to be Christ Incarnate. I'd make a very meager messiah.

As for the lying, what else is on offer—the truth?

Picture yourself chained to the bottom of a well, submerged in water whose surface lies just outside your grasp. It's always there, beckoning, rippling with sunlight. But no amount of strain can get you there. The ache in your lungs rages like fire, you'd give anything to breathe, but no matter how much you struggle, you can't reach the top. And there's no thought of going down, trying to free the chain from the bottom. It lies too far below in the darkness. You'll drown long before you get there. But, of course, you're going to drown regardless.

Welcome to my life. My helpless, immortal life.

Remember the wording of my curse: I am doomed to live and die and live again, over and over and over, until I acquire the wisdom of all the world.

At first, I believed the path to that wisdom lay in travel to the far corners of the globe, opening my mind and heart to every manner of living thing—oaks to oysters, not just mankind—the better to grasp what life and death, fear and hope, vigor and misery means for even the humblest of creatures.

Even after hundreds of years, however, I remained trapped in my cycle of existence, no closer to release from my curse than before.

I decided that the wisdom I lacked lay within. It was not the world I needed to know better but myself, and so I set about perfecting who I was: hunter, warrior, poet, friend.

I shed every ounce of hatred from my heart even as my skills in pursuit and killing multiplied in elaborate and ingenious fashion. I could move through a forest like a gentle breeze. I could snatch a man's life with a single blow, hit him with a dagger from twenty yards, or strike with an arrow from a thousand—all without a whisper of malice.

Like a wolf, a hawk, I simply embraced my nature—but that included kindness as well, fellowship. Love.

Yes, there were lovers along the way, and no small number, men and women, old and young. Was I betraying Niamh? The point was to learn, learn everything, and what lesson offers more than another's embrace?

And yet, given I do not age, few of these romances could last for long. Who, while growing older, feeling death inching nearer hour by hour, could possibly look at a lover untouched by time and not feel terror—or hatred—beyond imagining?

This weaving of the various strains of my nature into one cohesive self, predator and paramour, comrade and killer, would certainly earn me my eternal return to Tír na nÓg and Niamh's bed, yes?

Again, however, I guessed wrong.

Who I am would not be enough. I needed to transcend my nature, not perfect it. And since trying to be noble about it earned me nothing, it was time for a turn toward evil.

I helped Labhraidh crush the thirty subkings on the Hill of Flaming Death. I accompanied the sons of Dond Désa as they marauded Ireland in revenge for their exile to Alba.

As a mercenary for my Celtic kindred, I roamed the continent over numerous incarnations, wandering for the sake of war, joining the Senones in their pitiless sack of Rome, serving with Viriatus the guerilla during the Iberian War of Fire, riding with the bandit Charietto in his headhunting raids.

I didn't just serve devils, of course, though war is war, and seldom do the meek prevail. Yes, I helped Queen Boudicca mount her tragic revolt against Briton's Roman occupiers, but no one would mistake our methods for virtue.

My point: over the course of several hundred years, I didn't just embrace bloodshed, I exalted in it. Atrocity became an enthusiasm, desolation my state of grace. And no, that wasn't the worst of it.

That too, however, only led me back to this world, again and again, and though I now had a much deeper comprehension of my all-too-human soul, I only felt wearier, not wiser.

Thus began my years of monastic *peregrinatio*. I turned to earthly denial and solitude, plumbing the depths of simple things, diving headlong into the mysteries of silence.

I died and returned over countless generations in this fashion, mastering saintly humility and selflessness, even accepting the "green martyrdom" of Kevin of Glendalough, living in utter isolation in a cliff-side crevice of barren stone on Ireland's western coast, returning for three lifetimes, meditating, fasting.

It was there among the ancient rocks, bathed in the constant roar of the western surf, that I arrived at last at a state of absolute emptiness, in harmony with all things and one with creation, surrendering even my selfhood and my quest for wisdom.

Then, in the span of a heartbeat, I committed a fatal sin.

Once again, a mere a flicker of hope arose, incarnated in a single word: "Finally . . ." At long last, I would be released from peddling the wheel of my curse.

But that expectation, no matter how fleeting, condemned me.

And so I found myself once again on Tech Duinn, watching Donn Fírinne cull the worthy from the unworthy among the dead. Watching the former ferried to the Otherworld, watching the latter turn to dust. Watching a host of others undeserving of either fate sent back to the world as ghosts, where they wander the earth, seeking whatever it is their souls lacked while their bodies were alive, like travelers to the Island of Black and White, so they might somehow gain liberation and reenter the cycle of being.

Upon my return to this world after that epiphany, I surrendered all hope of making sense of my plight. Selfhood's a snare, enlightenment an illusion—such was the wisdom I'd discovered. And with that, I developed a whole new strategy.

Each time I found myself back in this mortal realm, I would head for the west country, the great siltstone cliffs they now call Hag's Head, where Macreehy found his giant corpse-eating eel, where the Mermaid of Moher bedded her fisherman.

Spreading my arms like the nattering Nazarene on his cross, I lunged from the top, momentarily joining the puffins and falcons and razorbills in my downward plunge.

I hit the water like an egg in a skillet. Every bone in my body cracked and twisted and broke apart, my skull burst open, my eyes and lungs and liver exploded. The rag that was left of me sank beneath the waves till I found myself in the sunken city of Kilstiffen, waiting for Niamh's great white horse, Embarr, to carry me back to happiness.

As you can imagine, Manannán, the architect of my misery, made short work of that plan.

Not that he told me, of course. He just let me try my little trick one last time, plunging off the cliff toward the granite sea. But on this occasion, even though crushed to bits, I did not die. Would not. Could not.

Washed ashore, I clung to the rocks, dragged myself to a nearby cave hacked into the cliff face. Over days and weeks and months of shivering, half-starved agony, I healed. After a fashion. I resembled a hideous jumble of sticks more than a man, all but blind, basically deaf, unfit for anything but beggary. Thus I lived for another three years, shuffling town to town, living off crusts, before the mortal veil at last descended, courtesy of pneumonia.

Lesson learned. But you may understand why, when Georgie asked if I was offended by her own suicide attempt, I found no fault whatsoever. How could I? I practically made it my personal art form.

It was only then I came to understand that wisdom is not a thing to pursue or possess. It is a way of being, a means of living. And from there it is a short walk to the realization that the wisdom *of* the world cannot exist independent of being *in* the world.

This was Manannán's cleverest, cruelest trick. He worded the curse so that I would believe there was an escape. But there isn't.

The wisdom of the world is inextricably linked to deeds in the world itself. One lives it here among the fallible beings of creation, trapped in time.

Just as things inevitably change, so wisdom never rests. Absent some great cataclysm that destroys the four elements and ends all mortal existence, I can never return to Niamh once and for all.

Given that's my fate, though, I can hardly just plonk down in a bitter sulk. Sure, from my perspective, life's no more a triumph than death a tragedy. Life gets lived, then it doesn't—there's the miracle, should you find yourself in need of one.

But since there's nothing to be done for me anymore, each time the brackish mist arrives to transport me from Niamh's bedchamber in the Land of the Ever-Living Ones, and I open my eyes to find myself in some forest or chapel or all alone on a desolate cliff, I rise to my feet, brush myself off, and set out in search of someone or something to care about other than myself.

More often than not, that means soldiering. For who deserves a comrade more than a terrified boy facing for the first time the wind of hate, or hearing the inhuman screams of a dying friend?

As with love, though, so with war. Given the specifics of my fate, anything requiring long service remains beyond me. Sooner or later, someone will wonder why I fail to grow older. And so I shuffle on. Or death pays his visit.

Nor does soldiering alone gratify my need to be of use anymore. At times I simply look for someone wounded or lost or beaten down, someone who can use a bit of honest concern and companionship—with a special devotion to the broken, lonely, gifted ones, the fawns of fate like Georgie.

I've watched the wolf devour the world not once, not twice—one loses count over time. And given the history of my ancient people, steeped as it is in discord and rebellion, who better to accompany Georgie on her reckless journey across America as it shatters?

Yes, of course, all well and good, I hear you say—but then why lie to her?

For the record, I did in fact spare Quinn McCann along the River Blackwater. That much is true. He wasn't a tout, just a loudmouth, a fool. A scapegoat. But my hands aren't clean. It is indeed a crime of deadly violence that brought me to America this last turn.

The man I killed was the real snitch—also the man who gave the order to put the blame on Quinn. Seemed to me, in the grand rapacious scheme of justice, he was the one more deserving of a verdict.

Meaning Bartosch isn't wildly off the mark with his suspicions.

Does that make me a monster? Perhaps. A monster chained to the bottom of a well, struggling forever to reach the surface, straining for the light, for a chance to breathe.

Then again, maybe that's all nothing but rubbish. Maybe I'm just barking mad.

113

THE WILDER SHORES OF SANITY

Throughout the whole absurd life I'd lived, a dark wind had been rising toward me from somewhere deep in my future, across years that were still to come...years no more real than the ones I was living.

—Albert Camus, *The Stranger*

20

ONCE beyond the Philadelphia megalopolis, abandoning the interstate seems wise. There's a better chance of avoiding trouble on the less-trafficked Old Lincoln Pike—fewer cameras, fewer cops, though not necessarily more agreeable ones. No choice of route is foolproof, of course, any more than our disguises are magical.

Case in point: a mere few miles on, a bridge condemned by the federal government remains open regardless. A sign along the approach to the structure identifies the local sheriff as the defiant authority. Why force honest people to travel miles out of their way to suit the whims of faraway pencil-pushers?

Two of his squad cars flank the road, rooftop strobes whirling in the gathering darkness. A torchlight crowd surrounds them, cheering us on as we proceed cautiously toward the dubious structure—it traverses a jagged gulley thronged with tents and campfires, an army of like minds drawn to the scene in solidarity with the sheriff's stand. Flames from the scattered fires create a shuddering play of shadow and light in the foliage of the ravine's pitch pine and rock oak.

A whispered aside to Georgie: "Care not, luv. This'll be over pronto."

The going's slow, the roadway cracked and potholed, the girders and guard rails scabbed with rust.

Protestors line the deck bearing placards—*Behold the Real America!* *Compromise = Surrender! This is Our Country Not Yours—And You Know Who You Are!*

What weight can the support piers bear? Not hard to imagine the addition of our car to the crowd might create just enough burden to plunge us all into the rocky scrub below.

Some of the demonstrators lean in as we inch past—hardscrabble women, work-worn men, onion-eyed with rage, fists pumping, voices hoarse from shouting, faces mere inches from the windows, their spittle smearing the glass.

Lucky for us, they're too self-absorbed in their righteous fury to give us more than a fevered glance.

At last we reach the far side, passing another pair of squad cars with their swirling misery lights. In the ensuing quiet, I venture a glance at Georgie. She's trembling like a fiddle string.

We pass through a succession of hard-luck townships, villages, hamlets, one blurring into the next, nothing between but scant woods riven by parched streams.

Here and there, through the dark trees, more campfires—not protesters, they'd be back with the others. Tramps, bolters, beghards. Fugitives on the run—like us.

The fact they're strangers, that's bad enough. Times like these, they could be long-time neighbors, family even, and still be hounded. When the rage begins to boil, the old ways resurface—the bodies of male suicides dragged through the streets to shame their kin, widows buried alive with their husbands for the sake of stealing their property, orphans offered up as human sacrifice. Mass conversions. Mass graves.

"Shane?"

I turn toward Georgie. She's staring back like smoke's purling from my ears.

"I can hear you thinking. You have a very noisy brain."

117

That's new, from her at least. Not since the era of machines put an end to the age of magic has anyone managed to read my mind. "My actual thoughts?"

"Not words, no. Just rumblings. That's bad enough, trust me. It's scary."

No doubt. "My apologies. I promise to make an effort to cogitate more quietly."

"Do you wanna, I dunno, talk about it?"

"And risk frightening you further?"

"So I was right. About what you were thinking. It was, like, nasty."

"Georgie—"

"You're right, sorry. Got it." Her gaze returns forward, hands folded so tightly in her lap her fingers practically glow.

They all but explode a moment later as we enter the next town.

A roadside billboard greets us—not the monstrous digitized kind so prominent in the city, more retro, good old-fashioned paper and paint. Lit from below with four upturned searchlights, it presents an image of a wholesome family, conspicuously Caucasian, riding merrily in a car—father, mother, girl, boy, a terrier pup with its head out the window—a near replica of one from the Depression, that one bearing the caption, "World's Highest Standard of Living—There's no way like the American Way."

This one reads merely: AMERICA AS IT WAS. AND SHALL BE AGAIN.

It's not the tagline, however, putting Georgie in a state.

"That has nothing whatsoever to do with your dream," I tell her gently. "The one from last night." Was it really only that long ago? "Mere coincidence."

"Stop reading my thoughts."

"You're one to talk!"

She swallows nervously. Her eyelids flutter. "Weird, though, right?"

Shortly, the thing's behind us. "As I remember, in your dream it was raining, the road led up a mountain, around a turn there came a blinding light."

"I don't need you to remind me of my own dream."

"To be sure. I'm merely distinguishing particulars."

In the center of the next town, an army-navy surplus store lies between two shuttered shops, its window blinds drawn but lights glowing within. The hand-lettered sign at the door reads "Open."

Despite concerns about being found out, I pull to the curb.

Georgie snaps upright. "We're stopping?"

"Thought to buy us blankets. For sleeping in the car."

"Huh." She stares out the window at the dimly lit storefront, blinks once, twice, then in a flash unbuckles her seatbelt. "I'm going in with you."

"It might be best if—"

"No. No!" She seems shocked by her own fervor. "I mean, long as we can, much as we can, let's stick together, okay? If these get-ups aren't going to work, better to find that out now."

Can't help but admire the pluck. Especially given the quaver in her voice.

"All righty, then. Look at me."

She obliges. I render careful inspection. "You're fine, nothing amiss. Me?"

She presses the edges of my fake mustache down. "Yeah. You're good."

"From this point forward, no glancing in mirrors, appraising our reflections. Give the game away."

"What about your accent?"

"I can tamp it down. Slurs and murmurs. Like a Dane." I open my door. "Ready?"

A teenager mans the register—bone-thin, hawk-nosed, slump-shouldered. Fiddling with some handheld device behind the counter, he offers not so much as a glance as a tuneless *ding* announces our entrance.

Only half the overhead fluorescents offer light, and half of those buzz and flicker. In the twitchy dimness we wander dogleg aisles with high metal shelves, stocked seemingly at random: ammo boxes, long johns, grenade pouches, tents. No telling where the blankets might be hiding. The teen clerk might know, of course, but let's minimize our face-to-face encounters, shall we?

Only then does it dawn on me—this place likely serves as outfitter for exactly the kind of militant riffraff we encountered at the crumbling bridge.

Be quick.

The dim maze of clutter leads us to a juncture where a small speaker perched high in a corner is broadcasting some sort of address in a raspy, orotund drone.

"We stand at the brink of moral, political, and material ruin. For over a century and a half, the two major political parties have competed—for what? Power and plunder!"

Georgie points up at the bodiless voice. "What *is* that?"

Warmed-over William Jennings Bryan, I'm tempted to say, just as someone else interjects, "It's Pastor Cole."

We both spin around. A short, ample woman has crept up behind us, dressed in a flower-print smock, her white hair cut short, reading glasses dangling from a chain around her neck. Her skin possesses an apparitional pallor, marred only by a rust-colored birthmark that stains one whole side of her neck.

"Hard-earned wages get taxed to the limit—to subsidize the undeserving, who show nothing but contempt for this great country, its history, its culture."

"You've never heard him speak?" Her eyes shimmer, her voice a saintly purr.

Georgie jumps in, sparing me the need to veil my brogue. "We're not local."

"Neither is Pastor Cole." Her gaze drifts back and forth between us. What is she trying to see—and why? "He's syndicated nationwide. A voice for us all."

"Divided into two stark classes—producers and parasites, makers and takers."

Georgie points back toward a rearward maze of shelves. "Might you be able to direct us toward the blankets?"

The woman says nothing, doesn't move, just closes her eyes, the better to listen.

"Burn down the cities, they will spring up again as if by magic. But destroy the small towns, the farms . . ."

I gesture for Georgie to follow me as I ease away. Before we can manage more than a step, however, the women reaches out to stop us.

"This part," she whispers.

"It is 1776 but again. We too must fight for liberty, like our forebears. Not as aggressors. To defend our homes, our families, our way of life. We have petitioned, and our petitions have been scorned. We have entreated, and our entreaties have been disregarded. We have begged, and they have mocked when disaster came. We beg no longer; we entreat no more; we petition no further. The time to rise up has come."

Sure enough, word for word, the Great Commoner himself—Cross of Gold speech, 1896. Pastor Cole's a plagiarist. Just like Reggie Feely.

A burst of static punctuated by a single hard click signals the end of the recording. The woman's bosom rises and falls in a deep sigh. Slowly, her eyes reopen.

"It's time," she says.

Georgie and I trade glances. Time for what—to confess?

"We all have our part," the woman adds. "For our country."

"Ah, indeed." Me, this time. "So true." The words come out in a mumbled slosh.

Her gaze frosts over. "You seem uncertain."

"No, not at all. Been driving, long day, slow on the uptake. Sorry."

I imagine the fake mustache fluttering. The desire to adjust it, straighten my wig, it's excruciating.

"When the people reclaim their voices, nothing can stop them. This country doesn't belong to the billionaires and the Hollywood hotshots, the lying media, the snooty professors. It belongs to Jesus our Lord and the common man. It always has. People forgot that. Well, they're waking up. They're remembering."

I can well imagine, at some less-rancorous time, this plump, prim, fastidious woman with her disfiguring birthmark at some sprawling church wingding, dishing out casserole, ladling cups of sweet tea, singing to herself like a schoolgirl. That's the way with politics, especially when wedded to a fiery creed—once it gets its hand up your spine, even the mildest of souls can become its puppet.

I'm mulling all that, struggling for words, when Georgie jumps in. "We were hoping to get a bit farther down the road before calling it a night."

She might as well have reached out and mussed the woman's hair. The frosty gaze refocuses. "You're from where?"

Burn down the cities.

"We're heading for coal country." To hell with the slurs and murmurs. A small adjustment of vowels, I sound vaguely southern. "Visit my sister."

"Wasn't what I asked." Her eyes rake Georgie up and down. "Why blankets?"

"Our car." Me again. "Not the latest or finest. Heater's on the fritz."

She turns back toward me and stares like I've turned into a stuffed giraffe. The silence drags on forever. Finally, another windy sigh. "Over here."

We follow her back into the warren of teeming shelves. She points out where the blankets lie in helter-skelter stacks, then vanishes without further word.

I snatch two off the top. Noticing a rack of clear plastic ponchos nearby, I grab a pair of them as well, one Georgie's size, one mine. Sooner or later, we'll face rain.

I head up front with our purchases; Georgie ambles toward the door, then stands there waiting.

A sticker the size of a playing card rests in the corner of the plastic sneeze-guard at the register cubicle. It bears the black silhouette of a pistol with the caption: *Speak Truth to Power.*

The hawk-nosed teen remains obsessed with something. Up close now, I see what it is—a handheld game console. The header atop the game space reads: *The Truth Against the World.*

"Excuse me. Might I get a glance at what you're—"

He quickly tucks the device away, begins tallying the total for our purchases.

"Didn't mean to be rude." I slide several twenties across the counter. "It's just that, well, I wasn't aware . . . is your video game based on the Fitzgerald book?"

One more cash cow in the enterprise, I'm thinking, amplifying my suspicion that Reggie's disappearance is wreaking havoc on someone's bottom line.

The youth fails to respond, just gathers my change, lays it on the counter, shunning eye contact. As I collect the coins and bills, however, he murmurs, almost inaudibly, "The game is taking its course."

I'm mulling that over on the way to car when Georgie says, "I almost blew it in there, didn't I?"

Given the drift of my thoughts, her meaning escapes me. "Sorry?"

"Cutting her off. When she was going on about—"

"Ah." I thumb the key fob, the car doors click open. "I mightn't go so far as that. But yeah, sure, courtesy's the ticket given the pickle we're in. Better yet, turn the focus around, feign interest, ask questions. Rare are those to resist the chance to go on about themselves. And absent a miracle, they'll scarce recall your face ten minutes later."

21

SEVERAL miles beyond town, a pair of sixteen-wheelers rest side by side in a modest rest area, having pulled off the road for the night. Needing a break from driving myself, I tuck the small sedan between the two tractor trailers. Seems a safe enough place to stop—if not here, where?

Trucks were supposed to be replaced by driverless upgrades by now, the so-called roborigs, but the things proved a hazard, baffled by jaywalkers, mistaking shadows for oncoming cars. When that proved not enough to forestall their deployment, truckers themselves rebelled—firebombing depots, blockading freeways.

Perhaps one or both of the drivers of these two specimens are similarly inclined, a small contingent in the rebellious multitude. Does that matter? Increasingly I'm coming to believe it's not so much which side a person's chosen in the political divide, but whether they're too wrapped up in their own obsessions to bother noticing us at all.

Georgie makes a bed by lowering her seat till it's all but horizontal. I nip into the back. We unwrap the blankets, slip out of our shoes, and drift off in our disguises.

Or try. Every sound seems a warning. More so every silence.

My mind keeps returning to the sulky teen at the army-navy surplus store—or rather, the game he didn't want me to see. *The Truth Against the World.* It has to be based on the Fitzgerald series. Video games rake in notorious sums, far more than even the most wildly successful book—billions, not millions.

A lot of the vets in the support group back in Philly talked about how addictive the games could get, how obsessive the players, themselves included.

They described how, inside the game space, you can find all manner of clues and connections, many the designers never intended. Apophenia, it's called—the discovery creates a dopamine rush. That rush creates ownership. *My God, I see it now, it's so obvious!* And that sense of ownership just triggers further searching. More time inside the game.

But the real action takes place in the chat rooms. There the clues are deliberate.

Recruiters from fringe groups seed the chat threads with short clips of black-on-white violence, border crossers, riots, jihadi beheadings. Maybe toss in clips from snuff films, kiddie porn. Messages follow: *They're coming for our guns . . . They're opening our borders . . . They're mocking our way of life . . .*

Gamers share the clips, echo the message, amplify it. Word spreads beyond the game space—sympathetic politicians, leaders of the anti-government movement, militias, religious nationalists, they all jump on. Their repetition acts as confirmation.

Participatory disinformation, it's called. It's how lies become true—become actionable, in the parlance of believers.

What was it the youth murmured as he counted out my change: *The game is taking its course . . .* Meaning?

And has Touchy Feely played a part in any of that? If so, it makes his disappearance all the more—

"Shane?"

Georgie peeks over the headrest of her reclined seat.

"Yes, luv."

She turns onto her side, the better to meet my eye. Her wig's gone slightly askew. "I can hear you thinking. Again."

Biting her lip, she seems about to ask what all the mental ruckus is about, but then just settles back around, lies flat, staring up at the car's ceiling.

A moment later, out of nowhere, she whispers, "Flouncy."

It takes me a second to make sense of it, but then it clicks. Our game. Naming the dwarves that never got a callback from Disney.

"That's a good one." I take heart from the unexpected levity. "Very visual."

"Your turn."

"Let me think."

"Quietly, please."

"Yes. Of course. How about . . . Minty?"

She sniffs, wipes her nose with the edge of her blanket.

"He's very fresh," I add.

"Haven't we used that one before?"

"Well, aren't you a stickler for the rules—and rules we make up as we go along."

"I've got one," she says. "Another one, I mean." She pauses, to amplify impact. "Dutch."

"That's it?"

"Can't you just see him?"

I form a mental picture—fisherman's cap, brass-buttoned shirt, knee britches and clogs. "Can I loan you a few bob there, Dutch. You're lookin' a bit short."

"No," she says. "Don't make fun. He's strong. And good. Someone to call a friend. Remind me, the word we're using now?"

"*Duine beag.*"

"That's it." She repeats the sound: *deena bee-ahk.* "Little person. Like me."

Like everyone, really. Standing before the great unknown.

Shortly before daybreak, the two semis roar into action, pulling away with the loud hissing groans of giant iron beasts.

As I sit up, rubbing the grit from my eyes, I notice it isn't merely the time that's prompted their moving on.

Beyond the roadside trees, beams from hand torches crisscross the undergrowth in the heavily shadowed dawn. Dogs whimper and yip.

Maybe the sulky teen and the birthmarked woman weren't so self-absorbed after all.

A coarse voice bellows, "Over here!" The dogs respond—even more frantic barks and howls. Someone, something is thrashing through the brush.

Tramps, bolters, beghards. Fugitives on the run—like us.

I scramble behind the wheel, not bothering with my shoes—turn the ignition, switch on the headlamps, get us on the road.

Georgie stares back over her shoulder as we pull away. "What was that about?"

The transmission clunks into a higher gear as we accelerate. "Not at all sure," I reply. "And feel no great need to stick around and find out."

Next town over, I venture a fill-up at the first service-station-cum-minimart we encounter—drab and dank and quaintly old school, no miniature screens on the gas pumps trying to sell me insoles or insurance.

More important, a mere two cameras, one directed at the fueling island, the other at the entrance.

I'm about to open my door when Georgie grabs my sleeve.

"Wait!" She licks her lips, eyes swimming fearfully behind the clear lenses.

"It's okay." I place my hand on hers—so slight, like gift-wrapped bone. "What is it?"

"I had . . . another dream. Last night. Sleeping here in the car."

"Bad habit you're developing, that."

"Don't make fun, okay?"

"Sorry."

Her grip loosens on my sleeve, the hand draws back. "It's nothing long or elaborate, just . . . I'm pounding my fists against a mirror, trying to get it to show me my reflection. Then I'm pushing on it, like it's a door. And it opens. Onto the sky. Nothing but clouds. Like rolling white hills and massive caverns. I want to step out. I want to explore. But something holds me back."

"Fear of plummeting to your death, I imagine."

"No. Something else. Something worse. But I don't know what."

She eases back into her seat, wraps her arms around her thin frame.

"We need petrol," I tell her. "Gonna to see to that, then step inside, check out the edibles. Care to tag along?"

She shakes her head. Pushes up her glasses. "Thank you. I'll be fine."

Last night she insisted on remaining together. The scene back at the rest stop, her dream, they have her spooked—and true to form, she's drawing back inside herself, wandering the hallways of her overactive mind.

"I'll just be a tick. Sit tight."

I fill the tank, then amble inside, wander the aisles, select a jar of peanut butter, another of peach preserves, a loaf of sliced wheat bread, some plastic utensils, picnic napkins, a flat of bottled water. No fruit to be had. Pity. Yes, we'll tire of it, same fare every meal, but eating in restaurants is out. And Georgie abhors fast food.

The cashier is freckled, twenty-something, strawberry blonde, and blatantly preggers. Perched unsteadily atop her stool, she pays me little mind, yawning into her palm every few seconds as she flips through a magazine.

As I approach with my purchases, she puts her magazine aside. Her eyes are fierce bloodshot—so difficult, sleep, with a parasite in your belly.

Counting out the bills for payment, I notice the TV monitor anchored to the wall above the cash register. My face and Georgie's flash across the screen.

Murder . . . Presumed dangerous . . . Irish . . . Reward . . .

The mom-to-be glances up as well while gathering my change. "That poor girl." She slams the cash drawer shut. "He's probably killed her already, buried her somewhere. Her family will never know peace."

I lower my head, sliding the various bills and coins across the counter into my waiting hand, tucking them into my pocket as she bags my provisions. Reminding myself to turn the focus around onto her, I nod to her protuberant tummy. "How far along?"

She flushes with pride. "Three more weeks. I'll be able to tie my own shoes again!"

I tuck the flat of bottled water under one arm, gather the bag with my free hand. "Brave of you—a child, times like these."

"Oh I'm not worried. Sure, things are, like, crazy, but aren't they always? Besides, I have faith. God provides. God protects."

Blame fatigue, but those simple words, echoing the remarks from the pious woman at the army surplus store last night, send my mind elsewhere, to when the famine struck. Scarecrow Irish, starving and desperate, condemned as thieves and idle liars by their free-market overseers, fleeing the blighted land for workhouses in the cities. Parsons offering parents a devil's bargain—your children eat if they surrender their faith. Pope or porridge, they say. Taking the soup, it's called.

I shake it off, smile. "Very best to you, then."

"You too." For the first time, she looks at me directly, just as I'm turning away. Maybe it's imagination, but as I head toward the door I feel her stare boring into my back, as though she too, like Georgie, can't help but hear my noisy brain.

—22—

WE plunge deeper into the rolling desolation known as Pennsyltucky. The asphalt buckles from long neglect, potholes a foot deep and yards wide. I slalom around them best I can, but when that's not possible due to oncoming traffic, the tiny car shudders from the slamming impact.

Weeds tall as goalposts erupt from the graveled berm, and except for the occasional crow circling lazily overhead, the sky is eerily empty of birds. I find myself reflecting on the regional hobgoblins—spook wolves, the sobbing squonk, Slag Pile Annie.

More billboards appear—again the old-fashioned variety, some rippled and faded with age, others spanking new—increasingly reminding us we've crossed the cultural frontier.

IT'S NOT RACIST
TO LOVE YOUR OWN PEOPLE
WWW.WHITEPRIDEONTHEWEB.COM

HE'S A CHILD—NOT A CHOICE
BEFORE I FORMED YOU IN THE WOMB,
I KNEW YOU—JEREMIAH 1:5
ADOPTION COUNSELING FREE OF CHARGE
FAITH & FOSTER CARE

STROKERS

DAILY DRINK SPECIALS—OPEN FOR LUNCH

GIRLS! GIRLS! GIRLS!

FULL NUDE—CUM SEE US!

POSITIONS AVAILABLE—PAY YOUR WAY THROUGH COLLEGE!!

LGBT:

LIBERTY—GUNS—BIBLE—TRADITION

In the distance, a thunderhead drifts low and dark over the windswept stubblefields. A massive shipping warehouse, large as a prison, windowless, grey, crowns a low treeless hill to the north. Its sprawling parking lot consumes acres, crammed with weather-worn cars, rusty pickups—is there anywhere else out here to work?

But destroy the small towns, the farms . . .

A mile or so on, off to the south, a sunken ravine serves as a local garbage dump. Trash pickers—children mostly, kerchiefs covering their small faces—scour the fetid swales of rubbish and the cast-off washers, freezers, toilets, searching for anything salvageable, dropping their finds into filthy bags. Dozens of them, like blowflies on a gutted sow.

"Maybe I'm overreacting," Georgie says, "but there's something going on out there, in the atmosphere, the zeitgeist. It feels personal."

I dart a glance her direction. Maybe the Old Black Dog's snuffling its way back into her graces. "Care to elaborate?"

"I'm trying not to overreact, Shane, seriously. I know it's been barely twenty-four hours. But I know myself. Know my weaknesses."

A few drops of rain splash onto the windshield, trickle upward with the airstream. The turbulent sky's grown darker, closer.

"It's like, if I reached out and touched the dashboard, it'd start to glow. I'm humming like a hot coil inside. And yet I feel better than I have in months. Years."

"There's bound to be a transition."

"Not for them." She nods as though at some multitude just beyond the nearest rise. "They're perfectly okay. Angry, but hey. Anger's power.

131

The crowd on the bridge, the men with their dogs at the rest stop, Pastor Cole—it's sinking in, you know?"

"In their defense, the folks out this way, they're suffering a transition of their own."

"You know this how?"

"Served with men from places like this. They grew up believing you don't ask, you earn. You only deserve what you're willing to work for. Demanding your rights, justice, that's whining. Responsibility, grit, discipline—that's what matters in a competitive world. Problem is, they've lost the competition. That's how the religious bit slips in—don't ask for more than God thinks you deserve. Stick to the plan, obey the rules—chin up, head down. Not both at the same time, obviously."

"Yeah, but they're not pissed at the people playing them for suckers. The hucksters with all the money may be assholes, but hey, they figured it out. They got rich. The enemy, it's people like me. Only thing easier to hate than an artist is one who's broke."

She's not wrong, of course. When change comes fast, people get scared. And start looking for someone to burn. Any witch will do.

"You're not alone, Georgie. I'm here. And I've known my share of trouble."

"Yeah, but you can't protect me from what I'm feeling. No one can. If loony lockup taught me anything, it's that."

Sensing a need to tread gently, I remark merely, "Fair enough."

"When it comes to your mind, you're on your own. But that's the weird comfort of it, nothing to think about but me-me-me. The rest is routine. Even Friar Daniel was, you know, predictable."

"I still wish you'd told me."

"Jesus, Shane. Seriously. So not my point."

She studies the rolling fields, some cluttered with lonesome machinery, a ramshackle barn, a low-slung clapboard house. Telephone wires, sagging low between tottering posts, sway in the wind like ghostly skip ropes.

"You can't just slap a slogan on chaos," she says, "and think it will disappear. It's still there, under the surface. And you know who wins when it's chaos. Men with money. Men with guns. They think chaos is swell. Puts hair on your chest."

I can offer no rebuttal. How many of the world's wonders manage to survive solely through faith in some illusion? America will prove no exception. History takes no prisoners.

After another moment, I say, "Can I tell you something?"

She eyes me the way a cat stares at a windblown curtain. "Maybe."

"I don't talk much about my tour of duty overseas. Never gone in for the 'soldiers and their sad and startling tales' bit. Believe me, there's no more chaotic place on earth than combat. Everything's wickedly out of control, nothing makes sense. You rely on your training, rely on your skill, but mostly you rely on each other. Find out who you can trust. You become not just a bunch of scared recruits but a unit. And that cohesion, that trust—it helps control the fear."

Her eyes look ripe with too much feeling, even behind the phony glasses. "You're saying you're just as crazy as I am."

"Well, that's a fair thought, but no. Not really my point at all."

"You're saying that everything, even this," she spreads her hand to convey the countryside, the storm clouds, "it's all just a kind of war. Everything, it's war."

"What I'm saying is you can trust me. We're a team. A unit of two."

She stares at me a second, mouth slightly ajar. "A unit." After a moment, she barks out a miserable little laugh, trailed by a whisper: "That's so incredibly . . . butch."

We pass another billboard:

EXTREME METH MAKEOVER
NO ONE WILL RECOGNIZE YOU

Beneath the caption, two pictures, the same woman, one before her addiction, pert and dewy-eyed, the other the rotted hag she became. Given Georgie's mood, I fear she might substitute "madness" for "meth," see herself in the Before and After. A ruin in waiting.

But that's not where her mind goes at all.

"Know what I can't stand about you?" She points an accusing finger, the damning effect amplified by the schoolmarmish disguise. "You turn every argument into an anecdote."

"That's a bad thing?"

She laughs. It feels like sunlight. "Wanna know a secret?"

"Surely. I'm mad for a good secret."

"After my mom died—I was, like, four—I couldn't sleep for more than twenty minutes at a time. Kept waking up in a panic, afraid my old man was gonna come in, throw me in a sack, chuck me down a sewer somewhere."

"For the love of heaven, why?"

"I was too much like my mom—she was a little off in the head too, they say it runs in families. Seeing things that aren't there, talking to them."

"You're not like that."

"Don't lie. Don't sugarcoat it."

"Not anymore. Not as much."

"Anyway, he was done with the whole business. Scared to death I'd end up just like her. Couldn't hit the road fast enough once he could pawn me off on someone else." She rests her hand on my arm, gives it a purposeful squeeze. "Honestly, ask me two years ago if I thought I'd ever trust anyone again? I would've laughed. But here you are."

That warms me to the kidneys. I cover her hand with mine. "I'm going nowhere."

"You're a gift. I don't tell you that enough. I can't imagine life without you anymore."

She takes my hand, places it to her lips, and plants a long, gentle, solemn kiss in the center of my palm. Folding my fingers over, as though to seal the kiss inside, she then holds my hand to her heart, meeting my eye with a look of lonesome, sacred fidelity.

A mere moment later, we encounter our first roadblock.

—23—

THEY'VE placed themselves on the far side of a blind curve, beyond a stony bluff rising up to the north on our right, so there's no chance to stop, reverse course, or otherwise escape. By the time the situation makes itself clear, I've advanced too far into the turn.

A number of mud-spattered cargo vans, pickups, flatbed trucks flank either side of the road, sporting an assortment of banners: Three-Percenter, Gadsden, the Confederate stars-and-bars. Fifty or so armed men stand scattered about, kitted out in backwater battle-rattle: jump boots, web gear, a full array of camouflage, from hunting fatigues to military-issue BDUs. A handful close ranks behind the car after we glide by, further guarantee we're trapped.

A miserable thought: We haven't even made it halfway across Pennsylvania. And that just the first quintile in our coast-to-coast jaunt.

Though I notice a good many deer rifles and shotguns among the weapons the men carry, I detect as well no small number of carbines, semiautomatic rifles, even a submachine gun.

For just a sec, Georgie's fingers once again commence their manic snapping, but she promptly tucks both hands beneath her legs.

"It'll be fine," I tell her. The world's most feckless mantra.

One of the gunmen gestures for me to reduce speed. We continue onward at a funeral pace, easing toward the end of a line of waylaid cars.

At the far side of the roadblock, another line coming from the opposite direction extends motionless into the distance.

"These costumes are a joke," Georgie mutters.

"You were mad about them before."

"That was then."

"No one we've encountered so far, the shop owner, the cashier—"

"Call me a pessimist, but these guys don't look like cashiers."

No, they do not. *Brigantes.*

"What was that?"

I'm unaware of having said anything aloud. *You have a noisy brain.*

"Latin term. It's what the Romans called this lot's forebears."

"This *lot?*"

"Reivers, moss-troopers. Originally from the borderlands, where England juts up against Scotland. Neither the Scots nor the English can manage to tame them, so they just ship them off to Ulster. From there they sail to America. Philadelphians hate and fear them so much they bribe them to settle out here, away from the coast. Take over most of Appalachia. Blood feuds, bootlegging, and the Bible—their trinity. Hate all forms of officialdom, mistrust all outsiders."

"If you're trying to make me feel better, try harder."

That's the problem with history. It so seldom reassures.

I nod agreeably to the men we pass. To Georgie, I say, "Principle of charity. Within reason, try to assume good intentions until given proof to the contrary."

"You mean what, like guns?"

I check faces, taking stock of each flinty, pugnacious, judgmental gaze. Some of the men wear arm patches bearing the Golden Tarantula, emblem of one of the more notorious militias out this way.

"Come now, all things considered, these fellas don't seem such a wretched lot."

I've seen far worse in my timeless time. No necklaces fashioned from human bone or belts strung with scalps, no bleached skulls dangling from a horsehair lanyard. And lest we forget, no severed Irish Catholic cocks pinned to their hats—the innovative touch conceived by Cromwell's Puritans.

Georgie says, "It's not their wretchedness I'm worried about. Not yet."

"Good."

"It's their powers of observation."

That, indeed, I cannot predict. "All the more reason to play our parts with gusto."

Wordlessly, we repeat our ritual from before, checking each other, like two facing mirrors, making sure nothing's amiss with our disguises.

The darkening sky hangs low. Despite the threat of rain, a squad of gunmen up ahead is forcing passengers to get out, stand to the side, as they and their vehicles get searched, even the kiddies.

Georgie's voice cracks as she whispers, "Remind me, what do I answer if they ask—"

"Let me do the talking." I shoot her a wink. "As they say in the movies."

"Shane—"

"My accent, I know. I'll keep it short. Slur my consonants. Every vowel a diphthong."

I glance about for any signs of wickedness—bodies on the ground, captives lynched, hanging from a boom hoisted in the bed of a pickup.

Any witch will do.

It's then I notice, spray-painted across the side of a van:

The Truth Against the World
The Game Is Taking Its Course

—24—

<hr>

TWO men in camouflage saunter toward us.

The gent on my side gestures for me to lower my window. He wears his gun sling fully extended so his semi-auto weapon rests at waist level, while a chest rack girdles his torso—meant for show. He can't seriously believe he'll need eight thirty-round mags at a civilian checkpoint in the middle of the Quaker State.

Can he?

The floppy brim of his boonie hat softens the rugged angles of his face, which he's smeared with eye-black. His gaze suggests a stoic heart with a stubborn streak, reminding me of sergeants I've known, not just during my recent deployment but long before, decades, centuries—the kind to administer merrily the punishment of decimation, strolling down a line of men deemed cowards or deserters, eerily whispering his descending count, "Ten . . . Nine . . . Eight . . ." Reaching Number One, he fires a pistol round point-blank into the man's face.

Lowering my window, I remind myself: be brief. "Yes?" *Yay-us?*

He says nothing, just leans down, his face mere inches from mine. Only then do I notice the tattoo on his neck—the spidery black sun of the Sonnenrad.

"Where you folks headed?"

The answer provided last night, "coal county," seems unlikely to satisfy.

"Little town called Horner's Mill. Visiting my sister."

The man says nothing, just keeps staring. Despite Georgie's checking my disguise, I'm wondering if my wig's awry, my mustache off-kilter.

"Given the general turmoil," I add, "it seemed best we drive straight through."

"No turmoil here," he says. "Just patriots. And this place, this Homer's—"

"Horner's."

"Mill. Whatever. Never heard of it."

"Due south of Gettysburg. Mere speck on the map, farm country."

"You mean Barlow?"

Has the place changed its name? Quite possibly. Last time I passed through was with the New York 69th, summer of 1863. "Can't say, honestly. I defer to my sister on such matters."

Georgie leans over and points to his neck. "That's an interesting tattoo."

She's employing the strategy we discussed: turn the focus around. And not a moment too soon.

He blushes ever so slightly.

"My wife's very visual," I remark. "Teaches art at the church."

He stands there blinking for a moment, and I wonder if he'll actually respond, tell her what the Sonnenrad stands for—the occult connotations specifically, linked to a mystical strain of Nazism whose followers consider Hitler an avatar of Vishnu.

"Y'all need to get your IDs ready."

"Of course." I remove my phone from my sport-coat pocket, scroll up the fake ID—Gerald Thomas Meyer, at your service—then turn toward Georgie to collect hers, only to notice she's now trading stares with the second of the gunmen, the one on her side.

Unlike his mate, he's rawboned, grizzled, older, thin—like somebody stuffed Ichabod Crane and Charles Manson into a giant blender, let it rip, then poured the results into an ashtray.

He wears a ball cap, not a boonie—the lettering reads *Pioneer Hauling*—and he seems transfixed, eyes as dull as hammered tin, staring intently at Georgie, like he's beholding some freakish creature.

I turn back to the gunman on my side. "Is something the matter?"

He ponders that a moment, then smiles like a judge relishing your sentence.

"No need to be nervous. We're the good guys."

"Of course. Thank you."

He squats down a bit more. Our eyes are nearly level. My disguise only makes me feel more exposed.

"You heard the news, right? You know why we're here."

No doubt there's a thousand wrong answers to that. "You mean, in general, or—"

"Family heading out of Harrisburg—mom, pop, boy and a girl—trying to reach our camp down in Seven Valleys. Never made it. Got stopped at the city limits by a gang of Muslim jigs. Turned their car into a fireball, burned alive. Kids were six and ten—sure you ain't heard this?"

I can feel Georgie shudder from across the car—her nightmare, the family in the car, the flash of blinding light. How many times, how many ways will it be brought back to life?

"We've not had the news on," I tell him. "Not much point. Can't trust the media."

I'm hoping for a nod of agreement, a muttered "amen." Nothing.

"Saying our prayers instead. Isn't that right, my dear?"

I turn to Georgie, wanting to offer some signal, a wink, a nod—*Snap out of it, hey, c'mon, just a bad dream, not a premonition*—but the other man, Ichabod Manson, is now leaning down even closer to her window, a look in his eye that could pop a clam.

At my window, Boonie says, "Do you believe America is the greatest country in the history of civilization?"

Rhetorical question, given the circumstances. "Certainly. Of course."

"Do you admit the fall from grace of White America has been caused by being untrue to the spirit of our Christian forefathers?"

We've apparently progressed from rhetorical questions to trick ones. "I must admit—"

"Do you agree that by strictly adhering to the principles of our Anglo-Saxon forefathers, and expressing in our life the spirit and genius of their ideals—then and only then can we hope to maintain the supremacy of the race, perpetuate our inheritance of liberty, and secure the existence of our people and a future for our children?"

The stone sincerity in his voice—like he's reciting from the family bible at his father's graveside. Meanwhile, the skinny grizzled one has pulled out his cell phone—he's glancing back and forth between it and Georgie's face.

He raps his knuckles on her window—hard—and gestures for her to get out.

"And demons shall disguise themselves as holy," Boonie says, "but their faith is corruption."

From up ahead, curses, shouts, a scream. A woman—dark-skinned, willowy, tall—struggles against two camo-clad men.

BOONIE and Ichabod reach for our door handles just as the distant roar of a giant transport aircraft rumbles overhead, beyond the low grey cloud cover. It's followed by a sound like that of a dozen airborne lawnmowers roaring to life at once.

I'm no stranger to the sound, having heard it often during my most recent tour. Apparently our Pennsyltucky patriots know it as well—they dive to the ground as though pitched off a roof. A pack of tactical drones have dropped to firing altitude and launched their payloads.

I lunge toward Georgie, pull her toward me, push her down across the console between us, and lower myself across her back, shielding her with my body.

The first blast shakes the northerly bluff overlooking the road, like a giant gave it a thundering kick. A geyser of flame and black smoke follows. Airborne dirt and rock shower down, then an avalanche of it tumbling from the broken cliff.

A second missile strikes one of the flatbed trucks, parked fifty yards behind us. Our small sedan shudders from the impact, skids across the pavement, fishtailing from the pressure wave.

The car stops rocking. I venture a look around. The flatbed's a skeleton of metal swallowed up in smoke. Trails of flaming petrol set off grass fires nearby.

Specks of something dark and sticky—oil, mixed with blood—rain down on the windshield along with more gravel and dirt.

Welcome to the dystopian now.

Everyone around us scatters—drivers, passengers, gunmen—shielding their heads, diving under vehicles.

Those not seeking cover freeze, stunned by the cinematic reality erupting before their eyes.

Others, American to the bone, huddle inside the protective sanctuary of their cars.

Some idiot opens fire, then guns start going off everywhere—shooting at what?

I catch the distinctive snap of a close-range miss and realize time's up.

"Hold on. And stay down."

I jam the car into gear, aim for a gap between two roadside vehicles—a dusty pickup and the van with *The Truth Against the World* scrawled across its side.

A third missile hits—this one a hundred yards or more up the road—then a fourth, a fifth. It seems they—whoever "they" are, presumably some renegade military unit stationed nearby—are trying to scatter the gunmen, break up the roadblock, with the hope they can spare civilians.

Good luck with that. There's probably a robot in the kill-chain choosing targets, and I've no more faith in pristine algorithms than in the tangled human minds that devise them.

I drive into the roadside field of waist-high grass, plowing through it like a miniature thresher, pointing us toward a gap in the line of trees beyond.

A few potshots aimed our direction zoom wildly past as the economy-sized hunk of plastic and metal at my command shudders, twitches, jolts, and rocks—lunging up, crashing down, like a chopper pulling pitch—with every rift and trough and mounded gopher hole obscured by the thick tall grass.

143

Meanwhile, the rapidly approaching line of trees reveals itself to be the beginning of many more—dogwood, red oak, maple, a small forest amid the pastureland.

Glancing at Georgie, I notice her staring up at me, eyes cloyed with fury.

"What's that look for?"

Her lips tremble as though from the force of what she can't manage to say.

The gap in the trees proves to be a mere rutted path through the underbrush, most likely left by an ATV or a small tractor, not an actual trail at all.

Saplings and thorn shrubs scrape the fenders and side panels as I plow through the woods, the car banging and leaping and veering off-course as we strike the various troughs, tree roots, and jutting rocks in our way.

I fear for the tires, the shocks, the transmission, the gas tank.

At last, after a mere few minutes—it feels like eons—the path opens onto a clearing of switchgrass patched with yarrow and sage in spring bloom. Then, a mere twenty yards beyond that: an honest-to-god fire trail, scattered with gravel, meant for real vehicles.

"You can sit up now." I rest my hand on Georgie's shoulder. "I think we're safe."

She doesn't move. "We're never going to make it, are we? To California."

"Not with that attitude."

"Don't be flip, okay?" Her hands ball into fists. "I'm not going back. No matter what. I'd rather die—here, now."

How to tell someone in the midst of the hardest thing she's ever done, who just came face-to-face with the kind of menace only her nightmares have conjured up to now, that things may look bad, sure, but it's not so long ago that men hung by the neck were cut down while still alive, disemboweled, shown their own bloody, stinking viscera, then either beheaded (if a gentleman) or drawn and quartered (if a peasant or a priest)—and that wasn't the work of camo-clad vigilantes. That was the English crown.

"Give me a tick, I want to look the car over."

I get out and do a quick tour of the vehicle, raindrops pattering the leaf cover overhead. The side panels look like Wyvern the dragon tore at the thing with its claws. The rear bumper appears dodgy and even gives a little to the touch, but isn't yet hanging free. No flat tires. I reach in the driver-side window to test the headlamps and taillights. All remain in working order.

Back behind the wheel, I put our humble chariot in gear and head for the fire trail.

Once she hears the rumble of the gravel beneath our tires, Georgie at last sits up. "Where are we?"

"The deep dark wood. Realm of mystery and magic." I study the crowns of the trees, discerning south by the thickness of their leaf balls. "We're once again headed west, give or take. Away from trouble, in any event."

She pulls down the visor to inspect herself in its underside mirror. Her wig sits awry. She rights it with a tug.

"Do you think it's true, what they said about that family?" The padding beneath her blouse has shifted oddly, creating a hump for a breastbone. She nudges it all back into place. "The one in the car, I mean. The one that was murdered."

"No way to tell. Either way, your dream didn't conjure it, any more than it did the billboard before."

"Stop reading my mind!"

"Stop listening in on my noisy brain!"

She removes her glasses, wipes the lenses with a tissue. "Touché."

Some sort of creature rustles in the underbrush to my left. It dashes off before I can make out what it is, but from somewhere in the overhead branches, a hawk descends in pursuit.

"Can I tell you something?" Georgie fusses her glasses back into place. "Way you acted back there. When everything went nuts. Like, not scared at all, unfazed."

"It's training, not lack of fright. Sad, miserable experience."

"Yeah? Well, train me then. Because I was so scared I almost lost it."

The shadows have deepened, I flick on our headlights. Tree trunks to either side of the rutted trail rise like pillars toward the leaf cover. It's like driving through a cathedral, made all the more solemn by the looming storm above, the sound of oncoming thunder.

"You'd hardly be the first—to lose it, I mean. I've seen strong men break down. Some hurl up their biscuits, others wet or mess themselves. It's called blowing ballast."

"But not you."

"I try not to think about it, is all." Bit of an old-hat factor. "Focus on the task at hand."

She turns toward me in the seat, begins to say something, checks herself. A minute passes, then another, gravel rumbling beneath our tires the whole while.

For the love of Saint Pete and his monkeys, I'm thinking, just spit it out.

"Remember me saying earlier," she says at last, "that I don't tell you often enough what you mean to me? That I can't imagine what it would be like, not having you in my life?"

"Of course. Not something I'd likely forget."

Finally, in the distance, an opening in the trees—the way out?

"Well, multiply that by a million, that's pretty much what I'm feeling right now."

—26—

THE fire trail empties onto a two-lane backroad in the middle of sprawling farm country. I try to maintain a westward direction, taking this turn or that down unmarked byways.

Soon enough, the long-pending cloudburst comes, and just like that, it's raining stair rods. I jack up the wipers to full tilt, but even then it seems our pitiful headlights are dragging us into an endless, cavernous car wash.

Various knocks and rattles from the undercarriage signal that our romp through the forest inflicted some damage after all, then the telltale screech of metal scraping asphalt.

I glide toward the gravel berm.

"What's wrong?"

"Need to get out, have a gander."

A stitch of lightning breaks the sky, then a second's pause, tagged by a rippling crack of thunder—so close, the ground trembles.

Georgie trembles as well, as though expecting to see some buried titan break free of his grave. "Sure you don't want to wait? You know, till the storm blows over."

"And when might that be? Too chancy just to sit here."

"What if you can't fix it?"

"I'm sure it's nothing."

"You're always saying that."

147

Well, yes. "Just some thingy or other knocked loose in the woods."

Grabbing one of the slickers we bought at the army surplus store, I stuff my arms into the sleeves, then shrug the rest onto my shoulders as I slip out the door.

Kneeling down on the rough wet asphalt, I examine the undercarriage. The muffler bracket has shorn away, the tailpipe hanger has snapped. I check the boot to see if Bartosch included a tool kit, or by chance left anything else behind that might prove helpful. No such luck.

Scanning our surroundings, I notice not too far ahead a rutted dirt and gravel path curving down to a tiny shack, so shabby it's most likely deserted, encircled by a thin veil of ground fog.

I crack open the driver-side door. "I'll check out the wee house down the lane here. See if someone or something can be found to help. You stay put."

"Hell, no." She grabs the second slicker from the back seat, drapes it around her. I'm wondering at the back-and-forth—one minute her wanting to stay in the car, the next desperate to remain by my side—when she adds, "I thought we were a goddamn unit."

I hold her hand as we mince our way down the sloppy path, and the closer we get to the homely shack, the more uninviting it appears.

The thing's all peeling paint and scaly metal. Made for seasonal farmhands long ago, not meant for long habitation. The porch, fashioned from bare wood planks, many of them warped or rotted, lies beneath a tarpaper roof of no use whatsoever. The rain leaks through in gurgling streams. Not a single window isn't cracked or slathered over with cardboard.

I venture to the door, find it open. "Anyone here?"

No answer. The place smells of rot and mold and, oddly enough, burnt coffee. Encouraging, that. The bare wood floor creaks beneath me.

"Hello!" Still no reply.

I ease further inside, Georgie tiptoeing behind. A tiny kitchen near the back stands empty, so too the bathroom lying just beyond it, both in need of a devout scrubbing. A pan filled with cold coffee, days old from the smell, lies atop the primitive cook stove, which at last explains the one odor that testifies to habitation.

The stillness in the place, like the bottom of the sea—then a murmur of sorts arises from a rearward room. Georgie and I trade worried, hopeful glances, then venture toward it, easing open the thin wood door.

A narrow bed lies deep in the corner, with nothing else there but a shabby old chest of drawers, a lampstand. Pools of rain from ceiling leaks lie scattered across the floor.

The bulb within the lampshade glows dimly, revealing a body in the bed—an old man, emaciated and motionless beneath a threadbare coverlet. Wispy white hair circles a freckled pate.

He stares as we approach, mouth agape, a scarp of broken, discolored teeth. But what truly catches my eye lies in his spotted, trembling hands.

It's a small ceramic sake bottle of particular delicacy, opalescent green and vivid white, with an angled spout like a teapot. Two stylized fish decorate the side, angled toward each other, like the two interlocking spirals of the *taijitu*, yin and yang.

The pottery type is Tsuboya, a specialty among the artisans of Okinawa. I saw quite a bit of it once upon a time, during a storm much like the one presently hammering down around us.

I sense them then, the restless dead, lingering like the swirl of dust moats in every shadow. There's something here they need to see, behold it for their own sake, a path to salvation, a way to move beyond Tech Duinn into the cycle of transmigration. For some obscure purpose they need this old man, or me, or Georgie, or the three of us combined—but why?

The old man's milky eyes widen. He takes us in with stark alarm.

The trembling in his hands grows violent. I go to lift the sake bottle away before it tumbles onto the floor and shatters. He holds tight at first, clutching it like a safety rope, but after a tug or two his hold weakens, and the item slips from his clutches. I place it on the dresser.

"We're not here to hurt you," I tell him.

That's when the closet door creaks open. The hovel's second occupant appears.

A giant of a lad, well over six feet tall, stoops beneath the closet header to enter the room. He's wearing a khaki ranger hat, like Smokey the Bear, plus a shirt of hunter's plaid, boot-foot waders, all of it mud-streaked.

Georgie eases behind me. "Hello?"

The young man's face is broad and strong; cinnamon freckles dot each cheek. Tufts of reddish beard scraggle his jawline. A scant mustache furs his upper lip.

He's holding an ax handle.

"You folks get lost?" A chesty baritone, no meanness in it.

"Not lost, exactly. Our car broke down. Sitting up there on the road right now."

That seems to strike him funny. A grin appears.

"I was wondering, actually, if you might have some tools I could borrow, just for a tick. Or even just a metal coat hanger. Muffler's dragging."

Georgie adds, gesturing toward the bed, "Does your friend here need any help?"

The big fella turns toward her. "He's not my friend."

"Your father?"

He laughs heartily at that. "Where's the thing?"

"Excuse me?"

"The thing, the little pitcher. It was right there." He nods toward the old man in the bed.

"The sake bottle?" I point to the top of the dresser. "I was afraid it might drop and shatter, so I placed it where I thought it safe."

He begins turning the ax handle in his grip. "Shouldn't touch things don't belong to you."

"As I said—"

"It's wrong to steal."

Oh, but I'm not the thief in the room, am I? "Agreed. But I didn't steal it. There it sits."

No warning, he swings the ax handle backhand, like it weighs no more than a switch. The blow catches me alongside the head, a blast of knee-melting pain. I'm tottering sideways, off-balance, reaching for a handhold that doesn't appear.

He charges me as I hit the floor, slamming the ax handle down on my back, then circling behind me, reaching around with it, pressing it against my throat in a choke hold, lifting me off my knees.

I aim an elbow into his crotch. It's just enough to get him to loosen his grip. I try to throw him—like trying to flip a bull—so I hammer away again with my elbow, this time landing blows to his knee.

His grip loosens a bit more as he emits a whining growl through gritted teeth.

Georgie's retreated to the far wall, paralyzed.

"Run, girl! Get help!"

She just stands there, staring. *Help? Where?*

If she stays, I fear he'll kill us both.

"Do it! For love of Mary. Go! Out! Anywhere! *Just run!*"

She scarpers off—the front door slams open, her headlong footsteps thump across the rotted porch planks.

Time to get serious.

I acquire some leverage finally, manage to gain my feet, make a quarter turn in his grasp, and slam my elbow into his throat, once, twice, three times, each blow fiercer than the last.

Finally, his hold on the ax handle weakens. He's gasping for breath as I break free.

I mentioned his size, his mass. You've no doubt guessed at his strength. Now—like Goll, son of Morna, Flame of Battle—comes his ferocity.

Still fighting for breath, he charges, left hand palming my face as he forces me back against the wall, lifting me off the floor. The ax handle's useless at such close quarters, so he tosses it aside, pins my arm to the wall with his right hand and starts going at me with his knee, aiming for the groin, missing, jamming my hip instead, the whole time fighting for air from my blow to his throat, eyes aflame.

Lightning stitches the sky beyond the window, followed by rumbling thunder.

His left hand slides down from my face and clasps around my throat, a chokehold. I'm hammering him with my free hand, but the punches land like feathers.

I can feel my own airway constricting. I have at best mere seconds before blackout.

Edges of my vision blurring, I nonetheless muster some ferocity of my own.

Left hand pinned to the wall, I put every ounce of remaining strength into my right and hammer again at his throat, quick fierce jabs, knuckles ramming his windpipe, like I'm nailing Christ to his cross.

His hold loosens just enough.

I regain purchase on the ground. Getting my balance, I slam a foot down his shin, rake an elbow across his face, then another hard jab to the soft mass of his nose. It turns to bloody mush and he buckles, wheezing horribly.

I search the floor for the ax handle, scramble toward it, collect the thing in my grip.

Taking up position in front of him as he leans and staggers, I say, "Truly sorry about this," then swing for the fences, catching him across the temple. The ranger hat flies as he drops to his knees. One more blow, slamming the back of his head, and he falls the rest of the way, face-flat on the deck, woozy and thrashing weakly, his skull oozing blood through his sweat-soaked hair. After a second or two, he blacks out.

My false mustache sags comically from my upper lip. The wig sits sideways on my head. The army-surplus slicker hangs off my body, ripped into shards. I peel it off like a second skin.

The sake bottle remains atop the dresser, the thing he feared I'd steal. It's beautiful to be sure, lustrous in color, its glaze smooth and even, the two bright fish on its side circling toward each other, mirroring each other, two aspects of the same whole—friend and enemy, guilty and innocent, living and dead.

I place it on the floor, lift my foot, and bring the heel down hard, crushing the thing into bits.

A barely perceptible sigh murmurs in the shadows. I glance about the room, as though to locate the uneasy spirits.

"Make of this what you will. Whatever you needed to witness here, it's not my concern."

Only then do I turn back to the old man in the bed. His mouth is upturned in a rictus of grim mirth. His aged eyes turn glassy, he trembles head to foot like a rustling sack of chaff, and a final harsh breath withers into a death rattle. He falls utterly still.

From underneath his pillow, a scrawny, yellow-eyed, smudge-grey cat emerges, tail swaying hypnotically black and forth as it blinks, eyeing me like I'm the enigma.

Quick as a whip-crack, it leaps from the bed, flees the room, and rushes toward the door, followed by an eerie whispering sigh as the ghosts follow.

I stand there like a man waiting to be hanged. On the floor, the giant man-boy moans and bleeds. What dark magic—magic that no longer has any right to exist—did I release by destroying that piece of crockery?

There's no time to ponder it. I finger the mustache back into place, right the wig, and head out into the storm myself, only to find that the low-lying fog has swallowed up all trace of the mystery cat.

Once I reach the road, I look back and forth in the downpour, hoping for some sign of Georgie. There is none. Nor is she inside the car.

A modest hill rises beyond the marshy roadside culvert. A trail of flattened grass ascends its gentle slope: tracks. I follow it upward, slipping and scrambling as I go.

Once I reach the top, a lightning flash momentarily brightens the landscape. A broad swale of pastureland, marked off with broken fencing, slopes away into the distance.

Tall grass everywhere. Beyond that, nothing. No sign of Georgie whatsoever.

She's gone. I've lost her.

THE WOMAN IN THE POTTERY SHOP

Perhaps life is just that . . . A dream and a fear.

—Joseph Conrad, *Under Western Eyes*

—28—

PERHAPS it's the unrelenting storm. Perhaps it's the Tsuboya sake bottle I crushed to bits, or the presence of ghosts, or the queer bit of sorcery I conjured, the smoke-colored, sallow-eyed, shapeshifter cat. The guilt of having failed to keep Georgie safe. Perhaps all these things combined. Whatever the reason, for one brief moment, a mere sigh of the mind, I'm no longer on a grassy hilltop in central Pennsylvania, but on a tiny island in the Pacific, the final scream in a horrible war.

I serve in the 27th Division, 165th Infantry, which for the course of the war has absorbed the Fighting 69th from New York.

During the previous week's fighting, all of it conducted in torrential rain, we've suffered brutal losses along what's known as the Machinato Line, a pinwheel of razorback ridges and barren ravines honeycombed with impregnable tunnels, bunkers, pillboxes.

All the men suffer boot rot from the non-stop rain and headaches from the unending artillery bombardment, both our own and the enemy's. Hard to convey the sense of grace even a moment of silence offers, let alone a dry pair of socks.

Reports emerge of "shadow men" seen rising slowly from the muddy craters, wandering about stoop-shouldered, dragging their feet, lips moving as they murmur something important but imperceptible.

158

The troops often attribute these apparitions to exhaustion, or the half-dream state into which we frequently drift instead of sleep. I lack the heart to tell them no, they've witnessed something quite beyond the realm of illusion. But what soldier in the midst of battle needs—or dares withstand—a tutorial on the reality of ghosts?

On the 25th of April, in the final push against what's known as Item Pocket, we enter the village of Gusukuma.

Despite a beating from artillery and mortar fire, the village remains an enemy stronghold. We struggle ahead edging wall to wall, tree to tree, if those are the proper words at this point. The landscape is apocalyptic—bomb craters brimming with dead men blown to butchery, houses crushed to rubble, all of it hazed with rain-swept smoke. Progress gets measured in inches, but one by one we clear out every tunnel, pillbox, and spider hole we come across.

Come nightfall, the worst is over. While two companies dig in along the village's western rim to guard against counterattack, the third moves back through the remains to mop up. The Japanese, geniuses at rear-guard ambush, never retreat without leaving commandos behind.

The chemical odor of artillery shells mingles with the stench of decay and death as we tread through the soft wet clay, keeping a five-pace interval in the blurring rain.

A bus station, victim of mortar shell and flamethrower, sits blackened and smoldering behind its ticket booth, which by some queer chance remains pristine.

In the street outside a small cosmetics shop, an old man's body, presumably the shopkeeper's, lies beneath a broken door that someone placed there out of kindness or piety.

Japanese dead lay scattered about as well, of course. One lies arch-backed across a low stone wall with his intestines trailing out like greasy bunting. Another has a leg missing; it lies by itself several yards away.

Our own dead and dying have been evacuated, leaving behind bloody battle dressings, discarded dungaree jackets or leggings or other clothing that mark where they fell.

We reach a cluster of huts that somehow survived the battle and begin our door-to-door. With the rain and sundown so near, we can barely see twenty yards ahead. It's easy to lose sight of one another.

Halfway through the sweep, I get an odd sense of something amiss. Noticing a broken door in a hut lying back from the road, I ease forward.

Reaching the wall just beside the open doorway, I press myself flat and shout, "Anyone inside? Call out!"

I get no response, just quick shuffling steps. I raise my weapon and enter, ready to fire.

A small ceramics studio greets me, lit by an *okiandon* lantern burning sardine oil, that greasy fish smell. Rain streams down through bullet holes in the thatched straw roof.

Two large, egg-shaped kilns sit at the back of the space, the walls covered with dozens of wood-plank shelves. The pottery is Tsuboya in design, much valued stateside—we've had officers inquire, willing to pay handsomely for any items we come across in our house searches.

Much of the pottery here lies scattered across the floor in shards, ruined, but not all. Some beautiful items remain. One in particular, a sake bottle not unlike the one I shatter decades later with my foot, rests in the lap of a tiny young woman propped against the far wall, legs spread out before her.

Straw-soled *zōri* sandals, the traditional white, split-toed *tabi* socks. Her black hair straggles from its bun. Her kimono's disheveled. A gaping cut, likely caused by the blow from a rifle butt, curves down the side of her face, the blood from it streaming freely.

Beyond her, lurking in the shadows, stands a member of my unit, a man named Pritchard, apparently hoping he'll remain unseen.

The man's made it perfectly clear, ever since day one, that he lacks any sense of what it means to be a soldier. We can never trust him if it means, even in the slightest, risking his own skin. Every man for himself and me first, that's Pritchard's creed.

"A civilian," I say.

"Fuck you. There ain't no civilians."

"A woman, no less."

"Don't preach to me." He eases out into the lantern light. "She had this." He holds an officer's pistol, a Nambu, the Japanese Luger. "Whaddya think she meant to do with it?"

I laugh at him. "You didn't get that off her."

"Hell I didn't."

"If she meant you harm, how'd you get close enough to thrash around inside her clothes?"

"That wasn't me."

"Sure. You just meant to rob her, not rape her."

"Listen to you, Leper-con." My personal slur—his rendition of Leprechaun.

"That gash is no joke, she's stunned and bleeding. If you mean her no harm, help me get her out of here. We'll take her back to the medics, make sure she's seen to."

I kneel down before her, check her eyes. There's life there still, but it's growing faint. "I'm going to do what I can, okay? But I need you to hold on. Can you do that?" I doubt she understands a word, but she blinks, and I take that as a signal.

"We've still got time, Pritchard. I'll take the right arm, you take the left."

There is an emptiness of gaze some men acquire right before they sink into their true nature. Pritchard has that look. A similar emptiness flattens his voice as he says, "I warned you."

He raises the pistol and fires twice. One bullet strikes just beneath my left eye, another carves open my neck. Once I hit the ground, he steps forward and adds a third round for good measure, aiming at my heart.

I do not die just that instant. In the few seconds remaining before I bleed out, I watch as he withdraws my Ka-Bar from its scabbard, sticks it into the woman's body—a whimpering moan, she's not quite dead—and then tosses it with her blood on the blade onto my chest. He fires his M-1, finishing her off, the better to perfect his claim of self-defense, then lifts the sake bottle from her lap and replaces it with the pistol. With that the light fades away into greyness, and this world gives way to the other.

OUTRUNNING HOUNDS

Watch him, watch him, the man on a hill whose spirit
Is a wet sack flapping about the knees of time.

—Patrick Kavanaugh, "The Great Hunger"

THAT wartime remembrance, fleeting though it is, redoubles my resolve. *Find her.*

Perched atop the roadside hill with its storm-battered knee-high grass, I take advantage of another flash of lightning to peer into the distance. This time I can make out the vague outlines of a muddy lane—it lies at the far edge of the pasture, leading up and over the next low hill.

As no better options present themselves, I surf down the hillside grass, trudge across the spongy meadow, then slosh and scramble upward again, dodging puddles and rain-slick stones.

Beyond the crest of that next hill, a farmhouse appears a hundred yards on, front windows lit dully behind red-checkered curtains. A lone dog in the yard, left to his miserable barking, lunges again and again at the rattling, chest-high, chain-link fence.

Despite the extra padding Michaela provided, I'm soaked through to the skin. As I march forward, a shock of harsh wind whips my sodden clothes like laundry on a line.

To the rear of the house lies a ramshackle barn, a few sheds, and the shadowed hulk of a flat-nose truck tractor, the kind used to haul freight trailers, parked on a concrete slab.

The truck, the barn, the outbuildings—places to run, perhaps. Spots to hide. Maybe Georgie scampered back there, found her way inside one or the other, a way to escape the rain while waiting for me, somehow, to show up.

The front door of the house slams open.

A tugboat in pigtails appears, silhouetted in the rectangular glow of the doorframe. From just her compact silhouette and her quick powerful stride, I sense a whole new round of trouble.

Then the shotgun tucked against her hip rises.

She bangs down the porch steps, thick-soled wellies clomping on the wet planks, muttering sidelong to the dog, "Hush now."

Astonishingly, it obeys.

I raise my arms, expose my empty hands. "I mean no harm. I'm not a threat."

She points the gun's twin barrels straight at my chin. "I already know what you are."

She squints into the darkness beyond me, and if I'd a mind to, I could take the gun away from her right there. But I lack the fire, the spite.

The fight with the giant, the spooky weirdness with that damned cat, the memory of failing that poor woman in her pottery shop, Georgie's vanishing—taken together, they've sapped something crucial from my soul. In some weary, despondent recess of my mind, I ready myself to die but again, this time at the hands of a pigtailed termagant.

The woman's fierce eyes come back and meet mine. "Inside. Now. I ain't asking."

Amazing how wrong one can be, even after thousands of years.

The instant I step inside the farmhouse, Georgie, from nowhere, leaps at me like a flying squirrel—wrapping her arms around my neck, pressing herself tight against me as though fearful I might turn to smoke.

I lay my cheek atop her head, the hair disheveled from toweling, the schoolmarm getup gone. Stroking her back through the thin cotton robe she's wearing, I can feel the trembling of her pencil-thin bones.

Whispering, she says, "I was afraid you were dead."

"It's fine. I'm fine. Everything's fine."

The tugboat closes the door behind us. She's younger than I first imagined. Stocky but not fat, strong in the arms, thick in the hips, thighs like girders. A broad face of weathered sheen—spinster lips and a double-jointed nose. The pigtails, like braided rope, hang to just below her shoulders. Her T-shirt reads: *I Don't Snore. I Dream I'm a Harley.*

"Best get out of those duds," she says to me. "There's some in back might fit."

I eye her up and down, appraising her size. No way we could share the same clothing.

"Belong to Goodwin, my husband. Clothes, I mean."

"Is he here?"

"Interesting question—you afraid?"

"No. Well, yes, but not of him. I think. Not yet, I mean."

"Shane," Georgie says softly, still shivering as she clings to me. "It's okay."

"I only meant that, if I'm to wear his clothing, shouldn't I ask his permission?"

"You got mine." The woman heads off with thumping footfalls to a rearward room. Over her shoulder: "Besides, he ain't here."

Once she's left the room, Georgie whispers, "Her name is Agnes."

"Of course it is."

"Meaning what?"

I reflect on her saintly namesake—a story even more harrowing than poor Dymphna's, martyred a virgin at age thirteen, dragged naked to a brothel, burned alive. Patron saint of girls generally, rape victims specifically. *Remember now the dangers that surround me.*

"It's a good old-fashioned name. Suits her."

Georgie says, "Take a wild guess at the dog's name."

Before I can venture a reply, St. Agnes of the Immaculate Shotgun returns bearing clothes and gesturing with a thumb toward the room where I can change.

"I think there are a few things I should tell you," I say, figuring I'll leave out the bit about the necromantic cat.

"No doubt. Ditch those wet clothes first. Wash off the muck. Then we'll talk."

The shower feels like grace, so I hum the Ambrosian *Te Deum* to myself as I lather and scrub, then towel myself dry. The clothes on hand are several sizes too large, but I cinch the waist of the jeans with my own belt and wear the red-and-black flannel shirt outside my pants, hanging free. I'm the clapper in a thick wool bell—but warm and dry, down to the socks and saggy briefs.

Checking the pockets of the discarded sport coat, I collect the damp envelope with the remaining reserve of the professor's generous gift of cash. The rest, with its evidence of Gerald Meyer, linking him to the abandoned car, will get left behind. I'm nobody now. Georgie, too.

As I come back out into the main room, she's just finishing getting dressed herself—straight-cut jeans, a simple button-down blouse, darted with three-quarter sleeves.

"They belong to Agnes's daughter," she says.

Across the room, reclined in a corduroy lounger, Tugboat Agnes adds, "Just hanging in the closet now. It's give 'em to you or give 'em to charity, way I figure."

I detect a tone of wistfulness in her words, and it matches the cast of her eye as she glances across the room at Georgie. Not longing. Grief.

"Your daughter's gone as well," I venture, wondering if some affliction befell the family.

"Welcome to farm country. Sooner or later, one way or another, everybody leaves."

She says this in a tone of voice that speaks of long, solitary endurance. Her eyes turn hard as glass. Worry lines pinch the corners of her mouth.

"Understood," I say.

"I doubt it. Anyways, just me and Nosy Barker now."

Georgie winks at me. Ah yes, the dog. He lies curled up now on the rug beside his owner's chair, quiet as a goldfish. As though to impress us further with his estimable presence, he treats us to a pungent fart.

"Back to what you said earlier," Agnes says. "There's something you want to tell me?"

"Yes, yes. We had a bit of bother in a shack just over the second hill."

"Your friend Georgia-lina here done told me that already. Told me just about everything, actually, all the way back to Father Scandal."

"Friar Daniel?"

She gives me that look: *Come on. Take a joke.*

"Yes, well, good. All out on the table then. But as for what happened nearby, there are parts she didn't witness, and which explain my delay in catching up. Parts which could make matters somewhat worse."

"You kill a man?"

Straight to the point, our Agnes. "No. He was alive when I left."

"Splendid. Because even I have a line when it comes to the law."

Interesting way of putting it.

"Wait," Georgie says. "There were two men."

"Yes, of course—I mean the younger man, the big one, he was alive. A little banged and bruised, couldn't be helped, but breathing. The old man passed, died in his bed, just as I was heading out. Nothing to do with me, he just . . . expired."

Agnes stares at me like a hanging judge.

"Already told this to Georgia-lina. I've lived here over twenty years. That old farmhand cabin's been empty all that time. Belongs to Ollie Bornhorst, owns everything that side of the township road. Begged him to tear the damn thing down, goddamn rat magnet, but there's no talking to that man. Now you two happen along and *poof,* it's some kinda hobo hotel. What am I supposed to make of that?"

Before I can answer, the dog sits up, ears pricked, eyes trained on the window.

—30—

I crouch near the curtain's edge. A half mile away, beyond the second hill, swirling red-and-blue strobes from multiple cruisers create a lawman's lightshow in the dark hazy sky.

They've found the abandoned car. Perhaps they've already checked the curious hovel as well—and discovered what? If the big fella's still there, he'll have a story to tell, and I have my doubts as to how much the truth will figure in it. And, of course, there's the old man's body.

Given the number of small-town police, sheriffs, even state troopers tied to the militias in this part of the state, whoever's there could prove little different than the mob we escaped at the roadblock. They might even be in league, meaning they're likely on the lookout for a man and a woman who managed to escape during the drone strike—a man and woman in disguise, possibly the crazed killer from Philadelphia and the poor young woman he kidnapped.

The Game is Taking its Course.

"They'll be here shortly." I turn away from the window. "Fifteen, thirty minutes at most."

"No kidding." Agnes fiddles with the rubber band knotting the end of her starboard pigtail. "So what's your plan, stranger man?"

They say the deaf possess three dozen words for silence. Actually, no one says that, I just made it up, but if they did, the silence that afflicts me this moment would most likely register somewhere near dumbstruck.

"Agnes works for a moving company," Georgie says, rescuing me.

"Took over for my husband when they put him inside."

That explains his absence—not suicide, not abandonment. Prison. Which likely accounts for her jaundiced view of the law. The daughter's absence, however, remains a mystery—as does the relevance of her mother's occupation. What am I missing?

"Got a pack-and-load job starts tomorrow. Gonna bobtail over to the yard, square away my trailer, then head for Ohio, little town called Lithopolis. Meet up with the shipper, pack up their stuff, and take it to their new home in Denver."

"She needs a crew," Georgie says. "To load the furniture and stuff."

"Ah."

"I have a number to call in Columbus, couple lumpers I know, but two more won't hurt."

Georgie meets my eyes, telegraphing her message. Our way out has presented itself.

"And in return . . ." I begin.

"I'll feed you and take you all the way to Denver," Agnes says. "But you work for free."

"Done," I respond. I check with Georgie. She's beaming.

Nosy Barker's head tilts sideways and he lets out a throaty snarl. I return to the window. In the distance, several torch beams crisscross the top of the distant ridge. And sure enough, the sound of distant barking. The lawmen are coming with dogs of their own.

"I believe we're running out of time."

Utterly calm, Agnes rises from her corduroy recliner, moves to the middle of the room, and tugs back a throw rug, revealing a trap door.

"Root cellar. You two go on down. I'll take care of this."

"No," I tell her. "Not me. Just Georgie. I'll create a diversion, head off on foot."

Georgie looks shattered. "Shane, no——"

"I'll draw off the dogs, make them chase me over the fields." Won't be the first time I've had to outrun hounds. "Can you point me in the proper direction, out the back and toward a stream if one lies near. And name a place where we can meet up later."

"You can follow the fence line," Agnes says, "heads more or less northwest. Mile or so on, the pasture ends in a crick. Take that downstream, cross over when you see a stacked stone wall. Follow that till you hit pavement. That's Westerwick Road. You'll see a windbreak of cypresses along a draw. You can hide in the hedge along there if need be. I'll wait there for you. Or you wait for me."

"There may be roadblocks."

"That ain't nothing."

"They'll search your rig."

"Let 'em." She nods toward Georgie. "Got a false-bottom bunk, she can hide in there. Won't be the first time I've used it, neither."

Maybe the husband isn't the only one who's flirted with incarceration. I put it to Georgie: "You okay with that?"

"Honestly?"

"I promise, this way is best."

She scans my face as though to memorize its features.

"The address in California," I say.

"The PO Box."

"Regardless what happens, go there. The post office where it's located." Yes, it could prove dodgy, her showing up alone, but . . . "Should we not meet up as planned, I promise, one way or another, I'll find you."

She wraps her arms around me. "Now, now," I murmur, stroking her hair. Turning back to Agnes: "Might there be a parka I can borrow? Something dark."

She points toward the back of the house. "Check the wall pegs in the mud room."

The dog's growling intensifies.

171

I give Georgie a courtly kiss on the brow. As I pull away, she stares back at me like I'm about to swan dive into my grave.

THE rain has stopped, but winds sweeping in from the north have turned the air cold, creating an even denser layer of ground fog. For the first time, I'm grateful for it.

The going is hard, the footing soggy. What I'm able to discern of the landscape resembles less a gentle, lovingly tendered greensward than a sprawling debris field. The wreckage comes not from a downed airliner or derailed train, but from the American experiment sabotaged from within.

Welcome to farm country . . .

Every rotting shed, rusting harrow, or mildewed hay bale brings the point home—not to mention a foul taint in the air, captured by the haze, like a bog full of bodies.

Shortly, that comparison reveals itself as more than mere happenstance.

It first appears as a freshly plowed section of a low-lying meadow, wreathed in mist. But then I spot the crosses, small and white, scattered across the upturned earth—a plague pit.

Mass conversions. Mass graves.

How many families lie here? The young, the old, everything in between—death by contagion, hacking up blood, drowning in their own phlegm, gaping sores oozing pus—too many to bury one by one.

Then again, maybe it's nothing of the kind. One hears the rumors—whole families setting themselves on fire in their barns once foreclosure becomes inescapable. Children pitched down contaminated wells, parents jumping in after, joining them in the poisonous water. Deaths of desperation. Sacraments of despair.

Sooner or later, one way or another . . .

In time I reach the creek—or crick, as Agnes would have it—allowing me to slosh downstream, obscuring my scent, till I come to the stacked-stone wall she identified, leading to the lonely two-lane road.

Once I reach the rendezvous point, I fear just standing there, staying in one place, like a prisoner waiting to get pinned mid-escape by a spotlight.

Instead I wander back and forth in the shadows among the windbreak cypresses and inkberry bushes, dipping in and out of the draw, which the rains have swelled, so I'm sopping wet to the waist and cold to the marrow.

My thoughts flee to unwelcoming places. *What's happened? Why aren't they here?* The curse of waiting, your mind tends to conjure disasters.

To ease my troublings, I select a nearby tree—not one of the cypresses but a wise old beech, as yet untouched by the leaf blight killing so many of his brothers throughout the region—and listen for his heartbeat, the hum of life within the wood, waiting patiently till the soft feathery tick creates an echo in my own pulse, and my mind grows quiet.

Finally, headlights appear in the distance, heading my direction, and the throaty growl of a massive diesel engine breaks the stillness as Agnes's machine rumbles up the narrow road.

She stops where the line of cypresses meets the asphalt. Scrambling out of the shadows, I catch the inscription scrolled across the door—*Doombuggy*—then pull myself up into the cab, a maroon velour cockpit glowing with dials and gauges.

"You look like something the cat dragged in." She hands me a towel. "A very sad cat."

"These are inclement times."

Surprisingly, we hardly need to raise our voices, given the cabin's insulation, despite the rumbling engine beneath us, nor does the smell of diesel penetrate. The impressive nature of the technology reminds me: "One hears that beauties such as this come loaded with surveillance gear now—cameras to make sure you're not dozing off, microphones to monitor your cell calls, automatic shutdowns to limit the number of hours in service."

She slips the rig into gear. A momentous hiss announces release of the brakes. "I took care of all that. Windshield, too. Got that funny business on it, distorts faces."

"Brilliant." I chafe my hands and face and hair with the towel, then press it against my trouser legs, hoping to dry them out just a bit.

Glancing out past the windshield, nothing before me given the truck's hoodless design, I feel as though I'm looking out the window of a hut-with-headlights high atop the oncoming road.

"Trailer yard's an hour away," she says. "Why don't you curl up beneath the bunk with Georgia-lina." A tilt of her head toward the back. "I'll let you know when the coast is clear."

I rise from my seat and turn, ducking into the sleeper area, which resembles a miniature apartment, complete with stove, microwave, stacked washer-dryer, slide-out desk, laptop, bookshelf speakers.

Christ in a cornfield, you could travel to the moon in this thing. I've spent no small amount of time in quarters far less inviting, and I picture Agnes on the road for weeks, even months, living in relative style, only returning to the farmhouse when—

"Where's the dog?"

"Nosy Barker?"

"Unless there's another I didn't notice."

"He don't come on the road with me. Needs to stop and do his business too often for my schedule. Dropped him off with Mrs. Widmer down the road. Whatever reason, she adores that damn dog."

As much as I want to tug off my wet clothes, the socks especially, that will have to wait, though I do discard the borrowed parka.

The bed, complete with goose-feather duvet, commands the back like an altar. Leaning down, I knock on the side of the bunk.

A moment's pause, then a clickity-clack from within—the mattress lifts, revealing Georgie's snug little hideout. "Hey there, sailor." Her eyes shimmer. "Come stow away with me."

I assume the spooning position, slipping in behind her. As she lets the mattress drop down again a small lightbulb switches on, which she quickly switches off again once the locks are refastened.

A wall of tight mesh at the rear of the box leads into a narrow filtering chamber, allowing us to breathe. Still, the air is close—I can smell the soap and sweat on Georgie's skin, even with my own wet fetor filling up the cramped space.

For lack of anywhere else to put my arms, I slip them around her waist, and she wraps them in her own, giving them a fond squeeze, then stroking them lightly, the way you'd pet a finch. As the truck gains speed, she eases back into me, relaxing into my hold, her body feeling fragile as glass against my own.

W E nap for a time, only waking when we feel everything around us shudder to a stop with another massive hiss of the brakes.

Shortly Agnes is thumping the side of the bunk with her boot. "Ally-ally-in-free."

We untangle ourselves and emerge from our hideaway.

Georgie eases up behind Agnes. "You doing okay? I mean, you didn't sleep at all."

"This line of work, you get used to all-nighters. I'll catch up tonight." Agnes collects a manila folder from the sleeper area's desk. "I'm gonna head on into the office, arrange for a trailer. You two stay put for now, I'll give Wally the story."

"About us," I say, "who we are. Who we're supposed to be, rather."

"You're quick, I like that."

Georgie says, "He won't wonder—"

"Once I tell him what I wanna tell him, the only questions Wally's gonna ask are which trailer I want and how I'm gonna pay. And he won't come out here for a look-see, neither. Man's fat as a walrus and lazy as they come."

She jumps down from the cab and heads over to the truckyard office.

The sun's just up, the sky clear, scrubbed by rain. Perhaps 20 trailers of various sizes line up across the yard, which is little more than a vast slab surrounded by a six-foot wall. It seems unlikely we'll be seen from the street as we work. If Fat Wally conducts himself as advertised, we should be okay.

Agnes returns with a sheaf of paperwork. "Incidentally," she says, "from here on out, your names are Turk and Misty." She tucks the paperwork into the manila folder, drops it onto the desktop. Sensing our mystification, she adds, "Lumpers never use their real names. Easier to skip paying taxes."

"Okay," Georgie says. "But, just wondering, why those two?"

"Know anything about jazz?"

Georgie turns to me for an answer, but I'm sensing none's required.

"My old man, Goodwin, he was a real fan. The older stuff mostly. Brubeck's 'Blue Rondo à la Turk.' Erroll Garner's 'Misty.'" Her eyes seem focused on something both intimately close and nowhere to be seen. "I dunno, just came to me."

For the next two hours we prep the 53-foot trailer we'll be using for the moving job.

First, open all the doors, air out the musty interior, then broom-sweep the floor, marveling at the dust, food, and sheer filth left behind from the last move.

"People don't clean house like they used to," Agnes says. "Least there ain't mice this time."

Once we're done, the floor shines. Even Agnes takes a moment to admire it. "You'd be surprised how many trailers get jacked just for the hardwood. Floor from a Kentucky 53 can turn even a meth lab into a showplace."

After a briefing on what to do next, Georgie and I hop to it: fill the belly boxes with cargo bars and plywood sheets; secure the humpstraps for moving large items down tricky stairs; roll up and stow away the burlap pads called "skins," used for covering the rough and dirty stuff—fireplace grates, charcoal grills, garden tools.

Though not exactly hard, the work is physical, and soon I find myself singing "Haul Boys Haul" under my breath.

Georgie finds the job equally therapeutic. I catch her humming as well now and then, wiping away a glisten of sweat. And she lacks nothing in the oomph department—the young lady is small but mighty.

It's not just the exertion improving her mood. The irony of depression—so much of it involves what lies in the dark: the unforeseeable, the unknowable, the future. But when the world's already going to hell, what's there to worry about? The air of disaster, it's self-confirming. *I was right all along.* Life may have its frights, but it finally makes sense.

Lying flat on a mechanic's creeper, Agnes checks the trailer's brake adjustments, then visits the "sneakers," measuring tread depth and giving them a knowing kick to gauge inflation level.

I wonder at her expertise. Given what she's told us, the job's come secondhand, a handoff from her incarcerated husband. Perhaps they did it together. If so, they spent years at it.

Before long we're on our way. Georgie scrambles back into the sleeper area, taking a perch atop the bunk, sitting cross-legged like a bonze. I ride shotgun.

"Next stop, Lithopolis." Agnes consults her GPS. "I'll assume there's no argument, we take the southern route."

Argument? Never. "Just how southern might we be talking?"

"Through Morgantown and Parkersburg. Roads aren't the best—Lord knows, they suck everywhere—but we won't lose much time. Plus we're less likely to hit checkpoints. And it's pretty country."

"Sounds grand," I admit.

Georgie says, "Super." Barely forty-eight hours beyond being locked up in an asylum, she practically bounces with glee.

THE GHOSTS OF GETTYSBURG

The air seemed literally thick with iron, and for more than
an hour it seemed impossible that man or beast could live
through it. Under cover of this *feu d'enfer*, Lee advanced his
columns of infantry, and made several desperate attempts to
carry our lines by assault . . . This, however, was repulsed
with slaughter.

—Capt. D.P. Conyngham, *The Irish Brigade*

—33—

BEFORE long, our route takes us through midtown Gettysburg. The battlefield lies beyond the southern city limits. Can't say I miss seeing it. After all, I've been there before.

By that time I'd shuttled back and forth across the Atlantic for more than a hundred years, having first arrived in America during the Seven Years' War , serving with France's Irish Brigade under Montcalm.

The uncharted country reminded me of the land of my youth— forests thick as a young bride's hair, the canopy overhead clamoring with birdsong, the underbrush teeming with pheasants and grouse, the streams cool and fresh and bursting with fish. It felt like home.

So once the French were defeated, I deserted my unit, made way to Philadelphia where the Friendly Sons of St. Patrick welcomed me, and in due course signed up for the next great fight, the Revolution—anything to get a whack at an Englishman.

Thus began my periodic exile, my white martyrdom, in America, returning to the old country only now and then, whenever the scent of rebellion arose—Ribbonman, Fenian, Molly Maguire. That last movement found its way to this side of the Atlantic as well, of course, and me with it. By then my stays here had grown longer and longer. Such a vast and restless country, this, easy to get lost in, perfect for a man in perpetual need of moving on.

As for the nearby battlefield, wandering souls throng such places, hoping to absorb some lingering valor or *esprit de corps*, like *lamiae* craving the flesh of children. I've had my fill of ghosts in recent days, thank you. Still, the mere proximity of the place, the simple awareness that so many men died nearby, men I fought with, men I knew, rattles the cage of my memory.

History books tell us it's on the battle's third and final day that the whole war turns. My unit, the New York 69th, the original Irish Brigade, having suffered heavy losses the day before on Stony Hill, digs in and mounts bulwarks against the expected rebel advance.

Cannon balls scream and hiss overhead nonstop for hours, crashing into trees, snapping them in two, or sailing far to the rear. We thank our luck for the enemy's poor aim.

Just shy of noon, Colonel Kelly pulls me aside, hands me an envelope. "Take that to Colonel O'Kane," he tells me. "Tell the men they have the whole of our hearts."

Colonel O'Kane commands the Pennsylvania 69th, Irishmen like us but from the ghettos of Philadelphia, not Manhattan.

The Philly troops chose their regimental number in honor of ours. Prior to that, they'd been a mere militia, formed to defend the immigrant community against Know Nothing vigilantes. Now they hold the middle of the line as Pickett's Virginians begin their advance in the teeth of our own artillery.

No point returning to my unit. I stay to join the fight.

Fight we do, like Kilkenny cats—grateful at last for the silent artillery, no longer afraid we'll be blown to shite—waiting till the enemy line advances within yards of our position, only then rising up from behind the low stone wall, hoisting the green silk battle flag, and expelling such a killing blast the entire rebel advance shudders and stalls.

Wisely, the Federal troops all along that section of the line, outnumbered three to one, have scavenged among the dead for extra rifles, so we use them to fire four to five shots in rapid order into the enemy ranks rather than waste time reloading.

Even so, despite the initial shock of those opening rounds, the grey wave just keeps coming, thousands reduced to hundreds but still thirsting for a fight.

Eventually they swarm over the low stone wall.

The fighting gets ugly and personal, hand-to-hand, muskets wielded like battle-axes. By the end of the day the Pennsylvania 69th loses two-thirds of its number, including Colonel O'Kane himself—born in Londonderry, perishing a mere few hours after the battle—but the Irishmen hold the line till reinforcements arrive.

Let the naysayers call them shanties, raggers, potato heads. That day they save the Republic.

If only that remained my firmest memory of that time.

First, there's the rain that night, the pure black darkness strangely common after a battle, and the lantern-lit tents never empty and never full, where severed limbs pile up outside, and the dying cry out to the dead.

Then, a mere two weeks later, we get the news from back home in New York. After their kinsmen have fought so valiantly, hundreds of our fellow Irish riot against the draft—not just men but women and raggedy brats as well—incensed against the use of their countrymen as cannon fodder in a rich man's war, where $300 can buy you out of the lottery just so freed slaves can take your jobs—so crow the Tweed and Tammany ilk.

More than fifty buildings burned to the ground, including the Colored Orphan Asylum, and anywhere from several hundred to more than a thousand people dead, eleven of them lynched.

With that, my devotion to the war falters. The original plan of the Irish Brigade was to teach the lads soldiering so we could all return to Ireland and fight for its freedom. Once we're mustered for battle, though, we routinely get placed at the front, fed into the breach. At Malvern Hill, we lose 200 men; Antietam, 200 more; Fredericksburg, over 500. Given such slaughter, whatever few of us remain post-war will never amount to the numbers we'll need back home.

I remain with the brigade for the sake of the men, feeling a sense of responsibility for the fresh-faced ones, ignorant of what they'll witness in the bitter months ahead.

Once the fighting ends, many not worn down by the war's misery feed off greed or hatred to muster on. Nor does it take a druid to predict that the slaves freed of their shackles will soon get betrayed for the sake of money and wounded pride.

All of which takes me back to the previous day, the roadblock militia, Klansmen in all but name. How can one not wonder: did Mr. Lincoln's war ever truly end?

As we reach the westerly outskirts of town, heading once more toward open road, Georgie leans forward and says, "I don't mean to pry, Agnes, okay? But I can't help wondering, given how you've taken over your husband's work and all, just how he ended up in prison."

Agnes stiffens—like the steering wheel just delivered a shock.

"Never mind." Georgie backs away again. "That was tacky, I shouldn't—"

"Stop, it's fine. I know about your troubles, guess it's only fair you know mine." She digs into her pocket for a breath mint. "How much you know about Civil War reenactments? One here at Gettysburg in particular."

Georgie looks baffled. "Not much."

Agnes turns toward me. Waiting.

Loaded question. You suffer through a battle—let alone thousands of others—you tend to find bringing it back to life for an ersatz encore a queer form of make-believe.

"Met a few reenactors, actually, sat and shared a pint. They seem a sincere lot, some overly so, but a handful genuinely know their onions, even if, on occasion, they tend to stray a bit too ardently into the footnotes."

"You don't find the whole thing just plain stupid."

I tug on my ear thoughtfully. "The whole thing?"

"Great echo in here, don't ya think?"

I cast my eyes across the low rolling hills with their lush grass, sparkling green in the sunlight, crowned by honey locust trees. "I'm not trying to be funny or unkind, all right? But yeah, I can't help but think of it as an open-air costume pageant. Grown boys playing war."

A long silence follows, nothing but the diesel's growling rumble, the thrum of the giant tires on the road, the rattle of the empty trailer behind. And the wind, of course, the constant oncoming wind. I wonder if I've been too strong. Or made some offense.

Agnes chews her mint into bits, swallows. "Goodwin was a reenactor."

Foot, permit me to introduce Mouth. "I should . . . I didn't mean—"

"Read every book he could get his hands on, joined every chatroom he could find. Took it real serious. Just not serious enough for some folks."

"Which side was he on?"

"Excuse me?"

"Your husband. Goodwin. As a reenactor—which side, Union or Confederacy?"

"Rebels. That's who carries the most weight around here these days, oddly enough."

She fishes out another breath mint, pops it into her mouth.

"This is about seven years ago now. Fella named Rollestone shows up, utterly drunk on that Lost Cause business. You know, Dixie shall rise again, southerners fought to preserve a way of life, slavery had jack to do with it—besides, slaves were happier before Lincoln showed up."

"Nothing spurs the imagination," I offer, "like defeat."

Georgie says, "This isn't just for the reenactment."

"Oh, hell no. We're talking *real* living history here. And the moment has come. Time for true believers in freedom and the Constitution to rise up against the socialist state, bring down the PC Stalinists and kick out the corrupt elites. Turn back the clock, right to the very day the tide turned against the rebellion."

"What did he plan to do?"

"Live ammunition." Agnes sucks thoughtfully on her mint. "He wanted to load their weapons with the real deal."

"Seriously?" Georgie's voice elevates an octave. "That's, like, insane."

"Everybody was taking the whole thing way too serious by then, both sides. Out-of-towners—they took the Federal side mostly—acting all superior, calling the rebel reenactors bigots, racists. Tourists who came to watch started chiming in." Another mint gets crushed to dust. "Whole damn thing went from dumb to ugly damn near overnight."

—35—

A N uneasy silence descends. Gently, I say, "Getting back to Rollestone
..."

Agnes shoots me a wincing glance. "Yeah. Him." Another search of
her pocket for a mint. It enters her mouth like a dart. "We left off where?"

"Live ammunition," I respond.

"So yeah, he says let's do it right this time. Draw blood, send a
message, start the revolution. Militias all across the country, they'll answer
the call. The uprising will commence."

And so it has. "Your husband went along with that?"

"Hell no. He thought Old Roll-Stone was utterly batshit."

"Why didn't he—your husband, I mean—report all this to the
authorities?"

"You don't do that out here. Nothing on earth folks hate more than
a stoolie."

Georgie and I share a glance—once again, the woman hanging from
her lamppost materializes in our shared remembrance. And what do the
Irish hate more than an informer?

"Besides, Goodwin has this confidence in himself, that if he just takes
the time, hangs in there, he can get his point across, make a difference."

"That's admirable," I respond, "in its own way. But I take it he didn't
succeed."

Agnes, staring straight ahead at the ribbon of asphalt winding through the Blue Ridge foothills, shakes her head slowly, as though she still finds the truth dismaying. "Turns out Rollestone was the stoolie."

Georgie lets out a low soft whistle. "That's sick."

"Yeah."

Agnes reaches up absently, begins twining a pigtail around her index finger.

"He operated a salvage yard down in Maryland. That's important—you cross state lines, the whole thing turns federal. Hadn't paid taxes in damn near ten years, the liens had piled up, he was due to lose everything to the IRS. He'd been involved somehow with the ATF way back when, acting as a middleman to the Pagans for some military hardware."

Anticipating a question from Georgie, I tell her, "The Pagans are a motorcycle gang."

"I was in the bughouse," she says, "not a time capsule."

"So he went to his ATF handler," Agnes continues, "said he knew this group of nimrods eager to arm up and make a stand at the Gettysburg reenactment. He made a deal: I reel them in, you get the IRS off my neck."

"Wait, wait." Georgie winces in disbelief. "Didn't the government see how, I dunno, stupid this whole thing sounds?"

"What does that have to do with anything? Whole point's to put people in jail. Lay off the stupid and crazy, prisons are empty. Besides, give Rollestone some credit. He could spin a tale."

A stab of sunlight through the low-lying clouds flares across the windshield. Agnes lets go of her pigtail, reaches up to flip down her visor.

"I know it sounds dumb. But like I said, Goodwin's got this belief in himself. Just kept trying, over and over, hoping he might get through, talk 'em all out of it, knock some sense into their heads. Then come one morning, six AM—*boom*—door busts open, agents in SWAT gear swarm on in like ants on roadkill, drag Goodwin outta bed, me sitting there hollering, 'Leave him be, what the hell you want?' Plant him face-down on the floor, cuff him right there on the bedroom rug and drag him out, then search the place."

"They show you the warrant?"

"Oh, sure. They were real polite about that part."

"How did any of this lead to a conviction? His lawyer surely must have—"

"Goodwin don't believe in lawyers. Thinks they're worthless as tits on a boar hog."

"Ah. Well."

"Gotta understand, flipside of loyal is stubborn. Goodwin dug in his heels, said no way they'd convict him on such a pile of lies. Sooner or later that jury of his so-called goddamn peers would see right through Rollestone. Justice would prevail. All he had to do was wait."

Georgie asks, "How long did the jury—"

"Two hours."

"Holy Hell . . ."

"Only holdup came when they wanted to hear the definition of 'conspiracy' again."

"How long will he—"

"Ten to fifteen. Over in Lewisburg. Could be worse. Get up to see him every now and then. When I'm not on the road."

We all fall silent for a bit. What's there to add? Is there anything as maddening, as ruthless and arbitrary, as the law?

"Worst part? Amalia, our daughter, she just lost her grip when all this went down. Was a senior in high school when it happened, and the other kids, well, you know. They were brutal. She's up at State College now, getting her master's. Anyway, she couldn't believe her dad could be so stinking ridiculous, or that I'd just sit there and let it happen. And it wasn't just Rollestone that lied—so many witnesses, including guys Goodwin's known half his life, saving their skins, then toss in the agents and the prosecutor and the media. Shakes your faith. Like something you didn't even realize you believed in hung itself in the closet."

Agnes takes in a slow, shuddering breath.

"Anyway, day the verdict comes down and they take her dad away, Amalia just comes home, packs up the last of the things she wants, heads back to school. Doesn't even say goodbye. Haven't heard much from her since. Even when she does call, what's to talk about?"

The silence lasts longer this time.

I glance back at Georgie. She answers with her eyes: *Say something . . . Do something . . .*

But Agnes beats me to the mark.

"Thing of it is, Amalia, she's adopted. Goodwin and me, we tried to get pregnant, God knows we tried, but you know? Things don't work out sometimes—they oughtta put that on the goddamn dollar bill. Anyway, Amalia's not our blood. Picked the little thing up at the hospital when she was two days old. Never met the mother, no idea about the father. No matter, raised her like our own, loved her to pieces. And damn if she didn't love us right back. But now . . . now, I don't know. Time will tell. I don't blame her. But I miss her. Miss both of 'em."

THE GAME IS TAKING ITS COURSE

Blood grows hot, and blood is spilled. Thought is forced from old channels into confusion. Deception breeds and thrives. Confidence dies, and universal suspicion reigns. Each man feels an impulse to kill his neighbor, lest he be first killed by him. Revenge and retaliation follow. And all this ... may be among honest men only. But this is not all. Every foul bird comes abroad, and every dirty reptile rises up. These add crime to confusion.

—Abraham Lincoln, letter to the Missouri abolitionist
Charles D. Drake, 1863

36

W E arrive in Lithopolis by late afternoon. Square, flat-roofed clapboard buildings line the main avenue through town, with lonely shotgun storefronts at street level—Hank's Home Hardware, The Knitter's Nook, Liberty Lock & Key—all in need of paint. And customers.

Agnes's GPS guides her to our destination, located mid-block on a side street. She banks to a stop out front, the curb-side ash trees scraping the side of the trailer with their sweeping, neglected branches.

The house stands two stories high with a steeply pitched roof missing multiple shingles. Sun-bleached red with faded white trim, it resembles a windowed barn with a massive brick chimney. Privet hedges, also in need of a trim, wall off the sloping yard on both sides.

An old and battered police-issue Harley, complete with sidecar, sits in the driveway, which is littered with thin brown wing-shaped samaras, seed pods from the ash trees.

Two figures command the top of the porch steps, still wearing helmets from the ride, faces obscured by the tinted visors. It gives them the look of blue-collar astronauts, for otherwise they're dressed for serious work: leather gloves, cargo shirts, steel-toe boots. They hug the pillars atop the stairs, one to each side, as though trying as much as possible to remain unseen.

"That's Jeep and Antonio," Agnes says. "Lumpers I told you about, from Columbus. Why don't you all get acquainted while I go inside, get the lowdown from the shipper."

She's just jumped down from the cab when a black Cadillac convertible zooms forward from the corner. It skids to the curb in front of the Doombuggy and jerks to a stop, the driver practically leaping from the car, barking out as his door slams shut, "Who do I talk to?"

He has the oily, pushy, dull-witted air of a small-town hustler—close-fitting slacks and silk shirt, gold chain, wraparound shades, leather car coat. He's combed his hair straight back and lacquered it with gel, which only emphasizes the whiskey sag along his jawline.

Agnes says, "I'm guessing you mean me."

He looks at her as though that's simply impossible, then glances my direction. When I just return his stare, he turns back to Agnes. He's breathing through his mouth.

"Fine, this way." He snaps his fingers, then practically sprints up the walkway.

"Excuse me," Agnes calls out. "Who are you exactly?"

The man stops, peering up and down the street, as he tugs a ring of keys from his coat pocket. "We'll talk inside."

Jeep and Antonio rise to their feet to make way as the man comes at them. His hand trembles as he fits the key into the lock, and once he gets the door open, he rushes inside as though trying to outrun a bullet.

Agnes stands there, chewing her lip. "Not getting a good vibe here."

She heads inside, leaving the four of us—Jeep, Antonio, Georgie, me—alone on the front porch. The sky has turned its usual twilight hue of late, a sickly red, less sailor's delight than a deathbed blush.

The two men lift the visors on their helmets. One is African-American, the other Latino, which perhaps explains their reticence about being too conspicuous in a town this size.

I stick out my hand to the African-American—he has that lean, ropey, muscular build that makes a man seem ageless. Add to that a stare like a chokehold. "You must be Jeep."

"He's Jeep." He nods toward the Latino.

"Oh. Beg your pardon." I introduce Georgie and me.

She wraps her arms around herself against the late-day chill, stomping her feet.

"So—you've worked with Agnes before?"

Jeep takes a small step back, deferring to Antonio, who apparently serves as spokesman.

"Oh yeah. Worked for Goodwin before that. Man was a legend. See that rig there? He could turn the whole damn thing around in a carwash, swear to God."

"You know what happened, then."

"Mm-hmm." He makes it sound of no great regret, as though prison's no worse than waiting in line at the DMV.

"Sad for the family," Georgie offers.

His eyes blaze. "When disaster comes, has not the Lord caused it?"

I try to place the reference: Amos? Isaiah? He might be an ex-con; so many wind up either radicalized or born again.

Meanwhile Jeep has produced a yo-yo from his pocket and is doing tricks—Walk the Dog, Rock the Baby, Hop the Fence. He has a thin, darkly freckled face, kind eyes.

"You like animals?" That soft lilting accent—Central American, not Mexican.

Antonio bristles. "Don't start, Jeep."

"I'm just asking, man."

"We're having a serious conversation here."

"I love animals," Georgie says.

"Once had a pet iguana, could ride a tricycle, no lie."

"Jeep?"

"You know rats are as smart as dolphins?"

"Jeep!"

"And you can train a snake to hold a flower in its mouth." He yanks back the yo-yo. It slaps home in his palm. "My *tío* had the gift."

The front door bangs open.

The nameless wheeler-dealer, stuffing a sheaf of papers into his car-coat pocket, flees the premises, making eye contact with no one, all but running toward his car.

As the convertible fishtails away, Agnes appears on the porch, staring after it, tapping a rolled-up set of papers against her thigh.

Antonio turns and spits. "Where's the *fire?*"

"You tell me."

"That guy," Jeep adds, "he's who?"

"Real estate agent." She gestures everyone inside. "Come on. We got our work cut out for us."

37

GNES'S assessment proves to be admirable understatement. In the sink, dirty dishes pile helter-skelter in a scum of greasy water. Napkins lie scattered on the kitchen floor. The dining room table bears two half-filled glasses, one with white wine, the other beer, plus more dirty dishes from a supper abandoned mid-course.

Antonio says, "Somebody up and left in one helluva hurry."

"Maybe they got abducted by aliens," Georgie offers.

"Or raptured." My contribution.

Agnes walks further into the house. "Yeah."

The same sort of haphazard clutter appears in every room—shoes with socks stuffed inside them sitting akilter by the couch, a rumpled sport coat dropped on the rug, a woman's silk scarf cast aside on the stair.

I sense no ghosts, however. Perhaps they fled with the inhabitants.

"Been seeing this more and more," Agnes says, glancing around. "Last virus outbreak, people couldn't hightail it out of the cities fast enough, like they're just a step ahead of the devil. Whole bunch of 'em ended up in backwaters like this—I know, I moved 'em."

"Weren't just that." Antonio lifts the half-glass of beer, sniffs. "Year ago, methane blowout south of town. Fracking company told folks to evacuate, six damn weeks. Some said, 'Screw it, why come back?' Property values tanked. Out-of-towners swooped in, made a killing."

"I'll bet, "Agnes says. "And the thought never crossed their pretty little minds they might not be welcome."

One more survey of the chaos, then with pinch-lipped suddenness she claps her hands. "Okay. Mess or no mess, we gotta load all this stuff. Let's bring in the cartons and packing paper and get to work."

Tasks get delegated: Georgie does the dishes, wraps them in paper, boxes them away. I collect the oddly shaped stuff—"chowder," in Agnes's parlance. Antonio checks the garage and patio for the rough and grimy items. Jeep heads to the master bedroom to empty the closets into garment cartons.

On occasion, glancing out a window, I spot neighbors gathered in small groups on the sidewalk across the street, staring up at the house, talking among themselves. Maybe it's us they find of interest—Jeep and Antonio specifically.

I put the question to Agnes as we're passing on the stairs.

"They got a problem with my crew, they can pipe it out their blowholes. Jeep and Antonio show up on time, work their tails off, and don't complain. Trust me, that's the exception. Neighbors don't like it, they can file their objections where the sun don't shine."

I'm on the second floor, boxing up the final bedroom, when I come across a gaming tablet tucked beneath the bed. When I pull it out, the screen flickers to life.

The Truth Against the World:
Battle of Gabhra—Celtic Civil War

I tap the space bar. The title page dissolves into a misty nowhere, then out of the fog comes the sound of clopping hooves. Horsemen appear, kitted out like the ancient *fianna*—bare-chested with body paint in the shape of spirals and raven wings, their heads heightened with lime-spiked hair. They carry round wood shields and arm themselves with broadswords, battle-axes.

The warriors are nearly identical to the ones so meticulously rendered in Georgie's purloined book. The border, all interlocking scrolls and tendrils and intricate Celtic knots, exactly replicates the one she designed. And the color palette matches almost perfectly—azurite blues, malachite greens, cudbear reds, buckthorn yellows.

So this is why Reggie's publisher didn't use the illustrations. They were saved for this. Given the production values, the thing must be a real money-maker.

Meanwhile, a synthesized orchestra provides aural atmospherics, shamelessly imitative of the Mars movement from Holst's *The Planets*. More plagiarism.

Atop the screen, a tool bar includes an icon for "Chat."

Let's see if my veteran pals are right, that this is where the real action lies. I direct the cursor to the icon, tap.

Gone are the stunning visuals—there's just a charcoal background, white text.

Scrolling top to bottom, I take in the various names, the acronyms. Some are gaily alliterative—Arian Aries, Bunds-fuehrer Bob, Adam Atomwaffen. All male, naturally, and I'd be astonished if more than a handful were over the age of twenty-five.

Further down, other names appear in Cyrillic lettering, Israeli *abjad*. As for acronyms, there's three I recognize: SRW, TOR, FL. Sacred Racial Warlords. Tower of Rage. Fortress Legion. Accused of courthouse sieges in seven states, assassination of two governors, plus the murder of school board members, nurses, poll workers.

One of the chat threads has a prompt for a video titled, "Stop the Globalist-Communist Takeover." Finding myself unable to resist, I click "Play."

It starts off with jagged clips of culture war memes—flamboyant drag queens, protestors rioting, mujahid clerics stoning a woman to death, immigrants wading across the Rio Grande.

Then the President appears, waving to an ecstatic crowd, which shortly transitions to images of beautiful blondes in virginal dresses, playing with children in sunlit fields.

I recognize the gamebook. Insurgency 101. Start with fear, identify the target, show what you're defending, rally with hope. Make it feel like victory hangs in the balance, annihilation is possible, no sidelines exist.

How outlandishly stupid, how horrifically effective. And who better to target with such bullshit than boys and young men? So needy, so malleable, so desperate for the Big Thing. History's suckers.

As the video draws to a close, the now-familiar anagrams materialize in blood-red lettering against a black background: TTATW. TGITIC.

The Truth Against The World. The Game Is Taking Its Course.

I return to the desktop screen. Bottom left corner, two windows have been minimized.

The first is a ledger: "Hate Speech/Disinformation Monitoring." A matrix lists names, dates, and times with messages, making a record of the ongoing stream of lies, vitriol, and recruiting efforts in the chat room.

Whoever lived here, they were keeping track. For whom?

The second window's a message—dated yesterday, early evening, about the time of the abandoned supper.

Beware the stranger
Look for the signs
Save the children
We know who you are
We know what you do
You got one hour

So it isn't us at all the neighbors are interested in, at least not directly, unless they think we're accomplices of some sort.

I consider sharing this information with Agnes, maybe Georgie, promptly decide no. Best thing, play dumb.

Don't blame us, we're just the movers.

I power down the tablet, wrap it in packing paper, box it away.

We work until well after dark, not even breaking for supper. Near midnight, we assemble in the kitchen, toasting our progress with tap water.

"Tomorrow morning," Agnes says, "we'll move it all out to the lawn, then load it up."

Jeep wipes his neck with a wet paper towel. "You sure this all gonna fit?"

"Got to," Agnes says. "I ain't paying for overfill."

I cast another glance out the nearest window, remembering the message: *We know who you are.* "Agnes, in case you were thinking of bedding down in the sleeper tonight, I wonder if that isn't a bad idea."

"I ain't scared of nosy neighbors."

"It's not their curiosity that concerns me."

"Well, save your concern for another day. Anybody wants to come after my rig, they're in for a rude surprise."

The night proves eventless. The following morning, we're back at work come daybreak.

No sooner do we begin loading up, though, than the neighbors once again gather, first a mere handful but then more, lining the opposite sidewalk, men and women and kids, a few wee nippers tucked into strollers.

No one approaches us, no one steps forward to explain. They just stand there, staring, on occasion murmuring among themselves, like we represent the end of something they've wanted gone for a good long while.

Agnes supervises the trailer's loading into tiers—large boxes first, then cabinets, dressers, sofas, mattresses, appliances—followed by the smaller stuff, the oddly shaped "chowder."

We wrap just shy of midday. The crowd across the street has thinned by half.

"Take a bow," Agnes says. "You all just did a nine-hour job in a little over five."

She digs her wallet out and thumbs through bills, passing one set to Jeep, the next to Antonio. Jeep tucks his away without a glance. Antonio counts his, then says, "You gonna fuel up before you weigh this monster?"

"Hell yes." Agnes signals for Georgie and me to climb up into the cab. "Add another thousand pounds. And I'll earn every damn dollar off that weight. If I haven't already." She glances across the street at the last of the onlookers. "Think it might be wise for you two to skedaddle."

Antonio nods. "Roger that."

Jeep scrambles into the old Harley's sidecar and Antonio kick-starts the chopper to life. They thunder off, trailing coarse black smoke, vanishing at the cross street.

Agnes cranks the Doombuggy and it starts up with a roaring whine. She lets the air build up, releases the brake, and eases away from the curb. Once again, the ash tree branches scrape the trailer's flank. Midday sun, bright enough to split stones, flares in the side mirrors.

She pulls onto the main drag that leads out of town, checking her mirrors as she tugs at the wheel, then lets it glide easily back through her fingers as the trailer straightens.

On the last stretch of road before the interstate, she pulls to the curbs outside a strip mall. She fishes a couple twenties out of her wallet, holds them out to Georgie.

"There's an art supplies store right over there. Go on in and get yourself a sketchbook—Turk here told me the one you had got left behind with the car you ditched back by my place—and get yourself some colored pencils, too, brushes, watercolors, whatever." There's a tone of fond surrender in her voice, and I can't help but think of the estranged daughter. Amalia. Georgie's become a kind of stand-in. "We got a long stretch of pretty much nuthin ahead of us, plenty of time to doodle and whatnot."

38

WITHIN the hour, we've reached the outskirts of Columbus. The flatland skies grow overcast, a blessing. We won't have to drive straight into the sun later in the day. But as we reach the outskirts of the sprawling city, it becomes clear the sun is the least of our worries.

Black smoke billows from the city's center. On the shortwave we learn riots are in progress all around the downtown area, in reaction to events from yesterday.

Three employees at a women's clinic were kidnapped by a tonk patrol—armed men in a pickup truck. Taken to a deserted spot along the Scioto River, they were stripped naked and tied to trees in a mock crucifixion, their heads shaved bald and slathered with red paint. A banner left behind read: *In the Name of the Innocent Unborn.*

"Not that I was thinking of heading straight through town regardless," Agnes says, turning the shortwave down, "but this pretty much nails it. We're taking the outer belt. Just wish I knew which direction is safest."

She decides on the northerly route, through the more upscale suburbs. Even here, however, we encounter the occasional roadside Humvee stationed at an exit, surrounded by armed men.

One stretch of sound wall is blackened from smoke where a fire-gutted van rests on its side. Beyond it, in red spray-paint: *Life, Liberty, and the Pursuit of Victory.*

As we reach the cloverleaf where the outer belt reconnects with the east-west interstate, a towering megaboard with its massive screen appears. Christ crucified commands the foreground, with sunburst clouds drifting behind. Text shimmers to life beneath the pixilated image:

TAKE HEART IN TRIBULATION
THIS ISN'T THE END—THIS IS WHERE IT BEGINS

In the upper left-hand corner, in gold block lettering, almost indiscernible against the gleaming rays of sunlight, the letters: TGITIC.

I consider letting Georgie know what the anagram means—*The Game is Taking its Course*—filling her in on what exactly "the game" is, the fact that it leads back to her book, meaning Reggie. Maybe even tell her what I discovered trolling through the game space in Lithopolis: the chat room, the extremist recruiters, the gullible players. So much resentment and rage, all in response to an innocent, beautiful book she meant as a gift.

Glancing over my shoulder, I find her immersed in her work, humming to herself, doodling and drawing, dashing down a line or two— a note, a fragment, a poem. Be a crime to disturb that. She looks happy.

Hours pass, the afternoon ripens, and before we know it we're circling Indianapolis along another outer belt, this one littered with abandoned cars, household belongings—clothing, blankets, toys—strewn helter-skelter in the shallow ravine flanking the highway, evidence of gunpoint hijackings.

West of the city, massive fires ravage the cornfields lying north of the interstate. Boiling clouds of grey-brown smoke churn skyward. Ash flutters down from the sky like snow.

The flames have turned the twilight a rusty orange color, something I've seen before. Not here. Cities blown to pieces by heavy artillery, the swirling dust of shattered masonry clogging the air. A fog of grit.

No firefighters in sight. Instead, armed men backlit by the flames stand guard in silhouette as the conflagration rages beyond them, white hot embers whirling high overhead, caught in the scalding thermals.

When Agnes briefly checks the shortwave and inquires of other truckers, she learns the fires are retaliation against farmers secretly selling their crops, their grain, their livestock to middlemen sending it on to the major cities. Time-honored strategy, rural rebels bringing their urbanite enemies to heel by starving them out.

"As you can imagine," Agnes says quietly, switching the radio off, "I'm no fan of the federal government. Lazy loudmouths, lying thieves—and that's being kind. Like a lot of folks, I had hopes for this President—self-made man, outsider, owes nobody nuthin. When he said he was gonna clean up Washington, put the snoots and shitheels in their place, I said, 'About time.' But promises are cheap. So far all I'm seeing is a lot of what's out there." She nods toward the acres of flame and smoke, the gunmen in its thrall. "People say, 'Hey, things always get worse before they get better.' And I gotta bite my tongue. 'Yeah,' I'm thinking, 'that's the first thing they tell you when you get to Hell.'"

Come midnight we pull into the brightly lit fuel deck of a truck plaza just beyond Missouri's western state line. Crossing into Kansas, I feel an oppressive foreboding, an echo from personal history.

Shake it off, I tell myself. Save the nightmares for sleep.

Agnes makes a spectrum-wide check of the various shortwave channels, listening for any mention of BOLOs or fugitive alerts: Irish male in his thirties, white female adult in her twenties. Maybe Bartosch's spoofing of our phones has the law believing we've split up, Georgie and me. In the end, there's no way to tell—there's no word concerning us whatsoever. If only that were a relief. The silence feels like a dare.

"You two go in and shower while I fuel up." Agnes opens the console between us, digs around for a moment, and lifts out a change purse. "You're gonna need tokens—each one buys you five minutes' hot water.

Georgie? Got towels in the cupboard right there by your elbow. Other elbow. There. And some soap."

Georgie withdraws two towels, two tiny bars of soap, individually wrapped, and hands one of each to me.

"Don't be scared," Agnes says. "Won't find glory holes bored through the stall dividers like you do at the pickle parks down south. But be careful if anybody comes up to you, ladies especially. Lot lizards, sleeper leapers—they may act nice, but they ain't. There's a notorious pussy patch just down the road. If business is slow, they'll come up here, looking for trade. Or trouble. We good?"

We're about to head off when Agnes places her hand on Georgie's arm. "Sorry. One other thing. I just freeze up whenever I try to put words to paper. If it's not too much to ask, I was wondering if you could help me put a letter together. To Amalia. Long overdue, but I never know where to start. I figure, maybe, with your help . . ."

Her voice drifts away into the fog of her hope. Georgie slips her hand into Agnes's, twines their fingers together. "Sounds awesome. Seriously. Can't wait."

Dozens of half-filled Gatorade bottles litter the vast expanse of asphalt between the fueling pavilion and the showers. "I've got a nasty feeling I know what's in those things," Georgie says, sniffing for the telltale odor. "Like a minefield."

"I'm sure stepping on one would risk serious unpleasantness, but not quite that severe."

"Figure of speech." Georgie spreads out her arms like an acrobat as she maneuvers among the discards. "You're always so literal when it comes to the army stuff."

We part ways at our respective doors—men to the right, women the left. It isn't till then, when I'm there alone in the doorway, that I get the feeling of being watched.

Stepping back out, I scan the plaza, or what's visible from my position. Agnes stands beside the Doombuggy, now tethered to a pump beneath the pavilion canopy's arc lights. There's a pair of other long-haulers fueling up as well, while along the far perimeter trucks sit backed into stalls for the night.

Off to my right, the all-night canteen glows like a spaceship, all manner of vehicles parked in front and along the side, more in the lot beyond. Inside, a counter and booths, customers at their meals, waitresses shuttling to and fro.

I fail to pinpoint the exact location of the scrutiny, but the hairs on my neck continue to bristle. Maybe I should go into the ladies' shower, grab Georgie, head back to the Doombuggy.

Then again, maybe I'm just away with the faeries. The unease melts away.

The shower room lies in a separate space beyond the urinals and toilet stalls. It's one large area framed in cinderblock—ten showerheads, ten drains, a concrete floor. I do my best to suppress all thoughts of Neo-Nazi gas chambers, truck-stop serial killers, marauding hookers.

I strip and toss my sorry socks and briefs into the bin, with hopes of maybe stopping somewhere along the interstate for a fresh change of clothes all around. I'm sure Goodwin is a fine man, but I'm weary of the oversize experience.

I'm standing there jaybird naked, testing the warmth of the showerhead spray, when I catch the distinct sound of rubber flip-flops slapping against the tile floor of the outer lavatory.

Maybe I'm not mad after all. I *was* being watched.

I know what you're thinking—what kind of killer trounces about in shower thongs?

The stupid kind, and their numbers are vast.

I glance about for something to use as a weapon. Like what—my wee bar of soap?

I'm still working that out when the man enters.

A rather short man, it turns out.

Duine beag. A dwarf.

—39—

I can only imagine that dwarves in the real world, as opposed to the World of Disney, must routinely endure what this poor soul suffers as he enters the shower room. To be sure, my being stark naked adds a certain *je ne sais quoi*, but I've little doubt my gaping stare is all too familiar.

Sure, we've all seen them in the movies: Burney Cullen or Angelo Muscat or Hervé Villechaize. But further back in time, when their novelty offered only the rarest few a chance of prestige—court jesters, jugglers, mystic savants—they had to fight for every crumb and crust while being cruelly mocked, beaten, tortured as demons, burned at the stake.

This comes snapping back in memory as he stands there before me— thick brush of hair a brick-red color, rugged features, heavy-lidded eyes. He's wearing a white shirt with bold, vertical blue stripes, charcoal dungarees—and the flip-flops, of course.

I shake off my daze, step beneath my showerhead. "Come on in, water's fine."

It's not the quip that pulls him up, it's my voice.

"You're . . ."

"Not from around here, yeah." Inwardly I'm cringing—how stupid of me. My accent. Too late now. "Welcome to Scrub Town."

He stands there for a second, working me out, then picks a spot on the bench along the wall and strips to the skin.

210

With a towel tossed jauntily over one shoulder, one hand jingling tokens, the other holding his soap, he steps toward the showerhead one down from mine. From within my cone of hot water spray, I reach over, extending a hand. "Call me Turk."

After stowing his tokens in the soap tray, he reaches across and clasps my hand. His is soft, a scholar's hand. Still, he's got a grip on him.

"I'm Roger. Roger Holbein."

His voice is rich, deep, resonant—easy to imagine him on the stage or in a broadcaster's booth. "Nice to make the acquaintance, Roger. Shall I call you that?"

He cranks the spigots, tests the water, steps in. "Funny you should ask." He lifts his face to the showerhead, lets the water run down him for a bit. "You know kids. They love to tease, not in a nasty way. It's really quite—"

"You're a father, then."

"Sorry, no, the kids aren't mine. It's a church group. Maybe you saw the restored Starliner parked on the other side of the canteen?"

"One of those big gleaming old-school buses?"

"Exactly."

"Brilliant! I'll look for it. Love those old beauties. Very art deco. I mean, for a bus."

"It belongs to the church. Paid a fortune to refurbish it."

"One can imagine."

"Anyway, I'm the driver."

"That must be grand. I'm sorry, I busted in. You were saying—about your name?"

"It's Holbein, but the kids call me Whole Bean or just Beanzy. What I prefer—and all of this is just to tell you the name I go by—"

"Indeed, quite a windup you've got going." Mocking up my best Vin Scully, I add, "And heeeeere's the pitch!"

He's scrubbing away now, all foamy and sudsy, squinting to spare his eyes the soap sting. "Dutch," he says.

No joke—my sliver of soap pops out of my hand. Once again I'm staring.

"Go on with ya."

"I'm sorry?"

"No, no, the sorry's all mine. Please. What I mean ... That's just, well ... That's an incredible coincidence."

He looks at me like I've sprouted feathers. How to explain—Georgie and me, our silly little sport: Name the Disney Reject Dwarf. Was her choosing 'Dutch'—like her dream about the family in the car, the blazing light—an actual premonition?

"A coincidence—in what way?"

"Bit of a shaggy dog, that story, and it'd be best if my friend, Misty, told it to you. I'll make sure you meet, she's just next door. She's brilliant. You two will get on like toast and jam."

With that we return to our respective showers, luxuriating under the scalding hot water. Toweling dry, we engage in idle chitchat and discover our ultimate destinations aren't all that far apart—both northern California, his a little town near the Oregon line called Devil's Garden.

"Not the optimal name, given we're a church group," he says, mastering the final button on his shirt. "But what's life without paradox?"

We step out into the cool night air and find Georgie waiting.

"Misty?" She blinks at first, then snaps to. "Meet Dutch."

Her mouth drops open, almond eyes all but popping out of her head.

Dutch turns to me, perplexed but not perturbed. Yet. "Is something wrong?"

She's gripping her head now, like it might explode. "You're kidding. Omigod ..."

"Excuse me?"

"Omigod, omigod, omigod ..."

Finally, she snaps out of herself and reaches over, takes both Dutch's hands, and gives them a hearty pumping, like he's a two-armed slot machine and she's desperate for a jackpot.

"You have no idea how amazing it is to meet you."

"I'm sure I don't." He looks back and forth between us. "What's this about?"

I defer to Georgie, and she does her best to put sense to it all. "I just always thought the movie made the dwarves out to be sappy. It made me wonder about the other ones, the ones that supposedly didn't make the cut. Because they were too real. They were *people.*"

"Wait," Dutch says. "It was a cartoon. There weren't, like, *auditions.*"

"Of course, I know that—*we* know that—it's just—"

"A game," I say. "Bit of fun. Made up."

"We started coming up with names for those guys. The ones who, if there *had* been auditions, you know, would have been told to go home. 'Thanks but no thanks.'" Her hands grip her head again. "God, you must think we're total assholes."

"Not really, no."

She leans closer for the next bit, as though to confide a secret. "What I'm trying to say is—one of the names I came up with was Dutch."

We all stand there a moment, like we're waiting for the séance phantom to speak.

"I mean, isn't that . . . *weird?*"

"A coincidence, as noted," I add, "to be sure."

"And I thought, like, it's a perfect name. *Perfect.* For exactly the kind of character a kitschy-schmaltzy Nazi like Disney would never want. And, I mean—here you are!"

Dutch seems at a loss for words. The heavy-lidded eyes blink twice. "How very . . . interesting." A grin appears, then he starts chuckling, like he can't help himself. When at last he recovers the power of speech, he says, "Kitschy-schmaltzy Nazi, that's rich," then reaches out for Georgie's hand, raises it to his lips, and bestows a princely kiss.

"You two are quite possibly the most charming couple I've—"

"Oh, we're not a couple," Georgie says.

"We're friends," I add. "Solid friends, trusted and true, but—"

"You're still charming," he says. "And it's been an unexpected delight meeting both of you. Maybe we'll meet up again in California." He turns toward the canteen. "Regardless, I better corral my brood. Before they create a problem even Dutch the Disney Reject can't solve."

—40—

ONCE again, we're obliged to navigate the dozens of piss-filled Gatorade bottles scattered across the asphalt. Stepping carefully, Georgie says, "Think the kids on his bus are, you know, like him?"

"*Duine beag,* you're meaning."

"Bingo."

"Interesting point. Why didn't you ask?"

"Are you kidding? I felt like enough of a nimrod as is."

"He said he was charmed."

"Yeah, and maybe that's his way of saying, 'Fuck off.'"

Agnes has backed the Doombuggy into a slot along the perimeter of the plaza, the area light enough for safety, dark enough for shuteye. We climb up into the cab, Georgie first.

As I'm reaching behind to close the door, it slams shut behind me.

There's a man on the pavement. His face is a mother's panic—furry unibrow, slits for eyes, piglet chin. He'd deserve a sliver of pity if it weren't for the gun.

A sound-and-flash suppressor extends the barrel. It's aimed at my head.

The light in the sleeper compartment clicks on. Another stranger— this one with a widow's peak and a gammy, oft-broken nose.

He's armed with a pistol as well—a Walther from the looks of it, the infamous PPK. In a space tight as this, however, make and model stand for little. It's deadly, that's what matters.

Georgie's stopped at the opening to the sleeper, frozen in place.

"Relax," Knuckle Nose says. "Show me your hands and we'll wrap this up quick."

Just what I'm wanting. Brevity.

Our hands rise, obliging his demand. I'm appraising distance, obstacles between me and him—the chief one being Georgie at the moment. Glancing sidelong, I notice Mr. Unibrow checking his surroundings now, making sure no one interrupts the proceedings.

I'm thinking: there's only the two of them.

Knuckle Nose has Georgie's sketchbook in his lap. "Been reading your"—he flips a page—"journal, diary. Whatever the hell this is. Because, you know, I've heard you're a genius."

That seals it. Our highly motivated adversaries are somehow, someway linked to the Rory Fitzgerald machine. And they've managed to pin down our whereabouts.

The Game is Taking its Course.

I edge up closer behind Georgie, hoping to slip past. Nodding toward her sketchbook, I say, "Bit private that, wouldn't you say, mate?"

Knuckle Nose glances up, eyes flicking back and forth between us. "Mate? Oh, right. Almost forgot. Hey, guess what? Got an Irish joke. You'll love it. What's a well-balanced Irishman?"

"One with a chip on both shoulders."

"You've heard it."

"Moses heard that one."

"What's the problem with the Irish boomerang?"

"Never comes back, just sings sad songs about how much it wants to—seriously, that's the best you've got?"

"Gee. And I thought you'd be pleased."

His gaze descends again, he reads another couple seconds. "To be honest, this stuff's not half as weird as what they found in the one you left behind—you know, the car you two ditched way back where."

"I wasn't well," Georgie says.

"Yeah, I heard that, too."

"I thought you meant to make this quick," I say.

His gaze turns toward me. The gun follows. "You're complaining?"

Georgie stiffens. "Where's Agnes?"

He doesn't answer, just returns his attention to the sketchbook. I have at best a second if I shove Georgie down, lunge over her, and if his impulses are quick he'll have a bullet in me by that time. Then what?

"I said *where* is *Agnes*?"

"I'm not deaf." He turns another page. "If you mean the bag who drives this truck, she won't be joining us."

"What does that mean?"

"Just what I said."

"What does that *mean*?"

"She's gone home. You're the genius, figure it out."

"Just tell her, ya manky fuck." I take note of a thick, glossy, magazine—*American Mover*—lying on the passenger seat to my left. Hefty thing, sturdy spine. "You killed her. Where'd you stuff the body?" I nod toward the hidey-hole, on top of which he's currently perched. "In there?"

He tosses the sketchbook aside. "Know what, Mick? You're right. I'm dragging this out."

His gun hand rises. The end of the silencer meets my eye.

I move to push Georgie down but nothing's there—she's the one who's lunged, quick as a hare, her hands outstretched and aimed at the bastard's face.

He gets off a pistol shot—it sails wild, she's clawing at his eyes.

Unibrow swings open the door, his own gun muzzle leading the way. I snatch up the *American Mover*, pitch it at him, the hard edge outward so it nails his eye—at the same time reaching for his gun hand, yanking him forward, slamming my free hand into his elbow, snapping it back, twisting the weapon from his grip as he screams.

I plant two bullets in him, point blank.

By the time I turn, Knuckle Nose has Georgie locked in a chokehold. She's squirming to get free, kicking, flailing, but he just grips her tighter, the whole time trying to draw a bead on me with his gun.

"Georgie. Enough now."

It's the eerie stillness in my voice that makes her stop, not the command itself. Small matter. I've got the shot off before she fully complies. The bullet whips past her head, missing by less than an inch. It slams dead square into the bridge of that eyesore of a nose.

I ease forward, reaching for her hand. Her chest is heaving, eyes all but bugging out of their sockets, staring at me, still wrapped in the dead man's hold.

"You—"

"It's all right now."

"You almost—"

"Give me your hand. We need to be off."

As though in a dream, she obeys, slipping herself from under the lifeless arm. I draw her past me, ease her into the driver's seat. "Stay down. There may be other men out there."

Despite the fact he's already dead, I feel a need to make a point. I move toward Knuckle Nose, put the silencer's tip against his forehead. "Know how you can tell Jesus wasn't from West Belfast? He fell three times and never filed a claim." One bullet. Through the brain. Good measure. "Now *that's* an Irish joke."

Turning to Georgie, I say, "I need you to stay put, okay? I'm going to check outside."

"No, no, you—"

"You need to listen to me, Georgie. It'll be all right. Just, please, do as I say."

She blinks, swallows, stares. At last, a nod.

I collect Knuckle Nose's Walther. It's the smaller of the two guns, easier to conceal. I check the magazine—only the two rounds gone, leaving me four. I slam the clip home and tuck the weapon under my belt at the small of my back.

Dropping from the cab onto the pavement, I gander about, under the truck, checking for a third man who's yet to show. Nothing. Cock an ear for footsteps. None.

As I climb back into the Doombuggy's cab, Georgie's shoved Knuckle Nose to the sleeper cabin floor, preparing to lift the hatch on the hidey-hole. I lunge forward, take her hand.

"You won't want to be seeing that."

"We have to help—"

"There is no help. Not now. Not for her. We have to hook off—*now*."

"What if she's still alive?"

"You heard what he said. And you've seen them at work."

I ease her from the cab, help her down onto the pavement. Like guiding a sleepwalker—and yet wasn't she fierce with Knuckle Nose? She's earned her shock, her black dismay.

We step around the body lying there, ease out into the open, crouching. All clear, or as much as it ever will be.

We scurry hand-in-hand across the tarmac toward the brightly lit canteen.

"How did they find us?"

Been wondering that myself. A banjaxed car abandoned in the middle of "way back where"—and Georgie's old sketchbook inside. A man in a wig and false mustache, ID'd by the giant farmboy I tangled with. From there it's not a leap to Agnes, a trucker, living nearby, and straightaway heading off. Who knows what means of surveillance, law enforcement penetration, or hacking skills they possess?

"I've some ideas. We'll talk it through later."

That's when the headlights flash on. An engine roars, the car leaps forward. Aiming straight at us.

"**R**UN for the showers!"

Georgie obeys, darting off, not realizing I've not followed. I'm running the exact opposite direction. The car veers my way—the encounter in the truck made it crystal clear: I'm the one to be done with. Georgie's to be taken alive.

I'm a swift runner—not Olympian rank, but reasonably fleet. I race off toward the refueling pavilion, the car's engine whining behind me as the driver accelerates.

He's maybe ten yards off when I make my jag, planting the right foot, darting left.

He veers to catch me but the turn's too tight, the left fender whips past me, inches to spare. He slams on his brakes.

As I guessed he would.

I reach the door, grab the handle, pull.

Locked.

If not for the glass, we'd be nose to nose. He's a pup, face all pink and shiny, dotted with two fierce, frightened eyes.

He's reaching inside his coat, going for his weapon, right as I'm going for mine. He's quicker, I duck the shot, it leaves a dime-size hole webbed with shards in the window glass. Out of his sight line, I move to where I doubt he'll expect me—jump up, pull the trigger.

The pistol jams.

I duck his next shot, taken with the gun barrel pressed against the window glass. The whole thing all but shatters.

I leap up, reach through the jagged opening, grab his pistol hand, yank it toward me, at the same time pounding with all my might with the butt of my gun.

I'm squatting to get the angle right, fit myself into the space with its rim of skin-shredding glass. This slackens the force of my blows. I make up for it with sheer savagery.

He fires twice, helpless shots, muffled by his suppressor.

Finally the gun clatters onto the pavement. I keep hammering away at his face, using the whole of my might. Bones splinter beneath my blows.

The youngster at last goes limp.

I draw myself back from the window. The shoulder of my jacket's torn from the broken glass. When I wipe at my face, the hand comes back bloody.

By degrees, the chilly snap in the night air registers, the rumble of idling trucks, the oily stench of diesel fumes—truckers refueling their rigs, only two at this late hour, but both staring, one already thumbing his cell phone. How long before the law arrives?

Don't run. Walk away easy. What's done is done. All's in order.

I head for the shower rooms. No need to call out—Georgie's seen the whole thing.

"You're bleeding," she says.

"Nasty habit, that." I wipe my face with my sleeve, take her hand. "I really mean to quit."

As we pass the canteen I do a quick scan of the patrons, don't find who I'm after, so I drag Georgie along to the parking lot beyond.

There the gleaming beauty sits.

A vintage Starliner, complete with torpedo lights front and back, the distinctive eyebrow window up top. It's painted a dark aquamarine with white trim, winged chrome panels along the side, slanting windows. The very sight of the thing conjures romance, like a giant retro fetish, feeding the myth, the American open road.

It's throbbing at idle. The front door stands open. I lead Georgie toward it.

Dutch sits perched behind the wheel—extenders rise from the pedals to meet his feet. He's studying his phone. I rap lightly on the antique doorframe.

"Hello again."

He smiles at the sight of us. The smile quickly fades. "Good Lord—what happened?"

I ease Georgie up the steps into the bus, follow along after. "I can explain, Dutch, and shall. The whole shebang. But at the risk of seeming presumptuous—"

"Your face, your hand, you're hurt, there's blood—"

"It's a favor I'm asking, seeing as we're headed the same direction and all."

His glance flips back and forth between us. "I thought—don't you already have a ride?"

"Well, to be brief, that's gone tits up. A third party entered the picture, and they were distinctly . . . unpleasant. Again, at the risk of seeming out of line, I think it might be wise if, as soon as you're able, we put some distance between this place and ourselves."

He doesn't respond, just stares at me as though I've got a hatchet sticking out of my neck.

Georgie gives my sleeve a gentle tug and whispers, "Shane?"

I turn, and she guides my eyes back toward the rear of the bus. The sides are lined with bunkbeds, three sets of two on either side. From the ceiling hangs a sign:

To Each His Zone

On each bed sits what appears to be a teenager, girls and boys alike.

Not good Christian lads and lasses at all, not at first glance anyway.

They're dressed in dark-hued costumes of garish complexity—Victorian collars and topcoats, high-waisted gowns with spider-web brocade, top hats with goggle hatbands—all in clown-face of a sort but wanton, merrily frightening, even demonic.

Twelve faces in all, staring at us with madcap eyes and lurid greasepaint smiles.

We're on a bus full of circus goths. Retro-futurist clowns. Toad smokers.

From the front, Dutch calls out, "Okay then, Foonies. Time to head off. Hold on!"

—42—

FOONIES—short for Loony-Foonies, fans of a Neo-Victorian-Byronic-Lovecraftian-steampunk (depends on who's yammering at that moment) rock band that calls itself the Lunatic Funeral Mafia.

Their fans, the self-monikered Foonies, follow the band cross-country, and the next tour begins in Devil's Garden, California, four days hence. As for this particular crew—none's older than 21, with two emancipated minors among them.

The kids.

That much I gather listening in on Georgie's enquiries of the group, who seem fascinated with her. No heartland hostility here. She might as well be a woodland nymph.

They're showing off their bustles and corsets, tailcoats and spats, parasols and pocket watches—along with an occasional gas mask, bandolier, hazmat gloves, some other touch of post-apocalyptic panache.

Meanwhile, in the air, the distinct scents of rosewater, candlewax, cinnamon.

Georgie plays the attentive guest, the entranced newcomer, though occasionally shooting me a worried glance. I nod in reply, assure her I'm fine, sitting on the floor in the front beside Dutch, facing the rear.

The mutual enthrallment, Georgie and the other young ones—I take provisional heart. I have an idea what's going on. The distraction provides temporary armor against what happened—three strange men hellbent on killing, Agnes likely dead, me lucky to be alive. Soon enough, it all will not just sink in. It will rise back to the surface with wicked intent.

Deal with that when it happens, I tell myself, then it's back to nursing the various cuts and scratches from all that broken window glass, dabbing with cotton balls dipped in witch hazel, courtesy of the Starliner's medicine kit.

"We're not traveling far tonight," Dutch informs me, "just another hour or so."

I sense an undertone. "You're wondering if that will be far enough. For safety's sake."

He rests his arms on the steering wheel, which is made of gleaming blond wood. His deeply lined face with its half-mast eyes, illumined by the dash lights, flares briefly from oncoming headlights, then falls back into soft glow and shadow once the car rushes past.

"If I honestly thought we were a danger, Dutch, I'd not impose."

"Meaning?"

"I believe the problem got solved back there." For now.

"Are we in any trouble, helping you?"

"You mean aiding and abetting? Harboring fugitives?"

He maintains his gaze on the dark road. "Something like that."

"Well, here's the way around that. How about I tell you nothing further. We're hitchhikers, is all. You felt a touch of pity, lent us a ride. That cover things on your end?"

He thinks on it a bit. "I suppose it will have to. For now."

"Seriously, you can drop us wherever. We'll venture on somehow."

The heavy-lidded eyes compress. Worry lines form. "Can I think about that?"

Not what I'd hoped to hear. "Of course."

"If it were just me . . ." He glances over his shoulder at the young ones. A chubby girl in a scarlet bustier, feathers in her coal-black hair, receives a clown-face touch-up while Georgie observes.

"You're a good man, Dutch. I wish no harm on you. Or them."

He goes quiet again for a minute or so. "The place we're heading, it's a farm outside a small town called Stull, not far from the state park at Clinton Lake."

"Touristy, this place?"

"Not at all, certainly not this time of year. Still off-season, at least until Memorial Day. Even if it were . . . My point—it's private, not public. We should be okay."

"If you don't mind my asking, given so little time before your final destination for the night, why did you pull up at the truck stop back there?"

That prompts another glance over his shoulder at the youths. "Let's just say I thought I stood a better chance of having some privacy there than where we're heading. The accommodations on the farm are a bit, shall we say, communal."

Makes sense. He's already noted the kids like to tease. And yet . . .

"You were looking for privacy in a truck stop shower?"

"You make it sound like something it wasn't."

Where my mind is going: He was on the hunt for a sleeper leaper, a lot lizard.

What my mouth allows: "Not my meaning at all, sorry, I just—"

"Most truckers, in my experience, end their day just after sunset and start up before dawn. I figured the timing was on my side. And I was right, wasn't I? Only person I ran into was you."

He looks at me with those soulful eyes.

"Yeah," I say. "Lucky you."

—43—

THE farm is small, quaint, tucked away off a two-lane road a mile or so beyond the borders of the state park. Lamplight glows in the windows of the rustic main house as the Starliner rumbles forward up the long driveway.

Dutch kills the engine, opens the door. The night breeze rustles through the leaves of the maples and poplars surrounding the house.

That quietude lasts but a second. With screams and hoots of youthful welcome a dozen or so other Foonies, all bedecked in a similar state of antiquated dress and frightful face paint, tumble out of the house. Shortly they converge with their visitors exiting the bus. Hugs and kisses and backslaps ensue, gasps of awe over stunning raiment.

Once again, Georgie gets petted and cooed over, introduced as a sort of newfound mascot, a possible convert to the cult. They're tugging her inside, everyone laughing, and she glances back inquiringly, wondering if I'll follow.

I give a little wave and point up the hill toward the shadowy hulk of a barn. She'll be perfectly safe among this crowd, and I'm feeling the tug of solitude.

I drift away in the moonlight toward a fenced paddock, drawn by the scent of horses.

According to Dutch, this place represents one of the last remaining farmsteads in the area, the others snatched up in the land grab that created the dam, the lake, the surrounding park. Valley farmers got conned into selling, only to watch their houses, kept in the family for generations, bulldozed into the newly swollen rivers and streams.

Progress, the fine minds in the capital called it. Devastation was what the dispossessed felt. Small wonder they're now rising up.

This place survived, transformed from a working farm to a riding school, offering trail rides along the manmade lake.

The stables lie to the left of the paddock, and shortly I'm standing in the wooden archway. Call it a need for respite, for something noble and simple and pure. Like a penitent venturing into a chapel, I make my visit.

The smell's the first thing—musty hay and horse apples, worn leather and rough cedar, the magnificent animals themselves. Next comes the sound— the slumberous breathing, like gods whispering in the dark.

A bit of moonglow hazes down from a dusty skylight, and my eyes adjust to the dimness. Scraps of hay and wood chips lie scattered across the hardpack floor. Harnesses, leads, and bridles hang from pegs outside each stall, as do buckets of carrots with their flowing greens.

I'm guessing it's mostly quarter horses here, retired from work to take a saddle for the city folk wanting a sunny ride through the park. But then one rises to greet me, second stall on the right, lolling his neck over the half-door—a Tennessee Walker, dapple grey, strong and tall, sixteen hands at least, that distinctive long lean face.

He's brushed and bright as a penny, keen as a hawk.

As I approach, his bulging eyes grow soft, the small ears recede, and his long muscular neck relaxes into my outstretched hand.

"Hey, big fella. And who might you be?" A brass nameplate hangs beside his stall: Pharaoh. Suits him—sniff of exotic royalty, that sad sense of long-lost time. Or is that me?

"And would you like to crunch on some carrot tops, Pharaoh?"

He beats me to the pail, snatches one in his cobbly teeth, and offers it to me to hold as he nibbles away.

"Oh, you're a fat and pampered one, Pharaoh, tell the truth now."

With my free hand I stroke his coarse black forelock, rub the felt of his ears, and after a minute I lean closer, place my cheek against his neck and feel the bristly warmth of his coat against my skin. The rough scent of him, the feel of his strength.

"Wouldn't it be grand, Pharaoh, you and me, riding off and away."

I'd like to say this all reassures me, calms my heart. But it's the state of Kansas I'm in, and Kansas and me and horses have a tragic history. It's the reason I've not been back to this godforsaken part of the world in a century and a half.

I tell myself to put that out of my mind and return to my devotions, sliding my hand down the long sleek peninsula of his face.

"So, Pharaoh, what say ye on the savagery of the civilized? Are we doomed?"

A horse blanket lies draped over the stall's partition—not much of a bed, but once I lay it down on the floor-strewn hay, it beckons like paradise. Shortly Pharaoh settles in himself, thumping down, sprawling onto his flank with a great harrumphing sigh.

Behold us now, horse and human, ready for the simple charity of sleep.

It doesn't come, of course. Instead I'm set upon by memories, the ones I've been trying to hold at bay ever since we crossed the state line.

THE WOMAN IN THE RIVER

"The past is the present, isn't it? It's the future, too. We all try to lie out of that but life won't let us."

—Eugene O'Neill, *A Long Day's Journey Into Night*

—44—

NO sooner has the Confederacy surrendered than rumblings arise among the Irish veterans regarding an invasion of Canada, with hopes of strongarming Britain into conceding the homeland's freedom.

At the same time, Fenian recruiters infiltrate the decommissioned ranks, mustering volunteers, whispering of an uprising planned back home.

To be sure, though the war's carnage has decimated our number, the drumbeat of rebellion against the Crown remains insistent. Nor am I immune.

But the sight of so many wounded and dying, Union and Confederate both, their cries for Mother or God or swift mercy, continue to haunt my mind.

Despite centuries of battle, what I've witnessed over the past four years stands apart: the scientific efficiency of "modern" war, the ingenuity of its weapons, the sheer wicked speed at which so many souls get churned into meat.

Needing to put some distance between myself and all that, I head west alone.

Traveling by railcar, buckboard, the back of a mule for one stretch through Illinois, I eventually find my way to Chouteau Island on the Arkansas River along the Santa Fe trail. There I fiddle up work as a teamster, helping guide the heavy freight wagons south through the sandhills of Bear Creek Pass.

It's during one such journey, as we struggle against the Cimarron's braiding midstream current in a mid-autumn drizzle, that I spot a commotion downriver.

Once the wagon makes it safely across, and the oxen stop their bellowing from the strain of dragging the overloaded buckboard up from the riverbed quicksand, I hand the reins to my partner and amble down the treeless riverbank, plodding through waist-high grass, hoping to get a closer look at what's causing all the ruckus.

A striking black woman—small but muscular, short-haired, with coarse grey whip scars crisscrossing her back—stands naked in the churning, sandy water, impervious to the rain, impervious to everything as she tenderly bathes an infant, singing to it softly.

A restive crowd watches from the river's edge, largely silent, except for a young Comanche woman in deerskin dress and knee boots, crying out angrily, even as the darker woman pays her no mind, cooing to the infant in her arms, continuing her plaintive song as she swirls back and forth, dipping the child gently into the water over and over.

A Mexican trader by the name of Cuchillo stands among the onlookers, chewing on a long blade of buffalo grass, face shadowed by the brim of his high-crowned hat. Having made his acquaintance during previous trips, I ask him if he has any details to offer as to what might be happening or why.

He glances one last time at the scene, then draws me away outside of general earshot.

He tells me the black woman is one of a half dozen wives for a Comanche head man named Three Wolves, whose band now occupies the river's south shore, waiting for the weather to turn before continuing on to the valley where they make their traditional winter camp.

The head man's main wife just died in childbirth, an all too common occurrence among the tribes, and the second wife, the one screaming on the riverbank, is too terrified of the swollen river to perform the ritual bathing of the newborn. The Negro stepped in, scooping the baby up and carrying it to the water, fearing that if she didn't the child would be just one more infant born "on the other side of the blanket." The second wife feels shamed—thus the intemperance.

The black woman's name is Na'ura, which translates as "someone found."

Come the Civil War, many blacks in Indian Territory decided to take their chances, make a break for Mexico, where slavery's abolished. Most never made it, like Na'ura. She alone survived among her family—both parents, three siblings—when they fled across the Red River into Texas. She was covered in tarantula bites and close to death from thirst and starvation when a hunting party from Three Wolves' camp found her.

A plan takes shape in my mind, for I can sense Na'ura has caused herself serious trouble, and the winds of time are not favoring Three Wolves and his people.

I have to act quickly, though. The Comanche band will move on in three to four days, heading farther downriver as soon as the rains stop.

I do not fear the tribes. Like them, the *fianna* were hunters and warriors—long-haired, expert horsemen, known for our keening war cry. We both esteem courage in battle to an extreme degree, something that appalls and horrifies our more civilized enemies.

The Celts and Comanche also share an awareness that not all that is real is visible, which explains the reverence for burial grounds. And a keen awareness of spirits.

With that sense of commonality in mind, I devise my way forward.

I already have the perfect gift in hand: a spanking new Yellowboy, the latest Winchester repeater, brass-plated with a fifteen-round magazine. The piece alone will make a stunning gift. Just to be certain, I add three boxes of .44 cartridges and a hand mirror, the latter alone worth a horse or a pile of buffalo robes.

I leave the ankle-deep mud of the smoke-filled town with its clapboard shanties and hugger-mugger tents to head downriver toward Three Wolves' camp, riding the gelding I've bought from the local blacksmith, knowing no Comanche can respect a man who owns not a single horse.

Word of my coming has preceded me—Cuchillo's handiwork—so once I arrive in camp, a few stern young men, accompanied by a swarm of mocking children, half drag, half shove me to the head man's lair.

Buffalo hides form the tipi's internal dew cloth, elaborately painted with scenes of battle and the hunt, while buffalo robes lie three deep across the dirt floor. Their dense black fur makes sitting luxuriant, despite the lingering haze of smoke from the fire.

A tall, sinewy man of indeterminate age, Three Wolves wears a headdress made of a buffalo scalp with the bull horns intact, from which his luxurious black hair, greased with bison fat, hangs loose to the middle of his chest. He's tattooed his battle scars, to make them stand out, and he bears himself with the sad severity of a man who knows war.

Na'ura wears a knee-length buckskin dress, festooned with beadwork and porcupine quills, high moccasins made of soft, chewed deerskin with buffalo-hide soles.

The clothing of the other wives is drab, a signal they do not think much of my visit. Their faces and arms are deeply gashed, wounds inflicted in mourning for the dead first wife.

I'm offered roasted elk meat by one of the lesser wives, in keeping with the Comanche belief one should never talk of serious things with a hungry man. Three Wolves and I agree to speak Spanish, a language we both manage well, and once I've finished a portion of the meat, he says, "You have a question."

"A request," I reply. "Yes."

With an air of indifference to suggest a position of strength, I present the Winchester, the boxes of shells, but hold back the mirror for now, in the event I'm obliged to haggle.

Three Wolves bobs the rifle in his hands, fingers the engraved brass plating, squints down the barrel to check the sight, racks the lever slow, then fast.

Though I know my principal leverage lies in the head man's immediate need to mitigate discord among his wives, I choose to frame the issue in starker terms.

"I have come," I tell him, "to help prevent any difficulties from the pony soldiers who, sooner or later, will come to take Na'ura away, offering nothing in return."

She sits there impassively, staring straight ahead, so stock-still I wonder if she's even bothering to listen.

I'm aware that Comanche women look forward to marrying great warriors, so I describe my exploits with the Irish Brigade—the great hand-to-hand battles, the valor of the men, the many fallen, the hope of returning to Ireland to fight for its freedom when—

Three Wolves stops me with a raised hand. Judging from his expression, he finds my exploits not so much unimpressive as irrelevant.

"Na'ura cannot bear children," he tells me. "The long rides on horseback battered her womb. So she does not want to leave the newborn infant, though the child is not hers, and she has no right to it. Still, she would help care for it well."

Out of the corner of my eye, I catch the second wife, the one who berated Na'ura so fiercely on the riverbank only days before, sitting passively. She says not a word, either on her own behalf or against her rival, from which I infer that it's time to negotiate.

"The Comanche are right to want more babies," I respond, "given that the drought years decimated their numbers. But as I said, the cavalry officers have orders to free all blacks believed to be enslaved."

"She is not a slave," Three Wolves thunders. "She is a wife. A good wife. She is needed."

"Yes, but whites are stubborn. They remain fixed on their ideas, all the worse when their notions are anchored in vanity."

I stop short of telling him that the settlers, inspired by their bibles and backed by their government, see this country as the Promised Land—meaning he and his kind are Canaanites, whom their god commands they dominate, drive out, destroy.

In the same way, they see the prairie as wasteland—an emptiness in need of dominion through work. Rather than coexist, they wage war—on native, nature, everything.

"It will only be a matter of time, and not much time at that, before the soldiers come and take her away. Forever."

And with that, I produce the hand mirror.

It's a simple affair—oval, made of unadorned silver, heavy in the hand—but it's often the simpler gifts that strike a chord.

Three Wolves grunts as he takes it from me, then studies his reflection. He runs a finger along his tattooed scars, grins puckishly, then hands the mirror to Na'ura. She declines to look at herself, instead passing it along to the next wife down.

Three Wolves says, "The Mexican, Cuchillo, says you sing well. The People love jokes and songs."

"As do the Irish."

"Sing for me, then, while I consider your offer. A song of your homeland, for I understand your people live far away, and have suffered."

Who hasn't—and what exactly qualifies as home anymore? But I know what he's after.

> *O Father dear, I often hear you speak of Erin's Isle*
> *Her lofty scenes, her valleys green, her mountains*
> *rude and wild*
> *They say it is a lovely land wherein a prince might dwell*
> *Oh why did you abandon it? The reason, to me tell.*

I doubt they've understood more than a word here and there, but sorrow translates, and it's there in the melody. At last, Na'ura turns toward me. Her eyes glisten, but not with melancholy. With grief.

I skip the other verses save one.

O well do I remember that bleak December day
The landlord and the sheriff came to drive us all away
They set my roof on fire with cursed English spleen
And that's the cruel reason that I left old Skibbereen

Three Wolves lets the last of it fade away, then waits, sitting there with that inbred stoicism unique to men of his kind. I wait as well, seconds bleeding into minutes, feeling Na'ura's eyes upon me but not daring to glance back, till it feels like all eternity is passing.

"If I learn you mistreat her," Three Wolves says finally, "I will find you."

He then extends his hand to Na'ura. She accepts it. He reaches out for mine. He crosses my wrist over hers, and chants softly for several moments, the sound deep in his throat, a tune that drifts like fog across a river.

We've ridden maybe half a mile—me on my gelding; Na'ura on a roan mare bestowed by Three Wolves—when she stops, turns in her blanket saddle, and stares back at the camp.

"I've heard talk of a couple Freedmen towns starting up," I tell her. "You might find yourself welcome there. They're very new, however, and a long ways off—San Antone's the closest, the others are around Dallas, Houston. It's too dangerous to travel alone. I can come along, make sure you get there safely."

She's still looking back the way we came. Nearby, the river churns, its mudbanks thronged with foraging birds, a brisk northern wind whipping the tall grass.

In time, she asks, "Where are your people?"

"I don't have any people," I tell her, then think of Niamh. "Not in this world."

She studies me like the sky before a storm. Moments pass, not a word, she hardly blinks.

"Then you and I, we are alone."

"It would seem so, yes."

Another infinite silence. I find myself remembering the scars crisscrossing her back.

"I know a place." She points northwest. "There are horses and buffalo. Good grass. Clear water." With a nudge of her knees into her pony's flanks and a click of her tongue she heads off, calling back over her shoulder. "Sing for me, Irish."

MASKED BALL

And in those days men will seek death and will not find it;
they will long to die, and death will fly from them.

—Revelation 9:6

—45—

I'M drifting somewhere in the haze between sleep and waking, images sifting through my mind of the Kansas badlands—*you and I, we are alone*—when a voice from the stable doorway rises above the thump of distant music.

"Shane?"

I rise from my bleariness, brush myself off, and make way barefoot toward the gate of the stall. Pharaoh pays me little mind—a mere one eye, dark and shiny, tracks my movement.

I gesture my visitor toward me, saying quietly, "Here, luv."

From her silhouette I can see the high-waisted dress, complete with puffed sleeves and flaring skirt, and as she draws nearer I can see the fabric's a vibrant purplish blue, like jacaranda blossoms.

The Foonies have performed their doll-work on her. Her face is coated in a bright white base, rimmed with a vivid red line. Celtic knots with their intricate interlacings predominate—eternity knots adorn each cheek, a Triquetra on her chin, two tiny matching lover's knots mark the edges of her mouth. She's planted a Nordic fire eye in the middle of her brow, so the downward dagger reaches the tip of her nose.

A sheen of sweat coats the bare skin of her neck—from dancing, I suspect. Her damp hair glistens.

I nod toward the facework. "Do all that by yourself?"

"Pretty much. Like it?"

"Working backwards, in a mirror?"

"Girls learn to master such things. Most do anyway. Jenny helped, admittedly, on the trickier parts."

"So there's a Jenny in our midst."

"Well, yeah, kinda. Her Foonie name is Spider Child."

"Cuddly."

"They all have names like that. Regina Mortalis. Professor Miserare. Countess Thundercut."

"And have you earned yourself a moniker as yet?"

"I have." Her almond eyes gleam. She holds out her arms. "I am Runaway Pearl."

"Well done." I clap my hands softly. "Suits you."

Quick as that, however, the mirth vanishes. She rustles forward, fingers rising to touch one of the deeper cuts on my cheek.

"How bad does it hurt?"

"Don't fuss now. It's all just nicks and nothings."

She withdraws her hand but not her gaze. "You're really not coming in?"

"I'm a crooner, Georgie, not a hoofer."

"It's not the kind of dancing that takes talent."

"Seriously, I cut a miserable rug."

"It feels good, though." She lifts her chin, rakes her hands through her wet hair, shakes them out. "Bouncing around. Working off the angst."

"I'm sure it's all grand fun. But me and Ol' Pharaoh here, we've reached an accommodation. Neither one of us intends to hog the stall."

"You don't mind the . . ." She crinkles her nose.

"Are ya mad? It's grand."

She rises on tiptoe to peek in at the beast. He greets her with that same glowing, indifferent eye.

"Native Americans," she says, "when they first encountered horses, called them magic dogs."

Did she somehow once again listen in on my thoughts—and from all the way down the hill? Perhaps my remembrances of Na'ura linger around me like a scent.

"So goes the story, yeah."

"You don't think it's true?"

"Unclear. I do know that among certain tribes—the Blackfoot, for example—the gift of a horse or a dog must be reciprocated. No questions. And generously, too."

She looks off down the stalls, biting her lip. "There's been a . . . development."

I settle in for a talk, drape my arms on the stall gate. "Tell me."

"Dutch knows who we are."

So ends the Ballad of Turk and Misty. "How did he find out?"

"Doomscrolling on his phone. He's a bit of worrier."

"He wears that on his face. And?"

"He pulled me aside. We took a little walk together."

"Alone, I'm hoping."

"Yeah, no one but him knows. For now, any rate."

And how long can that last? Unlikely he's the only doomscroller in that lot.

"I told him our half of it."

Could we even claim half the story anymore? Lord knows what else is out there.

"He's sympathetic," she continues, "but feels concerned for the others. It really is a church group, by the way. Slays me, that part. These are the wildings. No drink, no drugs, but boy—who knew people still slam-danced?"

"Back to Dutch, though."

"Yeah, yeah, sorry."

She turns and rests her back against the cedar column rising floor-to-ceiling at the corner of the stall, where Pharaoh's tack and the carrot bucket hang. She seems to be bracing herself for something, but no words come.

I prompt her with, "When him and me conversed on the bus, I told him not to worry. Drop us here—or anywhere—we'll find our own way west."

"He mentioned that. Said he appreciates it. He's thinking it over."

She sinks slowly to the floor onto her haunches, then settles on her rump, legs outstretched. Bits of hay cling to her billowing skirt.

"What in the name of hell are we doing, Shane?"

—46—

I lift the latch on the stall gate, slip out, and join her on the ground. "Don't expect a bolt from the cheap seats. No way to know at this point if we're doing the right thing, the wrong thing. That all gets sorted after, once it's done."

"I mean, it's just one book. And most of what's in it came from you. Sure, I added some touches here and there."

"Georgie—"

"And yeah, Reggie stole it. And maybe you're right, the people after us are involved in that somehow. But kill for it? I can't stop thinking about Agnes. She was murdered because of me—*me*. Mother of fuck—how did that *happen?*"

I consider filling her in on the game, its army of players, the recruiters trolling the chat rooms, the mountains of money that must be involved. Best, however, to scotch that idea. For now. Something else entirely is called for.

"First," I begin, "I want to put to bed for good this notion that the book somehow isn't entirely yours. Those stories awakened something in you. But you turned around and awakened something in them. I'm not messing you about. Far more of you in it than me. Or anyone."

Eyes closed, she takes a deep, tremulous breath.

"Second, the question now isn't what's happened or why. It's what's to be done. We're midway across a country turned upside down. Half the people we're likely to meet would gladly kill us or turn us over to someone else eager to do the job. If Dutch decides to take us all the way to California, may as well go."

I'm beginning to wonder, however, if Reggie's disappearance was voluntary. Or bloodless. If so, what's waiting for us in Napa?

"Then again," I add, "if Dutch feels compelled to leave us off somewhere along the way, we'll blunder on somehow."

Her eyes glisten in the Celtic clown face. "You're not afraid I'll flip out?"

"Hardly."

"Don't lie."

"Calling me a liar?"

"Shane—"

"And Agnes—she'd want you to live. To thrive."

That, at last, conjures tears. "She was just so . . ." A shrug where the proper word should be. "She didn't have to help us."

"You reminded her of her daughter."

"She wanted me to write a letter."

"Still can, if you want."

"And tell her what? Jesus. Those fucking fucks . . ."

I gather her to me and hold her tight. "None of this," I whisper, "none of it, is your fault."

She pulls away, rests her head in her hands, barely breathing.

"Every now and then? Especially after all that's happened—the roadblock, those two weirdos in the shack, the truck stop and Agnes and . . . I get these wicked jolts of nutso. I'm, like, seeing things in my head I really, really don't want."

"For instance . . . ?"

"Don't make me answer that, okay?"

I run my hand gently across the back of her dress, the bright blue taffeta damp with sweat. "You should get out of the cold night air. You'll ruin yourself."

She doesn't move. "I don't think I know who I am anymore."

You might imagine—the garish makeup, the antiquated dress—how those words land. I lean in closer. "I know who you are."

"Do you? How so?"

"I trust my judgment, if that's any comfort."

"It's not, actually." She turns to me, eyes like mineshafts. "Don't take this wrong, but every now and then, I'm not sure you even exist."

There's a jolt. "I do. I'm here."

"I'll be sitting there and your image will rise up in my mind and I'll wonder if I didn't make you up. And that scares me so much I—don't take this wrong, okay? But I tell myself you're the crazy one."

I lean back to get a better perspective on her face, the one I remember, the one beneath the muck. "You want to part ways?"

"God, no. I'm scared enough as is."

"Then—"

"I just don't know if I can live up to who you think I am. And then this awful loneliness sets in, like everything in the world is miles away."

Behind us, Pharaoh rises in his stall, as though wakened by some silent beckoning—shakes off the hay clinging to his coat, snorts with a twitch of his ears.

"Georgie, I've no set design for you or your life. Nor would I ever make you do something just because it suited some grand idea of mine. But we're in a spot. Your way out is far easier than mine. If you want to take it—"

"I go back, I die. Maybe not in a day or two or even a couple years. But what's waiting for me back there is an open grave."

"This Loonie Foonie lot, they seem to have taken a shine to you. Maybe you've found a home with these people."

"I'm not the churchy type."

"Their take on doctrine seems supple enough you might find some room to maneuver."

She takes my hand, caresses it, studies it. "And where would you be?"

"I'll be fine. A cagey fox is what I am, when the need arises."

"I wouldn't be fine. Not at all."

"Even though I might not exist—or if I am, I'm crazy?"

Her eyes turn misty. "What's the point of me?"

"I beg your pardon?"

"What's the point of me being alive? If I ever knew, I've forgotten."

I know that feeling. Hundreds of years of it.

Before I can think of something to say, however, she adds, "Am I just here to give you someone to protect?"

"You believe that?"

"I'm asking."

"You're here to flourish. Become the Georgie O'Halloran you're meant to be."

"What if she's a joke?"

"Georgie—"

"What if she's a monster?"

Pharaoh, standing at his gate now, shakes his mane, as though summoning us to some point we're both missing.

I gesture for Georgie to rise. "Up you go."

She just stares, so I reach out, take her hand, lift her to her feet.

"Pharaoh, I want you to meet my friend, Georgie. She's in a bit of a state tonight, troubled over her life. Could you lend her a bit of your strength?" I guide her hand to his neck. "It's all right, luv. Touch him. Feel him. He worries, too, believe me. None of us that answers to a heartbeat doesn't know fear. And yet look at him. Isn't he grand? Like a legend, he is."

I gather his halter from its peg, slip it onto his head, which he dips obligingly, tucking back his ears. Old soldier. Good soldier. I click on his lead and guide him from his stall, the scattered hay and wood chips softening the clomp of his shod hooves.

Georgie continues to stare, eyes like little moons.

"Hike your skirt up a bit."

"Excuse me?"

I take her by the waist, lift her off the ground. So light, like a trundle of bones and breath. It takes some adjusting with the voluminous skirt, but shortly she's sitting pertly astride the old boy's dappled grey back.

"Press with your knees. A bit of a walk about the barn, shall we?"

I lead Pharaoh toward the far end of the stable, Georgie clutching his coarse black mane.

A few of the other horses have risen from sleep and they poke their heads out of their stalls, watching the slow parade.

"Can you feel his power? It's not just his now. It's yours, too. Horse and rider. One."

She doesn't answer. It's all she can do to maintain her balance while strangling her fright. But we continue walking, slow, methodical. Only once or twice, and then but fleetingly, does my mind turn to another time, another horse and rider.

Sing for me, Irish.

Finally, Georgie leans down, strokes the horse's muscular neck. Tears stream down her face as she whispers, "Magic dog."

I help her down and guide Pharaoh back to his stall, unlatch his lead, remove the halter, place them back on their pegs. Once I'm done, Georgie lunges toward me, wraps her arms tight around my midriff and presses her face against my chest.

We stand there a while, saying nothing. Horse and rider. One.

"You're right," she says, disengaging at last. She swipes at her made-up face with her fingertips. "I should get back, I'm kinda chilly. Do I look all smeary and stupid?"

"You could stand to freshen up a bit, not much. Shall I walk you back?"

"I'll be all right. Thank you."

I watch as she heads toward the stable's double doors, glances once over her shoulder, then disappears into the moonlight.

A little past dawn, steps again. Not Georgie's—too heavy, wrong direction.

I rise from my modest bed, slip on my shoes. Pharaoh rises as well, gives himself a hearty shake, bits of hay flying off his coat.

Similar sounds arise from around the stable, horses rising from sleep, clomping their hooves, nickering in welcome. Our visitor is someone familiar—to the wildlife, anyway.

The bay doors at the far end of the stable creak open. Morning sunlight washes in.

I lean my head out for a peek—a mere silhouette at first, backlit, but then he clarifies: a workman, powerful fella, rumpled chore coat and overalls, duck boots, getting ready to let the horses out into the paddock for a morning romp while he mucks out the stalls.

I should have risen earlier. Will he recognize my face?

He attaches a lead to one of the horses, guides it out, murmuring to it, stroking its flank. It struts beside him happily. Once his back is squarely turned, I ease off the opposite direction.

I've all but reached the door when from behind: "Hey! Who the hell are you?"

Not wanting to give myself away with my accent, I say nothing, just continue walking—even as a stone the size of a walnut whistles past my head.

"Asked you a fucking question!"

I'm twenty yards outside the stable when he calls out again. "Tell those freaks and fairies you're with, when this is all over—you know what I'm sayin'—when decent people take this country back from the snobs and shit-heels, those creepy crazy friends of yours are gonna grow up fast. Mercy's gonna be in short supply. You tell 'em that."

He hawks and spits for the sake of punctuation.

The farmhouse greets me more cordially: utter stillness, just the lingering scent of sweat and perfume and candle wax, a whiff of apple from paper cups with dribbles of cider left behind.

I muddle my way back to the kitchen. Dutch sits by his lonesome in the breakfast nook, fiddling with his phone. Doomscrolling.

"I made coffee," he says quietly. He does not look rested.

Cups hang from hooks beside the sink, so I nick one, fill it, and slip in across from him.

"Judging from appearances, I gather your night was all toss-and-turn."

The stare he gives me, like he's the one in the crosshairs.

"I mean no offense, you just look weary."

"I guess you could say I'm something of an insomniac." He makes it sound like a confession. "How was it up in the barn?"

"Me and the ponies slept fine. Bit of a rude awakening, though. So to speak."

Another queer look. "How so?"

"Is anything wrong, Dutch?"

"You mean beyond... No, no, just... What happened? This morning."

"A workman, stable hand. Had a bit of a flea in his lug when he spotted me. Seems none too charitably disposed to your kids, neither."

He gazes off in the general direction of the paddock. "The owners of this place, the parents—they're away, obviously—well, I was led to believe there'd be no trouble."

"On the basis of only brief acquaintance, I'd call the man surly, not dangerous." Discounting a tossed rock. "He neither saw my face nor heard my voice, so there's that."

"Better get on the road as soon as possible." He tugs back his shirt cuff, checks his watch. "I'll give everybody another few minutes."

I sip my coffee. It's bitter and thin. "Gives us time to further our own acquaintance, then."

He nods like a man about to give blood. "That's . . . yes."

"Georgie mentioned, when she came out to the stables last night to visit, that the two of you had a bit of a chat."

"She told me about what happened. In Philadelphia. And, well, since."

"Quite a saga, yeah."

"She's really a remarkable young woman. Very open. Genuine."

"She's that and an ace-high straight. So—anything you'd like to ask me?"

"Ask?"

I respond with a smile. Wait.

He clears his throat. "Georgie mentioned you were in the service."

"I was, yes." Any number of times.

"Because . . . ?"

"I lacked for better options."

"But you re-enlisted."

"I did, twice. But I'm a wee bit superstitious. Figured three was the charm. Four's a famously unlucky number."

"Excuse me if this seems—"

"Nosy?"

"I don't mean to be rude." His wincing eyes, like he's just passed gas. "I'm just curious. You're not an American."

"You're catching on."

"Why fight in our wars?"

"Dutch, seriously—Irish been fighting America's wars from the very start."

Times like this, I almost wish I could tell him: who I am, how many times I've fought for this country—and once, in Mexico, defected to the other side, serving with John Riley's San Patricios.

"We've always believed in the *idea* of America, though admittedly we've had our qualms with how you yourselves live up to it. Wolfe Tone found the Americans money-grubbing phonies, not true democrats at all. O'Connell despised slavery and condemned America for letting it thrive. Both thought George Washington a pompous hypocrite." And there you have it—greed, bigotry, arrogance, the unholy trinity, America's original sin. "But especially since the famine, the great migration, Ireland and America, we're joined at the hip."

"But this war," he says, banging away at that same nail, "you did three tours—you must have believed in the mission. Why we're over there. Or—"

"I'm not a big-picture fella, Dutch. I only know what I know."

The eyes on him, I swear, they belong at a wake. "Such as . . . ?"

"All right." It's clear he's wanting a fuller account. "Once, after a truck bomb tears through an entire city block—people screaming, car horns blaring, smoke thick as fog all around—I come across this wee girl lying all alone, blue in the face. She can't breathe. I don't know why at first, but then I realize her whole mouth is clogged with dirt. I begin to scoop it out, trying to soothe her with my voice, saying, 'Hold on, darlin', stay with me, it'll be all right,' when this old man starts beating me across the back with a wooden staff. I shield the girl with my body, thinking he's aiming for her, then turn and shout over my shoulder, 'What the flaming hell?' He understands not a word, of course, just keeps on. I'm about to draw my sidearm when the company terp—our interpreter—stumbles onto the scene. The old man doesn't think I'm trying to help the girl at all. He thinks I'm trying to rip out her tongue."

"Good Lord—did she end up okay?"

"Never saw her again. What I'm meaning to say, no matter how many schools you build and wells you dig and roads you pave, to the people—the civilians, the ones you tell yourself you're there to help—you're just an occupier. Hearts and minds, it all sounds grand, but victory seldom belongs to the high-minded. War's a hate machine. I've watched it turn some quite fine people, men and women both, into something they themselves barely recognize."

"But not you."

What is he after? Maybe, like Bartosch, he suspects I'm not the man I claim to be at all. Of course, he's right. For all the wrong reasons.

An antique clock, shaped like a birdhouse and perched atop the kitchen doorway, gently chimes the hour.

"I'm no angel, Dutch, to be sure. But yeah, after what I saw and came to know, I decided there were better uses for me elsewhere."

—48—

THINKING it's time to steer the conversation in a new direction, I nod toward his phone. "Any news worth sharing?"

He's most likely been digging deeper, searching for anything under our names.

"Yes, actually." He thumb-swipes to a bookmarked page. "Turns out there was some sabotage to the freeway near the Colorado border."

Not at all what I was expecting. "Yeah?"

"The National Guard stepped in. Protecting the detour. There won't be any more roadblocks. Business community wants to keep traffic moving."

Sure. Bloodshed's one thing, losing money quite another. "Funny how messing with traffic always gets folks in a lather."

"It's not just that. Given how things are going, the European Union's issued sanctions against us, China's followed suit. Central banks around the world are calling in our debt. It's creating a run on our treasuries. Interest rates are skyrocketing, inflation too."

"Time for finer minds to step in. Assuming anyone will listen."

"There's talk of a nationwide truce, which is a positive sign. But the militias have made it clear—this is a ceasefire, not surrender."

From above, the shuffling of drowsy feet—someone has risen, they're dragging themselves to the jacks. The sound of a slammed door, then running water.

"So, Dutch, if you've no more questions of me, let me put one to you. How did you come to be the chaperone of this merry troop of rogues?"

His gaze drops into his cup. "Call it a sabbatical. While I figure out my next step."

"Your previous step being?"

"I was a librarian, small liberal arts college, New England."

"Sounds rather splendid, actually. But no?"

"A friend of mine was killed. Run down, at a protest."

From his tone of voice, I'm guessing more than a friend. "I'm sorry."

"The driver, he had a long history of, you know, mental issues, violent episodes, restraining orders. That came out later."

"How did—"

"Just plowed his car into the marchers."

"That's a coward's way."

"Put me in a tailspin. I ended up returning to the church, which is how I got this job, incidentally. I can only imagine what you think of that."

"I've no quarrel with belief, Dutch. Sure, I've known my share of holy hypocrites. Friar Daniel, Georgie's molester, leaps to mind. But I've known as well men and women of the cloth I'd happily nominate for sainthood. Some chaplains I've known in the service, for example. Nuns devoted to the misbegotten. It's fear of doubt, not faith, that turns the thing rancid."

"I mentioned a problem with insomnia. Before this job I suffered three straight months of it. Finally had to go to the hospital."

"There's grief for you."

"It wasn't just that. I couldn't stop thinking about what's happening. To the country. The violence, the hate. The insanity."

So you end up driving a bus for a passel of good Christian kids enthralled by a rock band called the Lunatic Funeral Mafia, kids who've decided to dance to the madness, like the doomed gentility of Venice with their masque balls as syphilis ravaged faces.

But what's life without paradox?

Not long thereafter, I'm outside helping Dutch load the Starliner's luggage compartment. As we arrange the various rucks and duffels, Georgie gathers a small group out on the front lawn for a morning session of the Krazy-Girl Kata:

> *Angel cradles hummingbird*
> *The moth devours the mountain*
> *Clutching the wheel of time*

I'm wondering if our snarky stable hand is secretly bearing witness from a distance. In the gathering darkness of my mood, I imagine him plotting some down-the-road misfortune, calling upon his own band of like minds.

Mercy's gonna be in short supply.

I glance toward the paddock. He's nowhere to be seen. And what does that foretell?

Soon enough, one and all, we trundle aboard the Starliner. Resuming my place up front with Dutch, I'm secretly dreading the landscape to come—the barren prairie of western Kansas, eastern Colorado.

I know a place. There are horses and buffalo. Good grass. Clear water.

—49—

MY mood darkens further once we return to the interstate. Sure, the highway's free and clear, state troopers stationed every mile or so across the flatland, the light bars atop their cruisers flashing like beacons of dread into the hazy distance, but just because the militias have mounted no roadblocks doesn't mean they and their supporters aren't out in force.

A tent city of sorts has arisen along the freeway, stretching for miles, and its denizens— hundreds, thousands, tens of thousands in scattered gatherings, old and young, women and men, displaced from midland cities—they line the road with banners and signs: *The Harder the Truth, The Greater the Faith . . . For God is a Consuming Fire . . . Because Fuck You, That's Why.*

The scene puts me in mind of the condemned bridge way back at the beginning of our journey, just beyond the Philly exurbs—the torchlight protest, the fist-pumping locals. That was a campfire jamboree compared to this.

One particularly voluble group shouts and chants and screams, red-faced, fists clenched. Others in the mix, perhaps grown hoarse from previous remonstrations, just stand in cross-armed silence, mean-mugging.

A khaki-clad press gang weaves its way through the bodies, clamping hands on shoulders. No secret what they're up to—dragooning men into militant scratch companies.

In the midst of all that, a lovely young woman—twentysomething, slim as a willow, lipstick the color of plums—stands at the very edge of the road, wearing a T-shirt blazoned with a swastika, offering a Seig Heil salute as we pass.

Farther along, a Christian contingent kneels in prayer, singing hymns, holding candles aloft while their free hands cover their hearts. Behind them, a primitive cross fashioned from rope-lashed lumber, high as a house chimney, crude as a gallows, rises above the drifting smoke from scattered campfires.

The rest of those gathered roadside just appear numb, standing at grim-faced attention as we ease past, traffic moving at barely half the speed limit.

It's not hard to sympathize. They've been betrayed—by their leaders, by history, by their own false hopes. Their misery's made bearable solely by the notion that a plan is at work.

Take Heart in Tribulation . . . The Game is Taking its Course . . .

Decency got them nowhere. Time to lock and load—what better consolation than the sacrament of revenge? I pity them the aftermath, when the blood settles, when they discover nothing's changed except having to live with the shame of what they did and why.

Our speed slows to a crawl for some reason, and the crowd, offered the chance, leaps from the roadside trench, approaches the Starliner, and begins hammering away at its flank.

Dutch calls out over his shoulder, "Everyone! Close the curtains on your windows, okay? And maybe sit toward the center aisle."

No point egging on the crowd with a macabre clown leering out through the tinted glass.

The thundering fist-falls continue, louder, angrier, the bus begins to rock from the force of impact.

Georgie works her way forward from the bunk area. "It's a little tense. I think we could all use a bit of a lift."

"A joke, you mean?"

"I'm not wild about your jokes. Maybe a song?"

Sing for me, Irish.

"Sure, give me a tick to come up with something."

I decide on a pair of upbeat dance hall tunes: "I Miss the Craic in Cricklewood" and "I'm Burlington Bertie, I Rise at Ten-Thirty."

Others shortly offer songs of their own, and it's something to behold, all these garish, painted faces, happily horrific, singing the likes of "Oh, What a Beautiful City" and "Where Have All the Flowers Gone." Hands clasp. Eyes soften. And by some odd bewitchery the pounding stops, though the furious, disconsolate chants continue.

In time, however, they too fade away in the distance.

Once we pass Salina, the crowds disappear. There's only the interminable prairie flatness.

Distant fires create a stench like singed burlap and an endless airborne haze. The late-day sun hangs in the sky like a lozenge of blood.

We hit the detour created by the bombed-out freeway and turn off onto an older, two-lane ribbon of asphalt stitching a path across the plain. Telephone poles totter off into the distance like abandoned crosses tethered together by lonely wire. The isolated towns resemble an afterthought, each with its line of whitewashed silos weeping rust, crying to be torn down, everything mounded with windblown topsoil, dry and fine as ash.

I try to conjure some sense of light, the *lux aeterna* pulsing within all things. The desolation prevails, however. My resistance falters, the present fading further and further away, and I suffer at last the rest of the nightmare I've been trying to fend off since entering Kansas.

THE WOMAN SACRIFICED
TO THE MORNING STAR

"Everything is always there, still unfolding, still happening."

—Sebastian Barry, *The Secret Scripture*

STARTING from Three Wolves' temporary camp along the Cimarron,
Na'ura and I set off on a sixty-mile trek north into the Ladder Creek
Valley, just south of the Smoky Hill River.

A freshwater stream, sparkling clear and cold as snow, carves a long,
jagged path among rocky bluffs tufted with buffalo grass and sage,
interlaced with yarrow, milkvetch, meadow rose.

No place for crops here, no need. Game abounds. Bison and elk,
whitetail deer and pronghorn antelope graze across the flatlands, scarred
here and there with rugged breaks and sloping valleys, while cacti and
yucca plants rise like sentinels from the llano.

Overhead, a dozen varieties of sparrow share the sky with orioles and
kingbirds, the humble meadowlark, the majestic eagle.

How many times, I wonder, while she traveled with Three Wolves
and his band, did Na'ura pass through this valley and dream of returning
someday, her life her own?

That night, we sleep beneath the night sky with its swarming stars,
while moonlight spills down across the cuts and ridges of the arroyo.

Come morning, she goes out to a spot of bare ground, cleans away
the stones and twigs, and makes a circle and a cross in the dirt. On the
cross she builds a fire, burns some tobacco, then cuts a place on her breast
and lets the blood drip into the flames.

After that, she lights her pipe, blows smoke toward the sun, and sits in motionless contemplation for nearly half an hour.

I've built a brush fire, made biscuits from flour and water and salt and tossed them into the skillet with some bacon, plunked a fistful of coffee into the kettle with water from the stream—supplies we brought by pack pony from Choteau Island, along with a Henry repeater and a pre-war Colt Dragoon six-shooter I finagled off Cuchillo, who hopes we bring him buffalo robes and horses for trade.

When Na'ura's done with her ritual, she rises to her feet, dusts herself off, and walks toward where I'm sitting. Squinting up at the sun, she takes note of its place in the sky. "Be careful," she says. "Do not let a human shadow fall across your food."

"Meaning your shadow?"

"It is very bad luck."

She declines my offer of bacon or biscuit, preferring instead to breakfast on pemmican, raw pigweed leaves, and a kind of wild turnip called dolios, also eaten raw.

Once we've finished, I kick out the fire and store our wares and prepare for a long day's journey to the stamping grounds.

"Watch the sky for ravens," she says. "They will tell us where to find the buffalo."

Over the next week, we hunt in the pocket between the Arkansas River and Pawnee Fork. Upon our return to camp, Na'ura cuts the meat into strips for drying, tans the hides, and stitches them together, flesh side out, then wraps them around a conical frame constructed of four tall red cedar poles to form a tipi, placing it on a sheltered rise above the creek bed, so the sound of downstream water never stops, like the flow of time itself.

She leads me inside that night and invites me to sit on one of two piles of buffalo robes. A dung fire burns at the center of the circle, surrounded by rocks from the stream, and its smoke rises lazily up and out through the portal at the top.

She's prepared a stew from the bison meat, mixed with wild onions and green pecans. For dessert she's made candy from mesquite beans and bone marrow.

She's unusually verbal as we eat, talking about her enslaved childhood, the arduous daily demands of survival with the Comanche, never in bitterness, but, as though it was a lesson, not her life, a story in search of a moral.

And, being me, with so much of my past beyond recounting, I offer a song in response:

> *But send round the bowl; while a relic of truth*
> *Is in man or in woman, this prayer shall be mine,*
> *That the sunshine of love may illumine our youth,*
> *And the moonlight of friendship console our decline.*

As she continues her work with the buffalo haul, I start ranging far and wide to every nearby stream and river, foraging for timber from the saplings that flank the water. Once I've felled one, I hack it into posts and rails, then load as much into the travois as the horse can bear.

In a week's time, I've fashioned a corral of just under a hundred square feet. Empty for now, but not for long, if all goes according to plan.

The Irish may not be the great horsemen the Comanche can rightfully claim to be—only the Mongols and Parthians measure up—but with the homestead set and the corral erected, the pair of us head off to the great grazing fields with a sack of Red River apples.

As before with the buffalo, our destination lies in the pocket between Pawnee Fork and the Arkansas, where spring streams bleed into the prairie, providing fresh water as well as new grass, both of which shimmer in the sunlight.

Not far from where we came upon the bison herd, we find a band of mustangs grazing on the gentle downslope of a creek-side knoll.

The work proceeds hard and slow, the ponies skittish and stubborn, but by day's end we have ourselves three, and that's enough to send us home. We camp midway back to Ladder Creek, beneath a solitary oak rising above the prairie like a gushing green wellhead.

As we sit by the fire over dinner, we discuss how we'll lead the horses into the corral using Na'ura's mare as a Judas horse. Then the weeks of training to follow. We'll take turns keeping watch for wolves who'll do their best to slip inside the perimeter at night. We'll move the band from pasture to pasture to allow new grass to grow, watching for wounds, broken hooves, festering horsefly bites.

Once trained, they'll be traded for supplies or hard cash, then the whole enterprise will start up again. Come fall, mesquite and grama grass will provide pasturage; if they're in short supply, we'll resort to cottonwood bark.

We both fall silent after a while, watching the fire's crackling flames. Overhead, the moon and stars peek through passing clouds. The horses seem at peace.

Then something miraculous happens. For the first time, Na'ura is the one to sing.

Her voice barely rises above a whisper, and so the words are hard to make out. The tune is a spiritual, a lamentation, something learned perhaps from her mother or the other slaves. That's what I'm imagining as the bullet pierces my neck, followed by the echo of the shot in the night.

The horses react first, neighing in terror, trying to free themselves. I try to stand but my legs won't work, they don't even seem to be there.

Na'ura jumps up only to get hit herself, a direct shot to the shoulder. She falls back away from the firelight. I'd call to her if I could, but my voice responds no better than my legs.

It takes a while for the men to appear—three of them, two deserters from the looks of their shabby blues, plus what I take to be a Pawnee scout.

Traditional enemies of the Cheyenne and Arapahoe, the Pawnee have thrown in their lot with the *taibo*—the list makers, the whites—and serve as outriders for the cavalry.

As they enter the radius of light from the fire, the three men mutter duties to each other—collect the horses, search for weapons, gather any food, tie up the woman if she's still alive—and from that I learn their names.

The deserters are Hecht and Overmarch. The Pawnee, Cosimo.

Overmarch appears to be the underling, doing the work of three men, a hulking, frog-eyed man with smallpox scars lurking beneath a scruffy red beard. He's tugged the dusty black brim of his kepi down low on his brow. The stub of an unlit cigar squats in the crook of his mouth. He speaks with a lisp veiled by a growl, and there's a tremor in his left hand—clearly not the sharpshooter.

That would be Cosimo, the Pawnee. He carries two Hawken single-shot hunting rifles on his back, their leather straps crisscrossing his chest. Spry on his feet like a bird, he's wearing a greasy buckskin shirt and striped dragoon pants several sizes too large, tucked into military-issue boots. When he comes closer, I can see—framed by his long black hair, spilling from beneath a camel-colored poor-boy hat—the glassy eyes, the sunken lips from rotted teeth.

The third man, Hecht, presents an even greater enigma. The face is almost scholarly, not just because of the rimless spectacles. It's his manner, the way his eyes drift from this to that, unhurried, untroubled. Philosophical. He's trimmed his beard, a fussy bit of tidiness out of place among the others, and a corporal's chevron adorns his ragged sleeve.

His hands belong to a different world as well—too slight and nimble for a horse soldier—but none of that's as queer as his voice, a basso profundo worthy of Mozart's Sarastro, despite his reedy, almost fragile build and the incessant cough. A lunger, cursed with consumption—he squats before me, tugs my head to the side to inspect the wound, his chest rumbling with pus.

He calls out, "Looks like Cosimo nicked his spine." He slaps my face, checking for any response. Punches me—there's no fending him off, my arms prove as useless as my legs and voice. I'm drenched in sweat and impossibly cold. "Paralyzed, I'd say."

Overmarch sidles over, my Henry repeater in one hand, the Colt Dragoon the other. "Supposed to blow his fucking head off," he says, the lisp furring his words as he scans the darkness for Cosimo, who's over among the horses, calming them.

"Yes, well." Hecht probes his mouth with his ring finger, loosens something from a tooth, spits. "Nobody's perfect, bucko."

Overmarch turns toward Na'ura. "What about her?"

Without looking, Hecht says, "That's the Injun's department."

He rises to his feet. Overmarch joins him. They stare down at me.

After a moment, Hecht says. "Thanks, ragger, for finding our horses."

So that's how they'll tell it. Should anyone bother to ask.

Hecht heads off into the darkness, returning a moment later with a leather saddlebag, from which he removes a razor, a cleaver, a bone saw, coughing all the while. He places the blade of the cleaver in the fire, then crouches beside me again.

"It's said the true test of one's humanity lies in the capacity not just to endure suffering—a beast can manage that—but transcend it. I'm not sure I subscribe to that view. But I do believe it warrants testing. Truth through experiment, that's my creed."

Cosimo and Overmarch plant themselves within the fire's circle of light, sitting down to bear witness. The Pawnee nudges Na'ura with his boot, kicks her for good measure, to make she hasn't bled out.

Meanwhile, using the razor, Hecht cuts through my pant leg just above the knee, exposing the skin, then removes his blue wool jacket, rolls up his sleeves, collects the bone saw.

"Then again, this could just be a waste of time. Worthless in terms of science, I mean. Given the state of your spine. Who knows, you may not feel a thing."

But I do—a lightning strike, white and scalding and total, the pain. I've watched field surgeons operate like this on men struck down in battle—and wonder if Hecht has as well, or performed the procedure himself—but there they had chloroform, ether, whiskey, a leather strap to bite. Here, now, despite centuries of self-mastery, I'm grateful to have lost the capacity to scream.

Time drags, seconds turn to hours, especially once the saw blade passes through muscle and digs into bone. For whatever reason, the mere effect of concentration perhaps, the man's cough subsides. To keep me from bleeding out, he lifts the cleaver, red hot from the fire, and cauterizes my arteries with the searing flat of the blade. I can smell my own flesh burning.

"Looks good," he says, studying the singed stump. "If I do say so myself. Really shoulda kept up with school."

As he works on the other leg, I begin to hallucinate, thinking I can hear the moon scraping across the night sky, feel the stars vibrating.

"Hurry," Cosimo snaps, a slight whistle due to missing teeth. "Sunup's soon."

"Stop worrying," Hecht tells him. "There's plenty of time."

Indeed, there seems to be nothing but time as the torture continues.

When at last Hecht rises from his work, specks of blood darken his shirt, his face, his glasses, his teeth—yes, he is smiling. He wipes his hands on a rag.

"Normally," he says, "that's just to make sure you don't go anywhere. But like I said, the truth matters, the truth about who we are. So tell me—what do you make of your transcendence? Worth it overall? I know you can't talk, a nod or a wink will do."

I'm trembling all over from shock. And the cold, or what feels like cold, grips me like death itself.

"Guess we'll just have to chalk this one up as inconclusive." He looks east to the horizon, glowing faintly with daybreak. "Good news? You're still breathing. Means you get to watch Cosimo work his magic."

❖

In the part of my mind not blinded with pain, I've been holding out hope they'd forget Na'ura, gather up the horses and all the rest and leave us both for dead. But cruelty is an appetite only gratified by escalation.

The two deserters arrange themselves near the fire. Overmarch lights his stub of a cigar. Hecht folds his hands, placing them over his mouth to muffle the hacking rasp of his cough.

Cosimo first builds a new fire of four logs arranged with ends touching to form a cross, pointing in the four directions. Next, he forces Na'ura onto her feet—when she almost collapses, Overmarch steps over to assist, propping her up—and strips her naked, cutting her buckskin away so he needn't remove her bonds. Her shoulder is caked with blood from the gunshot wound. Her black skin glistens with sweat. The whip scars crisscrossing her back all but glow.

Producing a small clay jar from a satchel, Cosimo smears a reddish paste over the right half of her body, murmuring incantations, his continuous singsong once again accented by the soughing toothless whistle, after which comes some kind of ritual purification with smoke from the fire before he and Overmarch drag her to the oak tree and lash her to the trunk.

Cosimo places his knife blade in the fire and lets it heat to glowing as he scours the night sky for the Morning Star, which in Pawnee lore means Mars, not Venus. Once he locates the small red planet, pointing with reverence, he intensifies his chant, bows in each direction, then retrieves his red-hot knife.

As he presses the blade into her armpits and groin, she begins her death chant in a shuddering whisper, which her torturer ignores. He then collects her bow, shoots an arrow into her heart, then cuts her chest open and smears his face with her blood.

Na'ura's death chant fades into silence, though her chest continues to tremble from ragged, shallow, unconscious breaths.

The men collect what they've claimed from our belongings, then douse the fire with fistfuls of dirt. As Cosimo and Overmarch mount their horses, Hecht takes a moment to come to my side.

One last look at his handiwork. One last time, that smile. The lenses of his spectacles flare in the midmorning sun.

"Whole goddamn territory's at a fever pitch, and you're out here playing bronc-buster with your half-breed whore. What in the name of God were you thinking?"

Over and over, those words hammer themselves into my mind, even as, come nightfall, the wolves descend, without malice or scheme, and finish the business off.

Na'ura, "someone found"—I meant to free her, save her. Instead, I end up ensuring a grotesque and hideous death.

What sort of fool—or monster—does such a thing?

IN THE SHADOW OF MOUNTAINS

But for my children, I would have them keep their distance
from the thickening center; corruption
Never has been compulsory, when the cities lie at the
monster's feet there are left the mountains.
And boys, be in nothing so moderate as in love of man, a
clever servant, insufferable master.
There is the trap that catches noblest spirits, that caught—
they say—God, when he walked on earth.

—Robinson Jeffers, "Shine, Perishing Republic"

—51—

"**Y**OU okay?"

Georgie's voice—she's kneeling before me on the ridged rubber flooring of the Starliner. The fog of memory melts away, the antique bus assumes shape and form—we're moving, the engine throbbing in some middling gear.

"I'm fine, sure. Brilliant." I pull myself up from a drowsy slouch, shrug meaningfully, wondering if we've left Kansas behind. And all that Kansas means. "Why wouldn't I be?"

She's staring straight into me. "You seemed, I dunno . . ."

Her face looms before me like a worried moon. She's all made up again—a whole new look, call it the Merry Concubine: ruby lips, eyes done up like peacock feathers, red dot cheeks.

I clear my throat. "Never felt better."

Dutch sits at the wheel, glancing down at me queasily, as though he's just watched me thrashing about in a seizure.

"You were muttering," Georgie says.

"Not even."

"Oh yeah. It sounded angry."

Beyond her, the nearest pair of Foonies pretend to be entranced by their handheld doojiggers despite clearly listening in.

"Like you were talking in your sleep. Except your eyes were open. And you were moving your head and shoulders a lot, kinda like this."

She imitates something that could readily be mistaken for a blind man trying to ward off an airborne chihuahua.

"Get out."

"I'm serious. It was spooky."

She takes my hand, laces our fingers together. "This is different."

"I'm not following."

She tilts her head, as though trying to be sure of something, a fresh perspective. "For once, you're the one who could use some looking after, not the other way around."

A short time later, we enter the Rocky Mountain rain shadow. The distinctively stark, massive, snowcapped peaks loom in the distance, while pristine clouds sail like schooners across a glassy blue sky. The Foonies draw back the curtains on their windows and stare.

The thing they're unlikely taking in properly—the parched grassland sprawling in every direction, a desert in all but name. Starvation Trail it got called by settlers who managed to cross it. If only those who want to resurrect the Wild West were even half-aware of what they're wishing for.

And with that I drift back into my reflections, sinking even deeper into the backlands of my mind, sensing a difficult truth just beyond reach.

In time, the pattern emerges. The woman in the Okinawa pottery shop, Na'ura—these aren't mere random flashes of remembrance, conjured by rain on the one hand, Kansas the other.

I've observed this often in certain vets, the ones especially shattered by what they've seen, what they've done. A kind of dark sacrament of memory. Returning over and over to the same tragic situation, the same brutal mistake, hoping to work out the destructive logic. Hoping to heal. Or it simply becomes irresistible, the need to lance the scab, watch the blood ooze up from below, feel it again—the horror, the danger. How else to know for certain you're still in fact alive?

Back at the horse barn last night, Georgie asked what she means to me, if she's nothing more than someone to save. I answered no. I meant it. But I'm seeing the lie in that now. She's wiser than she realized. I'm using her. To see if it all comes out different this time.

"You're doing it again."

I've utterly failed to notice her kneeling once more by my side, closer this time, studying my face like I've broken out in welts.

"What's going on? It's like you're daydreaming, except, I dunno, worse. Nightmaring?"

"It's nothing. I'm fine. Lost in thought, is all."

"Promise?"

"Swear on a stack of bible salesmen."

She plops down by my side. Stretching her legs out into the step-down well, then leaning in close, she speaks only as loud as necessary to register over the engine, wanting no one to overhear, not even Dutch.

"I've been thinking."

"Okay."

"About Reggie."

"Ah."

"It's no big surprise that he'd steal from me if it meant getting famous. If vanity were cancer, he'd be in his tenth round of chemo."

"Fame changes people, or reveals them for who they are."

"But then why step away from the spotlight?"

"Maybe he got sick of the charade. Or the fear of being found out got to a point—"

"No." A coltish headshake. "I think you were right before, what you said back in Philly."

"Remind me?"

"He's trying to get away. From his publishers, whoever else is making money off him. He's not strong enough to stand up to people like that."

"Not a point I'd argue."

"He's as much on the run as we are."

She goes on to describe what she intends to say once we finally meet up with him—an offer of forgiveness, laced with a demand.

Though a public statement of contrition is owing, she'll require no such thing. Rather, they'll team up, combine efforts from here on out, publishing their collaborations under the name of Rory Fitzgerald, fine, but choosing a whole new publisher, a fresh approach, returning to the brilliance of the first book . . .

I'm hearing her out, taking heart from the fire in her eyes, the strength of her voice. But what I'm seeing is a woman left for dead on the floor of her pottery shop. A woman tied to a tree, an arrow piercing her heart—waiting for the wolves.

"**S**LIGHT change of plans." Dutch is eyeing his handheld GPS. "Traffic's jammed up on I-70 this side of Denver. So heading back to the interstate from here makes no sense. Instead it's recommending we head due west to I-25, then turn north." He glances up from the device, stares out through the windshield at the dusty road. "I hope that's acceptable."

There's a hitch in his voice. When he turns toward me, his eyes retreat into a kind of fearful abstraction, as though he thinks I might not just object, but lash out in some way.

"Anything the matter, Dutch?"

"I just want to make sure the detour doesn't . . ." His voice trails off.

"Doesn't what?"

"You're okay with it, then."

"Shouldn't I be?"

"No, no, I'm just . . ." He swallows nervously. "Okay, please. Don't take this wrong. But the way you were acting a little while ago."

"My daydreaming, as it were."

"Pretty aggressive daydreams, to be honest. If that's what they were."

"And?"

"It worried me. A little. You know me, I'm a worrier. I just wondered. If something was, well, troubling you."

He's not the world's best liar.

"Nothing beyond the usual." I'm wondering now if maybe a bit of worrying on my part wouldn't be wise. "Sure there's nothing you want to tell me?"

He takes a moment to ponder that. "I don't know these roads." He glances sidelong at me, the distant fright now tinged with shame. "I don't know what to expect, I don't want to get us lost. But it seems, once we get beyond Wild Horse, if we take 94 due west, it's basically a straight shot to Colorado Springs."

"You're wondering if we'll be safe."

"It's the middle of nowhere. Just a lot of . . . emptiness."

"You're asking my opinion?"

"I guess." He closes up the GPS. "But it seems, even though it takes us out of our way, this route still saves us almost an hour."

"Seems you've made up your mind."

"It's all right, then?"

"You're sure there's nothing else you want to tell me?"

"No. Of course not. Nothing. Here comes the turn, excuse me."

He flips on his signal, slows for the left-hand turn onto another two-lane road, this one heading straight for the mountains.

I position myself just behind him in a half squat, half crouch, peering through the scummy windshield at the endless wasteland. Nothing anywhere stands higher than a fencepost. Airborne dust turns the horizon into a giant smudge.

A half hour goes by, nothing of consequence transpires, so I settle back into my usual place, looking backward at the parallel line of bunks, all the Foonies battling their boredom.

We pass through a place called Punkin Center, in reality nothing but an intersection marked by a pair of hardscrabble huts of rust-stained tin.

One of the young ones in the back calls out, "Hey, check it out. Two bikers just pulled out behind us."

Everyone crowds the back windows to look. Dutch stares straight ahead, barely bothering to glance in his side mirror.

In short order another pair of bikers appears, these two taking up position ahead of the Starliner. We have a formal escort now. To where?

Their leathers bear a distinctive patch: dark blue wolf's head in a white circle, the eyes a pair of blood-red slits. The words *American Nightwolves* appear on the upper rocker, with *Sangre de Cristo Nomads* along the bottom.

It's a Russian motorcycle gang, transported here, tied to the American Cossacks.

I lean down close so no one else can hear. "Something you're wanting to tell me, Dutch?"

He swallows hard, grips the wheel. "I told you I was worried."

Not worried enough. "Where are they taking us, Dutch?"

"I don't know that they're taking us anywhere, they've just shown up out of the blue. Maybe it's all just for show. They're taunting us."

I lean in even closer, so my lips all but kiss the middle of his ear. "I'm many things, Dutch. Blind, deaf, and dumb aren't among them. Now don't compound being a liar with being a coward. Tell me the truth. What are me and Georgie looking at here?"

He stares straight ahead, but his eyes glisten. Tears of guilt, of fright.

"They made contact last night."

"Who is 'they'?"

"I don't know. First, a text came in, when I was trying to sleep. It said the phone was going to ring shortly and I should pick up. So I did."

"And who was on the line?"

"A woman."

"Describe her voice."

"Husky, slight British accent."

Not Georgie's stepmum, unlikely a Philly cop—then who? "Go on."

"She said there were cameras at the truck stop outside Kansas City, they caught the two of you boarding the bus. She tracked down who it belonged to and got my cell number. She says she's concerned for Georgie's welfare. She may seem strong right now, but that won't last. She needs her medication. She needs care."

"Yeah, and these fellas on the motorbikes, they're nurses no doubt."

"Nothing was said about that. About them."

"Boy, there's a stunner. And then there's me, Dutch. This woman, the one with the accent—what might she have planned for me?"

"Listen, I really don't—"

"Dutch, Dutch, it's all right. It's fine. Just tell me."

"She mentioned the thing in Philadelphia. The murder."

"But Georgie explained that to you, yes? I had nothing to do—"

"Look, look, I really—"

"Okay, okay. It's all right. Let's move on to the real issue, yeah? This woman, I'm guessing she made a proposal of some sort."

He runs the back of his hand across his cheeks, damp from tears. "You know I can't let anything happen to these kids."

"Of course not. But if you'd been honest with me, told me this before we headed off this morning, I could have helped you devise a plan."

"She told me this is the plan. The only plan."

I rest my hand gently on his shoulder. I might as well have stuck a knife in it.

"Relax, Dutch. I mean you no harm—never have, never will." Your conscience will see to that. "But right now, I need you to help me find a way to keep Georgie on this bus. They can take me, I'm fine with that. But not her. Understand? We need to—"

"You're going to get us all killed." His voice darkens, half disbelief, half fury. "Make every kid on this bus pay for whatever it is you've done. You call me a coward—what's that make you?"

—53—

A NOTHER four bikers wait for us down the road. As we approach, they rev their engines, then join the motorcade—two on each flank.

One rides right outside Dutch's window: wraparound shades, a buzz cut, no helmet. Muscular, tan and taut—I pin him at maybe two hundred pounds. The thing about leathers, hard to fight in them, too stiff. But we won't be going at it, him and me. Nor any of the others. There's a holster fastened to his gas tank, the butt of a pistol pokes out.

He glances up at Dutch, at me, stares for a bit, then returns his gaze to the road.

Georgie joins us. "What's happening?"

"Tell everyone to just stay calm."

"What's . . . *happening?*"

"A woman got in touch with our friend here last night. English lady, he says, if her accent's any indication. Wants to have a wee chat. Do I have that right, Dutch?"

Some of the Foonies have edged forward now as well. Others peer out the windows along the sides, in back, a general state of high alert. Each of them, in one fashion or another, awaits a comforting word from their chaperone.

All he manages, however—and this in a barely audible whisper—is, "I'm sorry."

The bikers lead us off our westerly route onto a one-lane strip of unmarked asphalt heading south. A shallow ditch of parched dirt parallels the road to either side, flanked by lines of rusted barbed wire.

A few of the Foonies have chosen to pray—heads bowed, murmuring into their clasped hands. Others merely continue staring out the windows. Georgie, having wiped off her face paint, moves among them, murmuring apologies, offering goodbyes.

A house appears in the gritty distance—small, weather-beaten, single-story ranch-style. Not a shade tree in sight, just dust devils and scattered scrub oak.

Nor are any cars parked nearby. The place seems deserted—meaning what? Why bring us to such an isolated spot, except to do what best gets done with no one around?

At last the motorcade arrives at its newly scheduled stop. As the big bikes rumble and roar into the driveway and the riders dismount, Dutch opens the Starliner's door. He can't look at us, and I find myself pitying him, for just as one can never turn his back on a life's he's saved, only a psychopath can forget the people he betrays.

Forsaking goodbyes, we step down onto the cracked pavement.

The bus pulls away in a roar of soot-black exhaust and dust, the latter so saturated with silica from the over-worked earth it sparkles in the glaring sun.

Georgie turns, shading her eyes with one hand, waving with the other at the faces pressed to the windows.

"This way," Buzzcut says, turning toward the dust-blown house.

Inside, a sawed-off hallway gives way to what's meant to serve as a living room: oatmeal-colored carpet, walls a jaundiced beige. Sheets meant to preserve the furniture from harsh light and the relentless dust lie on the floor, only recently stripped away from the looks of the now-naked chairs—plump, upholstered, worn but clean.

Something else lingers, however, like a hint of wind among the dust motes—ghosts, hovering in the shadows, and ever so faint, that damp mutt scent. What do they expect to find here? What do they foresee taking place?

Two bikers remain out front, standing guard, two others block our path to the front door, the other four, including Buzzcut, wander back toward the rear of the house.

Muttered voices from that direction break the silence, and shortly a bedraggled figure stumbles into the living room, bruised, panting, wrists bound in front.

Robert Brown. Rory Fitzgerald. Reginald "Touchy" Feely.

54

So much looks strikingly different. The bramble of chestnut hair is now cut short, dyed ash blond, matching a furze-like beard. His eye color's different as well, no longer green but a muddy brown—contact lenses, no doubt. Gone are the Ivy League affectations—no tweed jacket, no starched shirt, no blue jeans ironed to a fatuous crease. Instead, a long-sleeved tee, drawstring pants, white trainers, no socks.

He could pass for a middling hipster, the kind always banging away at a laptop in some off-campus coffee shop. Only the bones, the vaguely vulpine shape, give his face away.

Looking up, seeing it's us, his mouth gapes open but no words emerge. His head darts back and forth—Georgie, me, Georgie again.

"Christ's codpiece, isn't this grand! Like old times." Sometimes I can't help myself.

In a quavering whisper, verging on tears, he says, "How did you . . . Where . . ."

I turn to Buzzcut. "Seems he's a bit distressed. Any problem untying him?"

Buzzcut looks at me like I'm mad. "You think I'm gonna hand you a knife?"

"I didn't say cut him loose, I said untie him." I wiggle my fingers. "Nothing to fear. It's just knotted clothesline, yeah?"

He gives that a think, then steps forward, removes his knife from its scabbard, cuts Reggie's bonds, and collects the rope. Apparently he doesn't want to leave me a possible garrote.

"Happy now?" He lopes away, heading toward the hallway that leads to the front door. "Just remember, I don't have orders to play nice."

"And who, if I might ask, would you turn to for such orders?"

He shoots me the one-finger salute and just keeps walking, out of sight, though not earshot—his shadow angles up the wall just beyond the doorway.

Reggie rubs his wrists. His breathing remains quick, shallow. His eyes turn to Georgie.

"You seem . . . different."

"Meaning?"

"You look, I don't know, well."

"No thanks to you."

"Look, I know, I know. There's a lot . . . to discuss."

"Boy golly." I shake my head, tsk tsk. "Where to begin?"

"Oh, right. Mister Glib. The Lucky Charmer."

"Don't call him that."

"What, you two an item now?" His lips curl into a lopsided grin.

She launches forward and slaps him—fierce hard, the sound a whip-crack.

"Little Miss Sad-in-the-Sack—remember calling me that? Surely you haven't forgotten that night. The night you threw me out."

I remember. Finding her beneath the great hickory on south campus, shivering from the cold, clawing her arm bloody.

"One-Woman Pity-Party. Come on, Reggie, you *remember*."

"I'm sorry." He cringes as though to duck the next blow.

"Couldn't have had anything to do with you. No, no, it was all my fault. Ms. Whiny Weepers. Gloria Gloom."

"I said I'm sorry!"

Buzzcut ducks in, snickers when he sees who's going at it—nothing to jump into—then draws back into the hallway again.

Reggie drops into the nearest armchair with a helpless thud. "I don't know where to begin."

"Why not start with how you made off with Georgie's book?"

He gazes out the window, as if there's something to see. "Okay, that was . . . a mistake."

"Bloody hell, a moral breakthrough." I clap my hands softly. "And so soon. Bravo!"

"I asked you not to be glib."

"Asked?"

"Just tell us what you did," Georgie says. "And why."

His face arranges itself into a sniffy petulance. "I didn't steal it. Technically. You gave it to me, remember? It was a gift."

"A gift of love."

"Yes, well, nothing lasts forever, sweetie, love least of all."

"Now who's being glib?"

"The point," he says, "is that you surrendered ownership."

"Not authorship."

"Well, possession is nine-tenths of the law, I'm sure you've heard that. And don't even think about taking these people to court. Their lawyers will eat you alive."

"Swell. So how did you hook up with these lovely people?"

"Writers' conference. An editor, a publicist, from a small publishing company with big money behind them, said they wanted something imaginative, something with heart, something they could break out."

"So you showed them the book. *My* book." Georgie's clutching her sides, as though to keep from exploding. "Go on."

"They liked it very much. Thrilled, actually."

"And you never thought to tell them—"

"I wasn't sure you could handle it."

"Jesus . . . "

"I shared the money, didn't I? Sent checks to—"

"My stepmom. Wow. Cool. So she'd keep me locked up, out of the picture."

"No, well ... No, that's—"

"Yeah, yeah. Whatever. Go on."

"I'll admit, all that attention, it turned my head. I should have been more . . . circumspect. I should have shopped it around."

"You think *that's* where you went wrong?"

"They were falling all over me—lunches in New York: Delmonico's, Scarpetta, the fucking Four Seasons. Like I was royalty."

"With my book as your—"

"The money was obscene. I had no idea they'd throw that much at a first-timer. I fell for it. Stupid, in retrospect, but everything's fucked in retrospect."

"Ah, we'll have to pass that one along to Wikiquote." Me again.

"Look, my point is they came on hard, told me the book was a bombshell, the market was huge—and no mainstream publisher would lavish the attention on me that they would. Anywhere else, I'd get a small advance, a pat on the head, and a lot of promises. The book would get published with little or no support and wither on the vine. They had bigger plans—whirlwind publicity, merchandising tie-ins, video games—"

"Yes," I break in. "Heard about the video game angle. Interesting, that."

He turns ashen.

Georgie glances back and forth between the two of us. "I don't understand."

"I've been meaning to tell you. Just discovered all this myself the other night, first at the army surplus store—kid at the register was playing an intriguing game called *The Truth Against the World* on a little handset. Then at the house in Lithopolis, there was a gaming tablet. The people who lived there, who ran off so heedlessly, they'd been playing as well— no, not playing. Monitoring. Taking note of who was lingering inside the game space, who was recruiting them. And for what. But why don't you take it from there, Reggie? Fill her in."

The look on him, like Cailleach the Hag is keening at the door. Georgie sits there blinking, waiting.

"I had no idea about that end of things," he says finally. "It held no interest for me. I had my nose to the grindstone, cranking out pages. Only connection I had with the game was getting story ideas from its designers. I'm not imaginative like our gifted friend here. For me it's a total chore."

Georgie, stunned: "You think it's *easy* for me?"

"When did it occur to your publisher," I ask, "that there was no way in hell you could ever reproduce the drawings in the original book?" Let alone the writing.

He glances up venomously. "You used to be a little faster on the uptake."

"Meaning?"

"What part about 'money' and 'lawyers' was unclear? They didn't care. Once the checks I sent got cashed, there was consent."

Georgie says, "I never cashed any checks."

"Your stepmother did. And she's got power-of-attorney, right? That's not implied consent, that's explicit, or so I was told."

A veil descends over Georgie's eyes. "Go on with your story."

"That's it, basically."

"I doubt that." I lean in a bit closer, lower my voice. "Or you'd be back east, working on the next book. Not here. A captive."

Before he can respond, Buzzcut makes another entrance. He looks each of us over, like he caught us plotting our breakout.

"Just catching up," I tell him. "Old times."

"Keep it up with that mouth. See where it gets you."

As a gesture of concession, I too select a worn plump chair and sit. He studies me a moment, then once again lumbers out.

55

REGGIE resumes his confession, his voice lower now.
"All that money, they knew I was in over my head, so they suggested a manager. Her name's Christina. Christina Harringale. She'd step in, take over the money end so I could focus on writing—and the contract demanded two books a year, which is harder than it sounds. That was the pitch, anyway. And as advertised, Christina . . . managed . . . me."

Color rises in his cheeks.

Georgie chuckles acidly. "She was your lover."

"Not at first."

"Like that matters."

"The *point* . . ." He pauses, blinking, as though unsure of what comes next.

"Go on," Georgie says, gentler now.

"She took over the accounting, the PR, the bookings, the travel—all of it."

"Wow. You finally got your wish. A kept man."

Reggie glances up scathingly. "Go ahead, mock."

Outside, a swirling harsh wind from the direction of the mountains scatters a barrage of dust and grit against the outer walls of the house.

Reggie props his elbows on his knees, makes a frame with his hands, rests his face there.

"One night in Albany, this man comes up while I'm signing books. Not much to look at—hunting jacket, plaid shirt, glasses. Some backwater bookworm, that's what I'm thinking. Out of nowhere, he starts getting into it with me, threatening me, says I'm preaching witchcraft, paganism—I'm not making this up. He gets loud, really ugly. Bookstore staff has no clue how to control him. Finally he just storms out, slams the door behind him. We're all thinking, fine, good riddance. But later, when I go to my car, there he is. He calls me the most stupid, disgusting things, then out of nowhere just takes a swing—*pow*, right across the jaw—and takes off."

The game is taking its course.

"When I tell all this to Christina, she says she was wondering how long it would take before something like that happened. The world's gone nuts, everybody's pissed about something."

Because fuck you, that's why.

"But not to worry, she says, she'll make sure I have security from there on out."

"Wow," I say. "A bodyguard. Now that's celebrity."

Outside, an approaching vehicle rumbles down the one-lane road. Everyone glances toward the front, waiting, like a family expecting the doctor to emerge from surgery with news. But the thing just bangs on, continuing past.

"His name's Mark Nicandro," Reggie continues. "Central casting—steely, silent, and smug. Worked for some heavy international mercenary outfit before teaming up with Christina, protecting her writers, the ones like me getting death threats."

"So it wasn't just this guy," Georgie says. "There were others."

"The online threats were just plain nuts. Anybody who thinks being famous is fun hasn't a fucking clue."

"'How dreary to be somebody,'" Georgie says. "'How public, like a frog.'"

"You're going to throw Emily fucking Dickinson at me now?"

"Count your blessings."

"What I didn't realize—not at first—was that Nicandro and Christina were an item long before I showed up."

She gets around, I'm thinking.

Georgie says, "Threesomes?"

"I'm not sure there's a word for what she's into. Or her. Polymorphous pansexual pervert from hell. Kinkiest person I've ever met. Any event, pretty soon it's one big happy orgy."

"Oh, you poor darling," Georgie says.

"Didn't realize till way too late the angry zealot at the bookstore was all a setup. I wasn't just managed. I was literally fucked."

Georgie's flummoxed. "But you were their moneymaker."

"Exactly. They were stealing, still don't know how much. But just as I was catching on to that there was another . . . incident. At one of my events."

I ask, "They stage this one as well?"

"That doesn't make sense, given what happened."

"Which was . . . ?"

"A woman in the audience stood up and asked how I could associate myself with the disgusting groups involved with the video games based on the books. Racist doesn't come close, she says, and the network's worldwide."

"So I've discovered," I say.

"Well I had no clue—I mean, I knew the games existed, I didn't know who they were targeted toward. Anyway, I try to get an explanation out of Christina and she blows me off, says the woman's obviously a crank, ignore her. Then I go online, check it out for myself. The games themselves are fine, I guess."

"Especially given the use of Georgie's drawings for inspiration. Free of charge."

"How many times do you want me to say I'm sorry?"

"I'll let you know once you've finished your story."

"So I confront Christina, tell her I want no part of any of that—cut all ties to these fascist gaming freaks, now. She laughs in my face. 'Who do you think's in charge here?'"

I'm almost sympathetic. "But you knew that was coming."

"That was the first night I tried to get away, but they were too smart for that. Nicandro was waiting. I thought he was going to rough me up, but he just dragged me back to the hotel and Christina sweet-talked me. Why rock the boat? Think of the money—and it's *a lot* of money. Do I really want to go back to teaching? So easy to be poor and virtuous in America. Then again, all I have to do is play ball and things can keep on going, same as always."

Georgie asks, "Did you?"

"For another couple months. Takes me that long to convince them I'm onboard while at the same time planning an escape that might actually work—the name change, new ID, new accounts. It's hard, that stuff's totally foreign to me, they're watching me like a hawk. But I'm too scared to fail. Then, one night, I manage to slip out, contact a limo service, pay the driver a thousand bucks to take me all the way to Boston. I catch a flight for the west coast."

"And end up in Napa," I say. "Or do I have that wrong?"

He settles back into his chair, glowering, spent. "That's where they found me."

"Who?"

"Nicandro, him and his goons. Grabbed me off the street, shoved me in a van, flew me here last night."

We fall into an uneasy silence. In time, though, we all three hear it—the down-sliding roar, like a trombone glissando. A single prop engine is passing overhead.

Reggie cringes, covers his ears. No stranger to the sound, it would seem.

56

I go to the window, look out, see the thing circling low over the flatland like a hawk coasting the thermals, dipping this way then that before easing down, using the one-lane road for a landing strip—a Cessna Stationair, gleaming white with turquoise trim, that classic, strutted, over-the-cockpit wing, almost as gloriously retro as Dutch's Starliner.

I turn back from the window. Reggie's face hardens into a mask of dread.

"Look." Georgie lowers her voice. "I'm going to make you an offer. In the event we make it out of here."

"Don't talk like that. Please. God."

"A way to make amends. I should make you come clean, publicly—"

"You don't understand—"

"Don't interrupt. I should do that, go public, but I won't. Instead, here's my proposal—we work together on a new set of books, using your pen name."

"That's impossible."

"I said don't interrupt."

"It can't be done, the contract's ironclad. They own the name Rory Fitzgerald and all proceeds connected to it. And I owe them six more books—I write anything, it's theirs."

"If Rory Fitzgerald writes anything."

"No. That's in the contract as well. No matter what name I use, they get the money. Period. End of story."

Outside, the Cessna's engine roars as it noses toward the house.

Georgie says, "How could you be so—"

"Why do you think I ran away instead of working something out? The publisher's in on it. They're all in on it—lawyers, accounting, the publicity flacks. Like a pack of cannibals. Not to mention the 'investors' I always heard mentioned in holy reverence but never met. It's a greed machine. I'm the piddliest part of the operation."

Georgie sits back in her chair. "I guess there's nothing left to say, then."

"Look—"

"You sent checks, good for you. To make sure I was 'taken care of.' I've got nothing coming except—well, there's the thing. I don't know. Getting murdered? But come on, one more time, let's hear it—you're sorry."

"Please, try to—"

"Sorry you were so pathetically gullible and desperate to be famous and *interesting*. I trusted you and you trusted them, and I guess we all get what we deserve."

The Cessna's engine winds down to a thrumming idle, then chugs to a stop.

Reggie hisses, "You want to talk about murder? I know what happened in Philadelphia. I know what he"—pointing my direction—"did to that priest."

"And you're crazy if you believe that. Crazy or stupid."

I say, "Interesting, though, your mention of that. Incidentally, he wasn't a priest. Seems no one gets that right. Regardless, I'd be fierce surprised if the people who actually pulled that off, the killing of Friar Daniel, aren't hooked up somehow with the same crew you're running from."

"What are you talking about?"

"I had no part in killing the man. Someone else did. And framed me for it. They've wanted to get me away from Georgie from the get-go. Isolate her. Use her for bait."

"Bait for what?"

"For you, is my guess. Turns out it wasn't necessary. They probably learned of your whereabouts from the same source I did, a sad little man at a bank." Or his wife. Maybe Djuna the Smitten. "Making it an open question as to what they want now from Georgie."

The look of sudden, abject terror. "So that's why . . . They're going to make sure . . ."

He sinks deeper into his chair, burying his face in his hands. I ease over, lean down. "Quick question, Reggie. This Christina woman—she worldn't by any chance happen to have an English accent, would she?"

Before he can answer I hear it myself, coming from outside, greeting the Nightwolves guarding the front, the consonants scrubbed, the vowels flattened from years in America, but the sniffy lilt and tick remain, like a rash beneath a layer of rouge.

In short order the front door opens, a woman's bootheels methodically hammer the bare floor of the entryway, shortly joined by the shuffling, desultory footfalls of several men.

57

BEHOLD, at last, the enemy.
Reggie rises uneasily from his chair, as though some macabre royalty has entered.

She presents a study in black: boots, gloves, long leather motor coat, even the silk blouse beneath. From there, however, the palette shifts—a red coral choker, earrings to match, eye shadow tinted somewhere between rust and blood. Her hair, side-parted, collects at her nape, its hue a coppery brown.

Christina Harringale, I presume. Humble business manager. Scheming mastermind. Polymorphous pansexual pervert.

Behind her, a man I can only surmise is her lover, chief of security, likely personal pilot—Mark Nicandro. He steps forward, then stands at parade rest, feet apart, hands clasped at the small of his back. The sneering air of a man who stole his lucky number. Small active eyes, widely set, so dark they're unreadable. Rugged jaw, scarred chin, face a blind dog might love, framed by raffish black hair. I pin him at fifteen stone and a whisker over six foot, all of it solid.

Three other men appear, dressed in identical dungarees and field jackets, the muscle—frontboys, roid rats, likely recruited from some pongy gym. I doubt they'll share their names, so I devise my own.

Big Fella—ginger hair framing a boiled-ham face, jacket zipper straining at his girth.

Sonny—barely out of his teens, if that. Scrawny, blond. Jangly as a pup new to his leash.

Spook—but for the freckling, white as death, with eyes like two piss holes in fresh snow.

Speaking of dwarves who didn't make the cut.

That's the extent of their distinctions. Beyond that, they maintain their drone-like solidarity with impeccable mindlessness. Sonny and Spook take up position at either doorway to the main room, blocking us in. Big Fella stands midway between them.

"Such a cozy little getaway," the woman says, that tamped down accent, a voice like smoke. She removes her gloves, tugging one finger at a time. "Shall we sit?"

Reggie remains standing at first, as though unable to move, the whole lower half of his face trembling. Nicandro comes forward, arranges the threadbare, overstuffed chairs so they all face the center, then nods for Reggie to sit. He dumbly obliges. The Harringale woman takes the final available chair, directly across from Georgie and me.

Nicandro remains standing, eyeing us like it's all he can do not to laugh.

"Aren't you going to introduce us to your friends, Rory? I've been dying to meet them."

Georgie reaches for my hand and grips it fiercely.

"No? All right, I understand. All a bit of a shock, I'm sure. Anyway, let me guess—you," nodding my direction, "must be the mysterious murdering janitor, Shane Something—do I have that right?"

"Murderer? Hardly. But you know that."

"And this little wisp of a thing must be the multitalented if somewhat fragile Georgina. How nice to make your acquaintance at last. Now—so much to discuss, hmm?"

Outside, a compound stuttered rumble erupts—the Nightwolves' motorcycles, kicking into action. They rev at full throttle momentarily, then the entire motorcade roars away.

"To begin," the woman says, "let me just say that I'm afraid there's been some terrible misunderstanding." Her manner, it's all jam now. "I know you weren't as happy as you'd hoped, Rory, but nothing's set in stone. Come to me, talk to me. We're friends, after all."

"I tried." Reggie's folded his arms tight across his midriff. "You know I tried."

"But you realize, don't you, that I have to keep your long-term interests in mind, yes? I'm not doing my job if I don't."

"I was a prisoner."

"You were a star—the centerpiece of the whole arrangement. Without you . . ." Her voice trails away seductively.

"I can't." Reggie shakes his head. "No more. Please."

"You're confused, my dear. That's fine. Confusions get cleared up. You'll see. We'll talk this all out and put your worries to rest and things will be better than ever. You need to get back to work. Deadlines, deadlines . . ."

Reggie lurches forward in his seat and vomits onto the dusty floor. Eyes closed, he's sobbing silently, clutching himself, a thin whitish spume trailing from his lower lip.

The Harringale woman reaches into a pocket, removes a cloth handkerchief, and waves it at Sonny, who's standing nearest Reggie. He rushes forward, collects it, passes it along. Reggie clutches it and nods. Only after a moment does he finally wipe his lips.

I decide it's time. Kick the dog.

"Given this little hiatus in the proceedings," I say, scanning the men, appraising body types, "why not identify which of you plonkers put the needle to Friar Daniel?" I gesture with a nod toward Spook. "Judging on body type and the psycho eyes, my money's on this one."

Spook bristles. Ms. Harringale remains unfazed.

"I'm not at all sure what you mean," she says. "You were caught on camera."

"Let's not be coy. Video was rigged. I was nowhere near."

Nicandro begins to move toward me. She stops him with a raised hand.

"Listen to me," she says. "I'm being perfectly honest. I haven't a clue what you're talking about."

"What about your man, there—Picanto—he got a tongue in that manky head?"

"There's no call for insults."

"You're dragging us here, to this house, middle of nowhere—there's the fucking insult. And let's not forget the three assassins at the truck stop on the Kansas-Missouri line—you remember them, yeah?"

The slightest nod from Nicandro—Spook makes his move.

I'm shooting up from my chair before he's wise, crash the heel of my hand into his nose, hear the cartilage mangle, watch the blood erupt, then take his wrist, bend back his arm, prepare to snap the elbow wrong-wise, but stop short. He's already on his knees, screaming.

I turn toward the others.

Nicandro's yet to budge, hands gripping the back of the woman's chair, eyes narrowing into mine. Sonny and Big Fella are gaping back and forth as though trying to decipher a code.

"Do hope that helps," I say, "clearing up confusions and all."

I let go of Spook, reach for Georgie's hand, lift her from her seat. "Come on. We've no part in this."

"Sit the fuck back down." It's Nicandro, finally. The voice is all chest, low and tight, like talking's a chore.

"Well blow me down. There is a tongue inside that head."

Big Fella makes a grab for me. I drop Georgie's hand in order to swat his away, then backhand him so hard the giant tub of blubber tumbles backwards.

"What the bloody fuck—were you not paying attention to what I just did to your chum?"

Georgie's trembling with fright.

I gesture for her to stay calm. I know what I'm doing. After a fashion. I'd venture none of these meatheads actually knows how to fight.

Over my shoulder, I tell the woman, "We're leaving."

She gives me a Borgian smile. "You can't be serious. On foot? Heading where?"

"I've walked longer distances. In worse places."

"What about your friend?"

"I'll carry her if need be."

"But you haven't heard my offer."

By now Nicandro's produced a small semi-auto pistol—Walther PPK, just like Knuckle Nose, Agnes's killer. No time to appreciate the symmetry. He's aiming not at me, but at Georgie.

"That settles that," I tell him. "No doubt whatsoever now. Just a common lowlife scanger."

"Let's all take a deep breath," the woman says. "And please, sit back down. There's so very much to discuss."

—58—

IT turns out the offer isn't that far afield from Georgie's notion, except instead of her and Reggie striking out on their own, they'll get teamed up in service to the ongoing franchise. Georgie will have sole command of the artwork and freedom to write as much as she likes—subject to editorial oversight, of course. And no need to return east—Rory, which is to say Reggie, has a lovely house in the woods outside Napa, and it would make a splendid writing retreat.

Georgie hears the woman out, then says, "I'd rather be dead."

"All things in good time," Nicandro remarks, the Walther still aimed at her skull.

The woman utters a dispirited sigh. "I can't help but wonder, my dear, if you aren't being misled."

"That's almost funny, given what's going on here."

"You don't you want to share your gift with the world?"

"With you, you mean. You and the others you're in with."

"You mean the kind of people who can actually help you, not just coddle your fantasies?"

"I mean liars and thieves and thugs and Johnny Jingo gamers and the money behind—"

"What in the world are you talking about?"

"Don't pretend you don't know. You stole from him." She points at Reggie, who sits there abjectly, working the hankie in his fingers like prayer beads.

The Black Queen laughs. "Did he tell you that? Honestly, that's rich. The truth is quite the opposite, my dear. He's the thief, not us."

She rises from her chair. Extending her hand toward Georgie, she lets it come to rest beneath her chin, then gently lifts, so their eyes meet. Her gaze conveys a sympathetic warmth utterly at odds with the femme fatale ensemble.

"You think I don't understand. We're not so different, really. I had a headful of sweet ambitions, cute little loft in the East Village, my whole beautiful life before me. But the world has a way of beating you up, stealing your dreams. You think you either have to give in or fight back but that's a false choice, because you have to do both. You've got to get inside the castle if you want to take on the king."

Reggie continues to sob quietly, and I can't help but believe he's no stranger to this presentation, or something much like it.

"You've not had it easy," the Harringale woman says. "Your luck's not the best. That won't change unless you let people like me help you. I can get you inside the castle."

"I'm fine where I am."

"That won't last, I promise you, not the way the world is going. Very soon, there will be only two types of people, the smart and the desperate. And you're smart, I know that—do you?"

Georgie just stares, chin still resting in the older woman's hand.

"As for how others respond to your work, that's beyond your control. No matter how noble your intentions, once the book leaves your hands it belongs to the world, not you."

"That's no excuse."

"People will see in it what they want to see. There will always be those who focus solely on the book's violence. But that's utterly faithful to the original stories, yes? And sure, the mopes, the losers, they'll take your portrayal as approval. Worse, permission. To do whatever. There's

303

no way to stop that, except to work harder, write more, but the key is to keep working. Let me help you do that."

Finally, she releases Georgie's chin, but neither of them breaks eye contact.

"Why should I believe you?"

"*The Truth Against the World* was a rare gem, one of those works that comes around so infrequently it actually changes the marketplace. And despite all his efforts, poor sad Rory hasn't managed to achieve that same level of excellence on his own, let alone surpass it. After a while, readers get antsy—worse, disenchanted—and they move on. You can bring back that special something, that magic, that's been missing. And if you do, I'll help make sure that the audience you want to reach, the one you can embrace and feel proud of, will be the ones who make your work catch fire, not the ones you find so disagreeable."

"Too late for that," I say. "Game's got a life of its own now. Crackpot conspiracies, bomb plots, kidnapping. Seen it with my own eyes—Tower of Rage. Fortress Legion. American Cossacks. Not to mention their friends—your friends—the Nightwolves."

The woman turns. The sympathetic warmth has fled. "You have a vivid imagination. Like your talented friend. I can see why you two get along so splendidly."

"We're inseparable," Georgie says.

"Why in the world would I want to separate you? Assuming you agree to join our little project, I even think we can fix his legal troubles. Maybe just hide him away for a while. No one remembers anything long these days. Not even murder."

"He didn't murder anyone, he told you."

"Regardless, given his little demonstration here the past few minutes, I can't help but think he'd make an excellent personal bodyguard for you."

"You seem to have a thing for bodyguards."

"Not sure what you mean by 'a thing.'" A vixenish grin. "But the world has turned ugly, people are mad, and there's so little one can predict. It pays to be careful. And rich."

304

Georgie points at Nicandro. "Tell that man to take his gun off me."

"Will your friend behave himself?"

Everyone looks at everyone else for a moment—all but Reggie, who remains staring at the rank pool of vomit between his feet.

"I'll do anything, to anyone, who tries to harm her," I say.

"I'd expect no less." She turns toward to Nicandro. "Mark, be honest now. How difficult do you think it will be to make our friend's legal problems go away?"

He takes a moment, conveying through his eyes he too is capable of anything to anyone, then drops his aim on Georgie.

Instead, he turns it on me.

Three quick shots, all to the chest.

There's no time to do anything except, for the slightest instant, take note of the chorus of sighs from the ghosts in the room, and glance one last time at Georgie. She's screaming.

THE WOMAN WITH THE GOLDEN HAIR

I must go away
With my terrors until I have taught them to sing.

—W.H. Auden, *The Age of Anxiety*

THE first thing you notice is the bodies, tens of thousands of them, tens of thousands more, shivering and naked along the low cliffs of Tech Duinn—young, old, craven, saintly—the day's dead, waiting.

From his dock at the base of the cliff, Donn Fírinne, master of the place, scans his eye across the multitude, not in appraisal, mere formality. He comprehends the logic of the matter no more than anyone else. But he understands his duty.

He lifts his great staff, and the low black clouds beyond the cliff erupt in rumbling thunder. Lightning cracks and flashes. The great wind from the center of time sweeps across the menacing sky.

Donn lifts his voice above the storm. "Each of you, ask yourself honestly—was I a body, or a soul?"

Some of the dead cry out their answer. Amazing how many believe that lying can still serve a purpose.

In an eyeblink, the vast majority of the assembled crumble to windblown dust, swept away into the vast nothingness.

Another group, nowhere near as large, see their bodies vanish as well, but a spectral essence remains. These spirits get swept back into the world as wandering ghosts.

The handful that remain, trembling all the worse—why am I spared, why not him, what now?—get summoned down the curving path cut from the jagged stone that leads to the black water's edge.

There, Donn shuttles them onto his longboat. Once all are aboard, he will ferry them over the waters of oblivion to an island off the coast of the Land of the Ever-Living Ones, where they'll set foot for a heartbeat, no more.

After just that instant on the ethereal ground of eternity, their transmigrations will begin anew, memories erased except in the most cryptic, inscrutable regions of their being.

And a handful of expectant mothers across the mortal world will feel a stirring in their wombs, a momentary shift in the life they carry.

Not even the gods can explain why this is—not that they'd bother—and don't expect me to try. The closest I've come to identifying what separates those who are spared from those who are not and those condemned to wander as ghosts, given my personal knowledge of some in each camp over the generations, is a vague recognition that those who move on possess that curious, ineffable quality known as imagination.

The spared are not uniformly virtuous—far from it, I've seen misers and cutthroats aboard Donn's boat—nor are they uniquely wise, kind, or brave. Morality seems to play no part whatsoever in the scheme, as though whatever higher wisdom devised it saw merit not just in decency, genius, and self-sacrifice but in cruelty as well, savagery, mendacity.

The key is creativity, not rectitude, combined with unflinching self-awareness. Those utterly lacking in this regard vanish for all time. Those who, when alive, recognize the need for such originality and honesty but shrink from the task, choosing instead comfort, compromise, acquiescence, return to the world as hungry ghosts.

Or, at least, that's the best I can figure. From what I can tell, whatever the power beyond the gods might be, it puts no stake in human life, or any life. It delights in perpetual novelty. It wants to be surprised.

I watch Donn's ferry vanish across the water. I am not meant for that journey. I wait for Embarr, Niamh's white stallion, for my transport.

Shortly he materializes through the haze, hooves grazing the water like flints striking flame. I would like to say my heart lifts at the sight, but I fear for Georgie, fear for what will become of her, what treachery awaits her back in the world. The world now beyond my reckoning or reach.

They will enslave her, torture her. They will bury her alive in a tomb of greed and steal her mind.

I can do nothing. Will do nothing. Just as I failed the poor woman in her Okinawa pottery shop. And Na'ura. And how many others?

I climb on Embarr's back and we return the way he came, into the whirling mist and across waves that turn to fire and past great cities that rise up and vanish like vagrant thoughts.

Finally, I find myself upon a rolling heath at the foot of the modest stone tower, surrounded by clover and roses, where my love awaits.

She sits atop the vast, rumpled bed like a woman tossed overboard on a restless sea, her white robe embroidered in scarlet and gold, making me think of blood in a chalice.

Soft light ripens the curtains at the window behind her, which stir in a fragrant breeze.

She's eating berries from a bowl. Black juice darkens her fingertips, her mouth, a trickling smear zags down her chin, which like the rest of her body is otherwise white as marble.

Her mussed hair spills down her shoulders, conjuring thoughts of stolen gold, and her gaze, the perfect blue of an empty sky, greets me with a knife-strike of unearned joy, a happiness haunted by countless shipwrecks and slaughters and mortal friends left alone to their terrors— my legacy of folly, my museum of skulls. Poor screaming Georgie.

How many thousands of times have I come to her like this?

She puts down the bowl and pats a spot beside her on the rollicking bed. "Come. Confide yourself to your bride."

I lay my head in her lap and she gently strokes my hair, humming a tune in a minor key.

"There's a secret I cannot tell you," she says. "Not yet."

"Why not?"

"You're not ready."

"Says who?"

She lifts my head, slides away across the covers, and gestures for me to follow her. "The bath—let us."

The water is scalding and scented with petals—dogrose, foxglove, *deora dé*. I lean my head back against the pitted stone of the giant tub and she rediscovers every curve of my body with her soapy hands, then joins me naked in the water, curling herself into me. Her long wet hair drifts across the surface like amber smoke.

"I too felt fond of this one," she murmurs.

"Georgie, you're meaning."

"So full of spirit, so wounded, so keen."

"If only I could tell her that."

"Would it make a difference?"

The answer is no, a thousand times.

When at last we lie together, the air trembles with her breath. How mysterious, her affection, how unthinkable the love of a goddess. She searches me out with her touch. I'm a pilgrim in a torchlit cathedral lost in a requiem. I'm a sinking frigate, drifting downward in the cold dark sea.

After, as we linger side by side, she traces her fingers across my chest in mindless spirals.

"You're sad. About the tiny, fragile one."

"She was not so fragile at the end."

"Because of you."

"Not at all. The thing I admired about Georgie, she had no use whatsoever for phonies. Could smell them out at first encounter. Well, except for one."

311

"No one sees their lovers clearly."

"There a message for me in that?"

"Yes, but it can wait."

Outside, finches converse in animated birdsong. The light in the window turns honey-colored.

"Regardless, nothing I can do for her now. By the time I return to the world she'll be dead. Or worse. In any event, she's on her own now. I failed her."

A light flickers at the back of Niamh's eyes like a match strike. "How do you know you failed?"

"I'm here. She's there. And in the hands of villains, no less."

"But you don't know what will happen. Maybe you underestimate her. Besides, fate doesn't play favorites. That's as true of villains as anyone."

I lie back and let all that trickle down to bedrock. She's right, of course. How arrogant to think Georgie's helpless, desperate, lost without me.

"I'm not as blameless in her fate as you make out."

"No?"

"I convinced myself I was trying to help her out of concern. But then, as things got chancy, I began remembering things. Episodes in previous lifetimes. Events I'd long put aside. Specifically, these two other women who came before her. Who prefigured her, in a sense. And I didn't see it. Until too late."

She's pouring her gaze into me now, like she can feel the regret eating away at me. "You're much too hard on yourself. Here, sit up." She rises in the bed, reaches for my hand. "Look at me. Let me be your mirror. What do you see?"

I oblige the request—as though I could refuse her—confronting for a moment my reflection in the night-dark pupils with their dazzling blue haloes, searching out what she believes I'm missing about myself. All I see, however, is me.

"You mentioned something about a secret."

"I did, yes." She smiles at me lovingly. Love I don't deserve.

Before she can divulge her curious little mystery, the brackish mist appears—so soon, why? It envelops my body, gathering me up in its filmy embrace, readying me for my return to the world.

The world of thirst and doubt. The world that lies beyond the mirror that is a door.

THE WOMAN WHO STEPPED INTO THE CLOUDS

The graves are walking.

—William Butler Yeats, "The Countess Cathleen"

—60—

THE heels of my hands rise up, dig into my eye sockets. I blink away the interstitial haze, like fine dust, and find myself in twilight, standing in a bed of pine needles and acorn chaff.

Overhead, oaks and cypresses join their branches like sisters locking arms, creating a profound depth of shade. A brusque wind rustles about in the dense green foliage as though in search of something—then, just as suddenly, moves on. A restless silence remains in its wake.

The understory is interspersed with madrone, manroot, wood fern, ivy. In the near distance, towering redwoods and eucalyptus give way to hillsides blackened from wildfires.

From these particulars I surmise I'm somewhere west, California perhaps. Napa?

He has a lovely house in the woods . . . It would make a splendid writing retreat . . .

Fifty yards or so away, a manmade canal and a long strip of asphalt provide a firebreak of sorts. On closer inspection, the asphalt, probably an access road for firefighting vehicles, reveals its other purpose.

A runway. And at its end, moored by guidelines to the tarmac: the Cessna Stationair.

They're somewhere near—the Harringale woman, Nicandro, maybe his gym rats as well. Perhaps Reggie, too.

Georgie.

Scanning the area in the dimming light, I can make out, about a quarter mile through the woods, the broad peaked outline of an impressive house. After a slow march through the underbrush, I'm at the edge of a clearing of scythed grass that serves as a backyard.

Lamplight glows in the window curtains. Smoke rises from the chimney. No one's posted guard at the back. Someone's assumed there's no one to fear.

How many days or weeks or months have passed? From the scent of the air, the feel of the earth beneath my feet, the alignment of the stars just beginning to take their places in the twilight, I'm guessing it's still early-to-mid spring. Usually, the elasticity of time between worlds works against returning in the immediate aftermath of the last incarnation, but that doesn't appear to be what's happened this time—what seemed like at most a day in the Otherworld mirrored a similar passage of time here.

Is this why my sojourn with Niamh was so brief, so I could promptly return? Is this part of Niamh's secret?

A great blue heron appears, backlit by the moon as it glides slow and graceful over the faintly swaying trees. The birds make their nests high in the upper branches, to protect their young from predators—raccoons and rats. And evil men.

At the far end of the clearing, a rickety shed stands open at the back of the house. Just inside the door I find what I'm looking for, tools hanging from a pegboard. Specifically, a hatchet. Not as sharp as I might like, but it will serve.

Around front, the large split-level house offers a modest stone façade with a picture window, curtains drawn. A patch of garden—rosemary, lavender, aloe vera—has been abandoned to weeds.

The rutted gravel lane that serves as a driveway curves away into the trees, probably toward some county thoroughfare. No sound of traffic in the distance, though. The road's most likely a good ways off.

No cars parked out front. Odd. They can't have only the plane for transport. There must be a vehicle of some kind, Reggie's if nothing else. Maybe someone's been sent on an errand.

Meaning, sooner or later, they'll come back.

I take up position behind a spiny juniper near the steps leading up to the elevated front porch, crouching down to remain unseen, testing the weight and balance of the hatchet.

Time passes. The darkness thickens. The moon drifts in and out of low, scudding clouds. From within the house, beyond the drawn curtains and the closed front door, the occasional sound of thudding footsteps, dull voices.

Finally, headlights flicker through the trees, then pass into the clearing. Tires crunch the gravel as the car eases forward. The engine clatters to a stop.

The interior light pops on as the driver-side door swings open. It's Sonny, the jangly pup. He's carrying two shopping bags, one in each hand, as he kicks the door closed behind him and ambles straight toward me.

He's about to step onto the first porch step when I rise, swing, and cleave his head open down to the neck.

The bags, filled with takeout cartons, drop. He crumbles into a pile of nothing as I yank the hatchet free. I'm spattered with gore, but make no move to wipe it away.

Let it be my warpaint.

Finding a hunting knife in a scabbard on his belt, I test the blade with my thumb—it's sharp—and decide to take it. In his pocket a pair of key fobs—one for the car, one for the house. Climbing the porch steps to the waiting front door, I've the bloody hatchet in one hand, bright shiny knife the other.

No need for the key, the door's unlocked. *There's no one to fear . . .*

Once inside, I slip off my boots, tuck the knife into my belt on the left, hatchet on my right. Shake the tension from my hands, nudge the door closed gently with my hip.

A male voice, not Nicandro's, calls from the living room: "'Bout fucking time, Sparknuts."

The entry's floor of Italian stone gives way to a parquet hallway lined with walnut paneling. I try to discern if there are ghosts about, sniffing for that distinctive scent.

Yes, it's there.

I'm almost to the pair of sliding wood doors that give way to the living room when one glides open, a head appears—Spook, the one whose arm I nearly snapped in half back at the house in eastern Colorado. It's now tucked into a makeshift sling. His nose is bruised and bent.

No time for the hatchet. I grab his head, twist hard and up, snap his neck. A slight wincing moan, nothing more, as he tumbles into my arms. Quietly, I set him down on the floor.

The fat one, Big Fella, sits at a game station, back to the door, stripped down to his T-shirt and pants and socks, absorbed in play, headphones canceling ambient sound.

I decide on the knife—slit the throat, sever the vocal cords, forestall his calling out. And I'm right behind him, ready to strike, when the queer intuition of the soon-to-die kicks in.

He glances up and over his shoulder. Our eyes meet, his bulge in fright—I'm the last person he's expecting to see—but before he can move I'm mid-attack, the blade ripping skin and carving deep, tracking the jawline. Blood streams down his lumpy tee in pulsing gouts as he clutches at the wound, fish-mouthed.

"Fair fucks to the lot of ya."

For just a moment, the game station screen distracts me: a scene of ancient war, with interlocking scrolls and tendrils and intricate Celtic knots along the border. Azurite blues, malachite greens, buckthorn yellows.

The Truth Against the World
The Game is Taking its Course

The long front hallway gives way to a kitchen of epicurean splendor—granite surfaces, red oak cabinetry, the gleaming cookware all copper, hanging from an antique iron rack above a central island.

Another hallway leads back from there. A voice drifts forward from a rearward room—Christina Harringale, that distinctive flattened accent—the tone soft, seductive, a kittenish purr.

Hatchet in one hand, knife the other, I silently make my way back.

Stopping at the doorway's edge, I peer in to get my bearings as to who's where.

It's the three of them—Reggie, Nicandro, the Harringale woman. She and Reggie lie side by side in the bed—she's stroking his face, kissing him, cooing to him, winning him back to the old arrangement. The three of them inseparable, lovers—and rich.

Nicandro sits in a chair pulled up close to the bed, leaning forward, fully clothed. The astute voyeur. Given his expression, he might just as well be an intern observing a biopsy.

Where's Georgie?

I wait a moment for her to appear, make a sound, anything, but I can't risk exposing myself in the doorway. One deep calming breath. Clearing the mind of pointless noise. Priming myself—element of surprise, certainty of purpose, swiftness in execution.

I've the hatchet raised and ready to fly as I enter the doorway, flinging it hard at Nicandro. It catches him square to the skull, knocks him off his pervert perch—he drops like a giant sack of misery, one hand clutching his face. The other flails in the air as he thrashes about on the floor.

The Harringale woman scrambles off the bed and staggers backward, staring in shock—no, it can't be, not possible.

Oh, but it is.

"Like a bad penny," I say.

Eyes alive with fright, she tries to flee. I switch hands with the knife, catch her with my left arm, lift her off the floor. To her credit, she doesn't just shrink in horror—she's kicking like a banshee, clawing at my face, biting my neck—but that's not why I drop her.

Nicandro has found his gun. He's waving it about blindly, still fuzzy in the head, but the danger's no less for that.

The woman can wait. She's scrambling to her feet and making way to the door when Bully Boy lets go with a lucky shot. It grazes my arm, but I'm moving too quick for him to get off a second.

In a flash I've torn the pistol from his fist, pinned his shoulders to the floor with my knees.

On the bed, Reggie sits up in paralyzed terror, as though remaining still might render him invisible.

I'm ready to drive the knife into Nicandro's eye when he makes his move. It comes out of nowhere, the blow a lightning strike—a kick of all things, up from behind, one shoe clanging the side of my head, hooking my shoulder. It drags me sideways, knocks the knife from my hand. Then he arches his back to buck me off, the whole of his force in it.

The scarred chin should've tipped me off. The man's solid, to be sure, but more to the point, he's a brawler.

We're at it on the floor, flailing around on the hardwood, me on top for now, him reaching up one-handed for my eye.

I get inside his arm, reassert my knee on his shoulder, the whole of my weight bearing down, my forearm as fulcrum, pressing down hard on his carotid artery.

Count of five, seven, ten.

He's a strong one, amped up on venom, slamming his fist into my ribs, but the chokehold finally does its work. His eyelids flutter, the eyes roll back. He goes limp by degrees beneath me.

My mind blazes white in the struggle's afterglow. A breath, a second, a third—the effect dissipates. Once again, I can see and think. I reach for the gun to finish him off.

"Shane?"

It's Georgie. She's in the doorway, tight in the grasp of the Harringale woman, who's clutching her own pistol now. It's aimed at Georgie's head—her eyes are swimming, her body seems lax. She's drugged.

"Whoever you are," the woman hisses, "whatever. Drop the gun."

"You're thinking a ghost, a zombie, the living dead, yeah? Maybe an avenging angel. An identical twin!"

"Drop the gun! I'll kill her, I swear."

"Christ's cunt, if killing's what you're after."

I fire one shot into Nicandro's skull. There. Done.

The woman tightens her stranglehold on Georgie, but her words are directed to Reggie. "Darling, listen to me—there's a gun in the bed stand drawer behind you. I need you to get it and point it at our intruder."

Reggie remains frozen in place, naked on the bed, glancing feverishly back and forth—me, the Harringale woman.

"Do as I say, darling. Now! We're in danger. Do it!"

Reggie snaps to life, turns toward the bed stand, opens the drawer.

I tell him, "Leave it. Just get up and stand near the wall. I won't harm you."

"He's going to kill you, darling. He's here to kill us all. Get the gun!"

"Who is he, what—"

"They tried using a gun on me before, Reggie. You were there. Look where it got them."

He's got the thing out now, raising it two-handed, pointing it at me—or trying, the barrel's waving all over the place.

"Shoot him, darling. Now!"

The gun goes off—the shot sails wide, not by much, and the next might not at all.

He's left me no choice. I turn my pistol on him, fire twice—the heart, the brain, so he's dead before he's even aware.

Even Georgie, high to the point of stupor, gasps at that. Then it registers in her eyes, the full reality, the fact it's me there—undead, back from the dead, never dead to begin with.

"Mother of fuck . . ."

I turn the gun toward the doorway, aim it straight at the two of them, their heads pressed close together.

"Georgie luv, remember that time at the truck stop, the man with the broken nose, inside Agnes's Doombuggy. Same type of scenario here. Same protocol, as it were."

"Shut the fuck up!" The woman's gun hand trembles.

"Christina—may I call you that? Ms. Harringale, then. A great blue heron flew overhead as I was walking toward the house a short while back. Upon my, you know, return. From the place beyond. Any idea what that means? The heron, I mean."

"I swear, I'll shoot, I'll shoot this little bitch dead you don't—"

"The heron's a symbol—represents determination."

"Shut up! Shut up, put the gun—"

"But also stillness, tranquility. I'm all of that, yeah? Even in the killing. Especially then. Georgie—be still, my love. Be calm. Trust me."

Whatever trust she might be mustering quickly surrenders to oblivion— she faints dead away, dropping like a deadweight, slipping out of the other woman's arms. Exposing her.

I fire just once—all that's needed. The bullet lands neatly between the conniving woman's eyes. She's not yet hit the floor before I'm rushing toward Georgie.

Pull her to the center of the room, clutch her shoulders, shake gently. "Georgie. It's all right. Wake up now. We need to go."

Her eyelids flutter. She flinches violently, lurching to one side as though trying to get away from something. Only then do her eyes shudder open.

She stares through the haze of her drugged state at my face, regarding it with a kind of mesmerized shock. Her eyes blink slowly once, twice.

I gently take her hand. "I can explain."

—61—

SHE faints away again almost instantly, so I carry her to the kitchen, set her down on the floor. This way, if she wakes up, she won't immediately encounter a dead body. Or me.

I start collecting what I think we'll need—weapons, ammunition, wallets, cell phones, laptops, powering off everything electronic to undermine tracking.

The wallets offer up some cash, not much, enough for a few frugal days. The credit cards bear the name of a corporate account, Creative Solutions—interesting, but academic. They'll provide a roadmap to our whereabouts if used.

I spot some mail on the kitchen counter, thumb through it, pocket a phone bill for the sake of the address. May come in handy, should I need to find my way back.

Searching through drawers—a small tool kit contains a screwdriver and pliers and a spanner, all potentially useful. I tuck it under my arm.

In the bathroom there's rubbing alcohol and antiseptic cream. Off with my shirt and its torn, bloody sleeve. I clean the wound on my arm—little more than a nick—bandage it up with gauze and tape. Bruises along my ribcage are beginning to effloresce, but I long ago recognized pain as more mental than physical.

The closet in the adjoining bedroom offers a small collection of men's shirts, presumably Nicandro's, given the size. I shoulder one on, button it up.

Back in the bathroom, a quick further search of the medicine cabinet reveals what they were using to drug Georgie: ketamine. Christ on crack, why? Probably thought it would help with her depression, it's been used for that, or maybe they just wanted her turned to putty.

I grab the remaining vials and a handful of needles and syringes, in the event she needs a little reboot to get through withdrawal.

I find a pair of duffels in a storage room, load one with the laptops and cellphones, the other with the weapons and ammo, throw in some clothes I think might fit Georgie or me, some blankets in case we need to sleep in the car.

One thing remains that I refuse to leave without, assuming it's here— the original book, Georgie's gift, *The Truth Against the World.* Checking every room, every drawer, every shelf—it's nowhere to be found.

However, a stand-alone floor safe stands deep inside the main bedroom closet. It's not bolted down—and it's surprisingly light. If not here, then where? A quick search for a combination written down anywhere proves fruitless, so I just carry it unopened out to the car.

Once it and the duffels are squared away in the boot, it's time to collect Georgie.

She's still flat out, curled up on the kitchen floor like a house cat. Groggy and moaning as I collect her in a fireman's carry, but no struggle as we continue to the car. I settle her down in the back seat, tuck her up in a blanket, her eyes still stubbornly shut.

Just as I'm about to engage the ignition, it occurs to me that all the car's computerized tracking software likely remains intact, and it will stay that way until I can find the right people to stealth-strip the vehicle.

Nothing to be done, not right now. I resign myself to the vulnerability.

Then another tech-related complication suggests itself. What if the phones and laptops I've nicked aren't just password protected, but require a retinal scan for access?

You're over-thinking things, I tell myself. Let it go. Get the hell away.

But then I consider the treasures those devices might contain—names of key figures in the chain of command, co-conspirators, secret investors, offshore account numbers, money transfers, recruiting memos, communiqués about plotting acts of violence, of terror—for I've no doubt Christina Harringale's "management" duties extended far beyond keeping Reggie in line.

Back inside the house, I collect from the kitchen a spoon, a pair of scissors, a couple of carving knives, plus several small plastic bags. There's no point in focusing on anyone but Reggie, Nicandro, the Harringale woman. I head back to the bedroom where their bodies lie.

I'm no doctor, and I have no time to waste. I retrieve the hatchet from where it ricocheted off Nicandro's head. The thing's proving strangely handy. Time to get to it.

Reggie first—using the blunt edge of the hatchet, I smash his right cheek till the bones around the eye socket splinter. That loosens things up. Slipping the spoon beneath the eyeball, I lift it out gently, like a poached egg, to surmise the state of the optic nerve behind.

The scissors won't fit, I'll need to cut.

A long, slender, serrated knife will serve, and I saw away at the rubbery cord. Once it's severed, the eyeball pops free. I drop it into one of the plastic bags, try not to look at the gory mangled crater I've left behind, then move on to Nicandro.

He's a little tougher, but the procedure's the same. By the time I get to Christina Harringale, I'm feeling downright surgical.

Back in the kitchen, I load ice cubes from the freezer into a mini-cooler found stashed in the pantry, then gently place the bags on top. The three eyes stare blankly upward: Shiva on ice.

Back at the car, Georgie snores ever so faintly beneath her backseat blanket. I slide behind the wheel and take one last glance at the house.

The temptation to burn it to the ground arises, but why draw immediate attention to the place? Hard to know how long before anyone comes snooping around for signs of Reggie or anyone else, but that's our window.

I start the car, put it in gear, and head off.

—62—

I look for street signs, so I can find my way back should the need arise, but we're way out in the boonies, the narrow winding roads unmarked.

Spotting a beat-up sedan parked all by itself under some shaggy redwoods, I pull over. The nearest house lies several hundred yards back from the road, windows dark. I crack a window, listen—but for the wind-rustled trees, not a sound.

Sure, there's nothing to be done about the car's tracking software, but the plates are a different matter.

Plucking the screwdriver from the toolbox found in Reggie's kitchen, I head back along the dark road.

If the car isn't abandoned, it ought to be—four flats, shattered windshield, the whole thing caked in sticky grime, littered with pine needles.

I nick the license plates fore and aft, return to Reggie's car, replace his plates with the ones I just stole.

For a moment I wonder if the house beyond the trees isn't abandoned as well. If so, it might provide shelter, at least for the night. If not this one, maybe another, temporarily empty, readied for rent or sale. But they'll likely have security systems in place.

Scotch that.

The idea of a hotel or motel seems dodgy, given the scrutiny of desk clerks, housekeeping. And yet the yearly wildfires have likely ruined tourism. Beggars can't be choosers, and if a motel happens to remain in business, anyone willing to pay for a room, no matter how sketchy or short-term, might readily be welcome.

For safety's sake, I find my way to the very north of the valley, the Calistoga Ridge. Turning off the main thoroughfare, I head up the grade to a spot called Jericho Canyon. The smell of char is stronger here, being so close to the blackened hillsides.

I spot a small motor court with a neon Vacancy sign glowing in the office window. No cars but one in the parking lot. I pull in.

Georgie remains unconscious in the back as I slip out of the car, close the door gently, and head into the office.

The walls are paneled in knotty pine, with randomly arranged photographs, decades old from the looks of them, of folks hiking and fishing. A waist-high bookshelf offers a quaintly random collection of hardcovers, their dust jackets worn and sun-faded. One giant chair of well-worn leather rests in the corner.

From a room behind the desk arises the sound of shuffling slippers.

The woman is birdlike, in her sixties or older, wearing a man's wool shirt, lumberjack plaid. A face that's seen plenty of wind and sun, reading glasses perched in her short grey hair.

A shotgun's tucked into a corner behind the desk—most likely to ward off coyotes and other critters chased down from the hills by the fires—raccoons and rats. And evil men.

"Might a room be available?"

She taps the keyboard of her ancient workstation. The screen flickers with light, dappling her face. "How many people in the room?"

"Two. My fiancée and I. She's asleep in the car, utterly knackered. Long drive today, all the way up from San Diego."

"Congratulations."

"On the drive?"

"Your engagement." A flat smile—she doesn't believe a word.

"Ah, yes, thank you."

"Name?"

"O'Shea." A favorite over the centuries. The sound, not so different from Oisín.

"That it?"

"Sorry. Michael." Plucked from thin air.

She key-taps it into her system. "And the lucky lady?"

"Lisa." Not far from her middle name, Laoise, meaning radiant. "Lisa Ryan. Any chance we might have a room near the back? Privacy and all." I take out one of the wallets lifted from the dead. "And would it be inconvenient, me paying in cash?"

"Money's money," she replies.

"Especially in times as troubled as these."

"Don't lay it on too thick, skipper. This may be the sticks, but I'm no fool." She gives me the once-over, a gaze hard as diamond. "You're not gonna make me regret this, right?"

"No, ma'am." How can I possibly promise that? "Not at all."

We stand there like that, staring into each other, for an unsettling while.

Her eyes narrow. The weathered lines of her face seem to deepen. She's the first to break away.

"Seventy-five for the night. Usually, with cash, I add a security deposit."

"I'll pay. Gladly."

"Let me finish. I said usually. I'm gonna let it go this time. Know why?"

Pity, perhaps. Or she plans to murder us come midnight. "No, I don't."

"Me, neither." She reaches into a drawer and removes an old-fashioned key on a plastic fob, half a century old at least. "Last unit down. Sweet dreams."

The room, like the office, is paneled entirely in shiplap pine, even the ceiling, giving it a woodsy coziness. Beyond that, it's clean and quiet. What more to ask? The mattress is firm enough, a touch of rust on the window frame, a bit more around the drain in the bathroom sink.

I sniff the air—sure enough, that telltale scent. Not mold or mildew. Ghosts.

No place is going to be perfect.

I head back out to the car, check to see if the old woman's watching—she's not, the cagey trusting soul—then lift Georgie from the back seat, heft her up in my arms, carry her in, set her onto the bed.

I plop down in the room's one chair and settle in to wait. Once she wakens, I'll have to act fast. Make sure she doesn't scream.

—63—

SOMEWHERE after 3:00 AM—wolf time, *inter lupum et canem*— Georgie stirs.

Her eyelids flutter and her limbs, bundled up tight to her body in sleep, begin expanding outward, like the petals of a moonflower. Rising on one elbow, she groggily drags herself upright and, at long last, opens her eyes.

Her gaze doesn't turn my direction at first. She's concentrating more on trying to counter the effects of dry mouth—working her tongue, licking her teeth, her lips.

"Glass of water on the bed stand there," I offer gently, pointing.

Her head snaps toward me at the sound of my voice. She stares for a moment, then scans the corners of the room, as though sensing we're not alone, the two of us.

She pulls herself to the edge of the bed, drops her legs over the side, and reaches for the water glass. A timid sip. Blinking.

"Are you really here," she asks quietly, "or am I dreaming?"

"Well, if this is a dream, there's still a chance I could lie and say it's not."

She nods. "That's so you. Saying that."

"There's your proof, then."

"I'm frightened. Should I be?"

"Not of me."

She slips off the bed, comes toward me, unbuttons my shirt and pulls it open. "I saw them shoot you," she says, pressing the flat of her hand against my chest. "But except for your arm, you're only bruised."

"The old wounds are gone. These are new."

"Your body's warm." Her eyes rise to mine, searching. Her hand follows, the fingertips tracing the outlines of my face. "The cuts and scratches are gone."

"Yes."

"I've died, that's what this means."

"No. Not at all. You're quite alive."

She shudders, taking in a breath. "Holy Hell . . ."

I gently guide her back to the edge of the bed, sit her down, then return to my seat so we're facing each other.

"All right. I said I can explain. Here goes."

Yes, the story I told her, about Oisín and his curse, his recurring incarnations, the tale she turned into her beautiful book, it's true. I've lived it.

I tell her what happened after Nicandro murdered me, what happens to the rest of humanity after death, the wheel of existence, the reality of the Otherworld, the paradox of time.

She listens dutifully, hands folded in her lap, looking at me all gone out, like she's not comprehending a single word.

Once I've finished, an uneasy pall hangs between us.

She swallows, a nervous reflex, then whispers, "Golly."

"Yeah."

"Now they'll really call me crazy."

"We needn't give them that chance."

"How can I believe in you, believe you're real, and not feel crazy?"

"Are saints visited by angels mad? Or do they simply, if only for a moment, peek beyond the veil?"

"I know you mean well, but you're scaring the living fuck out of me."

"If it's any consolation, this is queer for me as well. Believe me, this doesn't happen often."

"What doesn't?"

"Encountering someone who's watched me die."

We go back and forth some more over the next hour, her asking questions, me answering as best I can. Finally, daybreak glows in the curtains.

"Would you mind if I lie down for a short while? Feeling knackered to beat Jesus."

She makes room for me, then tucks herself against my flank, resting her head on my shoulder, one arm draped gingerly across my chest.

"One last question? Then I'll let you sleep, I promise."

"Surely. Fire away."

It takes her a second to work up her nerve. "So when I die," she begins, "I'll either disappear forever, or I'll turn into a sad ghost, or I'll be reincarnated as someone else and forget everything about me and this life."

A faint rustling in the shadows. The ghosts, listening in. "That's pretty much it, yeah."

Her head settles a bit more heavily on my shoulder. "Not really much to look forward to."

"If it's a stairway to heaven you're after, no. I suppose not."

"But the creative, the imaginative, they stand a shot."

"And the fiercely honest. The bold at heart. As I understand the logic."

She drifts away for a moment. "I don't think that's me. Not yet."

"Meaning?"

"I need to finish what I started. I didn't come west just to confront Reggie. I want to take back my work, my book, stop the creepy asshats from using it for their own fucked-up agenda."

"Not to let the cat out of the bag, but I've got something in mind on that score."

She rises up, meets my eye. "Like what?"

"A plan. I'll tell you all about it. Just, please, let me nod off. Not long, I promise."

64

SLEEP, of course, escapes me. What rest I obtain proceeds against the windstorm of my thoughts. Georgie can't settle in beside me, either. She's staring at the ceiling as though it's rife with stars.

I announce my intention to speak by clearing my throat.

"I've got some of the . . . medicine . . . they were giving you, if you're having problems with withdrawal."

"God. no, please. I feel like I'm clawing my way out of quicksand as it is."

Outside, from not far off, a lone robin offers its morning song. I check the time. Nine o'clock. "I should be off, run my errands."

"Should I tag along?"

"If you're feeling up to it."

She gnaws at her lip. Her eyes compress. "Maybe not."

"Got a lot on your mind, I imagine."

"Yeah." She chuckles bleakly. "Bingo."

She reaches out, runs her fingers over my face again, then moves her hand along my shoulders, my arms. "It still seems . . ."

"Impossible?"

"Crazy."

"Stop that. Seriously. Mysteries are mysteries because they're mysterious. Last thing you should be doing is finding fault with yourself."

335

"Force of habit." She settles back down on the rumpled bed. "I'll wait here then, until you get back." Her eyes glisten with fright. She swallows. "You are coming back, right?"

"I've said it before, it's no less true now. Don't think for a minute I'd leave you. Ever."

She stares at me all skittish, as though "ever" has some new, terrifying meaning.

"I'll not be gone long, I promise."

"It's not that. Or just that. I've been thinking. About what I need to do. To finish what I began. Hear me out before you go, okay?"

She lays out her plan. It's perfectly mad. And very much in tune with my own ideas.

First stop, back in Calistoga: a cell phone store, to purchase five burner phones, cash on the barrelhead. The store clerk—Julian, per the nametag, early twenties, electric red hair, a haze of black freckles alongside one eye—pleasantly pays me no mind whatsoever.

Once I've got the cell phones activated, I select one and dial the number I know by heart.

"Liguorian College—how can I help you?"

"Professor Hovstad's office, please."

A moment to manage the transfer, then several rings. Is he due in the office today? Could he be in class? Has he perhaps been visited by our enemies, have the police taken him away, is he even still alive?

More rings, eight, nine, then the stuttered click introducing his voicemail: "Hello, you've reached the office—"

A sudden clatter as the recoding breaks off. "Sorry, yes. Hovstad here."

Hearing that voice, live, it's like finding shelter. "Professor, it's your old friend. From Christ the King." The homeless shelter where we met. "In Point Breeze."

I can only imagine the suspicion, the disbelief. Has there been any word I was killed? Unlikely. Better to make my body vanish than let it be found. Still—

"Ah, yes. Christ the King. Been a while. Had to think."

"I'll make this brief. I need you to pass along a message to our mutual friend." I take out another of the burners, thumb the display screen to life. "Please have him call me at the following number—but please note, I'm three hours behind."

"Three hours behind, yes." He's confirmed he understands. I'm not talking about the time difference. Every digit I recite, he should subtract by three for the actual number, with two being nine, one being eight, zero being seven. It's a code I learned from him, after all.

"Very good," he says once the information's conveyed. "I'll pass that along. Three hours behind. Nice to hear from you, *kompis*. I trust all is well?"

"As well as can be expected. Thanks so much. For everything."

I find a grocery store parking lot where I can disappear among the other cars. The waiting begins. Knowing Bartosch, I imagine him taking his sweet time before responding. After all, we parted on terms of never-to-be-seen-nor-heard-from-again. And, of course, he's paranoid.

If I were in his shoes, having learned from the professor I am indeed alive, I'd figure something untoward has happened—arrest, abduction by a militia—and want nothing whatsoever to do with me. The likelihood he'll respond reduces to zero if word of my murder has somehow reached him. Why respond to some obvious impersonator?

As if those concerns aren't troubling enough, the longer I wait, the more I worry that Georgie, left alone with her thoughts, will succumb to panic. How to measure the shock I've inflicted—hard to imagine, impossible to know.

The second of my newly bought burners rings.

Picking up, I say, "Do I have the right party?"

Silence. Who else can it be?

"I've happened upon some items I think you might find of interest. Laptops and cell phones." Remembering the name of the company on the credit cards found back at Reggie's house, I improvise with, "Very creative. Possible solutions. Invaluable, perhaps."

No way of knowing if he gets the connection. I pause for a response. None comes.

"Independent appraisal is needed, however. If there's someone out here, the locale we discussed previously, who could look them over, evaluate their worth, he should call the following number—again, remember, I'm three hours behind."

I recite the digits for a third burner phone, adding three to each. Once I'm finished, he bangs off, having not said a single word.

More waiting. I watch the shoppers come and go. A weather-beaten sedan meanders the lot endlessly, like a rat hypnotized by its maze, before finally choosing a spot to park. A woman in a yellow pantsuit, wearing a wide-brimmed hat, plants her geriatric dachshund on an island of grass, imploring at the top of her lungs, "Do your business, Heinz! Your business!"

I'm about to begin singing to myself when the third burner rings at last.

Before I can say as much as hello, a digitally masked voice says, "Memorize this address. Call when you get there. You have an hour."

65

THE meeting spot turns out to be a dilapidated parking garage in an older section of midtown Napa—no ticket required, free to all, testimony to the desperation of nearby merchants.

The two-story structure stands virtually empty, a ghost town of oil slicks and skid marks and echoes bouncing off naked concrete. I pull into a slot with nothing else within thirty yards, and those vehicles are grimed with long-term filth.

Taking out the same burner used earlier, I hit my mysterious caller back.

A click, then the same altered voice: "Stand outside your car."

"Not going to shoot me now, are ya?"

The line's already dead.

I do as directed, resting my arms on the open driver-side door, making my hands as visible as possible short of hoisting them high in the air.

Overhead, in a corner, a shiny black spider tends to her web, the gossamer clotted with mummified moths and flies. A line of sleek black crows perches along the second-floor railing, like pallbearers awaiting the casket.

I'm about to re-dial when a voice calls out, "Don't."

A woman's voice. Young woman. She's standing near the graffiti-slathered door to the stairs, slender and tall, kitted out in a jogging outfit with a distinctly random, jagged pattern, the kind that can render her all but invisible to surveillance cameras.

She begins to walk toward me. As she does, another door creaks open behind me, thuds closed—a second figure, this one male, medium height but broad-shouldered, also dressed in anti-camera camo.

The two converge slowly on the spot where I stand.

The man is dark-skinned, Latino—gaunt, hollow-cheeked, deep-set eyes. He could be a martyr. Or an Inquisitor.

The woman's softly featured, amber-eyed. Her skin's a shade lighter than the Latino's. Mediterranean descent, perhaps, the Near East.

"How do I know for certain you two were sent by my friend?"

The Latino begins to reply, but the woman holds up a hand. She retrieves a phone from her pocket, thumb dials, waits. After a couple of seconds, she turns the screen toward me—she's connected to a video feed. It's Bartosch.

"Hello, again." It's all I can think to say for a moment. "Everything copacetic?"

"What do you want?"

"Can you vouch for these people?"

"Yes. Anything else?"

I reply with a shrug.

Pffft, he vanishes, the small shiny screen goes black.

She tucks the phone away again. "You supposedly have something we might find valuable."

"This way."

We reconvene at the back of the car. While the Latino readies to draw the pistol holstered at his hip, I make a point to move slowly while thumbing the key fob, opening the boot. I nod toward one of the duffels. "There's three laptops and six cell phones in there, belonging to people I can't help but think you'd find of interest."

"Who, specifically?"

"The writer known as Rory Fitzgerald, plus his business manager, his bodyguard."

"And that's 'of interest' to us why?"

"They're all deeply involved in the game *The Truth Against the World*, which is being used to recruit your enemies. There may well be links to a nomad chapter of the Nightwolves in Colorado, the American Cossacks, the Christian Caliphate, even the group that pulled off the Capitol bombing—a money trail, directives."

"You know this for a fact?"

"Not in the least. I never opened the devices up—give my location away. I just have my suspicions, given what I've learned about the game, the world it inhabits."

The two of them trade glances. She nods, and the Latino reaches in for the duffel.

The woman says, "And you came by these items how, may I ask?"

"I took them."

"By force?"

"No more than was called for."

"Oh right," the Latino says, "you were military."

"Irrelevant. Let's just say pity's a stretch for the victims, given their racket. Them or me, as the saying goes, especially seeing as I'd come for my friend, Georgie. But it does raise the issue of what got left behind."

"Meaning?"

"A bit of a mess. Could use a hand cleaning it up. Hide my tracks, buy some time."

"No. You'll go nowhere near. What's the address?"

I take out the phone bill found at the house, hand it over. "There's also a plane on a makeshift landing strip nearby. Mind you, I'm not wanting to tell you your business, but you'll likely want not only to make all trace of the bodies disappear, you'll want to spoof those phones and laptops and the plane to some other location as well—again, to buy time."

"Time for what?"

"I'm getting to that. But one other thing, first—see that safe there, in the trunk? The lock's digital. Any way you think you might be able to pop the thing open?"

The Latino leans in for a glance, says, "I'll be right back," then shoulders the duffel containing the phones and laptops and trundles off.

Once he's gone, I ask the young woman, "What should I call you?"

She studies me, like my motives are written on my skin. "Mavia."

"Brilliant." Like the warrior queen. Led the Saracen Arabs against the crumbling Roman Empire.

"You realize," she says, "you're being accused of murdering that truck driver back in Kansas, the woman, Agnes Tolliver, right?"

A ramshackle pickup clangs and thunders into the parking structure. I discreetly close the boot, Mavia turns her face away as the lumbering rattletrap chugs past. It heads to the opposite side of the first floor, the clamor of its ancient engine echoing against the concrete.

Once it's parked and its driver gone, I say, "I'll claim three other bodies left behind at that truck stop, men sent to kill me, take Georgie away. Not hers. I was quite fond of Agnes. Wouldn't have harmed her for anything."

"I didn't say I believed the reports," Mavia says. "We've a good idea who's responsible."

"What I just handed over, the phones and such, should remove any doubt. But there's something else to discuss as well."

She responds without a word, just a nod.

"Georgie wants to break into the game, take it over. Use it as a broadcast platform. She wants the truth out—how the original book was stolen, who's involved with its publication, who's behind the game, how it's being used."

"And what will that accomplish?"

One of the crows perched along the second-floor railing lets out an ear-splitting caw, flutters its long black wings, and heads off, soaring low across the pavement and into the sunlight.

"It's not a mere book they stole. Georgie bled stones to make it, only to see it not just pilfered but turned into something grotesque. For a purpose she'd never countenance, let alone allow. It's more than betrayal. It violates everything about her. She wants to speak out—needs to. Deny her that, you kill her."

"I understand, and I'm not unsympathetic, but why should we involve ourselves?"

"She'll shine a light on the violence being plotted in the chat rooms, call out the Sacred Racial Warlords, Tower of Rage, any other pack of deadbeats trolling for recruits. Maybe some of the knuckleheads inclined to sign on with those jackals finally realize it's them getting played, not the game. How many, who knows? But do it right, you could witness a turn in the whole sick business."

The Latino returns. Pulling a thin black device from his pocket, no bigger than a matchbook, he places it on the door of the safe beside the lock. It latches on magnetically, and then the digital readout begins spinning like the tumblers on a slot machine.

After ten seconds or so it stops, the lock clicks open. He pulls the door wide, withdraws a large velvet bag containing something angular.

"This what you're after?"

I untie the cincture knotting the sack, pull out what's inside—the book, the very one, the original. *The Truth Against the World.* One page has been torn out, it's tucked inside the front cover—the title page, bearing Georgie's name. Not even Reggie could face the shame of destroying it entirely.

I think of Parisfal, beholding the Grail. I find myself trembling.

Mavia says, "What you were talking about, breaking into the game— I think we might be able to help arrange that."

—66—

IN service of covering tracks, it's decided the Latino—"You can call me Daltón"—will transport Reggie's car to the remote house where he and his crew will conduct their cleanup. Even with the change of license plates, there's likely at least some record of the trip up to Calistoga last night, then down to Napa, in the event anyone's already onto us. Impossible to know as yet. Since our having travelled that route also reveals where we spent the night, Mavia's agreed to take me back to the motel, pick up Georgie, and deliver us elsewhere, a new place to stay.

"Incidentally," I tell Daltón, "you're going to find that three of the bodies left behind are in a somewhat gruesome state."

"Yeah?" He bites back a laugh, shoots Mavia an icy glance. "Care to be more specific?"

"They'll be missing an eye. You'll find them—the eyes, I mean—in that cooler there in the boot. On ice, which I freshened up earlier."

He looks at me as though I'm potted. Mavia's mouth hangs ever so slightly open.

"In case you can't access the devices without a retinal scan."

The silence between us feels like it's hardening the air. Then he can't help himself, the laughter spills out. "Very thoughtful, *güero*. But unnecessary. We have our ways."

On the ride with Mavia north to Calistoga, I try to imagine what Georgie's been up to in my absence—going stir-crazy? Has the Old Black Dog come sniffing around? Perhaps she's just lying there, staring at the ceiling, trying not to snap her fingers.

As we pull into the parking lot, I discover my fears misplaced. She and the motel owner sit side by side in rockers on the shaded patio beside the office. All seems laid-back and cheery. They're sipping iced tea. And yet I can't help but wonder what they've been discussing.

Mavia and I exit the car. Georgie comes down to greet us. A round of introductions and timid smiles, then the two young women saunter off toward the room. Mavia intends to make sure nothing gets left behind that might even remotely identify us.

I step up onto the patio, check my watch. "It's well past checkout. I assume we owe for a second day."

The old woman waves me off like I'm a nuisance. "I'm Delores, by the way. Your friend there calls you Turk. Calls herself Misty. Last night you were Michael and Lisa. God only knows what your real names are."

Oh, fiddle-fuck. I neglected to tell Georgie about the names. "May I sit?"

"By all means."

I take the nearest chair. "We'll be gone shortly. Hopefully we've caused you no bother."

"I figured you were in trouble the minute you stepped through the door last night. Wouldn't let you stay if I was afraid of being bothered."

"Thank you. For the hospitality."

"Kinda what I'm here for."

She picks up her glass but doesn't drink, just tilts it back and forth in her hand.

"My husband died last year of a heart attack trying to keep this place safe. Flames weren't more than thirty yards away, he's out there with a garden hose, making sure sparks don't burn through the roof. Once the fire crews arrived he came right here, sat down in the chair you're sitting in now, struck up a smoke, waved out the match, and keeled over dead. Married fifty-three years to the man. Never did listen to a word the doctor said."

"I'm sorry."

"Didn't know he'd secretly bought a million dollars in life insurance. So now he's a memory and I'm a millionaire. My sister wants me to move in with her in Visalia. I'd rather slit my wrists. Point is, I don't need this place, don't need to let anyone stay here. But I did. Last night I told you I didn't know why. That wasn't the truth."

"It's not really my business."

"You run a place like this for forty some odd years, you learn to read people. An imperfect science, for sure, but my take on you? Nice guy, good heart, can take care of himself. I've got no idea what your trouble is. Don't much care. But your eyes are kind. And sad."

> *From his eyes of flame,*
> *Ruby tears there came*

Good old Billy Blake. Again.

Mavia heads south along the Silverado Trail. One sorry winery after another passes by, the ones not burned to the ground lying shuttered, while the razed and barren earth stretches for miles along the ridgeline, century-old trees reduced to twisted sculptures of alligatored char, scorched arroyos etching down into the lowlands like jagged black scars. Not a single hawk circles overhead—what would it hunt? And yet the sky has turned such a dazzling blue it brings to mind a tranquil sea, smooth as glass.

Just beyond a turn-off heading for a place called Rector Canyon, we dip onto a side road that passes beneath an archway reading: Santa Yolanda Wines. The road shortly turns to gravel, winding uphill between Italian cypresses, many seared or withered, some half gone.

The driveway ends in the parking lot for a visitor's center somehow spared the rampant fires that destroyed nearly everything else around, though the terra cotta roof tiles remain singed in places. Queer thing about fire, what it chooses to devour, what it leaves alone.

Plywood covers the windows. A handful of outbuildings, blackened and gutted, stand roofless in the background, knockdowns waiting for the sledge.

"You'll be safe here," Mavia says, "If you can stand the smell."

"There's electricity?"

"A generator. Around back."

"Running water?"

"Last time I checked. But this is California, and water's never a sure thing. Come on, I'll let you in."

We follow her up a stone walkway dusted with ash. Using a digital key, she opens the door and gestures us into what once likely served as a tasting room—Italian marble floor, a massive cherrywood bar lining one wall, a mirror as big as a cinema screen behind it.

"The service quarters are back this way," she says, guiding us beyond a kitchen area.

"How did you come to know about this place?"

"Owners are sympathetic. After they were nearly burned out during the last fire season, they began to rebuild, hoping to get their workers back onsite. And that was happening, almost on schedule. Then five of the workers were kidnapped—three men, two women, all from Guatemala, lynched out there across the road, a note pinned to each one's shirt: 'No second warnings.'"

"You always hear California is different," Georgie says.

"It's not all boutique bourgeoisie and nouveau riche up here. You go five miles into the hills in any direction, you're in the land of the Roughneck Reich. Have a lot of the sheriff's deputies on their side, too."

"So the owners, they closed up shop and fled."

347

"Not exactly." She turns into a bedroom, tries the light switch, glancing up—nothing. "You'll need to crank up the generator. I'll show you where it is."

"If the owners didn't pack up and go, where are they?"

"Around. The bikers and hilljacks and bent cops around here think they run the show now. All it takes is guns and attitude. They're about to learn otherwise."

67

LATE-day dust devils tumble down the hillside arroyos, carrying with them a cascade of cinders and fine black soot. We huddle inside, but grit sifts through the cracks between the plywood sheets and the window frames and the occasional spy hole carved into the wood. It insinuates itself into our eyes and mouths, beneath our fingernails. The charred stench lingers.

I clean the pistols I took from Reggie's house, just to keep busy, but with no solvent at hand this amounts to little more than wiping them down, reaming the barrel with a pencil and a thin square of cloth. Georgie's writing away in a mad fury, jotting down her racing thoughts.

Come sundown, Daltón arrives. He's shouldering a stylishly techie, surveillance-proof knapsack, but before opening it up and revealing its contents, he pulls me aside.

"Man, you weren't kidding when you said you left a mess behind."

I picture the bodies scattered through the house like charnel castaways, imagine the gore, the insects, the stench. The bloody gaping eye sockets. "I was striving for efficiency, not effect."

"Yeah, well, remind me never to piss you off. As for the phones and laptops, even the plane's GPS, they're spoofed. Far as anyone can tell, them and their owners are all headed back to a little town called Punkin Center, last place they seem to have been before coming out here."

"That's where we crossed paths, them and their friends."

"Middle of bumfuck nowhere's the point. Hard to get to. Buys time, like you want."

"Understood. Anything else?"

"Yeah. Those laptops. Fuck me. I mean, we knew the game was a watering hole for malcontents, them and their millions of pals—not just here but Europe, Russia, Israel, Australia. Any given time, there may be a hundred thousand players all over the world engaged—whole bunch just as radicalized as the Nightwolves."

"They're involved, then. In the game. Recruiting."

"Not just them. But my point: the money, how much, from where— that was new. Revenue from this thing? Easily a thousand times what the books make. Means it's a great venue for money laundering."

"Yeah?"

"Inside the game, you can buy and sell virtual tool kits filled with special weapons, secret information, magic spells. You want to scrub a few million in ill-gotten gains—weapons trafficking, specifically—spread it around, buy up all the tool kits and drive up the price, then cash out. It's called gold-farming."

"What about the police, FBI?"

"Games remain largely unmonitored. One of the perks that bazillions of dollars can buy. 'Unregulated digital bazaars,' they're called. It's up to the manufacturers to police what goes on. Most do. Some don't."

"Like whoever runs this show."

"Creative Solutions."

"That was the name on their credit cards."

"They infiltrated Christian publishing couple years back. Huge market, virtually invisible to the mainstream. Began with niche books praising free markets from a biblical perspective—denouncing social democrats, internationalists, the scientific community, all because they're, you know, atheists. The initial Rory Fitzgerald book was their first attempt at mainstream fiction, and they hit it big, especially with the game as part of the platform. Again, incredible audience out there. Celts, Vikings, Goths, Cossacks, they're idealized as Great White Warriors."

"But they're all pagans. Well, except the Cossacks."

"Don't overthink it. They sure don't. That's the great advantage of conspirituality—it doesn't have to make sense."

That word, it's new to me. Apparently Daltón intuits that from my expression.

"Conspiracy theories mixed with spirituality. Life is meaningless chaos. Or it's all a sacred mystery. If so, what better code book than Revelation? If the bible's not your thing, try the game."

"Or even if it is, apparently."

"Everybody talks about the Russians, Chinese, Iranians. Hybrid warfare. Active measures. They're definitely involved, but they're not the main threat. Not now. There's a homegrown network with global reach—petrochemical sector, major-project construction, derivatives traders, defense contractors. They filter funds to troll farms and these fringe groups through bogus charities."

"But why?"

"Undermine the government, roll back regulation, all in the name of giving the country back to the little guy, the forgotten American, who tends to think of business as the good guys. There's even livestream telethons, to fund the movement, like they're pimping for muscular dystrophy, not a race war."

"And the game's a part of all that."

"Thing's a virtual parking lot for dark money. Plenty of it going to the militias, politicians in their pocket. Thought they were clever—numbered accounts, all offshore—but we ain't stupid. And, like I said before, we have our ways."

"Good to know."

"I've printed some of it out, so your friend can read it off when you commandeer the game. Share the skinny with the world at large, ya know? Tell them who's who, what's what, where the money comes from, where it goes. Fuckers."

"I'll be sure to pass it along."

"Just so you know, Mavia and me, the people we represent, we're grateful. For what you're doing."

"Anyone's guess what difference it will make."

"Can't think like that. They want us cynical, cuz cynics don't fight."

"Agreed."

"By the way, not to throw you off, and I can't say for sure if what we're hearing's true, but there's rumors the American Cossacks have surrounded Minot Air Force Base in North Dakota."

I know what that means. The weapons there. "Christ in Hell . . ."

"Right now it's a standoff—military for the most part leans pro-regime, but they're not batshit. No one's in favor of handing over nukes to those yokels. But things are tense. They're threatening to drive warheads into Minneapolis, Milwaukee, Madison, Chicago. Maybe they're serious, maybe it's blackmail." He shrugs. "Just thought you should know."

How ironic—or apropos. When terrorists at last get close to acquiring nuclear weapons, it's Americans, intending to use them against other Americans.

"Explain something for me. I can understand the anger out there, the sense of betrayal, it's directed at the wrong people in my view, but I get it. Even this nuke business—it's crazy, but that's the nature of rebellions. Nothing uglier than a family fight. Why, though, are the big money boys—not just here but around the world, from the sound of it—pouring millions into the enterprise through this stupid game? Isn't all this chaos utterly contrary to their interests?"

"They want to burn the system down, man. Build something else, something better—for them. Disaster capitalism, conflict entrepreneurs—you never read *Atlas Shrugged?*"

"Ayn Rand? Rather pluck out my eyes. *Nietzsche for Dummies.*"

He's brought a laptop for Georgie—not secondhand, courtesy of the dead, this one's a different creature entirely: sleek as a missile, thin as a blade, but with an impressively sizeable screen. He sets it up on the mahogany bar, so Georgie will have the giant antique mirror as backdrop while she's broadcasting.

"Okay," he says, gesturing for us to join him. "Let me explain what's going on."

Georgie and I take opposite sides, she on a barstool, me standing.

Daltón opens the game space. "One of the laptops you gave me? Belonged to one of the game's moderators."

"Christina Harringale, I imagine."

"Her, yeah. I cred-stuffed her login info to crack her password, which gave me back-end access to the gaming platform. You can take over the game any time you want but first, I'm going to tether this laptop to one of your burner phones, and that will act as your IP hotspot."

"Whatever you say." I catch Georgie's eye—she shrugs, baffled as I am. I hand him one of the as yet unused burners.

He fiddles with it, then the laptop, glancing back and forth.

"When you log on," he continues, "you're going to use a special browser. I've set it up for you. Fun fact—the original version was created for the Dalai Lama. To defeat Chinese cyberattacks, no joke. But, like, in a matter of months it became the favorite of the cartels, *sicarios*, human traffickers, you name it."

"Touching."

"Anyway, it spoofs your position continually among peers. Makes it virtually impossible to pinpoint your location. They'll try, of course, that's to be expected. And once they see the source of the intrusion is a burner, not a traditional access point, they'll start network sniffing, checking the application logs, try to figure out from the metadata who the intruder is, where you're located. Thanks to how I've set things up, though, you should be okay."

"Can't thank you enough, truly."

"If they don't just shut the game space down, it means they're still looking for you. That's the trade-off. The more airtime you get, means they're still hunting."

He collects his various gadgets and slips them back into his knapsack. Georgie stares blinking at the laptop screen, the reality of it all sinking in.

"If you want to hit the peak usage window," he says, shouldering on the knapsack, "I'd get ready to broadcast in about an hour. I'll monitor the online comments and track what other sites the players head to during your transmission. Some of that will be guys bailing because they don't like your message. But if others take to what they're hearing, you'll start seeing the broadcast spread all over the Internet, not just the game space. I'll text that to you in real time as best I can, keep you up to speed on what's happening."

Once he's gone, Georgie resumes her mad scribbling—reading from the printouts Daltón provided, adding that to her script, then reciting the words in a muted whisper. Practicing, revising, memorizing.

Outside, the winds are picking up. The gritty soot whirling down from the hills continues insinuating itself through gaps in the plywood at the windows. It conjures thoughts of nuclear winter, not so speculative now given the news from North Dakota.

Georgie stays focused, eyes glued to the words before her. Finally, she glances up, nods to let me know she's ready.

I use one of the burners to contact Daltón. "All set here."

"Cool. Nice crowd in play, you're hitting it just the right time. Give me just a sec . . . Okay. Log on. You'll enter the standard game space, but after a second or so your laptop will take over, the camera will come on and it'll be Georgie's image onscreen—every screen. All over the world. Good to go?"

68

GEORGIE sits up straight, squares her shoulders. She's the Maid of Orléans, standing before the citizens of Vaucouleurs, revealing to them her mission, anointed to save the realm. In the mirror behind her, I can see the game space go blank. Her image appears in its place.

Addressing the computer screen, she begins: "Not what you were expecting, I imagine. Don't go. You and I, we have a lot in common. We've had something stolen from us. Something we treasured. Something we want back. That's why you're here. It's why we're all here."

She lifts the book so it's visible.

"See the title? *The Truth Against the World.* It's the book this game is based on. The true original. Guess who wrote it." She opens the book, holds the title page, the one torn out by Reggie, up to the camera. "See? Georgina Laoise O'Halloran. That's me."

She sets the title page down, slowly leafs further into the text, pages facing the screen.

"Look at the drawings—notice anything? Check out the colors, the script and its embellishments, the figure drawings—warriors, gryphons, demons. You probably recognize them from the game. This is where they began. This book. It was stolen from me. Stolen by the man you know as Rory Fitzgerald. He was my professor. He was also my lover."

She holds the book against her chest, faces the camera squarely.

"My best friend, the most loyal and caring friend I've ever had, he's the one who told me about Oisín and his strange curse. And he gave me a whole new perspective on many of the other old stories. Admittedly, I embellished here and there, improvised, but what I mean is, it's his book too, more than I can convey. Which means it was stolen from him as well."

From her expression, I can tell she's wondering if I don't want to come stand beside her, share the spotlight. I shake my head. I'm baggage, a distraction—psychotic vet, mad-dog killer. Faithless ingrate.

"So, we all have that in common. Getting ripped off. Maybe it was your future they stole. Maybe it was your pride, your sense of belonging, your understanding of the world, your hope. Your faith in America. And what did they give you back? This game. This elaborate game, based on stolen stories, tortured to mean something they don't."

She resumes flipping through pages.

"Sure, many of the stories concern battles, but that's not really the point. The point is the mystery of existence. The sanctity of nature—the woods and rivers and hillsides where the *fianna* hunted and had their strange, magical adventures: The madness put on Finn by the goddess Daireann for his refusal to marry her. The terrible music of the man with no head, but a single eye in the middle of his chest. The lost magic stone with its golden chain belonging to the Woman of the Waves."

Her eyes begin to glisten. Tears of fright. Tears of passion. She wipes them away.

"That should inspire wonder and awe, not anger. But I know it's anger a lot of you feel, and the game gives you permission—you can kill, torture, maim, vent your rage at the enemies right there in front of you."

Something's stirring in the room, a rustling in the shadows—then the faint telltale scent, obscured at first by the overwhelming stench of cinders and char. Ghosts are congregating—here, in this room, around Georgie.

"And I know some of you have carried the fight beyond the game. Out here, in the world. Where so many others are urging you on, telling you it's good, it's right. Slaughter all the enemies you want."

One of my burners begins to vibrate. I thumb the screen to life. A text from Daltón:

> She's lost 30% of the audience. But that
> means 70% have stuck around. Not bad.

"The people behind the game, the ones bending the stories to their own purpose, they want you angry. Your hate is a goldmine—for them. And that's one more thing they're stealing from you. Your self-respect. They're playing you for suckers. They're using you as pawns."

She leans closer toward the camera.

"But you can resist that. You can take back control. Of your life. Of the game."

The burner vibrates again. Another message:

> Word's going out. You've got new people entering
> the game space, not just leaving. Good.

"After this book was stolen, I went into a tailspin, a depression so deep I thought it would never end. I thought I'd die inside that darkness, like a prisoner left to rot."

> About 20% are connecting to outside websites
> as they listen. Spreading the word. It's working.

"Funny thing about depression—know what it's like? Being brainwashed. You lose all control over your own thoughts."

> Someone with Admin status is trying to break in,
> close down the game. I've locked them out.
> Keep going!

"I'll bet some of you feel that way. Feel brainwashed. I'll bet that's why you're here."

> Chat rooms are going batshit!

"But there's another kind of brainwashing—the ordinary kind. When someone else, for purposes all their own, begins feeding you lies—seductive lies, empowering lies—so they can control you, manipulate you."

She's getting a following.
It's trending on other platforms.

"Lies that make you feel better for a while. Until they don't. And then they're ready with new lies—about what disgusting monsters and animals your enemies are."

Another attempt to shut down the game.

"It's time to see those lies for what they are. Time to take back what's yours."

She's reaching for her glass to take a sip of water when the computer screen goes dark. So does the display panel on my burner phone—the others have gone dark as well. But the generator outside continues chugging, the inside lights remain on.

Georgie whispers, "What's going on?"

69

I ease the front door open to head outside, have a look—pause first, waiting for the sound of a cocked gun, a rifle's report, an oncoming bullet.

Nothing.

Beyond the doorway, the night feels more absolute, not just because of our remote location. Glancing south, to where Napa should be, there's only a lake of darkness.

I head back in. "The power grid's down. That's why we have lights but can't connect to the web. The generator. But the cell tower—"

"I understand," she says quietly. "Let me prepare my thoughts for when we're back online and broadcasting."

Five minutes pass, then ten.

"Want to see something cool?" She gestures me over. Once we're side by side, she nods toward the laptop. "When the screen's not lit, it's like a mirror. A little on the dark side, but with it facing the mirror behind me . . ."

She leans to the side, glancing over her shoulder—her image multiplies endlessly, if dimly, into infinity.

"Remember the dream I had, pounding on the mirror, trying to get it to show my reflection?"

"It became a door, opening onto the sky."

"I wanted to step out into the clouds, but was too afraid." She stares at her reflection in the dark screen. "I'm not afraid anymore."

The laptop screen flickers and flashes to life. Almost immediately, one of the burner phones begins to buzz.

I pick up, saying, "What was that?"

"Okay, I've got good news and bad news. The good? Your girl made the news—cable networks, web outlets, online zines. She's having an impact. Already."

"And the bad?"

"They probably identified your burner from the metadata and tracked it to the outlet store where you bought it. That's why they focused on this area. They decided to bring down the power grid so you'd have to log back on. What they're doing—what I'd do—is insert tracking pixels into the game display while everything out here is dark. I also imagine they're operating one of the exit nodes for the browser I gave you. If so, when you log in to the game again or click on any element of it, they'll have immediate access to your location given the metadata in the application logs. They'll be able to locate you within a mile, and if they're good—and I'm guessing they're very good—they can triangulate probably within a hundred feet. If I were you, I'd call it a day. If you weren't finished, settle for what you got out there. Like I said, she had an impact. You go back in right now, you're basically saying, 'Come and get me.'"

"Give me a second to pass that along." Holding the phone to my chest, I relate to Georgie everything Daltón just said.

Her expression darkens. "Hang up," she says.

"Excuse me?"

"Hang up the phone."

To Daltón, I say, "Let me get back to you," then bang off. To Georgie: "What?"

Something looms in her expression I do not quite recognize.

"Those things you told me, about what happens after death—you weren't just making that up."

"Georgie—"

"There's nothing to be afraid of, not really. Right?"

"You don't have to die. Carry the fight to another place, another day."

"I won't be a prisoner again. I can't." Left unsaid, next time they won't just stick her in a room. They'll rape her, force her to carry the baby to term—same way the enslaved have always multiplied. "And I'm tired of running."

"It's not running. It's regrouping. Tactical retreat."

"Before you told me about who you really are and . . . I'd given up on stuff like angels, magic, the beyond. You've really fucked up my zeitgeist, buddy, know that?"

"Not my intention."

"Anyway, there's so much more to say, all the stuff off the phones, the computers, about the money, where it comes from, where it goes. I want to go back on, keep the message alive."

"Until when?"

"Until I can't."

"Georgie, no—"

"Promise me you won't let them take me. You won't let them torture me or—"

"And if I refuse?"

"Then you're a liar. A phony. A fraud."

"You mean I'm crazy. Like you."

"No." She shakes her head vehemently. "You don't mean that."

"To claim I've lived before, will again—what else can I be but utterly mad?"

Her shoulders tremble. Tears begin to gutter down her face. "No . . . Don't say that . . . Please . . ."

I hear what she can't—a faint, curious shudder in the room, animating the shadows, a silent cry—the ghosts.

"It's not madness," I tell her. "And I didn't mean to demean your condition. I was simply trying to shock you into realizing what you're asking me to do."

"I don't need that. I need your promise. You won't let them . . ." The rest fades away, into the needlessness of its being said.

Back online, inside the game, she starts reciting the information Daltón provided—the litany of names, linking them to their atrocities: the plutocratic sociopaths who bankrolled the Capitol bombing; the homegrown *sicarios* murdering governors, mayors, members of Congress; the freelancers targeting journalists, bloggers, filmmakers, poets; the paid provocateurs turning marches into riots, the arsonists torching courthouses, the saboteurs who brought down the Martin Luther King Bridge in East—

From the main road below, vehicles rumble up the winery's gravel drive.

Peering through a spyhole, I spot the caravan, five sets of headlights boring through the darkness, piercing the fog of airborne ash, aiming first this way then that as they follow the winding gravel road uphill.

Off with the overhead lights. The only illumination in the room now comes from the laptop. Its glow sharpens the angles of Georgie's face and creates a sea green aura in the mirror behind.

Her almond eyes are black with shadow as they search for me in the darkness. I click my tongue to identify where I'm crouching. She nods and resumes her recitation, moving on now to read aloud from the book, *The Truth Against the World.* Finn's search for a pup through the Valley of Swords and the storm of Druim Cleibh. The mysterious hospitality of Cuanna from Innistuil. The enchanted House of the Quicken Trees.

As the lead car pulls up at the top of the hill, it sprouts atop its roof a flashing lightbar. The law has arrived—local sheriff, most likely. Wise decision: lend an air of legitimacy to the violence.

I've loaded all the pistols collected from Reggie's house, six altogether—four semi-autos, two revolvers. I tuck two guns in my belt at the back, two more in the front, hold the other two in my hands.

There's maybe four pickups lined up behind the squad car. The posse. Courtesy of the Roughneck Reich.

A bullhorn voice breaks the outer silence: "Whoever's inside that building: You are on private property. You are to leave the premises immediately. Come out through the front door. Move slowly. Show your hands. There will not be a second warning."

I turn to Georgie, whirl my hand: Keep going.

She leans in closer to the laptop's camera and microphone.

"I'm going to be ending this broadcast shortly. Armed men are outside. They've discovered our location. They intend to put an end to this. To me. I've made my peace with that. But you shouldn't. If you're hearing my voice, rise up. Take back your lives. There's a movement out there, made up of people with the courage to hope, the courage to build something better for everyone, not just a few. A future worth sharing, not stealing. Join them."

Pickup doors slam shut. The posse is impatient—they're moving past the sheriff standing outside his squad car, about a dozen men altogether, armed with long guns, inching forward up the shallow grade.

I grip the pistol in each of my hands a bit more purposefully, breathing slowly in and out, emptying my mind, silencing what remains of my conscience.

"Don't let the hucksters play you for fools any longer. They don't believe in freedom, not yours. They believe in power. Stop pretending rage can save you, stop hiding behind righteous indignation so you can hate with a clear conscience. There's power in kindness, too, in care, in concern. In simple decency and honesty. Don't drown in your anger. Love one another. Welcome the stranger. Embrace your humble humanity. And that of others. Goodbye."

She glances up, searches for me in the dim light, finds me. "Shane?"

I turn toward the voice. Her voice.

"Remember," she says, "what I said back in Philly? How much I love your singing, how much it's what I want to hear when I die?"

"Georgie—"

363

"Sing for me, okay? Please. One last time."

I can hear the shuffling of feet just beyond the door, the thick, conspiratorial murmuring.

In my gentlest voice, I oblige her request.

> On a quiet street where old ghosts meet, I see her walking
>   now
> Away from me so hurriedly, my reason must allow
> That I had loved not as I should a creature made of clay—

A sledge hits the door like a thunderstrike. The wood, weakened by fire, splinters and shatters like scrap. I can see faces through the breach. See their weapons.

I turn back toward Georgie, my right hand raised.

Every movement has its martyrs.

"I love you," she says.

"And I you."

The bullet hits her square in the spot mystics have christened the third eye. Quick as that, she's gone.

The gunshot rouses the men outside. Gunfire pours through the shattered door. Then the inevitable, stupid silence—they wonder if they've hit anything.

That's when I charge.

I aim through the shattered door at every man I see, firing two-handed, killing the front four straightaway.

I kick what remains of the door open and walk out into the night, pistols blazing as I call out: "Behold Oisín of the Strong Hands, son of Finn mac Cumhal! My banner is Donn Nimhe, the Dark Deadly One. Kill me if you can. Die if you must. You'll not take me alive."

Once the first two guns are spent of shells I drop them, pull out the two from my front waistband, and resume the slaughter, even as a bullet from somewhere down the hill—the sheriff, likely—rips though my shoulder.

I'm firing at arm's length at the men around me, their shots sailing wide from panic at my coming on so close, so fierce. Then the second bullet from the lawman strikes, this one straightaway to my chest—hollow-point round, I can feel the gaping exit wound in my back.

"Come on, ya fucking coward! Come up here and look me in the eye if you intend to put an end to me!"

Of course, he doesn't. He merely fires once more, striking me again in the chest, blowing a cavern out my back. My heart flutters inside me like a torn flag. My pulse fades to a murmur, the dimness rises up in a surging wave and drags me under, into the black.

TORADH

And all times are one time, and all those dead in the past
never lived before our definition gives them life, and out of
the shadow their eyes implore us.

—Robert Penn Warren, *All the King's Men*

70

THIS time, on the sands of Tech Duinn, I do not merely stand idly by and watch the culling of the dead. Rushing to Donn's side on the dock beneath the cliffs, I tell him, "Wait, please, give me time. I need to find someone."

"That is not the way of it, as you know." His voice is kind, his eyes heavy with sorrow, but the terrible staff rises nonetheless, the skies turn pitch black—crack of thunder, lightning strike. The merciless wind.

I'm rushing up the stone path carved into the cliff, stumbling, dragging myself back onto my feet, in a fury to reach the top. I do, just as the bodies of almost all those gathered there wither into dust.

Was Georgie among them? I didn't see her face, but there were so many, and just that instant.

Next, those middling souls doomed to wander the earth as ghosts shed their mortal forms and drift back like a wave of fog to the world of flesh and death. Again, it all happens too quickly for me to ascertain whether Georgie stood among them.

Now just the transmigrating handful remains. Here, after all, is where I expect to find her, for if the rest of her life didn't reveal her worthiness, surely her final hours did.

I begin forcing my way through the crowd, searching every face.

Ironically, who should I encounter but one of the ruffians I just shot dead? Did I not say that morality plays no part in this business? His expression harbors no less fright at seeing me now than before.

"No worries," I tell him. "I can't kill you again. Not yet at any rate."

He joins the others, equally stunned and scared, shuffling toward the cliff's edge. One by one, naked, trembling, they head down to the haze-shrouded water. I continue moving, pressing through the flow of bodies, studying every passerby.

She's not there. The gunman who would gladly have murdered her earns himself a new incarnation but Georgina O'Halloran, a creative genius, bursting with imagination, honest to a fault, does not?

I agreed to kill her, shoot her dead, believing . . .

What kind of fool—or monster—would do such a thing?

I trail after the others down to the dock and try to force my way onto Donn's longboat, hoping for one last chance to find her. He stops me before I can board.

He implores me, "Think beyond yourself," his eyes more desolate than stern.

"What do you imagine I'm trying to do, old man!"

"You're not seeing things clearly. Now go!"

"And what punishment if I refuse? Death? A curse?"

"It's blasphemy!"

"Out of my way."

"You will come to regret—"

I push him aside, leap aboard his craft, and once again move among the trembling crowd, checking every single face, one by one, each of them staring back at me in mystified dread.

Nothing. She's not there.

Defeated, bereft, I step back onto the rocky, windswept shore. Donn pushes off from the dock. The low-slung craft drifts away through the whirling haze across the dark water.

In time, Embarr appears, charging across the distance, hooves striking sparks atop the waves. As always, I climb upon his strong white back and prepare to meet my love, though how will I hide this bitterness, this heaviness of heart?

Our journey differs from all the times before—no great cities or courts, no lime-white houses, no girl with a golden apple in her palm. Instead there is just the seemingly endless water, a requiem on the wind, until at last the darkness breaks as though we've emerged from a tunnel.

All is green and lush. Birdsong fills the branches of the forest, a rushing stream roars nearby, banging along its rocky course. The air smells fresh, and a valley of bright feathery grass weaves among low hills, while far beyond, in the distance, steep rock walls rise up on all sides.

Niamh stands waiting in the shade of an ancient, sprawling hazel tree. She kisses me in greeting. "Do you not recognize this place?"

The memory stirs from its dark resting place, shakes itself off.

How many times over how many years, after Finn and his hounds found me naked and alone on Beinn Gulbain, did I try to find my way back? I'd begun to believe it did not exist. Or was merely a trick of dreaming.

Niamh reaches out her hand. "Come. Indulge your bride."

Leaving Embarr behind, we walk through the dappled woods. With every step, the chime of remembrance grows stronger. At last we come upon a hillside rising up from the forest floor, a towering cliff high up. Set into the cliffside, a cave.

Niamh extends her thin white hand. "Wait now. Just a moment."

My eyes run thick with tears. I need to wipe them away to see.

At last she shows herself. A doe, tawny of hue with almond-shaped eyes. Gentle as a summer morning. Lovely as the moon.

I've returned to the place where I saw her last, a mere boy, paralyzed by a malevolent spell, as Fear Doirche dragged her off.

Sabdh, my mother. But also, I now realize, Georgie O'Halloran. The woman in the pottery shop. Na'ura, the one who is found.

"Your father," I murmur, struggling for words, "he has a hand in this. He—"

"At my insistence. He allowed me to intercede on your behalf."

The strange logic of it clicks into place: the dying old man in the abandoned shack, the mysterious sake bottle, the thieving brute, the shapeshifting cat.

"What did he make you pay in return?"

"Do not bother yourself over that."

"I have a right to know."

"No." She smiles sadly. "You do not."

Of course. Remember your place, mortal. I glance back at the cliff, the cave entrance, the doe, my mother. I feel fate shifting inside me. My blood runs cold—but like nightfall, not ice.

"Incidentally," Niamh says, "this latest turn in the world, be proud. People are rallying—thousands, tens of thousands. She touched a great many hearts, awakened their courage."

"That's good." I wonder which incarnation to picture: Georgie? Na'ura? Sabdh? Aren't they one and the same? "That's very good."

Something remains amiss.

"Does this mean it's over—the wandering, the endless . . ." I reach for the nearest tree for support, I'm shaking.

The doe looks down on me with tender eyes, eyes I should have recognized how many times but didn't.

"It wasn't about wisdom of the world, never, not in the sense—"

Niamh puts her fingers to my lips. "Guilt and shame, they too are a kind of curse. Like a hound licking a wound that will not heal—you were trying to redeem your honor, trying to atone. For not being able to save her. I saw that. You will no longer seek in vain for this place. It will be here, waiting. As will your mother."

"But my own curse, what—?"

"Only when you realized you could not save yourself were you able, once again, to bear the pain of caring so deeply for another. Why else your obsession with rescue?"

"Why did you never speak to me of this? How many hundreds of years—"

"No one else can guide you to your reckoning. There's the great mystery of your kind. Yes, it may seem I took too long to act, but remember: time, as you know, has no meaning here."

I glance up again at the cave, at my mother, Sabdh, who meets my eyes with such sad warmth, such affection. It feels like forgiveness. Except—

"She remains a doe. Why?"

Niamh does not answer. The terrible mist begins gathering. She strokes my hair, and through her tenderness, I realize Donn was right. I will come to regret my blasphemy.

No sooner have I atoned for one fault than I've blundered into another, trading guilt for arrogance. And it's my mother who must pay—again. What must I do? How many more lifetimes will pass before I've earned forgiveness for that?

And so once again I find myself back in the world. This world. Our world.

If you've enjoyed *THE TRUTH AGAINST THE WORLD,*
be sure to look into David's other titles:

FICTION

THE LONG-LOST LOVE LETTERS OF DOC HOLLIDAY

THE MERCY OF THE NIGHT

DO THEY KNOW I'M RUNNING

BLOOD OF PARADISE

DONE FOR A DIME

THE DEVIL'S REDHEAD

THIRTEEN CONFESSIONS (Stories)

THE DEVIL PRAYED AND DARKNESS FELL (Novella)

NON-FICTION

THE COMPASS OF CHARACTER

THE ART OF CHARACTER

GLOSSARY OF PRONUNCIATION

THESE ARE BY NO MEANS exact phonetic translations of the Gaelic words listed, but mere approximations at best, striving to mimic at least somewhat the subtlety of Irish vowel and consonant renderings, and to strike some compromise among the various dialect distinctions. As for the spellings, they conform to those that appear in Lady Gregory's *Gods and Fighting Men*.

Almhuin	AL-win
Beinn Gulbain	Ben GUL-ven
Bran	Brawn
Cailleach	CAH-lee-ahkh
Clanna Baiscne	CLAH-nah BWEE-shnyeh
Clanna Morna	CLAH-nah MWEER-nyeh
Cú Chulainn	Coo HOO-lan
Cú Sidhe	Coo Shee
Cuanna	COO-nah
Daireann	DARE-ee-ahn
Donn Fírinne	Don FEAR-neh
Donn Nimhe	Don NEEV-eh
Druim Cleibh	Droom Clave
Eamhain Macha	Ow MA-ha

Fear Doirche	Fahr DOR-e-ha
Finn mac Cumhal	Finn McCool
Gabhra	GAHV-ra
Laoise	Lee-sha
Manannán Mac Lir	MONN-aw-non Mok LUR
Muirthemne	Moor-HEV-neh
Niamh Chinn Óir	NEE-av Heen Orge
Oisín	Uh-SHE-un
Sadbh	Sahv
Sceolan	SHKO-lahn
Tech Duinn	Chagh DOO-een
Tír na nÓg	Tier-nuh-NOGUE

Other Gaelic words appearing in the text:

abhac	AL-luhk
duine beag	DEEN-uh BEE-uhk
Solas Agus Dorchadas	SUH-lus AH-gus DOR-ha-dus
Toradh	TA-rah

QUESTIONS FOR BOOK GROUP DISCUSSION

1. What are the various layers of meaning reflected by the book's title, *The Truth Against the World*?

   - How does the battle cry of the *fianna* speak to the challenge Georgie and Shane face in trying to confront Rory Fitzgerald (Reginald Feeley), his theft of Georgie's book, and all that theft has led to?

   - Professor Hovstad refers to Orwell's conviction that even if only one person stands by the truth, "being a minority of one against all the world," that does not make him mad. The professor disagrees with this, however—in what way? Why?

   - The gamers, militias, and other nativist elements have also embraced "The Truth Against the World" as their battle cry. How can two irreconcilable sides in a conflict rally under the same maxim?

   - How does the introductory quote by Ursula K. Le Guin, where she links the phrase "the truth against the world" to her conviction that "truth is an act of imagination," reflect the cosmology of the novel—specifically the logic of the afterlife as described by Shane?

2. Speaking of that cosmology, in which creativity rather than morality determines who earns reincarnation, how does it resemble evolution?

3. Shane comes to realize that the curse imposed on him by Manannán Mac Lir is a trick. How so? Specifically, what about Shane's understanding of wisdom justifies this realization?

377

4. What would motivate a god like Manannán to pull such a trick? Is there perhaps a benign explanation—for example, he and his daughter Niamh are trying to guide Shane toward the realization that his mortal ordeals someday will lead him to ultimately saving his mother?

5. Shane at one point admits that he too, like Georgie, has been institutionalized. At another juncture, he suggests that every fantastical thing he says about himself may just be nothing but rubbish. "Maybe I'm just barking mad." What indicates that this may be true, i.e., that he's an unreliable narrator suffering from delusions caused by Post-Traumatic Stress Disorder (PTSD)? What indicates that it isn't true?

6. At one point Shane says he fears America is falling into a period of protracted, tribalist violence like the Troubles in Ireland. He later revises this view due to the scope of the conflict. In each case, how is he right? How is he wrong?

7. What other aspects of the political upheaval portrayed in the story reflect on the current state of America? Do you believe another civil war is immanent—i.e., is Shane justified in wondering if Mr. Lincoln's war never truly ended?

8. Shane also reflects on how, in a mere two-week period, in July 1863, Irish Americans both helped save the Republic at Gettysburg and caused the death of an estimated 1,200 Black Americans during the draft riots in New York. How does this seeming contradiction reflect the wider history of race relations in America?

ACKNOWLEDGMENTS

No book is a solo effort. I owe a great deal of thanks to the many people whose assistance proved crucial in the writing and publication of this novel. Michael Torres, Joe Clifford, and the folks at Square Tire Books were invaluable in finding a home for the book. Lisa Daily, Carla Cruz, Kayla Compton and everyone at Swell Media made sure that the book gained the media attention it deserved. Thanks to Pam Stack at *Authors on the Air,* Hallie Ephron at *Jungle Red Writers,* Tony DuShane at *Drinks with Tony,* and Steven James at *The Story Blender* for helping get the word out. The cover design by Tim Barber at Dissect Designs and the interior text layout by Ellie Searl at Publishista have made the book a rewarding visual experience, while Zoe Quinton and Ellen Clair Lamb provided their considerable editorial expertise.

Thomas Pope, Vaughn Roycroft, and Emily Kimelman provided invaluable guidance on the ins and outs of the always evolving publication arena. Therese Walsh, Liz Michaelski, and everyone at *Writer Unboxed* provided so much assistance on so many issues it's hard to imagine the book reaching fruition without them. Robin C. Stuart, computer expert extraordinaire, provided insights into gaming, computer crime, and hacking that proved invaluable to the story. Deborah Crombie, Rachel Howzell Hall, Alex Segura, and Rob Hart all provided much-appreciated moral support. Adrian McKinty and John Connolly provided, sometimes inadvertently, cautionary advice on the perils of "Irishness," while Steve Cavanaugh did likewise on what is and isn't a good Irish joke.

Last, I simply can't overemphasize the importance of the daily love, support, and unfailing common sense provided by my exceptionally patient and forbearing wife, Mette Hansen-Karademir. And, to be sure, the wee Wheaten, Fergus.

References relied upon in the writing:

- *Lady Gregory's Complete Irish Mythology* (Preface by W.B. Yeats) and "The Wanderings of Oisín," W.B. Yeats

- *Celtic Myths and Legends*, Peter Beresford Ellis

- *The Celtic Book of the Dead: A Guide to the Celtic Otherworld*, Caitlín Matthews

- *History of Ireland*, Malachy McCourt

- *Ireland and the Irish*, Karl S. Bottigheimer

- *Ireland*, Frank Delaney

- *Tyrone's Rebellion*, Hiram Morgan

- *The Irish Brigades Abroad: From the Wild Geese to the Napoleonic Wars*, Stephen McGarry

- *'More Furies Than Men': The Irish Brigade in the Service of France 1690-1792 (From Reason to Revolution)*, Pierre-Louis Courdray

- *The Rogue's March: John Riley and the St. Patrick's Battalion, 1846-48*, Peter F. Stevens

- *The Immortal Irishman: The Irish Revolutionary Who Became an American Hero*, Timothy Egan

- *My Life in the Irish Brigade: The Civil War Memoirs of Private William McCarter, 116th Pennsylvania Infantry*, Edited by Kevin E. O'Brien

- *The Greatest Brigade: How the Irish Brigade Cleared the Way to Victory in the Civil War*, Thomas J. Craughwell

- *The Irish Brigade*, Captain D.P. Conyngham

- *The Forgotten Irish: Irish Emigrant Experiences in America*, Damien Shiels

- *Paddy Whacked: The Untold Story of the Irish American Gangster,* T.J. English

- *Duffy's War: Fr. Francis Duffy, Wild Bill Donovan, and the Irish Fighting 69th in World War I,* Stephen L. Harris

- *Connolly Column: The Story of the Irishmen who fought for the Spanish Republic 1936-1939,* Michael O'Riordan

- *The Fighting 69th: One Remarkable National Guard Unit's Journey From Ground Zero to Baghdad,* Sean Michael Flynn

- *Bandit Country: The IRA & South Armagh,* Toby Harnden

- *Say Nothing: A True Story of Murder and Memory in Northern Ireland,* Patrick Radden Keefe

- *The Earth Shall Weep: A History of Native America,* James Wilson

- *Bury My Heart at Wounded Knee: An Indian History of the American West,* Dee Brown

- *The Comanche Empire,* Pekka Hämäläinen

- *"The Origin of the Skidi Pawnee Sacrifice to the Morning Star,"* Ralph Linton, *American Anthropologist,* Vol. 28, No. 3, July-September 1926

- *Okinawa: The Last Battle,* Roy E. Appleman, James M. Burns, Russell A. Gugeler, and John Stevens

- *With the Old Breed: At Peleliu and Okinawa,* E.B. Sledge

- *The Next Civil War: Dispatches from America's Future,* Stephen Marche

- *The Long Haul: A Trucker's Tales of Life on the Road,* Finn Murphy

ABOUT THE AUTHOR

DAVID CORBETT is the author of seven novels, which have been nominated for numerous awards, including the Edgar. His second novel, *Done for a Dime*, was a *New York Times* Notable Book, and Patrick Anderson of the *Washington Post* described it as "one of the three or four best American crime novels I have ever read." David's short fiction has twice been selected for *Best American Mystery Stories*, and a collaborative novel for which he contributed a chapter—*Culprits*—was adapted for TV by the producers of *Killing Eve* for Disney+ in the U.K. His non-fiction has appeared in the *New York Times, Narrative, Writer's Digest* and other outlets. He has written two writing guides, *The Art of Character* ("A writer's bible") and *The Compass of Character*, and he is a monthly contributor to Writer Unboxed, an award-winning blog dedicated to the craft and business of fiction.

For more about David and his work, visit his website at
https://davidcorbett.com.

CPSIA information can be obtained
at www.ICGtesting.com
Printed in the USA
BVHW041605040523
663605BV00001B/1